The Falcon Takes Wing

Set in seventeenth century Siam, *The Falcon Takes Wing* is a stirring and authentic novel of politics, piracy, love and intrigue.

When Constant Phaulkon, Greek by birth and British by adoption, first rose to the dizzy rank of Pra Klang, first minister to the King of Siam, it was largely due to French intervention. Now, after several years in office, Phaulkon finds he has a debt to pay, as the French are still eager to pave the way for an alliance between Louis XIV of France, the Sun King, and his own King Narai, the Lord of Life. Their aim, ostensibly, is to convert the Siamese king to the Roman Catholic faith. But when the French 'guard of honour' arrives in Siam it consists of five hundred fighting men, whose demeanour suggests that the new 'ally' is bent more on conquest than conversion.

Meanwhile the piratical exploits of some of Phaulkon's own former colleagues threaten to poison his relationship not only with the British East India Company but also with his master, the ageing King Narai. Caught between his Catholic wife Maria and his beautiful concubine Sunida, his position threatened by the treachery of the French and his internal enemies – envious of the power he, a foreigner, has achieved – Phaulkon is taxed to the very limits of his strength and ingenuity.

by the same author

The Falcon of Siam

AXEL AYLWEN

The Falcon Takes Wing

METHUEN

First published in 1991 by
Methuen London, Michelin House,
81 Fulham Road, London SW3 6RB

Copyright © 1991 Axel Aylwen

The author has asserted his moral rights

Hardback ISBN: 0 413 63730 1
Paperback ISBN: 0 413 65170 3
A CIP catalogue record for this book
is available from the British Library

Printed and bound in Great Britain by
Mackays of Chatham PLC, Chatham, Kent

To Bennie, Sasha
and Christopher

Whilst Constant Phaulkon is an historical figure, documented in correspondence and records of seventeenth century Siam, this book is a work of fiction, based only loosely on actual events.

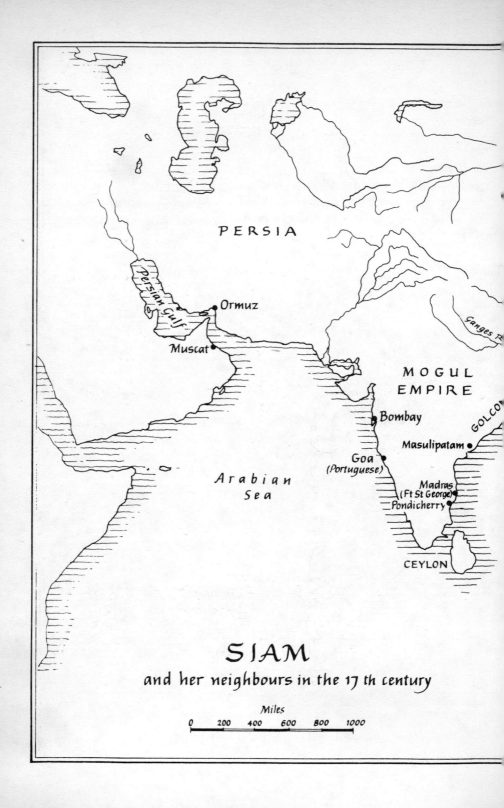

PERSIA

Persian Gulf

● Ormuz

Muscat ●

MOGUL
EMPIRE

Ganges R.

GOLCO

● Bombay

● Masulipatam

Goa ●
(Portuguese)

Madras ●
(Ft St George)
Pondicherry ●

Arabian
Sea

CEYLON

SIAM
and her neighbours in the 17th century

Miles

0   200   400   600   800   1000

Peking

KOREA

JAPAN

Nagasaki

CHINA

TIBET

FORMOSA

Canton

Macao

PHILIPPINE IS.
(SP.)

HAINAN I.

Hoogli

BURMA

China Sea

Manila

Chiengmai

ANNAM

Irrawady

Salwin R.

SIAM

Pegu

Lopburi

Bay
of
Bengal

TENASSERIM

Ayudhya

Bangkok

COCHIN-
CHINA

Mekong R.

Angkor

Tavoy

Mergui

CAMBODIA

Gulf
of
Siam

P. Kondor

Singora

BORNEO

MALAYA

CELEBES

ACHEN

Malacca (Dutch)

Pontianak

SUMATRA

Sukadana

Macassar

Batavia (Dutch)

Bantam
(Dutch)

JAVA

BALI

TIMOR

One

The Gulf of Siam, 30 September 1687

The little Siamese Ambassador climbed stealthily up the companion ladder to the main deck. He stopped just short of the hatchway and listened, cocking his head to one side like a bird. In the gentle pre-dawn breeze the ship's timbers creaked faintly. He edged higher until his black, slanted eyes peered cautiously over the top. He was dressed in full ceremonial attire, his flowing silk panung wound about his waist and his turquoise blouse with the mandarin collar loosely draping his deep brown torso. His pointed, conical hat with the three rings of gold round it was not on his head where it belonged, but strapped instead to his arm.

He glanced discreetly about him. The deck of the great French ship which had been his home for these interminable last months appeared deserted, a swaying leviathan wrapped in silence. In the half-light his eye ran across the nearest longboat and sought out the small but effectual hole he had painstakingly bored in its side in the darkness of the night. Now at last, he thought, he, Kosa Pan, mandarin of the first grade, with ten thousand dignity marks to his name, loyal envoy and slave of the Lord of Life, would escape ashore and disclose the treachery of the French invaders to his mighty sovereign. He filled his lungs with the warm, sultry air. Despite the problems confronting him, it was good to be back in Siamese waters again.

He was about to emerge on deck when he heard footsteps approaching. Quickly he ducked down, listening intently. Who could be up at this hour? Dawn was barely breaking and the ship's officers and crew were slumbering, ill and exhausted from the seven-month journey from France. Even the lookout had not arrived at his post.

The sound drew nearer. The tall silhouette of a man stopped just short of the companionway and then turned, muttering angrily to itself. The steps grew fainter. Kosa Pan eased himself

I

up a little, bringing his eyes level with the deck again. He stared at the retreating figure. It was unmistakable, even in the uncertain light. That elevated, lanky back with the stooping shoulders could belong to only one man: Simon de la Loubère, Ambassador Plenipotentiary from the court of Versailles and leader of the French expedition. Kosa Pan's fists clenched into a ball. The tall envoy was Louis XIV's insidious tool in the French plan to annex Siam.

Kosa watched as the Frenchman continued his fretful pacing and tugged irritably at the collar of his coat. Despite his annoyance at not finding the coast clear, Kosa Pan felt a strange comfort in the Frenchman's gesture. It showed him that what the scurvy and seven months' ordeal at sea had not accomplished, the climate of Siam soon would. For already, despite the early hour, the heat and the humidity were rising fast. The monsoon season would sap what little energy remained to the French troops.

Kosa thought again of the rigours of the journey, of the freezing northern temperatures and the stifling heat of the tropics, of the cries of the sick and dying, and of the mountainous waves around the Cape of Good Hope, the endless nauseous rolling and the interminable days of confinement in his monk-like cabin. The toll among the French had been high. A good third of the soldiers had died of the scurvy, he was sure. He had seen men's teeth fall out like leaves off trees in autumn. He had watched by moonlight the secret burials at sea from the little porthole in his cabin. And on dark nights he had listened to the splash of the falling caskets as they hit the ocean swell. Yet despite such casualties, he knew there still remained a whole army out there, hidden out of sight in four more warships of the royal French fleet.

Kosa Pan's features contorted with rage. It was essential he get immediate word of the treachery to his master, the Lord of Life.

The Frenchman, dwarfed now by a giant mast, reached the far end of the deck and turned. Once more Kosa lowered his head into the shadows. As the man approached, his muttering grew more distinct. Kosa strained to catch the French. '*Ce sacré Jesuite*

. . . Voilà déjà le quatrième jour . . . que le diable les emporte tous . . . '

The Siamese listened, secretly gratified at the Frenchman's displeasure. It was true. It was now the fourth day and still no sign of Tachard. The Jesuit had been the only one authorized by the French to disembark upon their arrival – no doubt to apprize the Siamese of their terms. Kosa longed to know exactly what those terms were; he feared the worst. The priest had been chosen because of his knowledge of Siamese and because he was supposedly a friend of Phaulkon, the all-powerful Pra Klang. But how far was Phaulkon to be trusted? Kosa had his doubts on that score too. The man was a farang, a damned foreigner. What had Tachard been instructed to convey to him? Would it be accompanied by a huge bribe? Would Phaulkon remain loyal to Siam, or would he become a willing tool of Louis XIV? One thing was certain. He, Kosa, had been present at Versailles when the court, in full regalia, had received Phaulkon's last letter. In it the Greek had requested an élite bodyguard of fifty men to be presented as a gift from King Louis to the Lord of Life. As the first Siamese Ambassador to France, Kosa had actually been shown the letter and nowhere in it was there a request for an entire regiment of troops. Was it possible that Phaulkon was as unaware of French intentions as the Lord of Life would surely be?

As always when he thought of Phaulkon, Kosa was forced to marvel at the astuteness of the man who had risen from a simple cabin boy on an English merchant ship to the most influential post in Siam. It was unprecedented. There were rumours that the Lord of Life no longer made a move without consulting him.

Perhaps Phaulkon had had Tachard arrested. It was certainly strange that the priest had not returned to report. Or at least sent word. The Jesuit knew better than any man how desperately provisions were needed, especially medicines for the sick. Not to mention la Loubère's fury at the delay. The impatience of the Sun King's impetuous chief of mission was proverbial. No, something had obviously gone wrong.

Ever since the French fleet's arrival at the bar of Siam four days ago, when all but his own vessel *l'Oiseau*, together with the *Gaillard*, had anchored out of sight, Kosa's repeated requests to go ashore had been politely but firmly refused. And always on

3

the same flimsy pretext. 'My dear Ambassador,' la Loubère would say, assuming his most engaging tone, 'you know how it was His Majesty King Louis' most explicit wish that his gift of an élite bodyguard should be first ashore to offer arms and allegiance to your gracious sovereign and to throw itself upon his great mercy.'

Kosa scoffed at the recollection. Since when did a bodyguard consist of four or five hundred men? Of course the French had not reckoned on the men being seen. He himself had not been expected to depart at all, especially as the Grand Monarque had expressly invited him to stay on. It had been put to him in the most flattering terms, how as the first Siamese Ambassador to the court of Versailles his continuing presence would serve as a token of everlasting friendship between the two nations. At first Kosa had appeared to accept, but when his alert ears had overheard rumours of the mighty force that was purporting to accompany the new French embassy to Siam, he had decided to turn up unannounced in Brest on the day before the sailing, with twelve carriages filled with trunks and a retinue of twenty mandarins bowing constantly before him. The officers in charge had been impressed and too embarrassed to turn such a potentate back. A senior officer had offered him the one remaining cabin, excusing himself for its smallness and explaining that the large contingent of Jesuits, mathematicians, astronomers, engineers, artisans and physicians – all gifts for the great ruler of Siam – had filled the ships to capacity. In the end only two of his mandarins had been allowed to accompany him and half his baggage had remained ashore. The ships' holds were filled with a treasure trove of gifts for the court of Siam: great crystal mirrors, ornate chandeliers, marble tables, mahogany escritoires, Aubusson rugs, bejewelled pistols, shotguns and swords, the latest chiming clocks and turning globes, watches encased in gold, leather saddles and harnesses, suits of armour, a magnificent gold crown encrusted with diamonds, rubies, emeralds and pearls, and three lifesize portraits – rich in symbolism – of the Sun King himself. One showed him on horseback at the head of his huge armies, another on his throne at Versailles receiving the prostrate Siamese embassy, and the third depicted him as the Defender of the

4

Catholic Faith, in conversation with his confessor Père de la Chaise, the head of the Jesuit order.

Nowhere, recalled Kosa Pan ducking lower, had there been any mention of soldiers, though he had seen hundreds of men embark. They were not dressed as priests, neither did they look like physicians or astronomers to him. No, this was undoubtedly an army of invasion and he must warn his sovereign or die in the process. It was time to make his escape before the ship came to life, he reflected again, as he observed the retreating figure of la Loubère. He would wait till the Frenchman reached the far end of the deck and then –

'Good morning, Your Excellency.' Kosa swung round, glaring down the companionway. The smiling, rotund form of Claude Cébéret du Boullay stood at the bottom, one hand on the ladder rail. 'Did you get your foot stuck on the rung, Excellency? Allow me to give you a hand.' The portly director of the French East India Company started up the steps, but in the next instant the Siamese's leg had shot out and Cébéret reeled backwards, losing his foothold.

Alerted by the noise, la Loubère turned and hurried back towards the companionway, just as Kosa darted past him. The Frenchman stood for a moment bewildered as the Siamese headed for the ship's side. He watched him swing a leg over the bulwark.

'Stop him!' shouted la Loubère, coming suddenly to his senses, 'Guard!' Surely the little man was not actually going to jump overboard in his silk panung, his conical hat under his arm? 'After him!' he screamed, as two drowsy sailors appeared on deck rubbing their eyes. Following la Loubère's frantic gestures, they rushed to intercept Kosa, but the lithe Siamese had already swung his other leg over the side and disappeared. There was a splash. The sailors turned and looked at la Loubère.

'Well, what are you waiting for, you fools? After him!' shouted the Frenchman, beside himself.

The sailors hesitated. Then the taller of the two stammered: 'We...er...we don't know how to swim, Your Excellency.'

La Loubère looked ready to burst. 'Then lower a boat, you numbskulls. Hurry!' He followed them to the nearest longboat.

5

'That man must not be allowed to reach shore, do you understand?'

There was a flurry of activity as several men now appeared, a dozen soldiers and some crew. All began to help detach the boat. As they worked, la Loubère ran to and from the side to observe the progress of the Siamese. He swore repeatedly. The little envoy was clearly an experienced swimmer, distancing himself from the ship with regular, effortless strokes. Yet the shore was a good half-mile away and it wouldn't take long for the boat to catch up with him. If only these louts would get a move on. He glanced again at the distant shore. A man probably couldn't swim that far anyway. And then he remembered reading that these damned Siamese were all brought up along the banks of their chief river, the one they called the River of Kings, and they learned to swim almost before they could walk. He cursed again and turned to spur the men on.

Cébéret du Boullay now emerged on deck, clutching his head.

'What's the matter with you, Claude?'

'That unpredictable little devil let fly at me without warning,' said the director of trade, impressed despite his pain. 'He's got a kick like a mule, I can tell you.'

'He swims like a fish, too,' said la Loubère bitterly, pointing out to sea. He turned to address the men grappling with the boat. 'Hurry up, for pity's sake. We'd be in fine fettle with you lot if this ship were sinking. Where the devil's your captain anyway?'

The sailors redoubled their efforts and the boat was finally lowered into the swell. The chief of mission looked out to sea again, amazed to see how far the swimmer had progressed. Still, it would only be a matter of minutes now, he thought; with six men rowing, the boat would be alongside him in no time. 'I want only the strongest rowers,' he ordered. 'And make sure you bring him back alive. Try not to hurt him. If he resists, you'll just have to subdue him somehow.'

The boat set off with six burly men pulling vigorously at the oars. At first it surged forward, but in the next instant, inexplicably, it began to fill with water. Quite a crowd had now gathered by the ship's side and their initial cheers soon trailed off as the boat began to sink lower and lower into the water. There was a gasp from the spectators as a wave washed over it and the men began to jump overboard.

La Loubère, with Cébéret beside him, looked on in disbelief. 'Don't just stand there!' he shouted to the group of onlookers. 'Lower another boat, for God's sake. Hurry!' Several men ran to prepare another boat while others dropped ropes to the floundering rowers.

La Loubère raised his telescope to scan the ocean again. He found himself raising it ever higher in his search. 'Well, I'll be damned!' he swore, as the lens finally alighted on Kosa in the distance. He was almost halfway to shore. His stroke seemed as steady as ever and whenever he raised his right arm, la Loubère could just make out the conical hat still strapped to it.

The second boat set out in pursuit. A huge sailor led the chanting oarsmen. The boat was propelled forward, and watching the swiftness of its progress, la Loubère smiled for the first time that morning. Despite the gap, such a team would have no trouble catching up with the swimmer long before he reached shore.

'Boat ahoy!' The sudden cry of the lookout, high up on the main mast, burst in on his thoughts.

La Loubère stared upwards. 'Where?'

'Over there, Your Excellency.'

He followed the direction of the man's arm and raised his telescope. A dark speck was moving in the distance, seemingly close to shore. He gave silent thanks to God. 'Tachard at last,' he muttered. 'About time, too.'

The ship's longboat was rapidly gaining on the swimmer while the new craft seemed to be heading in their direction too.

'It's a strange looking boat, Your Excellency. Long and sleek.' It was the voice of the lookout again.

La Loubère raised his glass once more, but all he could make out was a dark blob on the horizon. He lowered his instrument in frustration, envying the younger man his vision. 'You mean it's not Tachard's boat?'

'I can't make out the faces yet, Your Excellency, but it's certainly not the boat the Reverend Father set out in.' Tachard had taken the smallest of *l'Oiseau*'s boats, with two oarsmen to help him row. The sailors had instructions to await the priest's return at the point of landing. Only Tachard was to proceed ashore.

La Loubère turned angrily on Cébéret, as if he were in some way responsible for all this. 'What the devil is going on, Claude?'

'Damned if I know. But we have been warned against Phaulkon time and again. Now if Tachard is on friendlier terms with him than we thought – '

'Oh, come on, Claude. Not that old refrain. Tachard hasn't even seen the Greek for five years. You're not suggesting that the priest is going to give us away, are you? We're the best bet he has of achieving his lifelong dream, for heaven's sake. Did you not see his face light up when anyone spoke of the King of Siam's conversion, or the millions of his subjects that would follow? What did he liken it to, now? Oh yes, he called it potentially the greatest coup since St Paul's conversion on the road to Damascus.' La Loubère shook his head. 'No, the priest would be the last to jeopardize the successful outcome of this mission. And he knows full well how important the element of surprise is.'

Cébéret looked unconvinced. 'Well, I never did trust those Jesuits. Their religious zeal has too often stood in the way of our nation's commercial interests. They are obsessed with converting everyone, no matter what the odds – or the damage.'

'But you are not forgetting, I hope, that that is precisely the object of our mission: to convert King Narai of Siam to the Catholic faith and to use whatever means necessary to achieve that objective.'

'While commercial concessions, which might have been readily obtained, must suffer in the process.'

'With Siam in our hands, Claude, you will be free to dictate French commercial policy however you see fit.'

'But at what price? How much blood will have to be shed first? When we could simply dominate the country through our gradual hold on trade.'

'That is a consequence of our objective, not a means to it.'

'With due respect,' responded Cébéret, eyeing la Loubère askance, 'it is also a consequence of the divine inspiration of our most Catholic King. For only with divine assurance could anyone presuppose that the ruler of a dynasty as old as France and six

8

thousand leagues distant would consider adopting the faith of a country he has never even set eyes on.'

La Loubère raised himself to his full height. 'You forget that we are not just any faraway country. We are France, the beacon of the civilized world. Word of our greatness, and the reasons underlying it, has spread far and wide.' The trade chief remained unmoved by his words. 'If you seek more practical reasons, Claude, then I must point to Phaulkon. Do you not find his presence in Siam more than a mere coincidence? That we should have at our disposal the services of a Catholic at the pinnacle of power, a favourite at court who has clearly hinted in his letters that he would be instrumental in persuading his master to adopt the true faith?'

'Perhaps, if he is really on our side. But if he turns out not to be, I believe he could twist Tachard round his little finger if he is only half as canny as he is made out to be. All he has to do is suggest ways to the Jesuit of achieving the King's conversion. The worthy Tachard will melt like butter in the sun.'

The two men fell silent and stared out to sea, their minds on Phaulkon as they watched the gap between the swimmer and their boat gradually narrow. They had had this discussion often enough before, dissecting, arguing and mostly disagreeing. The facts were that the official invitation of the Siamese King to his French counterpart, splendidly inscribed on a sheet of gold, had not only requested the dispatch of a great embassy to Siam but offered the Grand Monarque, as a special mark of his affection, the southern port of Ligor from which to trade. And Phaulkon, in his accompanying letter, filled with declarations of the true faith, had hinted at 'more concessions to come'. He had added confidentially that his sovereign was a secret admirer of the French King. Not only had the Lord of Life, as he called him, ordered translations of French histories to be made into Siamese, but a portrait of Louis XIV, requisitioned from the Jesuits, actually hung from the wall of his private apartments in the innermost sanctum of the Grand Palace.

Cébéret was intrigued by the commercial possibilities of this mission but sceptical of its religious outcome, ever fearful that an insistence on the latter would jeopardize the former; while la Loubère was adamant that both must go hand in hand. The

9

policies of the Defender of the Catholic Faith could not be satisfied by mere trading concessions granted by a pagan king. Yet despite their differences, both men were agreed that Phaulkon was the key and that the answer lay in his willingness, and his power, to co-operate. Was he a true Catholic intent on converting his monarch and assisting France in its subjugation of Siam, or was he just a political adventurer using the prestige of France to thwart the ambitions of the Dutch and keep himself in power? Time and again during the long voyage the two men had gone over the mass of rumours that surrounded Phaulkon, trying to sift fact from fantasy.

He was known to have been born on a small Greek Island, and to have stowed away on an English ship as a young lad, eventually winding up in the employ of the British East India Company, the greatest trading monopoly on earth. Twenty years later he had resurfaced as the most powerful mandarin of a great Oriental kingdom. After throwing in his lot with the English for so many years, he had now converted to the Catholic faith and was openly courting the French. He was known as the Barcalon – apparently a Portuguese corruption of the Siamese title of Pra Klang; his authority was that of foreign minister and treasury minister rolled into one. He wielded enormous power and was a legend in these parts. He lived apparently in two palaces, waited upon by some six hundred servants. No foreigner in Asia had ever held such exalted office. It was said that he was virtually fluent in every trading language in Asia and as cunning as a clan of foxes and at least as ruthless, yet with a charm and persuasiveness that was equally powerful.

The French traders for the most part disliked him and spoke ill of him, complaining of his high-handedness. One report had described in detail his incarceration of the French trader, Monsieur de Rouen, on the grounds that he had refused to sell the Barcalon a cargo of sandalwood at a price dictated by the Greek himself.

The Jesuits, on the other hand, swore by him, pointing proudly to his exchange of correspondence with the Pope in Rome, and calling him the key to their long cherished goal of converting the King of Siam to Catholicism. Whatever the truth, la Loubère and Cébéret had concurred, it was certainly remarkable that a foreigner should have risen to the rank of prime minister in a distant Oriental kingdom, larger than France and England combined, whose host of vassal states was second only to the Middle Kingdom of China itself. And however different their approach, both men could not help marvelling at the daring of this Greek. He had written to the Sun King pointing out the great advantages of an alliance and stressing the religious possibilities arising from his position as the King of Siam's chief minister, but he had not awaited a reply. Instead, aware that his letter to King Louis would take seven months to arrive and the reply just as long, and apparently fearful of an imminent Dutch move on the country, he had taken it upon himself to announce a grand Alliance between Siam and France, forging the necessary documentation with the connivance of the local French Jesuits, who were ready to assist in any project which might hasten the day of King Narai's conversion. Copies of the concocted alliance were passed to the chief Dutch factor in Siam, with such brilliant results that the Dutch decided against risking confrontation with Europe's most powerful monarch. For the moment, at least, they continued to confine their activities in Siam to trading.

When, inevitably, the ploy had come to light in France, the wrath of King Louis was greatly mitigated by the intervention on Phaulkon's behalf of the Father de la Chaise, His Majesty's confessor. He persuaded King Louis that the Catholic Phaulkon was acting only in good faith in promoting the cause of Catholic France against that of the Protestant Netherlands. Through all the intrigue, the ambitious Sun King had discerned a God-sent opportunity to add to his imperial conquests. And when Phaulkon had further proposed the élite French bodyguard of fifty men, the Grand Monarque devised the scheme of sending an army instead, under the command of a marshal of France. The offer of the port city of Ligor, with 'more concessions to come', soon grew into a demand for the strategic ports of Bangkok and Mergui instead, as Louis XIV pored over the few existing maps of the area with his advisers. The first, Bangkok, was a small but strategic port near the mouth of the great Menam Chao Phraya, the River of Kings, at the very entrance to the Siamese heartland, and the second, Mergui, was the great western port on the Bay of Bengal from which all trade to India and Persia emanated.

11

Finally, King Louis decreed that though the ceding of these ports to France was of considerable importance, the ultimate aim of the mission and the jewel in its crown must be the conversion of the Siamese King.

Simon de la Loubère, a high ranking diplomat and accomplished scholar, was placed in overall charge of the expedition, with orders to oversee the native sovereign's spiritual conversion, while Claude Céberet du Boullay, naval commissioner and one of the twelve directors of the French East India Company, was in charge of all France's commercial interests. General Antoine Desfarges was placed in command of the troops with orders to defer to the other two in matters of general policy.

In the event that the King of Siam should declare himself reluctant to adopt the Catholic faith or should resist diplomatic requests to cede the two ports, General Desfarges was to take them by force and set up fortified garrisons from which to subjugate the entire country. Although the Siamese troops would vastly outnumber the French, it had been estimated that their regiments of war elephants and the lances and harpoons of their fighting force would be no match for the cannon of the French fleet or the muskets of the French garrisons. In a matter of days, at most weeks, France would hold sway over the Kingdom of Siam, militarily, commercially and spiritually. France would gain an important new colony where Holland had so far failed.

And now, less than a year later, the Jesuit Father Tachard was ashore putting these very terms to Phaulkon, while the Siamese Ambassador was racing to divulge the true size of the French army to his King.

A whistle from above distracted the two men.

'Well, what is happening?' demanded la Loubère, staring up at the lookout.

'Your Excellency, the other craft is gaining rapidly on the swimmer. More rapidly than our own boat. Its design is beautiful. Long and narrow and very swift. I've never seen anything like it.'

'Damnation,' cursed la Loubère. 'Are you sure Father Tachard is not on board?'

'It doesn't appear so, Your Excellency. The faces all look Siamese to me. Though at this distance it's hard to be sure.'

La Loubère turned to Cébéret. 'Tachard better have a damned good excuse if he's not on board. He's two days late as it is.'

'It is apparently a long journey upriver to Siam's capital, Simon,' ventured Cébéret placatingly. 'Over fifteen hours, I'm told. And we have heard how slowly things move in the Orient.' Cébéret had read all the reports on trade in the East, and the Siamese were described as not overly concerned with matters of time. 'Perhaps His Siamese Majesty is considering our demands at this very moment.'

'What is there for the King of Siam to consider?' asked la Loubère gruffly. 'Did he not send us an official invitation? We should at least be invited to disembark. Is this the celebrated Oriental hospitality? And how dare Phaulkon ignore us? The Siamese may be slow to react but a Greek should know better than to keep an embassy from the Sun King waiting.'

'As I said before, Simon, Tachard might well have been coaxed or tricked into revealing the true extent of our armed forces. In which case the Siamese could be deliberating their next move. It would explain the delay.'

'If Tachard has been arrested,' observed la Loubère, clenching his fists, 'there will be war. Those people will soon learn what it means to thwart the will of France.'

'I'm not so sure about that. Their numbers must be prodigious, and if their spirit is anything to match . . . I understand their nation has never been subjugated by a foreign power before. They're not likely to sit back and watch us take them over.'

'They won't have a choice.' La Loubère mopped the sweat from his brow. The heat from the rising sun was damned uncomfortable.

'What if the King of Siam reverts to the Dutch for help? Holland is still the greatest power in Asia.'

La Loubère scoffed. 'It is precisely to curb the ambitions of the Dutch that the King of Siam has turned to us. He trusts the Dutch least of all.'

Cébéret could not refrain from smiling. As if the Siamese King were better advised to put his trust in the French instead! Still, la Loubère was right about the ambitious Dutch. They were too powerful and greedy to be trusted. In the half century since they had taken over from Portugal as the dominant trading power in

13

Asia, they had absorbed Malacca, Java, Sumatra, the Celebes, the Spice Islands and countless others into their burgeoning empire. And it was probably true that only the timely ploy of Phaulkon had stopped them from swallowing Siam. They were now surely biding their time until the outcome of this much-heralded embassy from France became clear. If only everything could be resolved peacefully. How would the Dutch look upon the supposed grand alliance with France anyway, if the two countries were seen to be at each other's throats?

'Hey, you up there!' cried la Loubère. 'Keep us posted. What's happening?'

'I can see the faces clearly now, Your Excellency.' The lookout sounded nervous. 'The Reverend Father is definitely not among them.'

'How close are they to the swimmer?'

'Not far, Your Excellency. They don't appear to have spotted him though.'

'Perhaps they won't pick him up,' observed Cébéret hopefully.

La Loubère turned and glared down his long nose at him. A sudden breeze ruffled the curls of his voluminous grey wig. 'The swimmer, Claude, is an ambassador plenipotentiary from his country, just as I am. Do you seriously expect his own people not to stop to collect him?'

'I was not questioning the etiquette, Simon. I was merely wondering whether they might spot him or not.'

'The swimmer is gesticulating now, Your Excellency, and the native boat appears to have sighted him. Yes, it definitely has. It's changing course. It's propelled by a dozen oarsmen all clad in red,' the lookout added conversationally.

'What the devil are our own fools doing then? Having a rest?'

'They're still rowing, Your Excellency, but they're some way away. They just haven't the speed. The other boat has caught up with the swimmer now. He's climbing aboard. Good God! All the oarsmen have fallen flat on their faces. He's speaking to them now. The boat's turning round. It's heading back to shore, Your Excellency.'

La Loubère raised his arm and for a moment it seemed as if he were about to smash the telescope on the deck. Then he appeared to think better of it. With an effort he controlled his voice. 'This

14

is a disaster, Claude. We'd better rouse General Desfarges. How is he?'

'Still poorly. He needs rest.'

La Loubère's expression soured still further. 'Let's go to my cabin. Are you sure we shouldn't rouse the General?'

'I'd leave him be. In his present condition he wouldn't contribute much to the conversation anyway.'

'Very well, then. We'll just have to formulate a new plan without him.'

Two

Father Tachard looked around him in awe as he waited by the main gate. So this was the new palace of the chief minister, he reflected as the messenger left to announce the arrival of the foreign priest in the long brown robe. The sprawling edifice was built strictly in the Siamese style, raised on a score of stilts with triangular tiled roofs and thick walls of panelled teak. Numerous windows allowed for maximum ventilation. In the far background rows of smaller wooden huts on stilts indicated a large retinue, and on closer inspection a multitude of servants and slaves, like ants in the distance, could be seen going about their business. Lush gardens surrounded the central structure, while lotus ponds, fountains and small streams lent a pleasing freshness to the scene. A beautiful fan palm stood majestically in the forecourt while clumps of bamboo, clusters of mali shrub, beds of yellow champa flowers – which he remembered the children of Siam were so fond of wearing behind their ears – and bright vermilion bougain-villea added a chorus of fragrance and colour.

Tachard caught his breath. This was not just a place of grandeur and beauty but one of peace and serenity at the same time. The scented air and sound of running water seemed somehow to render the heat more palatable. He was glad to be here. It had taken him long enough. He was already two days behind schedule. He had been held up for an inordinately long time before being allowed to proceed upriver to Ayudhya. The Siamese officials had given no particular explanation for the delay, but despite their meticulous courtesy and their assurances that it was just a routine check, he had the distinct impression that they were delaying him purposefully. In any event, he had lost over a day in the process.

Then, on reaching Ayudhya, he had not been able to resist calling at the Seminary. His Jesuit colleagues there would not hear of letting him go until they had fêted his return. When, finally, he had reached Phaulkon's palace he was informed at the outer gate that His Excellency the Pra Klang would be away until morning. The priest should return then. So Tachard had retraced his steps to the Seminary, perturbed by the delays and fully guessing la Loubère's frustration, yet equally aware that there was little he could do to remedy the situation.

At the Seminary he had listened avidly to the reports of progress regarding His Majesty's conversion. He learned that Father Brouet had been summoned a number of times to the palace to interpret difficult passages in the Bible which had excited the King's curiosity, but other than that, the situation remained unchanged. The King still appeared uncertain. And Phaulkon, the real key to progress, had indicated that he wanted to await the arrival of the French delegation before pressing the matter too strongly.

It was now the fourth day since he had left the ship, and Tachard was anxious to complete his mission and return aboard. He must present Phaulkon with the French terms without delay.

'His Excellency the Pra Klang will see you now,' said the bare-chested guard, as he returned to the gate. He bowed low, smiling courteously and displaying a row of teeth rendered dark red by the constant chewing of the betel nut. As Tachard followed him along a broad stone alleyway bordered by flowers, he was reminded of what a handsome race the Siamese were. They were generally slighter than Europeans, well-proportioned and not prone to obesity. Their dark eyes were less slanted than those of the Chinese and their deep brown complexions and straight, jet-black hair seemed in perfect harmony with the bright colours of the tropics. Their ears were usually larger, their lips thicker and their noses much squatter than those of the European, but their bodies were lithe and supple and they held themselves with a matchless grace.

Tachard sighed and ran a hand through his thinning grey hair. It had been five years since he had left these shores and his journey up the Menam Chao Phraya had brought back a flood of memories. The river banks were lined with the familiar wooden houses on stilts, bare-chested men and women bathed in the river and shrieking children jumped into the water from the terraces of their houses. Fruit orchards ran along the shore, and a myriad of canoe-like boats travelled the river laden with produce like some floating market, the smiling boatwomen declaiming their wares. The prows of the mandarins' barges, raised high in the shapes of mythical birds, all aglitter with gold leaf, glided past.

Tachard had been captivated anew by this exotic land. He had awaited every new bend in the river with childlike delight, exclaiming aloud as some golden spire or orange roof of a temple, shimmering in the sun, made a sudden appearance tucked between clumps of palm and banana trees. The time had slipped by unnoticed until, towards the twelfth hour, rounding a bend that was dotted with little islands, he first sighted the majestic skyline of the City of Paradise, Ayudhya.

Though the memory of his earlier visit was still vivid and he had been mentally prepared for the sight, it nevertheless took his breath away. Rows of golden spires shot up into the sky, glistening in the sunlight like so many jewels, while a host of colours vied for his attention: the rust red of the thick walls surrounding the island city, the oranges and browns and greens of the temple roofs, the blue and mauve tiles of the houses, the sparkling gold of the spires, and the infinite blue of the heavens. Not for nothing had the first Portuguese travellers been awed by the sight. They had called the city, criss-crossed as it was by a maze of canals, the 'Venice of the East'.

The guard escorting Tachard now led him up a series of broad steps that led to two large, open, wood panels, decorated with mother-of-pearl and forming a central doorway. Apprehension gripped him as the guard, bowing low, beckoned him inside. How would Phaulkon react to the French proposals? Would he not see they were but thinly disguised threats? At the threshold, two more prone servants awaited him, leading him obsequiously towards an anteroom whose floor was covered in thick Persian carpets. Tachard stared around him. The walls were lined with a rare collection of lacquered cabinets, some black, some gold, others with decorative animal designs. Early Ayudhya, probably fourteenth century, he noted. The servants fell silently prostrate in the far corners of the room while Tachard sank into some cushions and waited, his mind now focused entirely on Phaulkon.

He felt distinctly uneasy at the prospect of having to conceal the fact that instead of the fifty soldiers that Phaulkon had

18

requested for His Majesty's bodyguard, two French warships and four further frigates, with five hundred soldiers under a marshal of France, lay at anchor beyond the bar. For the initial phase of the French plan, it was essential to obtain permission to disembark.

For the first time, too, faced with the reality of the moment, Tachard began to question Phaulkon's allegiance. Supposing he really was a mandarin of Siam, in soul as well as in rank? The priest glanced around the room. The evidence would seem to point that way. It was truly the house of a Siamese overlord: apart from the priceless wood carvings and Persian rugs, sumptuous Burmese tapestries hung from the walls, delicate Chinese silk screens and Ming vases graced every recess.

Tachard recalled how some of the Jesuits – admittedly a minority – had expressed doubts at the time about the sincerity of Phaulkon's conversion from the Protestant faith of his English masters. Could he have become a Catholic merely to satisfy the requirements of his Portuguese-Japanese wife, herself a dedicated believer, or to further his own career? When he stressed his staunch Catholic beliefs to Louis XIV, had he been attempting to gain the French sovereign's confidence and predispose him in his favour? If that had been his intent, the ploy had certainly worked. Tachard was aware of the significant honours that la Loubère was charged with conferring upon Phaulkon in the name of France – as an added incentive for his co-operation, of course. Such coveted awards as the Order of St Michel were not given lightly and only to those who had rendered great service to the Crown. In His French Majesty's eyes, Phaulkon was clearly the key to the successful conclusion of his plans for Siam.

It made Tachard nervous to think how crucial his own role had now become. How successfully would he be able to influence the course of events? Had Phaulkon's thinking changed over the last five years? Was he able, or even willing, to make King Narai see matters the French way? He shuddered at the thought of the bloodshed that might ensue if he didn't.

He looked up as the sound of footsteps echoed in the corridor outside, and with an effort he willed himself to remain calm. Perhaps he was worrying unduly. After all, was the man not

Barcalon of Siam, and were not these Oriental surroundings but the outward trappings of his position?

Two slaves, bent almost double, appeared in the doorway, one bearing his master's diamond-encrusted betel box – a gift from His Majesty King Narai – and the other his ceremonial sword. The sword's scabbard, resting on the slave's right shoulder, glittered with rubies and emeralds.

The slaves entered and fell prostrate on either side of the doorway. In the next instant, a lithe, imposing figure stood framed in it, gazing across the length of the room. Tachard could feel the magnetism of the man. He seemed physically little changed from five years ago, although there was an aura of strength and command about him now, that the Father thought had not been in such evidence before.

Phaulkon was dressed in a grey silk coat and a black panung, the edges of which were embroidered with gold thread. He held himself very erect, giving the impression of being taller than he really was. His thick, dark hair was swept straight back from his forehead and his alert chestnut eyes settled unflinchingly on his visitor. Then the air of gravity diffused and a warm, generous smile lit up his features.

'My dear Tachard,' he said, with that ready charm that Tachard recalled so well. 'Is it really you? You won't believe how they pronounced your name.'

Tachard rose, but Phaulkon greeted him unexpectedly in the Siamese manner, cupping his hands in front of his face and maintaining his distance. Nonplussed, Tachard returned the greeting. Then to his increasing surprise he watched as Phaulkon slid down, sweeping his legs behind him to one side like a mandarin, his left palm resting on the rug in front of him and bearing most of his body's weight. His right hand lay loosely on his thigh. It was a position that any European would have found excruciating, but Phaulkon seemed to have adopted it with ease. Were it not for the Western features, reflected Tachard, he might have been sitting opposite any well-to-do Siamese aristocrat. He lowered himself onto a cushion and crossed his legs like a tailor.

'What a pleasant surprise,' continued Phaulkon affably. 'I could not think of a more welcome visitor. I long to hear your tidings, Father. But first let me offer you some refreshment.'

20

'Not for the moment thank you, my lord. I am delighted to be back, and especially pleased to find you in such good health.'

'I am well looked after, Father.' Phaulkon smiled conspiratorially at the priest. 'Dona Maria thinks of everything. She does not even let me over-eat.'

Tachard knew Phaulkon's wife well, far better in fact than he knew Phaulkon. He was one of the Jesuits who had brought her up and it was they who had arranged her marriage to Phaulkon. Though it was against the Jesuit code to bring up a girl, there had been extenuating circumstances. Her great-grandfather had after all been one of the first Christian martyrs in the terrible purges of sixteenth-century Japan. She was an exceptional woman, imbued with all the resolve of her tenacious ancestors.

'But do tell me, Father. You did not arrive from France alone?'

Tachard chuckled. 'Indeed not, my lord. I have been sent ahead to inform you of the ambassador's arrival.'

'And who is the leader of your delegation?'

'Simon de la Loubère, a prominent intellectual.'

Phaulkon appeared to consider for a moment. 'Simon de la Loubère? The name is familiar . . . Was he not a senior French diplomat in Switzerland at one time?'

'Indeed, my lord. He was assistant to the Baron de St Romain,' said Tachard, marvelling at Phaulkon's knowledge. 'This time he has his own deputy, Claude Cébéret du Boullay, one of the twelve directors of the French East India Company.'

Phaulkon appeared impressed. 'It sounds as if the French have serious plans here. But tell me, did His Majesty honour my master, the Lord of Life, with the élite bodyguard I requested?'

'He did indeed, my lord. The guard is waiting to pay its respects now, just as soon as the men are given permission to disembark.'

Phaulkon eyed the priest steadily. 'And how many soldiers did King Louis favour us with?'

Tachard felt a sudden hollow in his stomach. Phaulkon's eyes seemed to be boring into him. 'Fifty élite men, my lord, as you requested.' Even as he said the words, Tachard felt their awkwardness. Was the attempt at sounding casual overdone? He thought he saw a shadow cross Phaulkon's face.

'And who is in charge of this bodyguard?'

Tachard hesitated ever so briefly.

'General . . . General Desfarges, my lord.'

'General Desfarges? His name, too, is known to me.' Phaulkon's voice registered undisguised surprise. 'King Louis has indeed been generous with his favours to place a marshal of France in charge of a fifty-man bodyguard.'

Tachard detected a note of sarcasm in the last sentence but he had come prepared. 'His Majesty of France wanted to show his special regard for the King of Siam by placing a high-ranking soldier in his service,' he said, just as he had rehearsed countless times during his journey. 'And there are a score of engineers and artisans on board as well. Unfortunately their original numbers have been sorely depleted by the hazards of the voyage.' Tachard made the sign of the cross. 'The scurvy mainly,' he added, by way of explanation.

'I am indeed sorry to hear that,' replied Phaulkon, 'as I know the Master of Life will be.' He gazed at the Jesuit in silence for a moment. 'And how many ships of the royal fleet do we have the pleasure of welcoming?' he enquired, his face expressionless.

'Two, my lord, headed by the six-hundred-ton flagship *l'Oiseau.*' The other four ships were to remain out of sight before proceeding to Mergui as soon as that port had been officially ceded to France. They would slip out, head south along the Malay peninsula, sail round the point of Singapura and then turn north again through the straits of Malacca, into the Andaman Sea and the Bay of Bengal. Their sudden appearance at Mergui would come as a complete surprise. The troops would disembark, garrison the town and take over the western provinces of Siam.

It would be the same with Bangkok. Surprise was the crux of the whole French strategy. Once the river port was ceded to France and they were given permission to disembark, the men would occupy the fort there before the Siamese had recovered from the initial shock of their numbers.

Tachard did not like the way Phaulkon was staring at him. He uncrossed his legs and adjusted the cushions beneath him.

'You're not keeping anything from me, are you, Father?'

The priest froze.

'I mean,' continued Phaulkon, unexpectedly breaking into a smile, 'you haven't any surprises up your sleeve, have you?'

Tachard felt a little reassured by the smile. 'Surprises, my lord? What do you mean?'

'Oh, come now, Father. You know I hate surprises. If you have any in store for me, tell me now.' He leaned forward, lowering his tone, as if someone had entered the room. 'I'd far rather hear them from you.'

Tachard squirmed in his seat. There was something ominous in the way Phaulkon stressed the 'you'. How he detested lying and how uncomfortable this whole charade was making him feel. If only it could be over with and he could return to the ship.

He was about to speak when Phaulkon forestalled him. 'So, Father, tell me.'

'Yes, of course, my lord.' Tachard paused. 'The fact is, though His Majesty King Louis is most grateful for your master's kind offer of the port of Ligor in the south, he respectfully requests that it be exchanged for the ports of Bangkok and Mergui. His Majesty feels that with a base at Bangkok, France would be better able to contain the Dutch and protect your trade routes in and out of the country. While Mergui, with its gateway to the west, would better serve his own trading interests – which your master so kindly expressed a wish to see expand, through the granting of Ligor.'

The same dark cloud Tachard had seen earlier crossed Phaulkon's face. Then he broke into a gracious smile. 'The reputation for military planning of your sovereign is well founded,' he remarked, 'for Bangkok and Mergui happen to be our two most strategic ports.'

'His Majesty considers you a special friend of France, my lord. He wishes to lend you every assistance in keeping the Dutch at bay and what surer deterrent than to place these strategic enclaves in French hands? As a token of his particular esteem for you – whom I have heard him call his greatest friend and ally in Asia – he has charged Ambassador de la Loubère to confer upon you the Order of St Michel. He has further granted you honourary French citizenship and made you a count of France.' Tachard bowed his head respectfully as he allowed the words to sink in.

Phaulkon's expression barely changed. 'It would be difficult

23

for any man to remain unmoved by such great honours, bestowed furthermore by Europe's greatest monarch,' he said, careful to mask his exhilaration. 'But I cannot see what I have done to deserve them, unless it is that I have yet to merit them by my good deeds.'

Tachard smiled. 'I will not deny, my lord, that King Louis is counting greatly on your assistance in leading your master onto the true path, but I know that as a Catholic, you yourself could have no greater aspiration.' The priest leaned forward eagerly. 'What hope do you hold out at present for His Majesty's conversion?'

Phaulkon's expression suddenly hardened. 'Until a moment ago, a great deal, Father. But you surprise me. The Jesuits, and you in particular, have worked long and hard in Siam to achieve your one overriding ambition. Yet now that you are close to your goal, you come to me with demands that will destroy everything and set the Jesuits back a hundred years. Tell me, Father, when you receive a gift, is it your custom to exchange it for another or to return it and ask for two in its place? Do you think the King of Siam is in the habit of handing out vital ports to his visitors like so many New Year gifts? He deliberated long and hard how best to distinguish France from other nations and how best to express his great esteem for your king and country.' Phaulkon paused. 'In a gesture without precedence, he gave you the gift of a port on his shores. Yet your only thanks is to ask him to exchange it, nay, even to demand two in its place.'

'But, my lord, your letter mentioned more concessions to come and—'

'I have not finished yet, Father,' cut in Phaulkon, his indignation seeming to build on itself. 'If I were so much as to hint at your suggestions to His Majesty, you would not only incur his outrage at your lack of manners, which you well know are all-important to a Siamese, but his everlasting contempt as well. And as for any progress in spiritual matters, words fail me. Do you honestly believe that my master, or any ruler worth the name, would be disposed to embrace the faith of one who was asking him to hand over his two most strategic ports? Those that hold the key to the defence of his very kingdom? Little do you

24

know the Siamese spirit, my friend, or the wisdom of my master, the King.'

Tachard was visibly shaken by this verbal onslaught. 'My lord, you must know that it is not the Jesuits who dictate such policies. Nothing would grieve me more than to undo all we have striven for. But I have my orders.'

Phaulkon observed him quietly. The storm which had darkened his features was gone almost as quickly as it had appeared. 'I am aware, Father,' he said more gently, 'that you cannot return to your ship empty-handed. For your sake then, and for the sake of the great esteem in which I hold the King of France, I shall offer you a compromise. But know that my offer is final and not subject to barter. It is a gift, Father, and you should impress that fact upon the Ambassador.' He paused. 'I shall recommend to His Majesty that you be granted the port city of Bangkok, in lieu of Ligor, from which to trade, and I shall take it upon myself to give a suitable explanation to His Majesty. The generosity of Siam shall never be insulted by the demands of France. Mergui, however, is out of the question. His Majesty has already appointed Englishmen to conduct trade there on his behalf, and their performance has in no way been wanting. It is not our custom to reward success with dispossession.'

Tachard's face lit up. At least it was a compromise and the bloodshed might yet be averted. 'Thank you, my lord. Your generosity is equalled only by your wisdom. And what should I inform the Ambassador with regard to the prospects of your master's conversion?'

'That it is close to realization, but can never be concluded under pressure. The Lord of Life is impressed only by deeds, not by words. If he were in any way to become suspicious of French intentions – a response which your original demands would inevitably have aroused – you would lose his trust and with it his growing respect for the true faith.'

'I understand, my lord.'

'Very well then, I shall request my master's permission for the men to disembark. You had best remain here until you can convey the answer. I shall recommend that Cébéret du Boullay be allowed to set up his trading headquarters in Bangkok, and that General Desfarges be authorized to bring his bodyguard to

Ayudhya to present arms and allegiance to His Majesty.' Phaulkon's expression hardened again. 'But know one more thing, Father. By being forced to maintain silence on the question of your demand for Mergui, I shall have failed in my sworn duty to my liege to apprize him of everything that concerns his realm. And it is with a heavy heart that I deceive him.'

There was the sound of approaching footsteps and a moment later the figure of a European, clad in grey breeches and a blouse, prostrated itself in the doorway.

'Your Excellency, I beg to forgive this intrusion but a messenger is here from the palace. Your presence is required there most urgently by His Omnipotent Majesty.'

'Thank you, Bashpool. Well, Father, you may have your answer sooner than expected. I don't think you have met my secretary, Bashpool. This is Father Tachard.' Both men bowed to each other. 'I would like you to see to the Father's needs until my return, Bashpool.'

'Very well, Your Excellency,' said Bashpool.

Phaulkon entered his private apartment, wondering about the pressing nature of the summons he had received. He was due to see His Majesty later that morning anyway in barely over an hour, so the matter must be urgent indeed. He began to change quickly into his obligatory palace clothes: his gold-embroidered silk panung – a gift from the Lord of Life himself to be worn only in the royal presence; a cream-coloured coat with a mandarin collar and filigree buttons; and his conical hat with the three rings of gold round it. But, above all, it was his ceremonial sword and diamond-encrusted betel box that denoted his foremost position in the rigid hierarchy of Siam. In a moment he would summon his escort, one hundred and fifty retainers who accompanied him everywhere, as befitted a man of his rank, for the higher the number of dignity marks, the greater a man's escort. Long gone were those exciting days when he could stroll alone and wide-eyed along the bustling canals of Ayudhya, marvelling at every sight. Now, he could only venture out with all the pomp and fanfare attached to his elevated position.

He glanced up, surprised, as he heard a subdued knock at the door. 'Who is it?'

26

'Forgive me, Constant. I did not mean to intrude,' replied a gentle voice in Portuguese. 'May I see you for a moment?'

He smiled. His wife did not usually venture into his private apartments, let alone his dressing quarters, in the middle of the day. Perhaps she had heard of his summons or been notified of the arrival of Tachard. She was clearly fascinated by the advent of the Catholic French and no doubt hoped to learn more.

'Come in, Maria. I am in a hurry, but so unusual a visit must be given full honours,' he said banteringly. He looked at her for a moment as she stood framed in the doorway, a refined, porcelain-like figure, half Portuguese, half Japanese, wrapped in an elegant blue kimono whose wide, three-quarter-length sleeves exposed the fair skin of her slender arms.

'You would grow tired of me, Constant, if I were always too predictable, I am sure.' Despite the jesting tone he thought he detected a shade of anxiety in her eyes, as if she had unwittingly stumbled upon some awkward truth.

'You are never predictable, Maria, except when it comes to the strength of your faith.'

'Ah, my lord, would that yours were as great.'

He looked up at her quickly, almost aggressively. 'Thank God it is not. For if I were so blinded, I should be at the mercy of your scheming Jesuits.'

She observed him quietly through dark, vaguely slanted eyes, not wishing to aggravate him. He seemed to her tense and overwrought. What did he mean about the Jesuits? If only he would work less, she thought, relax occasionally and spend just a little more time with her. But now the French had arrived and the pressures of state would increase further still. The pleasure she felt at the prospect of being in the company of so many educated Catholics was offset by her fear of losing her loved one to yet more distractions, yet more commitments to keep him away from her, when he had so little time for her anyway. Was it her imagination or had he grown more distant still of late? He was always so perfectly correct towards her that it was difficult to admonish him directly, but she seldom felt that she had his full attention. She touched her stomach lightly as she felt a slight movement. Perhaps this long-awaited blessing would change everything, bring him closer to her again. She hadn't told him

27

yet. She wanted to wait for the right moment, when they would have time to enjoy their good fortune and celebrate. But when would that ever be?

She observed the deepening frown on his handsome face as he wound his beautiful silk panung through his legs and about his waist, tucking the ends in neatly. What was troubling him so? She had not intended to voice any doubts about the strength of his faith, but of late she had been forced to question it. Then she chided herself for entertaining such disloyal thoughts. This was, after all, the man she loved and it was wrong to question his motives thus. He was walking a political tightrope as it was, and he needed strength and support from her, not doubts. He might be a little distant but he had done nothing to deserve such suspicions.

'I meant, my lord,' she said, 'that I wished God to give you strength to overcome your burdens.'

'My burdens would be more manageable, Maria, if the Jesuits didn't do their best to increase them.'

She hesitated, not wishing to question him before he was ready. 'Can I be of help, my lord?'

'Perhaps,' he replied. 'By keeping Tachard firmly ensconced in this house. He only gets up to mischief when he's let loose.'

'Father Tachard?' she asked excitedly. 'Is he here? The one who married us?'

'The same.' Phaulkon smiled drily. 'You two should have plenty to talk about. He's in the anteroom with Bashpool at this moment.'

'Is it permitted to know how he has displeased you, my lord?'

Phaulkon's dark eyes flashed. At first he ignored the question, busying himself with the last of the filigree buttons on his coat. 'I wouldn't know where to begin, Maria.' He paused. 'Perhaps a good place would be with the shameful fact that he lied about the number of French ships that have arrived. Lying is not one of the Catholic virtues I was taught to emulate, Maria.'

'Indeed not, my lord.' She appeared shaken. 'How many ships have then arrived?'

Phaulkon controlled his fury. 'Six, my dear. Not the two he so innocently claimed.'

'Six ships? Are you sure, my lord?'

'Of course I'm sure, Maria. Do you think my spies are fools?' he retorted, and almost immediately regretted his tone as he observed her pained expression. She stood there silently between two beautiful jade figurines on pedestals, as vulnerable and graceful as either of them.

'Why would he lie, my lord?'

'That is precisely what I intend to find out, Maria. My men are reconnoitring now. In the meantime, I shall prevent Father Tachard from returning to his ship until we can establish the truth. The French must be anxiously awaiting his news. I must go to the palace now, but I will be back as soon as possible. Make sure the Father doesn't leave.' He started towards the door.

'Oh Constant,' said Maria despondently, 'why must there always be problems? Will we ever lead a normal, Godly life, as human beings were meant to?'

He paused for a moment. 'I suppose, my dear, that some of us are called upon to ensure that others may lead just such a life.' He smiled kindly. 'And for better or for worse, you are the wife and trusted confidante of one of those.' He put his arm affectionately about her shoulders. 'You just don't realize how miserable you'd be without all the intrigue. Or how crippled I'd be without your help.'

She returned his smile, wanting so to believe him. Then she held her head high and spoke with determination. 'You tell His Majesty that if the French are here with anything but honourable intentions, then Catholic or not, they must be repelled.' She held his hand and squeezed it. 'You see how reasonable we Catholics can be?'

'You and I share a great love for Siam, Maria, that is certain.' He kissed her lightly on the forehead and departed, fastening the strap of his conical hat about his chin as he went.

Three

'Mighty Lord and Master of Life, thy slave craves permission to speak and implores Your Majesty to suffer his unclean and defiled voice to reach the doors of thy divine ears.'

Prostrate, Phaulkon addressed his master and then raised himself on his knees and touched his forehead to the ground three times in the direction of the upper balcony. Though he could feel the royal presence above him, at no point did he dare look up. It was strictly forbidden. No mortal had ever gazed upon His Majesty's countenance, not even, it was rumoured, the ladies of his harem. It was customary at this point to shuffle forward three paces on knees and elbows to enable His Majesty to distinguish the person of the petitioner, and then to make three more obeisances. But on this occasion the ritual was superfluous: the forty mandarins of the first grade who normally attended the daily audiences were conspicuously absent.

Despite the daily meetings in the palace's panelled audience chamber, with its massive walls lacquered in red and gold and its nine tiers of ornate parasols hanging above the royal balcony, the King's chief minister still felt awed on those special occasions when he found himself alone with his liege in the vast hall, without the customary ranks of prostrate courtiers and their rows of betel boxes to keep him company. Though there were five grades of mandarins in the kingdom in descending order of importance, only the first, and occasionally the second grades, were allowed to attend the royal audiences. In matters of protocol, Siam was rigorous in the extreme.

It was clear that on this occasion His Majesty wished to discuss confidential matters with him alone. Phaulkon felt a tremor of excitement not unmixed with anxiety. He had not yet reported the sighting of so many French vessels by his Dutch spies; he had wanted to elicit an explanation from the French first.

He adjusted his white conical hat.

'High and Mighty Lord of me, thy slave,' he continued in the

30

royal ritual, 'I desire to take thy royal word and put it on my brain and on the top of my head.' Phaulkon remembered the ripple of astonishment that had greeted his first such address in the royal tongue. It was six years ago, almost to the day. The assembled mandarins had been stunned as he had started to speak, for no foreigner had ever mastered, or even attempted to master, the exclusive language of the court before. Few farangs, as foreigners were known, even spoke the vernacular and fewer still were of sufficient standing to be ushered into the Lord of Life's presence. Even His Majesty had been rendered momentarily speechless by the sounds of those lofty syllables emanating from the mouth of a farang. It was not till some time later that Phaulkon learned how profoundly affected the Lord of Life had been by his efforts. It had certainly been worth the struggle.

From the moment he first arrived in Siam Phaulkon had sensed his own special destiny with the fascinating country and he had set out to master every aspect of it. He had travelled deep into the provinces, shaved his head and entered a Buddhist temple where for six months, clothed in saffron, he had led the life of a novice monk, meditating upon the scriptures and going forth alone at dawn with his begging bowl. It was from an ancient monk there, who had at one time been in the service of the late King, that he had painstakingly learned the grand and ringing phrases of the ancient Pali tongue. His Majesty, after all, could never be addressed in the common vernacular and if ever Phaulkon were to fulfil his dream of one day coming into the royal presence . . .

'Vichaiyen,' the commanding voice from above interrupted his thoughts, 'we wish to know what news there is of the French.'

Phaulkon had grown used to his other name by now. At court, and throughout Siam, he was known as Pra Chao Vichaiyen, or Prince of Knowledge, a name conferred upon him by His Majesty. Only the farangs still called him by his former name.

'Mighty Sovereign, I receive your orders on my hair and on my head. The priest, the Jesuit Tachard, came to see me, your slave. He wished humbly to request the Master of Life's permission for the French to disembark.'

'We see. But are they to be trusted, these French?'

'August Lord, as much as the English or the Dutch. Only we need them more.'

'And do they bring with them the bodyguard we requested for our protection?'

'August Lord, your unworthy slave believes so.'

'You are not sure, Vichaiyen?'

'Mighty Sovereign, the dust of your foot would not wish to impart information that has not been verified.'

'A wise precaution, Vichaiyen. But are there then no facts at your disposal?'

'August Lord, I can only repeat what the priest told me. That a distinguished delegation from Your Majesty's esteemed colleague King Louis of France has arrived. The chief emissaries are Ambassador de la Loubère, a veteran senior diplomat, and Claude Cébéret du Boullay, one of the twelve directors of the French East India Company.' Phaulkon paused. 'And there is a General Desfarges, Your Majesty.'

'A general, did you say? Our generals command regiments of war elephants, Vichaiyen. What do French generals command?'

'August Lord, I, a speck of dust on the sole of your foot, understand that the General has been sent as a special gift to Your Majesty, a mark of King Louis' particular esteem for the Master of Life. For Your Majesty's added security, in lieu of the customary captain, the élite bodyguard has been placed under the command of a marshal of France.'

'We see. And what numbers did the priest tell you this General will be commanding?'

'August Lord, he said fifty.'

'And these are the same numbers you, Vichaiyen, requested from my brother, the King of France?'

'August Sovereign, the same.'

Why this persistent questioning? wondered Phaulkon.

His thoughts were interrupted by the sound of wheezing and coughing from above. Phaulkon was reminded sharply of Father Brouet's recent diagnosis. The priest had been charged with interpreting passages from the Bible for His Majesty, but he was also the most experienced of the Jesuit physicians. On his last visit he had asserted that the King was showing the initial symptoms of asthma, that terrible disease which rendered the

32

breathing ever harder until one's energies were wholly consumed in the effort to inhale air. It was alarming news, for the illness had no known cure and progressed rapidly. Besides, rumours about the royal health could provoke an instant upsurge in the endless intrigue and conspiracies of the various factions rivalling for the succession. The matter had been immediately hushed up.

'And what of our royal gift to King Rouee of the trading port of Ligor?' enquired His Majesty, still breathing heavily.

'Mighty Sovereign, I, a speck of dust on the sole of your foot, have the temerity to suggest that the French King has been over-liberal in his interpretations of Your Majesty's offer.'

'Over-liberal? Explain.'

'August Lord, I receive your orders. Not having accurate maps of the area, but being informed that Ligor is far from Your Majesty's seat of government, King Louis has requested the Lord of Life's gracious consideration in granting him facilities at Bangkok instead, a port which is known to him by reputation and whose proximity to Your Majesty in Ayudhya he finds particularly agreeable. The King of France has sent engineers and artisans, draughtsmen, astronomers and cannoneers to serve Your Majesty, and he asks to lodge them near you, the better to serve the Lord of Life.'

'We offered him Ligor not Bangkok.' The voice was firm, and the breathing regular again. 'Bangkok is not a trading post, Vichaiyen. It is a river fortress, a strategic port guarding the entrance to Ayudhya, the gateway to our very heartland.'

Phaulkon detected a rising note of irritation in His Majesty's voice. He was glad he had not brought up the question of Mergui. Though he had nothing but admiration for the wisdom and far-sightedness of this monarch who seemed to comprehend matters beyond his own sphere and who, by the standards of an Oriental despot at least, was surprisingly tolerant, yet there were limits, thresholds beyond which loss of face reached such unacceptable levels that behaviour became governed entirely by pride.

'August Lord, it is so,' replied Phaulkon, 'but I, a hair of your head, dare to suggest that the King of France is not so much mindful of Bangkok's strategic value as of its favourable proximity to the Lord of Life.'

33

'We shall find it easier to be touched by the King of France's concern when we discover precisely what his intentions are.'

'Mighty Sovereign, your unworthy slave is ascertaining that at this very moment. I shall bring the answer to your divine ears before today's sun is down.'

'Not a moment too soon, Vichaiyen.'

Phaulkon remained silent, his head pressed to the thick Persian carpet.

'After all,' continued His Majesty, 'it can't take long to investigate two ships.' The voice paused. 'You did say there were *two* ships, Vichaiyen?'

'August Lord, I receive your orders. The priest said there were two ships anchored off the bar.'

'You speak almost as if there might be others lurking somewhere.'

These continuing innuendos were becoming increasingly disconcerting. It was as if he were being tested, thought Phaulkon. What if His Majesty knew more than he was admitting? Withholding information from one's sovereign was punishable by a severe caning of the soles of the feet. In extreme cases, deception could even incur the death penalty.

'August Lord, this speck of dust's spies are verifying these matters at this very moment.'

'Which matters, precisely?'

Phaulkon hesitated. 'Mighty Lord, the possibility that there might be more ships of the French fleet than they are admitting to.'

'More ships? How many more?'

'August Sovereign, my spies working in the Dutch outpost at Little Amsterdam have claimed to have sighted four others. Several men disguised as fishermen are heading out towards them now and –'

'Four more ships?' interjected His Majesty. 'But that would make six in all! We are outraged. And our displeasure is barely mitigated by the fact that you have at last revealed what we already know. But it is time for you to learn more, Vichaiyen.' Phaulkon's heart froze as he heard His Majesty give an order.

In the next instant, the light from the four open bamboo shutters high in the panelled walls illuminated a prostrate figure crawling on knees and elbows into the audience hall, his conical hat tilted forward like the horn of a unicorn. He took up his position to one side and slightly to the rear of Phaulkon. As a mandarin of the first grade with ten thousand dignity marks, Ambassador Kosa Pan could not lie as close to the King's balcony as the Barcalon, who had fifteen thousand dignity marks. Whether on land or on water, in the cortège accompanying the royal elephant or the royal barge, the higher a nobleman's rank, the greater his proximity to his liege.

With an effort Phaulkon controlled his surprise and the anger that accompanied it. How dare Kosa Pan go straight to His Majesty without reporting to him first? It was highly irregular. The man had deliberately circumvented him. Worse than that, His Majesty appeared to have accepted the breach of protocol, making it impossible for Phaulkon to object openly. What the devil was Kosa doing back in Siam anyway?

Kosa Pan dipped his already bowed head slightly in Phaulkon's direction. He was the younger brother of the late Kosa Lek, the last Barcalon, whom Phaulkon had greatly admired and eventually succeeded. Pan, however, had spent most of his life travelling abroad as a royal emissary and Phaulkon did not know him well, though he had heard of his astuteness and knew that he had distinguished himself on numerous occasions in the diplomatic service. He would, however, pay dearly for this insult.

'Pan,' commanded the royal voice, 'you will tell us what you know of the French arrivals.'

'Mighty Sovereign, I receive your orders. I, a mere hair of your head, am distressed to report that there are six French ships anchored beyond the bar, four of them out of sight to avoid detection. At least two of them are superior warships with fifty-two and forty-eight cannon respectively. There are several battalions of troops in their bowels.'

Phaulkon felt his stomach churn. So Tachard had indeed lied about the number of troops just as he had lied about the number of ships. Why? he wondered. Why would that blighted priest deceive him when it was above all *his* assistance the Jesuits needed in bringing about His Majesty's conversion? The French designs must indeed be sinister. The truth descended on him like the blow of a sledgehammer. The French must be planning an

35

invasion. Fear and fury gripped him at the same time. Why, those God-cursed –

'It seems the élite bodyguard we requested from King Rouee has multiplied greatly on its journey, Vichaiyen.' His Majesty's tone was both indignant and sarcastic. He addressed Kosa now. 'How large a bodyguard would you say has now come to serve us?'

'Mighty Sovereign, I receive your orders. I, a speck of dust, judge their numbers to be between five and six hundred. There were many deaths on board, of some farang disease they call the scurvy. I saw men's teeth fall out before they died. They generally threw the corpses overboard at night, but I stayed awake to watch and counted a good thirty dead on my ship alone. I could not observe the extent of the casualties on the other ships, but when the epidemic was at its height, I overheard the crew discussing the great number of 'soldiers' who had succumbed on the other vessels. One crew member offered the opinion that at least a third of the entire force had been wiped out.'

'What, then, are your conclusions, Pan?' His Majesty's voice shook slightly, though it was difficult to tell whether from anxiety or suppressed rage. Phaulkon's heart had beat faster throughout the Ambassador's speech and his mounting fury was now almost choking him.

'August Lord and Master,' answered Kosa, 'by the power of the dust of your feet which covers my head, I conclude that the intentions of the French towards our sovereign nation are far from honourable and that they have sent an entire armed force to carry out their evil schemes.'

'And what might those schemes be, Pan?'

'Mighty Lord, the French have not made this worthless slave privy to their designs, but I believe they dare to imagine they can subjugate us by military force and impose upon the Master of Life their Christian faith – a matter which seems to obsess equally their King, his courtiers and his priests.'

'Is that so?' The royal tone was mocking and defiant at the same time. 'Pan, you will inform our Pra Klang of the degrading manner in which you reached our shores.'

'Mighty Lord, I receive your orders.' The Ambassador's head twisted slightly in the direction of Phaulkon. 'Your Excellency,

36

despite my repeated requests, the French were at great pains to prevent my going ashore. I had finally to escape by jumping overboard and swimming. It is quite clear to me that the French were anxious not to risk my alerting the Lord of Life as to the true size of their force.'

Phaulkon was genuinely shocked. A distinguished emissary of His Majesty of Siam forced to swim ashore? Had the French gone mad? Were they that desperate? The element of surprise in their plans must indeed be crucial. A sudden thought struck him, as he heard His Majesty now address him.

'What have you to say to all this, Vichaiyen?' The royal tone implied that Vichaiyen had some explaining to do. It had, after all, been his idea to invite the French to Siam.

'Mighty Sovereign, I receive your orders on my hair and on my head. I am indignant at the treatment of our esteemed Ambassador here, and only sorry that he did not come to inform me of his plight earlier. I am furthermore surprised by the behaviour of the French emissaries, who from their names and ranks I know to be people of some distinction. If the Lord of Life will permit me, I should first like to put a few questions to Ambassador Kosa before drawing any further conclusions.'

'You may proceed, Vichaiyen.'

'Mighty Lord, I receive your orders. Ambassador, may I ask whether anyone else left the boat with you when you so deftly made your escape?'

'No one, Your Excellency. I instructed my servants to remain below so as not to draw attention to my own movements. After my escape I was picked up by a barge heading towards my ship with a message from the Jesuits at the Seminary. They were reporting the delay of their colleague Tachard in returning to his ship. I identified myself and promptly ordered the boat to turn back.'

'So that, my lord, Father Tachard would not have been aware of your escape?'

'Indeed not, Your Excellency. He could have had no way of knowing.'

Phaulkon's mind was racing. It was all fitting into place. Tachard thought Kosa was still safely aboard the French ship. Damn these conniving Jesuits. They, and Tachard in particular,

37

would pay dearly for this. It was essential that he vindicate himself in the eyes of his master immediately. His relationship with the King might be one of mutual, almost filial esteem – the late Barcalon had once told him that His Majesty frequently referred to him as 'our farang son' – but the tenuous nature of power in an Oriental court did not allow for slips of this kind. Many a courtier, whose envy had long been aroused by the appointment of a farang to the supreme position of influence in the realm, would seize the first opportunity to topple him. No one might yet dare speak ill of the King's favourite in the royal presence, but this could soon change if the right occasion presented itself. It was essential that he come up with a suitable plan to counter this serious threat. He addressed Kosa once more.

'Ambassador, could you tell me something of the condition of the troops you saw? You mentioned that a large number had died on the voyage. Would you say that the rest were in reasonable health or generally worn down and out of spirits?'

'I would say, Your Excellency, that a combination of the long journey, the torrid climate and the death of so many of their comrades has left the majority much weakened and depressed. Many are still sick. General Desfarges himself has been bedridden for the past three days. Those that are well enough seem desperate for a change of scene and I heard many of them clamouring to go ashore.'

'So that, for the moment, they would hardly seem in a position to fight?'

'Not at this stage, Your Excellency.'

'Then time is on our side. Now, Ambassador, if we were to take advantage of their present weakness and dictate our own terms, the French might be forced to accept at least part of them, would you not agree?'

'Perhaps, Your Excellency, depending on the terms, of course. But that wouldn't alter their fundamental objective – the armed invasion of our country.'

'Only if we allow them to undertake it, Ambassador. Now you mentioned that their General was indisposed. What about his second-in-command? Who is he?'

'A Lieutenant General du Bruant, Your Excellency. I do not know his condition as he was not on my ship.'

'I see. I am sorry to have had to put so many questions to you, Ambassador, but you will appreciate that this is the first opportunity I have had of speaking to you about this crisis,' said Phaulkon pointedly.

He paused but Kosa kept silent. Phaulkon addressed His Majesty.

'Mighty Lord and Sovereign, I, your unworthy minion, beg to suggest a plan. It would seem unfortunate that though I requested fifty troops the French have seen fit to send five hundred. Yet do I see a way in which we might turn this to our advantage. We have but to harness such a force to suit our own purpose. Now, their men are weak and tired, their provisions undoubtedly low and their leader bedridden. This is the time to press our own demands.'

'And what might those be, Vichaiyen?'

'Mighty Lord, I receive your orders. In the first place, we should refuse any Frenchman, from the Marshal down to the lowliest corporal, permission to set foot on Siamese soil before the entire force has first agreed to pledge its allegiance to the Lord of Life, for as long as a single soldier remains on our territory. Such allegiance is to be pledged unconditionally in a grand public ceremony immediately upon the landing of the troops. In the second place, for every French soldier permitted to land, a Siamese soldier must be placed next to him, as a trainee. And let it be made perfectly clear from the start that the French army is here as the guest of our country, to train our troops in the art of warfare, as part of a joint military exercise to deter the Dutch, all within the framework of our grand alliance. Our people will thus know that this is no army of occupation. To this end, August Sovereign, I humbly advocate that we welcome the French arrivals – just as soon as they have accepted our terms.'

There was a moment's silence, interrupted by Kosa.

'May I be permitted to suggest, Excellency,' he said with barely hidden sarcasm, 'that the French are bound to reject such terms?'

'Not when they have considered the alternatives, Ambassador,' replied Phaulkon firmly. 'Half their men are demanding to go ashore and the other half are desperate for food and medicines, and their ships are too large to cross the bar even at high tide. The alternatives, therefore, are gradual starvation on board or instant massacre on shore. They would be forced to land in boats, where our waiting armies would outnumber them a thousand to one.'

'The terms you suggest, Excellency,' insisted Kosa, 'are too bitter a pill for the proud French nation to swallow.'

'Ah, but I intend to sweeten it, Ambassador.'

'In which way, Vichaiyen?' asked His Majesty in a tone that indicated growing interest.

'August Lord, I receive your orders. I have it on good authority that the principal objective of the French mission is to see the Master of Life converted to the Catholic faith – '

A short laugh from above interrupted him. 'What strange creatures indeed, these farangs, so advanced in matters of science and yet so backward in matters of the soul.' A note of concern crept into His Majesty's tone. 'You don't suppose, Vichaiyen, that King Rouee thinks us a fool for not instructing our ambassadors to attempt to convert him to the Buddhist faith while they were in Paris?' He paused as if contemplating the strangeness of such a mentality. 'Why, Vichaiyen, we would not even dream of constraining you, who are our chief minister, to renounce your faith in favour of our own. Surely every man has the right to his own belief? But we digress. Pray proceed with your plan.'

'Mighty Lord, I receive your orders. We must offer the French a prize. And with Your Majesty's gracious participation we could offer them the greatest prize of all: your own conversion. We could dangle that carrot before their hungry eyes till we have achieved our purpose. I have already taken the liberty of explaining to the Jesuits that Your Majesty is keen for your religious instruction to continue, but that it would be detrimental to their cause to press Your Majesty unduly. I have furthermore stressed that Your Majesty's attitude will almost certainly be influenced by the behaviour of the French delegation, especially if Your Majesty were to be favourably impressed by them. French military intervention will hardly predispose Your Majesty in their favour. Father Tachard will relay this to the leaders of his delegation.'

'We are indeed fortunate, Vichaiyen, that the blind zeal and fervent hopes of your Jesuit priests make it so much easier for us to mislead them. For if the French demands are indeed restricted to the matter of our conversion, and their leaders can be satisfied on so trivial a point, then we shall be happy to persuade them of the imminence of our conversion, which shall, of course, never take place. But will this be sufficient to entice them to accept our terms?'

'August Lord, not quite. The hair of your head begs to suggest that despite its strategic importance, we also appear to cede them the port of Bangkok for trading purposes, subject of course to their agreeing to pledge their full allegiance to Your Majesty.'

'Forgive me for interrupting, Your Excellency,' interjected Kosa Pan, barely masking his indignation, 'but to allow an experienced foreign force, equipped with the latest weaponry, to garrison the fort at Bangkok would be tantamount to military suicide.'

'Not while that force is recuperating, and while there is one Siamese for every Frenchman in the fort. We will place our best fighting men there and they will not be slow to learn. In addition, I know that the French soldiers, like any soldiers, will have only one thing on their mind after seven months at sea. The men will be starved of female company and will fall easy prey to the delights of our women, especially if we set the right trap for them. The women of Siam are probably the most beautiful in the world, and if they can just exercise their charms on them, military matters will soon fade from their minds. You can hardly garrison a fort with a contingent of lovesick soldiers.'

'But who is to say, Vichaiyen, that our women would be willing to undergo such sacrifices?'

'Mighty Lord, I receive your orders. With Your Majesty's gracious permission, we could spread the word through the marketplaces that the French troops are the honoured guests of our country and that the Lord of Life has expressed the wish that they be received with every mark of hospitality.'

'And who, Vichaiyen, is to spread this word and ready these female legions for battle? We trust that your own extensive

duties, if not the feelings of your Catholic wife, will not personally allow you to perform that task?'

Phaulkon managed a smile, despite himself. In less serious
moments, His Majesty always derived pleasure from teasing him
about the Catholic insistence upon monogamy, not least because
Phaulkon had requested permission to house his beloved concubine, Sunida, at the palace on account of his wife's intransigence.
His Majesty believed this restriction to be one of the most absurd
precepts of the Catholic faith, and his own extensive readings on
the various mistresses of the French King had only served to
confirm him in his view. While no Buddhist monk could touch a
woman on pain of death, here was the supposed Defender of the
Catholic Faith behaving like any normal mandarin.

'August Lord, this unworthy minion believes that someone is
needed whose loyalty is unquestioned, whose tongue is persuasive and whose mind is quick to grasp. I would humbly recommend Sunida for the task.'

'A wise choice, Vichaiyen. Sunida is a pearl among women,
and we approve. But she must see to it that our women appear
hospitable and not loose, anxious to please yet not fawning.'

'Mighty Lord, I receive your orders. Sunida will see to it that
they succumb to the troops of France with creditable modesty
and appropriate reticence.'

'If well prepared, such a plan could perhaps keep the troops
distracted. But be warned, Vichaiyen, that its greatest chance of
failure comes from your legions of interfering priests. They will
not be subject to the charms of our women and they will upbraid
the soldiers for their dissolute living, threatening them with
eternal damnation. For the conduct of the troops will interfere
with their plans, and they will not rest, these Jesuits, till they
have seen me a Catholic. They are ruthless connivers, dedicated
to their cause, obsessed with overthrowing governments who do
not see things their way, bigoted zealots who believe their duty
on this earth lies in supplanting peaceful religions that have
existed in harmony with life around them for a great many
centuries longer than their own. We fear them more than we do
the French army.'

After a suitable pause, Phaulkon asked, 'August Lord, do I

take it then that your humble slave may offer the French Bangkok?'

'We are anxious to avoid bloodshed, Vichaiyen. Though we are incensed at the treatment of our Ambassador here, and appalled by the ignominious manner of his arrival ashore, yet are we reticent to start a confrontation even on that account. Not the least because it would defeat the whole purpose of inviting the French to our shores: to put an end to the ambitions of the Dutch. It would be senseless for the Hollanders now to see that we are not the great allies of France after all. But rest assured, Pan, that the insult to you will one day be avenged. In the meantime, we thank you for your diligence.'

'August Lord, I, a hair of your head, thank you for your gracious words,' replied Kosa. 'But my loss of face is greatest in that the French will know my advice has gone unheeded and that my entire escape was in vain.'

'Furthermore, Ambassador,' said Phaulkon drily, 'I am afraid we will need to spread the rumour that the reason we did not take your warnings to heart was because we believed your suspicions to be exaggerated and your vindictiveness aroused by the unfortunate mode of your escape; that we are on the contrary delighted by the size of the French contingent which will put paid once and for all to any aspirations the Dutch may have. But know, Ambassador, that while your loss of face will be temporary, your service to the nation will be permanent.'

'History will one day be witness to my warnings, Excellency,' said Kosa Pan, his voice quivering.

A fit of coughing resounded from the upper balcony. Phaulkon determined to have another word with Father Brouet about His Majesty's condition.

'So be it, then,' said His Majesty hoarsely. 'The French emissaries shall be invited to disembark under the conditions previously stipulated. If they agree, they will be received with full honours. No expense will be spared and we ourselves will receive their chiefs of delegation in audience. Vichaiyen, you are authorized to offer them the facilities of the port of Bangkok and to inform them that our nurses will be at their disposal to care for their sick. We will assemble their troops in the fort there, the

43

better to keep an eye on them. And while receiving them with open arms, we will pretend to be unaware of their real intentions.

'We thank you for your wisdom, Vichaiyen, and recommend you prepare the ground thoroughly with Sunida before the troops disembark. And know too, Vichaiyen, that we are gratified in the knowledge that so strong a bridge as yourself stands between French interests and our own.'

'Mighty Lord and Sovereign, your bounty knows no limit,' said Phaulkon, touched as well as relieved to be back on course again.

'Let us then see to it together that the ancient sovereignty of Siam is maintained for a further thousand years. The audience is at an end.'

The sound of trumpets and the clash of cymbals announced His Majesty's departure, and Phaulkon and Kosa Pan crawled reverently backwards out of the chamber.

As usual a flutter went through Phaulkon's stomach as he approached Sunida's door and saw it had been left ajar. She must have heard he was with the Lord of Life earlier than planned.

In the next instant, a wide-eyed, silk-skinned little Eurasian girl dressed in a miniature blue sarong ran out from behind the door and jumped into his arms. Her ankle bracelets chimed pleasantly as he lifted her up. No child in Siam could escape far with that noise following it about, he reflected. She pulled affectionately at his chin and giggled. 'Surplise,' she repeated again and again, happily, barely able to say the word. He laughed out loud. How he doted on his daughter.

He hugged Supinda to him and carried her into the apartment where a royal nurse immediately prostrated herself. The room was sparsely but tastefully furnished. Apart from the variety of musical instruments that had once served Sunida's trade, there was a lacquered gold cabinet, a couple of bamboo screens and a cotton quilt on the floor. Two large Burmese tapestries adorned the walls. The apartment was situated on the first floor of the palace, just before the maze of corridors that criss-crossed the royal harem. This enabled Phaulkon to visit Sunida without passing through the women's quarters, which were strictly out of bounds to all but the scores of eunuchs and dozens of young pages who had not yet reached puberty.

44

'Well, you scion of a goddess and an adventurer,' Phaulkon tickled his daughter's toes, 'how are you today?'

Supinda fastened her chubby little arms about his neck and squeezed. Even at the age of four he could see a lot of Sunida in her, especially in the high cheekbones and the large almond eyes. He continued to play with her for a while, tossing her up in the air while she whooped with delight, until a discreet cough from the nurse told him it was feeding time.

He handed her over with regret, while she showed no sign of complaint. The children of Siam were held in such special affection by all around them that they seldom had time to feel neglected or abandoned; it was not uncommon for the extended families to bring a child up. Phaulkon watched his daughter leave, and then Sunida stood framed in the doorway, like some tall, exotic goddess.

She never failed to take his breath away. Her long, black hair, freshly washed and scented, fell in dark streams to her waist and the top of her multicoloured silk panung clung tightly to her waist, accentuating its narrow girth. Her skin, the colour of light teak, was as smooth as silk without a blemish on it. Her breasts were covered loosely by a cotton shawl, not out of any feeling of modesty but because she knew that her master liked it that way. He had once told her that one of his most sensual moments – and there were many between them – was when the shawl slipped away from her shoulders and revealed her firm breasts to his rapt gaze. She was proud too, he knew, of the look that infused his eyes, a mixture of admiration and animal desire. It was a voluptuous moment for her, she had once confided in him, to see so powerful a man bend and surrender to her will.

Sunida smiled radiantly at her lord, gracefully lowering her whole body to the ground like a gazelle, her hands cupped in front of her in the Siamese fashion. She was pleased, too, that he favoured her own customs. So much more erotic, he had assured her, than rushing into one another's arms like the farangs did.

He closed the door and knelt on one knee before her. It never ceased to fascinate him how this coy, graceful woman, raised in the traditional ways of Siamese composure, could in the next instant turn into the most uninhibited creature that ever clawed its way through a man's defences.

45

'Sunida, you are a goddess,' he said.

She let the shawl slide gently from her shoulders and knelt before him, her head bowed.

'That cannot be, my lord, else I would be in better control of my emotions each time I saw you.'

Phaulkon remained on one knee, devouring her with his eyes, savouring the moment. How wondrous it was that such strong emotions could be fully reciprocated. She looked so genuinely pleased to see him that once again he found himself thanking the gods for that day almost six years ago when he had met her. What a quirk of fate had brought their paths together. And what an eventful career they had had, ever since the days when she had been a classical dancer at the court of Ligor, and he, ostensibly working for the East India Company, had been smuggling cannon to the rebel Queen of Pattani. His ship had run aground off the coast of Ligor and during the investigations that followed, the Governor of that province had given a banquet in honour of the English traders and Sunida had danced before them there. She was the leader of the dance troupe, and had been statelier and more talented than the rest of the performers combined. He had been unable to take his eyes off her. She, for her part, had never seen a farang with straight black hair, good looks and fine manners like her own people, and his smile had quite entranced her.

When the Governor had finally cleared him of any charges and granted him leave to return to Ayudhya, Phaulkon had requested permission to take Sunida with him. But the wily Governor had refused. It was only afterwards that Phaulkon had found out that she was in fact the Governor's niece. When, two months later, he had resigned from the service of the English Crown and thrown in his lot with Siam, the same Governor, aware of Phaulkon's infatuation, had recommended to His Majesty that she be sent to spy on him. They had been deeply in love, the spy and the farang, but she had performed her duty to her King nonetheless while he, apprized of her role by a stroke of good fortune, had been able to feed suitable information through her to the highest levels of the palace. It had worked wonders for his career.

Now, of course, he was the Pra Klang, the leading notable in

46

the land, and she had no need to spy on him any more; but to this day he had never revealed to her that he had known of her role, nor she that she had ever undertaken it. It was the only secret between them. He wished it could be the same with Maria. But there were too many things that could not be spoken between them, like little Supinda, whose existence was known only to the bevy of palace nurses who looked after her by royal order. It was in moments like these that he could not help asking himself why he had married Maria. But he quickly chastized himself for such uncharitable thoughts. He had married her for a variety of reasons – and he did not regret it. The reasons were partly political because circumstances had called for a Catholic wife, partly intellectual because he enjoyed and respected her wit and wisdom, and partly emotional because she, like him, was a Eurasian. The fact that she was one by blood and he only by temperament did not make any difference. It was a mental bond they shared, strong and intimate.

Phaulkon saw Sunida regularly every day following his audience with the King and he was convinced that his love, which seemed to grow continually in strength, was nurtured by the brevity of their moments together. There was none of the bickering so common to those who shared a household. Sunida and he had time only for love and they had so much to tell each other during that brief period each day that it was as if they had just met after a long absence.

Sunida, for her part, was the envy of every girl in the palace, being the honoured minor wife of the great Pra Klang. Sure of her master's love for her and conditioned by her Siamese upbringing, she felt no jealousy or bitterness towards his major wife. If anything, she felt only mystified that the major wife did not seek her help in looking after the husband. After all, a man was such a complex and demanding creature. Why would any one woman want to assume the whole burden of pleasing him for herself? Was it not obvious that two women could do a better job than one?

She sat next to Phaulkon now, stretching her long legs outwards to one side and resting her head gently in his lap. Her fingers drummed lightly on the underside of his thighs and he felt an instant stirring. His thoughts dissolved and his hand slid over her bare shoulder, slowly tracing the contours of her breasts. They were a shade lighter than the rest of her torso, having had less exposure to the sunlight. She sighed with pleasure and then, raising herself onto her knees, stretched her body to its full height like a cat, bringing her voluptuous breasts, their dark nipples erect, in line with his hungry mouth. She arched her back, threw her head backwards and with eyes closed abandoned herself to the sensations that flowed through her. Then, aching to reciprocate, she sought the knot of his panung and while her long delicate fingers loosened it, her tongue met his in a frenzied embrace.

He pulled her to the ground now, clasping her tightly to him until, lost in the fever of their passion, they rolled about the floor, oblivious to its hardness. And when, at last, they were spent, they lay together panting in one another's arms, still clinging to each other as if they were fearful that the spell might be broken.

After a while she put her nose close to his cheek and inhaled him deeply in the Siamese fashion. In the heat of passion she would use her mouth and tongue as he had taught her, but when they were calm again she liked to kiss him in the way of her people, gently sniffing the texture of his skin and savouring its scent. The Siamese were nonplussed by the joining together of mouths, the same mouths which the gods had given them for swallowing food, and they looked upon such customs as gross and unrefined. Phaulkon suspected that Sunida only succumbed to such barbarity to please him. There wasn't even a word in their language for 'kiss'. They used the word for 'sniff' or 'inhale'.

He put his own nose to her cheek now and inhaled her in turn. She purred with pleasure at the delicacy.

He tapped the end of her dainty nose playfully. It was straight and flared only gently at the nostrils, without the squatness of many of her countrymen. The beautiful almond eyes set in the high cheekbones stared back at him expectantly.

'Sunida, I have news for you. A project.' She raised herself up on one elbow, her face suddenly bright with anticipation. She loved nothing more than an adventure in the service of her master. It had been a while now since the last mission.

'Tell me, my lord. What is it to be?'

48

'Where is your Buddhist virtue of patience, Sunida?' he teased.

'I knew it once, along with several others, before my master came and took them all away.'

He laughed. 'Sunida, the farangs are coming again, whole shiploads of them this time.'

She screwed up her nose distastefully. 'I don't need whole shiploads, my lord. I have the one I want.' She tapped the end of Phaulkon's nose playfully in turn and laughed with childlike delight. 'Where will the exclusivity of my specimen be, if there are hordes of others running about the place?'

'They won't be running about for long, Sunida. With your help we're going to turn them into vegetables. Every one of them.'

Sunida cackled delightedly. 'Vegetables? Farang vegetables! Tomatoes, no doubt, to match the colour of their skins. How is my lord going to achieve that?'

'Sunida, these men are French soldiers and do not come here with good intentions. Yet we must receive them with every show of courtesy and deflect them from their purpose.' He paused. 'Siam must seduce them by its charm.'

Sunida considered for a moment. 'How many of them are there, my lord?'

'About five hundred.'

'Five hundred! Lord Buddha save us. I hope you haven't singled me out for this project, my lord?'

He laughed. 'You'll have help, Sunida. All the help you need.'

'But what do they want, all these farang soldiers?'

He looked at her steadily, his expression serious now. 'I think they would like to take over our country.'

Sunida's expression turned to horror. She raised herself indignantly onto her haunches, taking care not to bring her head above the level of his. 'Never!' she cried. 'Never will we allow it. The Lord of Life's armies would rather depart this life's cycle than suffer such shame.' She prostrated herself at the mention of the King.

'Our objectives will best be achieved by peaceful means, Sunida, not by war.'

She looked up at him penitently. 'Of course, my lord. Forgive me. We must make them welcome, make them feel at home until they relax their guard. We must make them love our country and

49

its customs, so that the aggression will be drained from them. We will sap their strength by showing them our qualities.'

Phaulkon stared at her, marvelling at her astuteness. She was so quick to understand and so fiercely loyal to King and country – had she not after all spied faithfully on him, the very man she loved? But this time, thank God, she was on his side. There was no one he trusted more in this world.

'That is precisely what we are going to do, Sunida. And I want you to organize it for me. The farangs will be disembarking in a few days and we must be ready for them.'

'We will be, my lord. I will devise a plan. I already know just who to go and see. For I think we need some very special girls.' She smiled coquettishly. 'And rather than fail you, I promise to take the whole lot on myself.'

'I didn't know how to ask you,' bantered Phaulkon, smiling in turn. 'But don't forget that our knowledge of the real reasons the French are here must not be revealed. The farangs must be taken by surprise and any girls you use must be oblivious of our motives.'

'Don't worry, my lord. They will be asked to welcome the farangs as a matter of hospitality. We are famous for entertaining visitors, are we not? Why should our girls suspect anything anyway? But who are these farangs, my lord, and where have they come from?'

'From France. They've been seven months at sea.'

Sunida laughed roguishly. 'Seven months? Why, they'll be like kapok in our hands. Leave them to me, my lord.' She looked up at him enquiringly. 'Will you take me to France as my reward if I succeed?' She was only half joking, he knew. Like her sovereign liege, Sunida had an insatiable desire to see the world and to learn of other nations and other races.

'When the last man is reduced to inertia, we will speak of your reward, Sunida.'

'Thank you, my lord. But I want to ask you, are we to deal with the leaders as well, I mean the men in charge?'

'No, you don't have to worry about them. I will handle them myself.'

'Very well, my lord.' She half rose to her feet and, bending her body low out of respect, she crossed the room to a little

50

recessed corner which served as a bathing area. A large earthenware jar with dragon designs painted on the sides stood full of
water. She dipped a cloth in it and returned to sponge her
master's body.

She was gentle with him, as always, and he looked up at her,
his expression full of love. 'I am fortunate to have such a woman
as you.'

'And I thank the Lord Buddha every day of my life for having
delivered such a fine master into my hands. Yesterday I took
some offerings to the temple.' She paused a moment in reflection.
'Forgive me for asking, my lord. I know your honoured major
wife still wants you all to herself, but will it always be so? I mean,
will she one day tire of shouldering all the responsibility and call
in others to help? For instance now, could we not have worked
on this project together?'

'I fear not, Sunida. Your two worlds must remain for ever
apart.'

'In that case, my lord, I shall worry about it no longer.' She
smiled resignedly.

He rose to leave, relieved that her feelings were not those of
envy or jealousy but merely of bewilderment and incomprehen-
sion. It was one of the few things this bright and eager child
could not truly fathom. 'I must go now and prepare to deliver
those farang hordes into your hands.'

'And I, my lord, must prepare their downfall.' She remained
respectfully prostrate until the door had closed behind him.

Four

The two Frenchmen sat opposite each other across the large mahogany desk in the main cabin of *l'Oiseau*. Gilt chairs stood in each corner and a portrait of Louis XIV hung from one of the walls. Despite the heat, la Loubère was still dressed in full European clothes, though the less formal trade director had abandoned his coat and wig, allowing his corpulent form to spread itself across a chair in its shirt-sleeves. The gaunt figure of la Loubère, by contrast, was stiffly erect, and every now and then he raised a hand to pull at the collar of his coat. His face was beaded with sweat beneath the heavy wig. The open porthole provided little comfort, and though it would have been less oppressive to remain on deck, the two men needed the privacy of the cabin for their talks.

La Loubère adjusted his wig and eyed Cébéret quizzically. 'Well, Claude, what is our next step?' The question was largely rhetorical. In matters concerning religion and politics, la Loubère's views took precedence, and the present crisis was certainly more political than commercial. 'Tachard, I'm sure, has been apprehended. We cannot just sit here and await his return. The Siamese will probably be arming now and the longer we give them, the better prepared they'll be to face us.'

'In my view, Simon, the Siamese army will be just as reticent to face the French soldiers as our own beleaguered forces will be to confront them. The Siamese must be as uncertain of the sophistication of our latest weaponry as we are of their numbers. I think our best bet is to sit it out and await the arrival of Tachard or some other messenger. Besides, the Siamese have not yet turned down our requests for Bangkok and Mergui, and our orders from the King were to exhaust all diplomatic channels first, before proceeding to more forceful means. We can hardly be said to have done that.'

'Before Kosa Pan's escape I would have agreed with you, but everything has changed. Any delay now can only be to our

52

disadvantage. If Tachard is not back by tomorrow, I advocate we attempt to sail across the bar at high tide.'

'Duquesne said he was sure the water was not deep enough for vessels of this size. What if we run aground?'

'Damn Duquesne. Vaudricourt told me we might make it. He reads Portuguese and he has been studying their charts carefully.'

'Why don't we send another emissary to investigate instead?' suggested Cébéret, anxious to present any plan that might delay a confrontation.

La Loubère screwed up his nose in disdain. 'Another emissary? Why, they'll only delay him like Tachard, if that is their tactic. No, the Portuguese charts state clearly that the monsoon season is the time when ships can cross the bar, and once over it, they can sail all the way up to Ayudhya. We'll take *l'Oiseau* and the *Gaillard*. What a display of strength could we not put on with our cannon pointed at the heart of their capital city! Why, we might not even have to fire a single shot.' La Loubère observed the look of doubt on Cébéret's face. 'Don't misunderstand me, Claude, I'm not seeking war any more than you are. On the contrary, I believe that now that the truth has been exposed, the best way to avoid a conflict is by speaking from a position of strength. Diplomatic niceties would be superfluous at this stage.'

'Kosa may suspect the object of our mission, Simon, but he has no positive proof. He is hardly privy to the details of the French plan. He can only assert to having seen a large number of men whose presence on board we have anyway explained. They are artisans, draughtsmen, engineers, physicians, Jesuits – all non-fighting men – sent as gifts to the King of Siam.'

'I think you underestimate that wily little envoy, Claude. He is reasonably conversant in French and I saw him on several occasions talking to our officers and even to some of the deckhands. Who knows what they might have let slip? Every last man was aware there were battalions of troops aboard.'

'Perhaps,' conceded Cébéret. 'But I still maintain we cannot be sure.' For a moment he looked despondent. La Loubère was right of course. The Siamese Ambassador was no fool. His sojourn in Paris had clearly shown that. The great Siamese embassy to the court of Versailles, which Kosa Pan had headed in the summer of 1686, had been a glittering success. There had

53

been much talk of the splendid gifts sent by the King of Siam: the twin baby elephants, the rhinoceros sedated with opium, flasks and chests of gold, Chinese and Indian rugs, Japanese screens, animal horns whose powder provided powerful aphrodisiacs, not to mention the fifteen hundred pieces of exquisite porcelain. Every dignitary in France had scrambled to fête the Siamese more lavishly than the next man. Tales of their gallantry towards the French ladies abounded, and considering that they weren't French, they were deemed to be remarkably witty! The French nobility had been titillated by Kosa's anecdotes about his twenty-four wives. The Siamese had had their portraits painted in one of the salons of Versailles, and their state entrance into Paris had consisted of a cortège of no less than sixty carriages drawn by six horses apiece, seating the cream of French aristocracy. In Paris they had attended theatres, balls and operas. Louis XIV himself, clad in formal robes of brocade, had received them in solemn audience in the Salon de la Paix, while Ambassador Kosa, prostrate throughout, presented him with a letter from King Narai and eventually crawled out backwards to avoid turning his back on him.

But all this grand reception, reflected Cébéret bitterly, however it might have impressed Kosa at the time, would not count for much now.

'I am not suggesting that Kosa was aware of the exact orders of our sovereign, Claude.' La Loubère fidgeted yet again with the collar of his coat. 'What I am stressing is that he will advise his sovereign strongly against the French terms as a matter of principle. And if the Siamese authorities are to be forewarned anyway, we might as well show our hand openly, before the enemy has time to prepare himself fully.'

'Siam is not the enemy yet. Just a nation we are attempting to subjugate,' said Cébéret wrily.

'A nation we are trying to civilize,' corrected la Loubère, 'by bringing to it the true faith. There is a difference.'

'A very thin one, if I may say so, and the end result is much the same. It would be more practical, and more beneficial to both parties, simply to enter into a series of trade agreements. Especially when we know the Siamese are prepared to make valuable concessions.'

'There you go again, ignoring the main purpose of our mission. We are here to convert the King.'

'But do you not see that we are dependent on Phaulkon for that? And if he is on our side, why has he not released Tachard yet?'

'No doubt the King has intervened after being warned of our intentions by his Ambassador. Phaulkon has been overruled.' La Loubère gave up the battle with his sweat-soaked collar and took off his coat.

'Phaulkon is a trader by profession, Simon. And traders are generally pragmatists. Which is why we should concentrate on our commercial demands instead. They will be far easier to obtain than the King's conversion. The Siamese King is not likely to adopt a new faith just to avert a war, but he might well give up two trading posts to that end.'

'Bangkok and Mergui, as I keep trying to tell you, are but secondary objectives.'

Cébéret controlled his frustration. Why was la Loubère so stubborn? Could he not grasp that policies had to change with circumstances? 'It puzzles me how you can continue to believe that Phaulkon, already wielding ultimate power in Siam, should risk his master's displeasure by trying to convert him against his will.'

'Because he is a Catholic, Claude, and true Catholics share only one desire, a desire he has clearly indicated in his letters to our sovereign King.'

'Letters written under duress, while the Dutch were hammering at his door. He had to think of something fast.'

'You're not a true believer, Claude, which makes it difficult for you to judge.'

'Phaulkon was a Protestant when he worked for the English and now he is a Catholic. Convenient, don't you think, when he needs the French?'

La Loubère banged his fist loudly on the table. 'Your constant lack of faith infuriates me. The sincerity of Phaulkon's intentions will be put to the test soon enough. In the meantime I will not be provoked by your endless pessimism.' His voice was rising. 'Neither will I be swayed from my mission. I will give Tachard

55

one more day to return. After that we take action. My decision is final.'

There was a long, heavy silence, interrupted at last by a knock at the door.

'Who is it?' demanded la Loubère brusquely.

The door opened slightly. 'It's me, gentlemen, Desfarges. I was looking for you.'

In the next instant the General's portly frame stood encased in the doorway, blocking the light. His chest was heaving spasmodically and strands of his thinning grey hair were stuck in an uneven patchwork to his perspiring forehead. His light blue eyes shone feverishly and he looked drained and weak.

'Come in, General,' said la Loubère. 'How are you feeling?'

'Not so well, I'm afraid. I've been having nightmares about Father Tachard. He hasn't returned yet, has he?'

'I am afraid not,' replied la Loubère. 'We were just discussing the situation. Won't you join us? We were reluctant to disturb you earlier.'

'I find it hard to rest at a time like this, gentlemen.' Desfarges pulled a chair out of the corner and sank heavily into it, filling it completely with his bulging sides. 'I hear the little Ambassador has escaped.' He mopped his brow with a handkerchief and dried the corners of his eyes. Perspiration stained his blouse. 'Who would have thought he would have plunged overboard in full ceremonial attire!'

'What do you make of Tachard's continued absence, General?' asked Cébéret.

'I cannot believe he would have disobeyed orders. It was his duty to return to this ship with the minimum of delay. It smells of foul play to me.'

'And what do you think should be done about it?' pursued Cébéret.

With an effort Desfarges pulled himself upright in his seat. 'We came here with a mandate from our great sovereign – long may he reign – to impose certain conditions, did we not? If those conditions are not met, or if we encounter resistance, as far as I am concerned we should take appropriate action to enforce them.'

'Quite right, General,' agreed la Loubère readily.

'But the Siamese haven't resisted yet,' pointed out Cébéret. 'All they've done is show no sign of life.'

'Well, I find it intolerable,' said Desfarges, his voice cracking, 'that after seven months at sea, with one hundred and fifty of my men dead of the scurvy, we are left to lie here within shouting distance of shore while not one Siamese comes to greet us. I can only conclude that they're preparing some act of treachery.'

'But is your army in any condition to deal with it, General?' asked Cébéret, looking him straight in the eye.

Desfarges lowered his gaze for a moment. 'My men are not in the best of shape perhaps, but I'm sure it's nothing that the impetus of a little skirmish couldn't put right,' he said, his tone bragging.

'Even though we no longer have the element of surprise?' Cébéret persisted.

'Ah! But we still have the cannon, and the French soldier his lion-heart. Every man knows he must carry out the orders of King Louis.' He paused, his brow puckered in concentration. 'We could perhaps send another emissary ashore to request the handing over of the ports of Bangkok and Mergui. If our request is refused, we could then give the Siamese an ultimatum and if that ultimatum should expire, we could open hostilities. By the time we have exhausted all those possibilities, my men will have had a few days at least to recuperate.'

'But what if the Siamese refuse us permission to land and our ships are unable to cross the bar?' insisted Cébéret.

'We have not yet established that,' interjected la Loubère.

Desfarges considered for a moment. 'If we cannot cross the bar, we will have a problem, gentlemen. Our provisions are running low and the truth is, my men are getting restless on board. We would have to attempt a landing in small boats, which would expose us to great risk. The troops would be subject to every sort of harassment on unfamiliar ground and we do not yet know the size of the enemy forces.'

'So that the only reasonable course to pursue at the moment would be to attempt to cross the bar?' put in la Loubère.

'There would seem to be little alternative, sir, if all else fails. We can hardly let the Siamese starve us out on our ships.'

The three men looked towards the door as the rapid tramping

of feet was heard coming down the companionway. It was a private stair that led only to the main cabin. There was a hurried knock.

'Come in,' called la Loubère.

'Forgive me for interrupting, sir,' said a young officer, 'but the Reverend Father has returned. His boat is coming alongside now.'

The three men rose and headed rapidly for the door.

Five

Sunida smiled at the guard in the smart red tunic as she walked up to the palace gate. The guard wai'd to her, always pleased to see the honourable minor wife of the exalted Pra Klang. She was very popular with the palace guards. Not only was she lovely to behold, but her manner was gentle and open. There was none of that haughtiness so common to many of the mandarins, and she always bestowed a radiant smile of recognition on even the humblest of palace minions. She was the only one of the palace females allowed beyond its walls, for none of the King's consorts would ever see the outside world again.

Soon Sunida was happily mingling with the throng, walking barefoot like the rest of them. Only mandarins wore slippers in the Muslim fashion, their points turned up like the prow of a small boat. Sunida wore a mauve panung that descended to her knees and a matching cotton sash that was loosely draped about her breasts and shoulders. Her hair was oiled and scented, and done up neatly in a bun in the style of the day.

She enjoyed these outings from the palace, the more so since they were occasional, and their very infrequency caused her to take in every detail of the surrounding scene as if she might never see it again.

The Lord Buddha had indeed been kind to her, she reflected, as she crossed a humped bridge that straddled one of the city's many canals. She entered the tree-lined alleyway where the artisans plied their trade: silversmiths, weavers, wood carvers, gilders, jewellers, lacquerware painters, and countless others. She sighed happily. She belonged to the foremost mandarin in the land and she was devoted to him. He visited her every day and the strictures of palace life were relieved by these occasional but exciting sorties into the outside world. She had a child to care for and her master's well-being to watch over. She was a valuable listening post for him within the palace, where gossip and intrigue, enclosed as the occupants were within its thick walls, seemed to flourish all the more on account of it. The palace was a world unto itself, a separate kingdom where not a day passed that did not give rise to a new rumour, which gathered momentum as it passed from mouth to mouth, heading always towards the sensational. It was her job to sift rumour from reality, especially when the talk centred upon her master, which it so often did.

Last week it was Kanika, one of the Lord of Life's more recently acquired concubines, who was rumoured to have seduced the twelve-year-old Tong, the third gentleman of the royal bedchamber, and initiated the trembling page into the use of his love lance. If the rumour were true and they were discovered, they would both be roasted alive on a slow-turning spit, observing each other's agony side by side, just as they had lived their ecstasy. For in Siam, as was only fair, the punishment was always appropriate to the crime.

Rumours about the arrival of the French farangs had already begun to circulate. Some said it was a small bodyguard dispatched by the King of France as a gift to the Lord of Life, while others – and here was the worrying aspect – maintained it was a large army sent to control the country with the connivance of the Pra Klang. As always, it was impossible to trace the source of the rumours, but many claimed that these were the very thoughts of General Petraja, the Commander-in-Chief of the Royal Regiment of Elephants and the distinguished Chairman of His Majesty's Privy Council. Despite his impeccable manners and his air of sincerity, Sunida had no doubt that the General, who had certainly expected to be named the next Pra Klang, greatly resented the Lord of Life's choice of her master instead. She sensed that Petraja might only be awaiting the right moment to bring his challenge out into the open.

Sunida was now anxious to reach the marketplace and confer with Sri whose peasant wisdom she had come to trust and whose admiration for Phaulkon she knew to be unquestioned. Sri had once been her conduit to the palace during that trying period when Sunida had been recruited to spy on Phaulkon. How often had the two of them not prayed together that he would not incriminate himself and force them to report guilty thoughts or actions to the palace. Throughout the ordeal, and probably on account of it, Sunida and Sri had become fast friends and Sunida enjoyed nothing more than visiting the vendor at her little market stall. Sri's jovial good humour and her raucous laughter were contagious and there was always so much news to catch up with.

Sunida passed under the flowered arch that marked the entrance to the marketplace. Immediately the crowd seemed to double. Various aromas filled the air, scented flowers, pungent durian, dried fish, exotic spices, while the whole market was abuzz with the noise of bartering and the shouts of gesticulating vendors.

Sunida made her way past endless stalls covered with mulitcoloured umbrellas to shield them from the sun, until she reached the fruit and vegetable stall that was Sri's domain. The plump, goodnatured vendor was extemporizing loudly, enticing the crowd to come closer and then abusing those who would not buy from her. On sighting Sunida, she broke off her harangue in mid-sentence.

'Little mouse, what an unexpected surprise! What happy wind brings you here? I thought your spying days were over,' she added in a hushed tone.

'Pi Sri,' said Sunida, addressing her middle-aged friend affectionately as elder sister, 'our days of conspiracy are not over. We have a new project.'

'Another project!' exclaimed Sri, slapping both her thighs at once. 'Oh merciful Buddha, thou hast heard my prayers. How often have I not begged to be relieved of the boredom of successfully overcharging my poor customers. A project, you say? I am all ears.' She tapped the ground beside her.

Sunida settled down comfortably next to Sri, crossing her legs like a tailor, while the vendor rolled up a large tobacco leaf and stuck it between her betel-stained teeth. She leaned forward to light the end in the flames below the insect roaster, took a deep puff and then sat back expectantly.

Sunida was about to elaborate when a customer ambled up to the stall and began examining a large water melon. Sri glanced menacingly at her, as if she had no business intruding at a moment like this. The old woman, however, seemed not to have noticed and took her time. She was obviously the choosy type.

From time to time she cast an appraising glance at Sunida and, before long, Sri was exasperated.

'You can't afford that one,' she exclaimed irritably. 'It's overpriced and I won't come down a single salung.'

'Is it now? That's for me to judge.' Undeterred, the old lady continued examining the fruit, turning it over and over in her hands. As she brought it close to her nose to sniff it, she again glanced at Sunida.

Sri was losing all patience. 'You're wasting your time. That stall over there has all the good bargains.' She pointed over her shoulder.

The woman now looked straight at Sri and smiled. She was slim and graceful and had aged well. Her deep brown complexion was set off by her grey hair, cropped short, and the wrinkled skin surrounding her fine features gave her an air of weathered dignity. She must have been a very handsome woman in her prime.

'The other stalls have already informed me that your goods are overpriced,' she said, still smiling. 'But in my business I have learned that it is often wise to pay more for the best.' She paused, as if to give Sri time to enquire what her business was. But Sri had no intention of obliging her.

The old lady motioned towards Sunida. 'Your daughter?'

'Yes, but she's not for sale.' Sri chuckled, pleased with her retort.

'A pity,' replied the old lady unexpectedly, and in the next instant she had moved on to a neighbouring stall.

'Merciful Buddha,' said Sri grimacing. 'I thought she'd never leave. Now tell me about our project, little mouse. I'm shedding weight from curiosity.'

'Well now, Pi,' began Sunida, 'this is all highly secret.' She edged closer to Sri. 'The master has confided in me that a farang force has arrived here in several big ships. There are at least five hundred soldiers waiting to land.' Sunida paused to observe the effect of her words. But Sri merely shrugged her shoulders matter-of-factly.

'Why, little mouse, I could have told you that myself. The rumours have been floating round the marketplace for days.

Well, perhaps not days, but since yesterday anyway. What does the master say they want, these farangs?'

'He's not sure yet, but to be on the safe side, we are to find ways to distract them, to weaken their resolve, whatever that might be.'

Sri burst out laughing and then glanced about her. 'Weaken them, did you say? Why, I know some stalls here that sell such inferior produce that the farangs would be in a squatting position all day long!'

Sunida giggled delightedly. 'That would be one solution, Pi Sri, but the master thinks our women might do the best job. I mean, lure the farangs away somehow from their task.'

'Our women?' Sri appeared to consider the matter. Then she smiled, clearly enjoying the thought. 'You mean remove all their farang juices until their bodies dry up like fish in the sun? I like the idea, little mouse. But where would we find such volunteers?' She wrinkled her nose distastefully. 'They don't exactly smell like the kadung flower, these farangs, do they? The master excepted, of course,' she added quickly.

'Our women are resourceful enough, especially if we turn to the butterflies of the night. Don't they always cleanse their customers first?'

Sri emitted a great belly laugh. 'The poor farangs. Hardly landed before they're scrubbed, rubbed and loved! Erotic bathing, our girls could call it. They could say it's part of the Siamese welcome ritual.'

'Pi Sri, you are incorrigible.' Sunida never failed to enjoy her time with Sri. She looked at her impishly now. 'In your younger days I bet you could have taken them all on single-handedly.'

'What do you mean in my younger days? I was considering offering my services now.'

Sunida's expression grew suddenly serious. 'The main problem we face, Pi Sri, is time. There isn't much of it. The farangs will be given permission to disembark at any moment and the master wants us to be ready for them. They've been seven months at sea, you know.'

'Seven months at sea!' exclaimed Sri. 'It hardly matters who we find for them then.' She giggled. 'My own prospects are looking brighter by the minute. Ah, but see who comes here. A sure candidate, that one. If I know her, she'd give away the entire contents of her stall to be able to volunteer.'

A plump, grey-haired woman was ambling over to them now, her fat arms swinging like windmills. She was a great crony of Sri and the owner of the stall Sri had earlier pointed to.

'Greetings, Sri. Thanks for the tip. That old lady bought half my stall. What's the matter with you? Are you getting generous in your old age? I couldn't believe you actually sent her to me. You know who she is, of course?'

Sri pretended to be uninterested, but curiosity got the better of her. 'Remind me,' she said.

'Why, you don't even know!' exclaimed the fat woman, relishing her sudden advantage. She shook her head in disbelief, as one might at an ignorant child.

'All right, Soong. That's enough. Who the devil is she?'

'Khun Prateep, of course, the owner of that famous floating house of pleasure, the one outside Samut Songhkram. She is said to be richer than any mandarin. She didn't even bother to bargain my prices. No wonder you didn't grab her for yourself. You didn't know!' The woman cackled delightedly.

But Sri was no longer listening. She rose to her feet with remarkable agility, crying: 'Which way did she go? Quick!'

'I don't know,' exclaimed her friend, taken aback. 'She probably went home. She couldn't have added another package to that pile of hers if she'd wanted to.'

Sri did not hear the end of the sentence. She rushed off, bumping into customers and vendors alike, leaving a trail of protests in her wake.

Sunida rose too, wondering whether to go after Sri. She turned to the fat woman who was following Sri's retreat with wide eyes. 'Pi Soong, what exactly is a floating house of pleasure?' Though she had an open mind and was quick to learn, Sunida had led a sheltered life, first at the provincial court of her uncle, and then at the royal palace. Apart from the butterflies of the night whom everybody had heard of, the seamier side of life in the capital was an unfamiliar world to her.

Soong looked at her affectionately. 'It's the domain of the willow world, my child. The countryside around Samut Songhkram is famous for its maze of canals that run alongside the rice

64

fields. The boatwomen row their customers through the isolated paddies at sunset when the farmers have gone home. They work in pairs. One rows while the other takes care of the customer. Often, I have heard, they switch places.' Soong smiled. 'They say it is especially uplifting to travel through the rice fields by moonlight.'

Sunida understood now. With a 'wai' to Soong, she rushed off in pursuit of Sri. She eventually found her at the main gate, asking questions of everyone around. From her frustrated expression, Sunida could tell that her enquiries had led nowhere.

'It's no use, little mouse,' said Sri sadly as Sunida came up to her. 'With all those purchases, she must surely have hired a boat. But where to? She could be staying just about anywhere in Ayudhya. Or perhaps she went straight home to Samut Songhkram, although it's a long way, I hear.' Sri shook her head disconsolately. 'And to think I actually sent her away when I had her right there in the palm of my hand. No wonder she was eyeing you so keenly, little mouse. What a prize you would have made! And what a shock she would have received when she found out who you were. Oh well, we'd better get back to the stall and dream up another plan. I must say the idea of a floating house was a good one. But around here? The capital's canals are so crowded, there could never be enough privacy. I don't know of any local floating houses, do you?'

'Pi Sri, until a few moments ago I'd never heard of a floating house of pleasure.'

'Of course, little mouse, how stupid of me. You have always lived in another world. As you rightly deserve.' She rested a hand affectionately on Sunida's shoulder as they made their way back to the stall.

'In less of a hurry this time, eh Sri?' shouted a voice as they passed.

'I'm sending you a bill for my bruises,' cried another.

'You'll have to lose weight if you're going to tread on people's toes like that!' exclaimed a third, amid general laughter.

When they arrived back at the stall, the old lady was standing there, fingering the same water melon, as if she'd never left.

'I've still got a few baht left,' she said pleasantly. 'I thought I'd come back and be overcharged.'

65

'It's on the house,' cried Sri joyfully. 'Have whatever you want.'

'My, my,' said Khun Prateep, 'but you are unpredictable. A veritable chameleon, I should say.' She turned kindly to Sunida. 'Is your honourable mother always so changeable?'

'My honourable mother is just happy to see you again,' replied Sunida grinning delightedly. 'And so am I, now that I know who you are.'

The old lady's fine features lit up at the sudden prospect of such a prize. Her eyes devoured Sunida, scouring her body unabashedly from head to toe. She could not wait to make sure. Edging closer to Sunida she whispered: 'Every girl is given her own boat, on loan of course. But she has the right to buy it for herself in time. You'd earn yours soon enough, I can assure you. And then you could pick your own assistant.'

Sri, who throughout this description had been at pains to keep a straight face, now burst into uncontrollable laughter. When eventually she calmed down she beckoned to Khun Prateep to sit next to her and began to speak to her in hushed tones. The old lady's eyes grew wider with every sentence, while every now and then she glanced across at Sunida. When Sri had finished, the old lady remained silent, apparently deep in thought.

'But how can I close my operation down?' she asked eventually. 'I have many important customers. Mandarins even. Some of them travel dozens of leagues to see me.'

'You could say that malaria has broken out in the area and that the girls have been put in quarantine. They must be isolated for a while,' suggested Sri.

'But such rumours will cause havoc to my business.'

'So will the French army if they are not dealt with,' retorted Sri. 'Besides,' she added importantly, 'the order comes from the palace.'

'Of course, of course. You're right.' Khun Prateep quickly turned in the direction of the Grand Palace, whose golden spires rose up in the distance, and prostrated herself. 'I will close down the premises until further notice. But I am not sure I can have the boats moved to Bangkok in so short a time. It's a long journey and some of the boats are lavishly adorned and heavy to

66

paddle for any distance. They're specially constructed, you know, quite different from ordinary canoes.'

'But the girls can be moved easily enough?' It was Sunida who spoke this time.

'Indeed, my lady.' Khun Prateep lowered her head respectfully before the honourable minor wife of the Pra Klang. 'They can be moved at any time. It is only the boats that present a problem.'

'My master will send all the men you need to have them moved,' said Sunida decisively. 'They will work in shifts if necessary.' She paused. 'But will the farang soldiers not see that they are different from the other boats in the floating market? We don't want their presence to appear anything but natural. The boats should look alike really. Perhaps, mother, your boats could be laden with market produce, like the real ones?'

'While, in fact, they'll be selling much more,' quipped Sri.

'Oh no, Pi Sri, not selling,' said Sunida quickly. 'They will sell only market produce to the farangs. At least at first, until they can entice them back and gradually ensnare them.'

'You mean my girls won't get paid?' asked Khun Prateep anxiously.

'They'll be paid handsomely, don't you worry,' said Sunida. 'But by us, not the soldiers. You can rest assured that His Excellency the Pra Klang will be generous. He will rent your entire establishment for as long as he needs it. You can present your bill to me every week in advance. Under no circumstances must any of the girls demand money of the farangs.'

Khun Prateep bowed her head. 'Your slave, my lady.'

'My master once told me that the farangs found the smiling boatwomen with their blue panungs and broad peasant hats quite irresistible,' said Sunida. 'Your girls, mother, should be dressed like that.'

'As you command, my lady.'

'But how will the farangs know who is who?' enquired Sri. 'There could be terrible scenes if they laid their hands on the wrong boatwomen. Some of our peasant women are paragons of virtue.'

'If a few mistakes are made, Pi Sri, it will look all the more genuine. After all, not every woman should appear to give herself up to the farangs. I am confident that the real boatwomen

67

will know how to defend their honour while the false ones will learn to play their parts and succumb gracefully to the advances of the farangs. And those that have can point to others among their friends who might be "willing" too. The farangs will be channelled in the right direction sooner than you think.'

The old woman bowed her head again. 'My lady, your plan is subtle indeed, but if you will permit an old woman a humble suggestion, I would recommend the use of the ganja plant as well. It is highly pleasing and quickly addictive and in the end has quite a stultifying effect. It would certainly help to sap the will of the farangs, if that is indeed your purpose. My customers often request it and all my girls are adept in its use.'

'An excellent idea, mother,' put in Sri. 'You wouldn't have room for one more in your establishment, would you?'

Khun Prateep chuckled. 'I have eighty-five girls now, younger sister. What's one more or less?'

'That's a good number, mother,' observed Sunida thoughtfully. 'Just the right amount for the farangs to fight over. They will end up quarrelling with each other.'

'My girls will know just how to fan their jealousies too, my lady. They are very skilled in the ways of the flesh.' She bowed her head again. 'I am most honoured that you should have chosen my humble establishment.'

'It was a difficult choice, mother,' observed Sri, winking slyly at Sunida, 'so make sure you don't let us down.'

'I will not, younger sister, you can count on it.' She turned to Sunida. 'When do you want my girls to arrive in Bangkok?'

'As soon as possible. I will go to Bangkok myself tomorrow to search out a suitable location and to bring you your first week's payment. I shall await you by the great fort at sundown.'

'You do this slave great honour, my lady.'

68

Six

As Father Tachard's small boat pulled up alongside *l'Oiseau*, the priest glanced up apprehensively at the grim line of faces leaning expectantly over the ship's side: la Loubère, tall and indignant, Cébéret du Boullay, portly and frowning, and General Desfarges, towering above the others, his face pale and his eyes watery. Every now and then he raised a handkerchief to his brow and mopped the moisture. The humidity was heavy even for this time of year and rain clouds were gathering ominously as far as the eye could see.

'So you have finally returned, Father,' observed la Loubère in a strained voice as the priest clambered aboard. 'No doubt you have good reasons for this extraordinary delay.' It was all la Loubère could do to restrain himself from demanding an explanation there and then, but there were crew and officers present. 'Shall we go to my cabin?'

Tachard exchanged greetings with Cébéret and Desfarges while a handful of officers welcomed him from a distance. Most of the ship's crew was below decks resting or sulking, as low in morale as they were in provisions. Tachard raised a hand to the officers and followed la Loubère down through the aft hatchway.

No sooner had the door of the cabin closed, than the Jesuit turned resolutely to face the three men. 'Gentlemen, before we go any further, I want to assure you that I did everything in my power to return sooner. But I was thwarted at every attempt.'

La Loubère smiled thinly and motioned them to some chairs. 'Were you then forcibly detained?'

'Not forcibly, Your Excellency, but I was not given any answers. I would have had nothing to report had I returned earlier. Things do not move very fast in Siam. I did send a message through the Seminary to inform you that I was delayed.' He looked around him enquiringly. 'Did you not get it?'

'The boat bearing your message was no doubt the one commandeered by Kosa Pan,' said la Loubère. 'You know, of course, that the Ambassador escaped?'

69

'I do indeed, Your Excellency. He has in fact made some very strong accusations against us. Lord Phaulkon was summoned to the palace to hear them.'

The three men looked grim. 'And what exactly transpired?' asked la Loubère who, as head of mission, continued to conduct the inquiry.

Tachard emitted a nervous cough. This was not going to be easy, he knew.

'Well, Father, we are awaiting your report.' La Loubère drummed his fingers impatiently on the edge of the desk.

'Of course, gentlemen,' said the priest, quickly pulling himself together. 'First I bring you good tidings. Lord Phaulkon defended France vigorously against the Siamese Ambassador's accusations, assuring His Majesty that the bulk of the men were non-military and that the whole contingent was a gift from King Louis. His Siamese Majesty, who has great faith in his chief minister, then graciously consented to grant us the port of Bangkok in lieu of Ligor.' The priest smiled. 'His Majesty has furthermore invited the French troops to disembark and has expressed the wish to receive the leaders of this distinguished delegation with full honours. Your Excellencies are to be granted a royal audience shortly after landing.'

There was a sigh of relief all round.

'And what of the Siamese King's conversion?' asked la Loubère eagerly.

'I am happy to report that His Majesty is so well disposed towards the Catholic faith that there now stands little between our goals and their realization.' The priest cast his eye over the now smiling assembly. So far so good. He felt a glow of warmth as he recalled how immediately upon his return from the palace, Phaulkon had insisted that Tachard accompany him back there. It was most unusual and highly irregular. Official audiences were formal affairs arranged weeks in advance, yet Phaulkon had managed to secure one for him at very short notice. He was determined that Tachard hear for himself the King's feelings towards Christianity. Phaulkon had entered the royal audience hall first to speak privately with His Majesty and emerged minutes later with the news that the King would receive him. Tachard had been flattered by the unexpected honour but even

70

more favourably impressed by the manner in which His Majesty had spoken of his innermost spiritual desires. It was clear that the monarch was closer to God than he had ever been.

'What precisely?' enquired la Loubère.

'I beg your pardon, Your Excellency?'

'What precisely stands between His Majesty and his conversion?'

'Two things. First, His Majesty wants to be assured of the lasting friendship of the great King of France. He wants to be certain that his esteemed colleague will help defend him against his enemies. You must bear in mind, gentlemen, that it will be no easy matter for a sovereign, whose kingdom has followed the same faith for over a thousand years, to explain to his subjects so momentous a change of heart. It is essential, therefore, that his mandarins see for themselves the superiority of the French in both temporal and spiritual matters. Which is why His Majesty welcomes this distinguished delegation with especially high hopes and expectations. He trusts that by their fine comportment they will impress his people with their elevated beliefs.'

'Did Phaulkon tell you all this himself?' asked Cébéret, eyeing the priest carefully.

'No, my lord,' replied Tachard with pride. 'His Majesty summoned me to the palace in person. I speak enough Siamese for His Majesty to communicate with me directly. Everything I am relating now came straight from the mouth of the sovereign.'

Cébéret muttered something under his breath. 'But you make no mention of Mergui in all of this. Is His Majesty aware that we have requested the port of Mergui?'

Tachard looked down at his feet for a moment. 'Lord Phaulkon told me he has not broached the subject with His Majesty yet for fear of overstepping the bounds of good manners. His Majesty has, after all, just offered us the port of Bangkok, which is of great strategic importance, and it would not be seemly to request a further concession so soon. Besides, Mergui is presently in the hands of the English. There are trade agreements in existence.'

'Mergui in English hands? Since when?' enquired Cébéret, surprised. 'That's the first I've heard of it.'

'I am afraid I did not ask that question, my lord.'

'The English,' exclaimed Desfarges frowning. 'Always the

damned English. We are the most powerful country in the world and yet we still find the English everywhere. *Nom de Dieu.*'

'Does that mean we will have no trading rights in Mergui?' enquired Cébéret gravely.

'Not for the time being anyway, my lord.'

'Unless we stand and fight for them,' remarked Desfarges.

Tachard turned to the General. 'I must point out, sir, that Lord Phaulkon has an intimate knowledge of the workings of His Majesty's mind. If he advises against such a request at this stage for reasons of diplomacy or etiquette, it is only because he does not want to do anything to aggravate the ruler at a time when we all are so close to achieving our goal.'

'You mentioned that there were two points on which His Majesty was seeking our assurances before agreeing to convert,' said la Loubère. 'What is the second one?'

The priest smoothed the long sleeves of his brown robe. 'Indeed, Your Excellency. His Majesty wants the same assurances from you as have been given to him by his chief minister, that this delegation has come in peace and that France and Siam will be allies and partners on equal terms. You can understand, I am sure, gentlemen,' continued Tachard, 'how this request has arisen, when you consider that his Ambassador has informed him of the arrival of a far greater force then he had either requested or wished for.'

There was a moment's silence.

'I am confused on one point, Father,' said Desfarges. 'Is this man Phaulkon not concerned that a contingent of the finest army in Europe could simply take by force whatever it desires, whether it has been granted or not?'

'Since he is offering you what you want anyway, General, the issue doesn't arise, surely?'

'It would hardly suit the current Siamese position to allow a conflict to erupt with France,' observed Cébéret.

'That is true,' agreed Tachard. 'It suits everybody's purpose for peace to be maintained. But speaking of the Dutch threat, His Majesty expressed to me his great desire to see his army trained by Frenchmen in modern warfare. On that score he welcomes the unexpected size of the French contingent as it will enable him to send more of his troops to the fort for training. If every French soldier could train one of his men, then in no time – '

'Enemy soldiers in my fort!' burst out Desfarges. 'Are you suggesting that five hundred Siamese are infiltrated into my fort under the guise of training? The enemy within our very ranks? Absolutely fatal. They could muster their armies outside while they turn on us from within. A classic ploy. Never, sir! Whose side are you on anyway, Father?'

'The Father is on the side of God,' remarked Cébéret drily, 'and it seems God is with Phaulkon, for the time being at any rate.'

'Siam is not our enemy, General,' said the priest quietly. 'Siam is our ally. We have a treaty of friendship, remember?'

La Loubère now raised a hand, demanding silence. 'It seems to me, gentlemen, that what we have been offered is a compromise. Let us take the question of Mergui first. It is, we now learn, in English hands, not Siamese. Are we then to fight the English for it? It is not in our mandate from King Louis. And the English are fierce fighters.'

'Since when have the English worried the French army?' scoffed Desfarges.

'All too often in history I am afraid, General,' replied la Loubère.

'But Mergui is a crucial part of our plans, Simon,' said Cébéret. 'The English already have Madras and if they control Mergui too, they will be in effective control of the Bay.'

'We must find out more about the situation,' said la Loubère. 'We must discover if there is a treaty with the English and, if so, how long it is valid and what their troop strength is.'

'How will we find all that out?' asked Desfarges.

'In Ayudhya, if we ever get there,' replied la Loubère. 'But let us proceed for a moment to the question of the King's conversion. Though Father Tachard has heard of the King's leanings from his own lips, we must ask ourselves how far we can trust Phaulkon to see them through. Is he telling the truth, or is he playing for time?'

'I am delighted to hear you pose the question, Simon,' said Cébéret.

73

'Lord Phaulkon is a true friend of France, believe me, gentlemen,' said Tachard eagerly. 'And he has turned to us, not to the English. His goals differ little from our own. He seeks the King of Siam's conversion as fervently as any of us. His only advice to us is that we approach the matter with caution. He told me, and my colleagues at the Seminary confirmed it – '

'So you stopped at the Seminary too?' interjected la Loubère caustically. 'No wonder you were so long in returning.'

'It was on my way, Your Excellency, and I only wanted to verify Lord Phaulkon's story. His Eminence the Bishop confirmed to me what Lord Phaulkon had said, that His Majesty is well versed in the Holy Scriptures and eager to learn more.' Tachard leaned forward and looked round the table. 'His Eminence was also of the opinion that the arrival of so distinguished a delegation would serve as a final catalyst to His Majesty's conversion. The noble bearing of so sophisticated and refined a people could not but influence him towards the final step. Furthermore,' pursued Tachard, once again eyeing each of them in turn, 'when I mentioned your names to him, Lord Phaulkon knew every one of you by repute, and he was greatly impressed. He is well informed on French affairs, for it is our nation, gentlemen, that both he and the King of Siam admire the most. Lord Phaulkon assured me personally that nothing would give him more pleasure than to see France firmly established in Siam as the dominant trading power in the region. But one thing is certain, gentlemen. We will never achieve King Narai's conversion by attacking his country.'

'It seems that Lord Phaulkon has been most persuasive with you, my dear Father,' observed Cébéret with a thin smile. 'You sound quite converted yourself.'

'I am dedicated to only one cause, my lord. France and the Catholic Church, which I consider one and indivisible. And I strongly suggest in the name of France that, despite any initial reversals, we carry out the foremost wish of our King by the means which now lie before us. For if we are foolish enough to choose confrontation, we will be doomed. We no longer have the element of surprise. We must adapt to a changed situation. King Louis would surely not wish his troops to be slaughtered.'

'That will never happen, sir,' objected Desfarges indignantly.

'I believe it will,' retorted Tachard. 'And so does Lord Phaulkon. It is quite easy to comprehend, even for a non-military man. Our ships are too large to cross the bar and if the King of Siam were so much as to suspect our real intentions, he would refuse us permission to land. Our choices would then be to return home, to remain on board until we starved, or to attempt to land ashore in small boats. Correct me if I am wrong, General, but I believe that Siam's forces – which I was assured both by the chief minister and our own Bishop number over twenty thousand war elephants – would have little difficulty in picking off our men one by one as they emerged from their boats.'

There was an ominous silence, broken only by the wheezing of Desfarges.

'I see,' said la Loubère eventually. 'So if I understand you correctly, Father, the only viable course of action you see for us would be to abandon the idea of Mergui, to present five hundred troops to His Majesty of Siam as a surprise gift from our King, and to agree to place one Siamese trainee next to each French-man in the fort. Is that so?'

'Indeed, Your Excellency. For you must understand that from the Siamese government's point of view, the French army cannot be seen to be an army of occupation. The mandarins would all be up in arms. The French troops must be viewed as a defensive force operating under a joint venture with their Siamese allies, with the aim of deterring the Dutch.'

'You have put the Siamese government's case most ably, if I may say so, Father,' said Cébéret stonily. 'It is a pity we do not have you on our side. We could do with a man like you.'

The Jesuit ignored the jibe and looked instead at la Loubère. 'There is one more thing, Your Excellency.'

'Yes?'

'In order for the Siamese people to understand that the French troops are a gift from the French government to their King, they must swear allegiance to the King of Siam and to Lord Phaulkon, as his chief minister. General Desfarges must place himself and his troops officially under their command.'

'Never!' exploded Desfarges.

'You have surpassed yourself, Father,' Cébéret remarked.

All eyes now turned towards la Loubère who remained for the

75

moment silent. He drew a deep breath and then fixed his narrow eyes firmly on the priest. 'Father Tachard,' he began, 'until a moment ago, though I was not quite sure whose side you were on, I was willing to give you the benefit of the doubt. But now those doubts have evaporated. I feel we have been listening to Lord Phaulkon all this time. I shall therefore give you the French point of view now.

'Much of what you say may be true and the situation we find ourselves in may not be unlike that which you describe, but you have touched upon it only from the Siamese angle, seemingly ignoring our own. What you have failed to consider are the consequences following upon the various options you believe are open to us. The first option was to return home, was it not? What if we did so? The alliance with France would be seen to be worthless, and the Dutch, with no one to stop them, would lose no time in realizing their ambitions. Siam would in all likelihood end up as a Dutch colony whose Protestant governor would be anything but eager to see the King a Catholic. The second option was to remain on board and face starvation. The lack of merit in this plan is so obvious that I will not bother to discuss it. The third option was to go to war. Now if, as you suggest, Father, our troops would be trampled under the feet of twenty thousand war elephants, then the Siamese would win a Pyrrhic victory. For no sooner had they defeated us than the Dutch would swallow them up instead. So in that respect the Siamese would almost be better off having us emerge the victors: at least then the King would be able to fulfil his apparent desire to become a Catholic and forge his irrevocable ties with France.

'But before I send you back to Ayudhya with my response, Father, let us hear the views of my distinguished colleagues. Claude, which option would you favour?'

Cébéret crossed his hands in front of his voluminous belly. 'I reject the first option on the grounds that we have come too far to turn back now. I recommend instead that we persist in our quest for Mergui which is vital to our future interests in the area. As to vowing allegiance to the King of Siam and his minister, though I believe there are few instances that would justify war, I think this might be one of them. For French soldiers to pledge allegiance to a foreign power is unthinkable.'

'Thank you, Claude. General?'

Desfarges had been desperate to speak for some time. The words shot out of him like a salvo from a cannon. 'I reject the first option out of hand, sir. It is inconceivable that we should even consider turning back at this stage without attempting to fulfil our objectives. But if we stay, it would be madness to invite five hundred enemy troops into our fortress. As to the French army swearing allegiance to anyone but the King of France, why, it would be nothing short of treason. I subscribe, therefore, to the last option, war. And I take this opportunity of admonishing Father Tachard not to underestimate either the strength or the resolve of the armies of France.'

'Thank you, General.' La Loubère turned to the Jesuit. 'Well, Father, there you have it. I suggest you return to your new master with the following message. Tell him that the French can be both gracious and resolute. We graciously accept the port of Bangkok instead of Ligor and even consent to train the Siamese army within the fort.' La Loubère ignored the General's splutter of dismay. 'For the moment, we will let the issue of the ceding of Mergui rest. We rejoice greatly in the knowledge of His Majesty's imminent conversion, and are even prepared to pledge temporary allegiance to him – in the form subscribed by King Louis – but under no circumstances will the French army swear an oath to his chief minister. If this is unacceptable to Lord Phaulkon or his pride, then we have no alternative but to open hostilities.'

As he finished speaking, there was a loud clap of thunder and moments later the sky opened up. Torrential monsoon rain began pelting down on the deck above them and through the porthole of the cabin they saw a wall of grey envelop the ship.

La Loubère smiled despite himself. 'Now go, Father,' he ordered.

Seven

Samuel White, Shahbandar of the port of Mergui, swept back his mane of straw-coloured hair, bleached lighter still by the tropical sun, and smiled. It was a smile of satisfaction, directed at no one in particular but at the pleasing course that his life was taking. He was thirty-three, harbour master of the greatest port in Siam, a mandarin of the third rank, and his friend and patron was none other than Constantine Phaulkon, the most powerful man in the kingdom. In matters of foreign trade, His Majesty King Narai left matters very much in the hands of his Pra Klang, who in turn entrusted them to a handful of close friends, which meant that he, Samuel White, managed all the King of Siam's interests in the Bay of Bengal and beyond: India, Persia and Arabia. The nation's coffers were bulging, his personal strongbox was full to bursting and with another year or two's plunder he would be ready to return to England and live the life of a squire. How many times had he not envisioned the country estate he would buy, nestling in rolling hills, with a stream running through it, a few hundred head of cattle and sheep, the grand manor house, manicured lawns, carefully tended flower beds.

Fortune had indeed smiled upon him, he reflected, as he sat on his wooden verandah overlooking the magnificent natural harbour of Mergui, a view that was rendered the more breathtaking by the considerable elevation of his house on the hill. Phaulkon had appointed Richard Burnaby Governor of Tenasserim, the province in which Mergui lay. It was hard to believe that Burnaby had once been Phaulkon's superior in the East India Company's Siam office. But Phaulkon was loyal to his old friends and when he became Barcalon, his former chief had found himself catapulted into the post of Governor of the country's strategic western province. Gradually, however, White was able to take over the new Governor's responsibilities. He exploited Burnaby's lethargy and began to relieve him of the chores of government, allowing him more time to indulge in his sybaritic pursuits. Encouraged by White, a host of women, slender Burmese, dark-skinned Tamils, graceful Siamese or hybrids of mixed blood, generously offered him their favours until he could only laugh at the thought of life in rural England where he might otherwise have retired – married to the likes of the vicar's daughter.

On the Governor's behalf, White was before long collecting all of His Majesty's revenues in the province – a most lucrative activity as he soon discovered – while Burnaby was content to lie back and wallow in the knowledge of his exalted position. He sat daily on his throne-like chair listening to prostrate petitioners address him as Your Excellency and watching them grovel before him. Their outward servility and their apparent adulation, together with the listless climate of the tropics, gradually conspired to remove the last vestiges of enterprise from him. Comfortable with his present revenue, he lost interest in amassing further wealth and stopped interfering in White's increasing extravagances, which, despite his bemused state, even he could not fail to notice. When Tenasserim's Council of Five met, of which he was the nominal head, he inevitably endorsed White's proposals. The other three members were Moors, for Muslim traders of Indian and Persian extraction had settled in Siam generations ago and had traditionally conducted trade with their cousins to the west. The Moors had at first been infuriated by White's intrusion into their domain, but their subsequent uprising had been so severely crushed by Phaulkon that their position and influence were now all but eroded. Despite the majority of their numbers on the Council of Five, a system devised by His Majesty to check the abuse of power, their voice was subdued and their spirit cowed. They invariably, though sometimes reluctantly, added their seals to White's decisions. It had become quite obvious to all that His Excellency the Governor was content to remain a figurehead.

White's daring increased in direct proportion to Burnaby's indifference, and only the fear of discovery by Phaulkon kept him from throwing complete caution to the winds. He smiled as he recalled how Phaulkon, shortly after his accession to power, had declared his intention to promote Englishmen whom he trusted to key positions in Tenasserim, for the Siamese were not by inclination a seafaring nation and the English were better suited to oversee the trading routes across the Bay of Bengal to India and Persia. And now, four years later, English captains appointed by White commanded the vessels of the Siamese Crown and traded under its flag.

Although he had had to resign his commission in the East India Company to enter the service of the King of Siam, White had maintained his contacts with Madras across the Bay; the officials of the Company's headquarters were delighted that an Englishman, a former employee to boot, was in control of the strategic port of Mergui on the easternmost shores of the Bay. On the high seas of Asia, where every man was out for himself and where the line between trader and pirate was a thin one, this augured well for English commerce, both official and private.

White's sky-blue eyes twinkled. It had been so easy really. His orders had been to fly the flag of Siam and make the kingdom a force to be reckoned with in the trading world of the Indian Ocean, but he had stretched this interpretation to suit his own restless pecuniary ambitions and he was soon trespassing far beyond the boundaries of the law. His ships began to exact tolls from defenceless traders in return for their freedom, though he was always careful to avoid intercepting ships of the East India Company, concentrating instead on Mohammedan and other commerce.

His strategy at this stage took on a well-worn pattern. The crew and passengers of the captured merchant ships would be asked to make a substantial contribution to his coffers and then to sign a declaration that they had had to put into port for repairs, where they had been well treated before departing. Those who protested at this policy were thrown in prison whence they soon emerged more receptive to White's demands. He was meticulous in filing the declarations in case at any time he should be called upon to account for the number of ships 'putting in' at Mergui. He was aware that the merchantmen would lodge strong protests on their return, but he was counting on the fact that time and distance were on his side and that he would be rich and out of Mergui before the mass of complaints pointed too damning a finger at him.

Yes, he pondered happily, in this year of 1687 he, Sam White, was virtual master of the Bay of Bengal. The one thorn in his side now was that little despot Ali Beague, the pockmarked Governor of Masulipatam, Golconda's chief city on the eastern seaboard of India. For some time now Siamese ships manned by English captains had been trading with the Indian Kingdom of Golconda, but that thrice-cursed devil Beague had been extracting exorbitant tolls from them, and causing White's captains costly delays, all of which was cutting heavily into the profits of the Siamese Crown, and consequently his own. Not only did White resent anyone emulating his tactics, he had an old score to settle with Beague from his days with the East India Company. White's face broke into a sudden grin. At that time he had been only a junior employee in the English Company; now he was a mandarin of Siam in charge of the King's whole western fleet.

White had written to Phaulkon three months ago explaining the state of affairs and requesting permission to take action, omitting only the less savoury reasons for his proposal. He had waited patiently for the reply until at last, six weeks ago, permission had arrived. But while he was awaiting the reply, a strange rumour had reached him from Batavia in Java that a large French fleet had put into port there for provisions. What had excited his curiosity was the fact that the fleet was apparently on its way to Siam. What was it up to? Had the powerful French decided to take a greater interest in the area? With their base at Pondicherry on one side of the Bay, would not Mergui be an ideal place for them to set their sights on at the other side? You never knew. Instinct told him to play his hand while he still held all the cards. As soon as Phaulkon's official sanction had arrived, he had instructed his secretary, Francis Davenport, to write to Thomas Ivatt, the King of Siam's trade representative in Golconda, to take action. He had in fact sent him two letters. In the first, he had asked Ivatt to submit a claim to Ali Beague for compensation based on a list of grievances he had drawn up; in the second, confidential, letter, he requested Ivatt to submit bills so far in excess of damages incurred as to warrant Ali Beague's certain refusal. Not that that two-faced brigand would have even considered the demands of the first letter, but White wanted to play it doubly safe. To encourage Ivatt's co-operation, he had insinuated that the second directive, though perforce unofficial,

81

had come from the 'highest source' in Ayudhya. It was a risky thing to do, but rumours of the French fleet were worrying him and he was banking on the fact that any query from Ivatt in India would take several weeks to reach the capital.

White leaned back in his chair, deep in thought, wondering whether Ivatt had received his letters. From the vantage point of his broad, wooden house high on the hill he could observe all the activity in the teeming harbour below, the bare-breasted Burmese women balancing earthenware jars on their heads, the graceful Siamese with their colourful panungs, the gesticulating hawkers, the long rows of food stalls, the naked brown children chasing the mangy pariah dogs. The vista was sweeping, with wooded hills descending down to the sea from every side and the meandering coastline forming countless inlets and sandy bays. Little palm-fringed islands dotted the horizon as far as the eye could see. He clasped his hands behind his head and stared dreamily out across the Bay.

Somewhere over those sparkling waters lay the Kingdom of Golconda, and perhaps at this very moment his most unscrupulous captain, that daredevil Coates, at the helm of the *Star of Ayudhya*, was preparing to teach Ali Beague a lesson. His secretary Davenport had objected of course, though White had to admit that the New Englander's puritanical scruples were sometimes a good balance to his own extravagant impulses. White had wanted Coates to sail straight for Golconda. He was impatient of the time it would take for his letters to reach Ivatt, for the claims to be submitted, for the deadline to expire and for the response to reach him. He would suffer months of lost revenue. But Davenport had pointed out the folly of attacking Ali Beague before he had had time to respond to the demands. Had not Phaulkon's directives clearly stated that Ali Beague must be given reasonable time to reply? In the end, though White had refused to be swayed, he had at least agreed to certain concessions, of which the most important was that Coates should first apprize Madras of his intentions, before proceeding to Golconda.

In his letter sanctioning action, Phaulkon had stressed that under no circumstances was the East India Company, with its trading posts in and around Golconda, to be in any way molested.

The whole affair must remain a private matter between Siam and Golconda. By apprizing Madras first, White saw a way of possibly implicating the East India Company in his activities. For it was known that the Company, too, considered Ali Beague a thorn in its side; it might welcome – unofficially of course – Coates's mission to the extent of providing him with ammunition and even a few volunteers ready for a brawl. It was a good ploy and Coates had been sent to Golconda via Madras.

White felt content. Another of his cherished plans might soon be brought to fruition. With Ali Beague out of the way, he would be the unchallenged master of the Bay. And with the added revenues that Ali Beague was depriving him of, he would be that much closer to his goal. Of course he would continue to send monies to Phaulkon and the Treasury – though the greater split would go to him, with neither Phaulkon nor the Treasury any the wiser. It was only fair, after all. Phaulkon had an entire country to milk whereas he, Samuel, had only a single province.

What a stroke of fortune had brought him into Phaulkon's orbit, he reflected. What a Godsend that George, his very own brother, had been Phaulkon's friend and mentor. That had given him, he knew, a special place in Phaulkon's heart. It was, after all, George who had first brought Phaulkon to the East as his apprentice a dozen years ago and taught him the ropes of Asian trade. Although there were twenty years between them, the two men had been inseparable, more like comrades than master and pupil, and White had observed certain traits in Phaulkon today that reminded him strangely of his own brother. Both men considered that when the law was fair you followed it, but when it wasn't you simply ignored it. Even now, instead of enjoying a tranquil and well-earned retirement, George was back in England challenging the very concept of a royal monopoly and fighting the East India Company in court to obtain a liberalization of the trading laws. No one else would have dared to challenge a royal edict, but George was a legend, considered by many the greatest trader Asia had ever known, and his voice was not easy to silence. He had returned to England for good, for he was old now, in his mid-fifties, yet there he was, still fighting for the Asia he loved.

White recalled his brother's words, when George had stopped

83

off to see him in Madras, on his way home. 'Mark my words, Sam, you hitch your wagon to Constant Phaulkon's. That lad's star is on the rise and ye'll do a lot worse than to follow in its wake.' That was six years ago and, by God, George had been right. When rumours had spread across the Bay that the great King of Siam was seeking English captains to enter the service of the Siamese Crown, he had immediately resigned his commission in Madras and headed straight for Ayudhya. Phaulkon had welcomed him as a long lost friend and to this day White knew that it was thanks to his brother George that Phaulkon placed a degree of trust in him that he would not otherwise have given so readily. There were not many who could claim a hold over the canny chief minister.

White picked up a bronze bell that lay on the wicker table by his chair and rang it loudly. He would have a word with Davenport, then he might order one of those spicy Burmese curries he was so fond of. Finally he would summon his masseuse. He stared out to sea again. He had servants and slaves, clerks and guards, and even a private secretary at his beck and call. His eye swept across the harbour to the south of the town where another of his sloops was being built in the busy shipyards near the mouth of the Tenasserim River. Thank God for the excellent stocks of local timber and the skill of the native carpenters and shipwrights who were daily building him an ever larger fleet. How he loved his little domain and the power he wielded here. Though of course nothing could compare with the honour and prestige of being a great squire in England. But you needed money to live well in England – lots of it. And with a bit of luck, he would soon have amassed more than enough. He would become a power to be reckoned with in his native land and people would listen to his opinions as they did to his brother's. It was not that he didn't enjoy Siam or that he was homesick – he had adapted well to the country; he had even learned a few words of the language and didn't suffer from the heat the way so many of his compatriots did. And his surroundings afforded the most pleasant activities. The island forests were full of wild pig and the fishing there was unsurpassed. But a man had to move upwards in this world, climbing the ladder of life to reach its highest rungs.

Davenport emerged onto the verandah.

White turned his head round briefly to observe his secretary. 'Ah, Francis.'

Francis Davenport was an American from the colonies, a Bostonian by birth. He was tall and lanky with grey, almost wild eyes, and his rumpled chestnut hair and ill-fitting clothes gave him a perpetually dishevelled and distracted air. His appearance, however, belied his methodical and tidy work habits, in particular the meticulous record-keeping that in a short time had made him an indispensable part of White's daily life and schemes. He had recently been ransomed from slavery in Burma. While returning to India, where he was in the employ of the British East India Company, his boat had been seized off the coast of Pegu by one of White's captains. The ship he was on was carrying Hindu merchants back to Madras, and whereas the merchants were all able to settle their score on the spot, the impecunious American had been brought back to Mergui where he was 'persuaded' to offer his services to White in lieu of payment.

Davenport was a literate man familiar, among other things, with accounting. By offering him a substantial wage, half of which he held back as an 'investment' – though the real reason was to prevent him from accumulating sufficient funds for his passage home – White had inveigled him into staying on in Mergui as his secretary. His detention had the added advantage of preventing Davenport from revealing at first hand in Madras the acts of piracy he had witnessed. Though White was aware of the Bostonian's objections to the excesses of his behaviour, yet he sensed the man was somehow drawn to his flamboyance, however reluctantly. The acquisition of Davenport was one of White's more astute moves.

Davenport shuffled about uncomfortably, staring at the back of his master's head. White seemed to have forgotten his presence. It was a while before he spoke.

'Francis, it is my intention to go to England to see my brother in the next few months. I would like you to see to it that the *Resolution* is taken into dry dock for a thorough careening. On completion she should remain in port at all times.'

'Very well, my lord,' said Davenport, addressing the back of White's head. This was certainly interesting news, he reflected.

85

But if White was planning to go, where exactly would that leave him? Absolutely exposed, he reflected, unless he could find a way of salvaging his position very soon. He determined to escape White's clutches before he was dragged down with him.

His thoughts froze as White suddenly turned to face him. 'You look rather pale, Francis. Perhaps you worry too much. You should learn to relax. And, Francis, send Aung Min in to me, would you? I could do with a little relaxation myself.' He smiled his debonair smile, showing off his fine white teeth. It always managed to infuriate Davenport. With his handsome blond looks and his devil-may-care attitude, the swashbuckling Englishman represented everything that Davenport despised – and could never be himself.

He bowed and walked silently out into the house.

Moments later a tall, lithe Burmese woman with smooth brown skin and straight black hair slid noiselessly onto the verandah and crouched quietly at White's side. He looked at her expectantly and she smiled at him knowingly. Then, with a deft movement of her hand, she let the sash slip from her shoulder to expose a pair of perfectly formed breasts. The nipples were dark in the glossy skin and he stroked one of them gently until he felt it expand between his fingers.

'*Nuat*,' he said, smiling. 'Massage' had been one of the first of the few Siamese words he had taken the trouble to learn. She took him by the arm and laid him gently down on some cushions on the floor of the verandah. She began to undress him. A trellised bamboo awning kept the overhead sun out but the sides were open and a welcome breeze wafted through. He loved the feel of the warm wind caressing his naked body. A bamboo rail surrounded the verandah but did not obstruct the view even from floor level.

Slowly and sensuously she began to massage him, her long slender fingers kneading his joints and muscles and applying just the right amount of pressure. Her touch was firm, just below the threshold of pain, yet erotic enough to make his whole body tingle. As her practised hands descended to his stomach, he felt his excitement grow and she smiled down at him and gave him a look full of feminine understanding.

He stared up at her like a child now, bemused as always by the silk-like texture of her skin and the graceful curves of her body. It would be a while, he knew, before she would unwind her multi-coloured panung and climb on top of him to bring him the final relief.

White closed his eyes, savouring the moment. Lulled by the perfect rhythm of the masseuse's hands, he let his mind drift. It seemed to him in that relaxed, unguarded moment that nothing could disturb the smooth course of his life.

Eight

Father Tachard gave his name to the guard at the gate and waited for his arrival to be announced. He had reacted with mixed feelings to the news that Lord Phaulkon was at home. For while he was anxious to get this meeting over with, he was most apprehensive as to its outcome. How would the Greek receive the news that the troops under General Desfarges would not pledge their allegiance to him but only to the King of Siam?

The guard now returned and, bowing low, beckoned to Tachard to follow him. Once again the priest found himself in the awesome surroundings of Phaulkon's palace with its multitude of slaves, whose duties would include escorting their elevated master everywhere, announcing his passage, clearing a path for him and ensuring that no stranger's head was inadvertently higher than his own.

He was ushered into a different anteroom this time. Its walls were lined with intricate Burmese tapestries depicting scenes of the great Hindu epic, the Ramayana, while lacquered Japanese screens pictured the life of geishas and the exploits of fierce Samurai warriors. In the corners of the room, prostrate slaves lay in statue-like immobility. As their master's footsteps resounded in the corridor outside, he saw their heads sink even lower into the thick Persian carpets that covered the room from wall to wall.

Preceded by two more slaves carrying his ceremonial sword and his betel box, Phaulkon entered the room. He was wearing a long, Moorish robe, a kind of Muslim kaftan that seemed an incongruous garment in which to greet a Jesuit priest.

'My dear Tachard, you have returned,' he said smiling. Then, seeing the look on the priest's face, he added, 'You must excuse my attire, Father. I have just been in conference with two emissaries from the court of Persia. Would you believe that the Emperor, Shah Suleiman, is now openly exhorting my master to adopt the Muslim faith. In anticipation of that happy day, the

Persian envoys have presented His Majesty with a most exquisite copy of the Koran, embossed in gold.' Phaulkon's eyes twinkled mischievously. 'I have just learned that a third emissary drowned in the Tenasserim rapids while holding the Holy Scripture above the water to save it from getting wet. Such was the will of Allah.'

Phaulkon saw the look of consternation on the priest's face. 'Have no fear, Father. I am only doing my diplomatic duty. His Majesty is not likely to turn to the Mohammedan religion while his feelings for Christianity are as warm as they are and while so distinguished a delegation from the Defender of the Catholic Faith is here to impress him with its example. But won't you sit down?'

'I am aware, Your Excellency,' said Tachard, lowering himself into a pile of cushions, 'that His Majesty in his generosity has donated land and money to the Mohammedan cause. But I trust it is more in a spirit of religious tolerance than from any desire to embrace their faith.'

'That is so, Father. And I am sure the French delegation will do nothing to give His Majesty cause to reconsider his own inclinations. But tell me, how did your Ambassador greet my proposals?'

Tachard emitted a nervous cough. 'Well, my lord, they have . . . been accepted for the most part. There is only one small question . . .'

'Which is?'

'The matter of allegiance, Your Excellency. Ambassador de la Loubère feels that his authority does not extend beyond pledging the army's allegiance to any but the King himself.'

A shadow flitted across Phaulkon's face. 'But my dear Tachard, I am the Lord of Life's chief representative. His Majesty will not himself come to Bangkok to receive the allegiance of the troops. It is not the custom. He will delegate me to act in his place.'

'I told Monsieur de la Loubère that, Your Excellency. But he nevertheless feels that he would be overstepping his bounds.'

Phaulkon stared across at Tachard in silence. He watched the priest lower his eyes. He felt certain, looking at him now, that Tachard had argued his case genuinely. If there really were no

89

other obstacles, he had not done badly. It must be as he had suspected. The French troops were in no condition to fight. La Loubère would never have backed down so readily otherwise. But things could change once the army had recovered its strength. He had to be ready to manipulate them, to use them to his advantage, to ensure they served both as a deterrent to Dutch ambitions and as a vehicle for his own designs. For with such a fighting force behind him, subservient to his will, there was no limit to what he might achieve in the Gulf of Siam and beyond. In the Bay of Bengal Samuel White was looking after his interests, and now the means were within his grasp of sitting astride a growing empire, of becoming the powerbroker between East and West, a mighty figure astraddle two continents, revered by two monarchs, holding the balance of power.

But the King's asthma was another reason why he needed the French force behind him. His Majesty was approaching his fifth cycle – he would be sixty next year – and if he were soon to become incapacitated by his asthma, or for any other reason unable to govern, Phaulkon's enemies would snap at his heels like a pack of hungry wolves. It was essential that the French army be seen to pledge its allegiance unreservedly to him as well as to his monarch. If they declined or even hesitated to give him that pledge, it would become clear to the disgruntled factions within the establishment, notably General Petraja and his son Sorasak, that the French army was wavering in its commitment. The King's heirs, his younger brothers, were weak and quarrelsome, fit only for puppet leadership. Phaulkon would need every support to deal with the ensuing crisis; it would not be easy to govern the country under a weak successor.

But why were the French balking at pledging their allegiance to him? Was it out of pride or did they not trust him? Or was it a combination of both? Perhaps they felt the need to draw the line somewhere, especially after so many concessions, and no doubt such a pledge had not been authorized by Louis XIV.

Phaulkon's eyes hardened. 'The Lord of Life, my master, will never allow so large a French force on Siamese soil unless it pledges its unconditional loyalty to him and his appointed government. I am the chief of that government. I am His Majesty's mouthpiece. We speak with one voice. You cannot owe allegiance to the one and not to the other. You are well enough acquainted with the ways of our land, Father. His Majesty sees no difference between us. I am but a hair of his head.'

Tachard shifted uncomfortably in his bed of cushions. Phaulkon stared at him unsmiling and his expression became colder still.

'If the French army will not bow before the hair of the King's head, it will not be allowed to disembark. And if it attempts to do so without permission, such a move will be construed as an act of aggression. And an act of aggression will mean war. You had best not return to your ship, Father, if you value your life. Return rather to the Seminary to console your brother Jesuits. For you may be sure that in matters of creed, the King will never adopt the faith of an aggressor.'

The blood drained from the priest's face. 'You . . . would . . . declare war, my lord?' he stammered.

Phaulkon nodded gravely. 'We would starve the French on their ships until they grew weaker than they are already. We would evacuate our people from the river banks so the French cannon would fire on empty spaces. If the troops attempted to step ashore, our armies would descend on them and smother them in their thousands. We would enter into an alliance with the English who have been courting us of late. We would survive, Father, and my master, you can be sure, would be irrevocably confirmed in his Buddhist faith.'

Tachard was distraught. 'But my lord, there must be some compromise, surely?'

Phaulkon appeared to consider the matter. He remained silent for a while as the Jesuit fiddled nervously with the sleeves of his robe. Then slowly the warmth returned to Phaulkon's eyes and he smiled again – that familiar conspiratorial smile. 'There might be a way, Father, with your assistance.'

Tachard leaned forward. 'How? Tell me.'

'You are aware, I am sure, of the importance of a royal letter in Siam?'

Tachard hesitated. 'I know that it is always engraved on a sheet of gold.'

'True enough. But that is not the point. A royal letter is the very word of the King. It is his will, his command. The population

91

prostrates itself before a royal letter as it would before the person of the King himself. When a royal letter travels on the river, it lies in a golden vase on a golden dais in a royal barge of its own, with four mandarins of the first grade prostrate at each corner. The entire population lies face down on the river bank as if the King himself were passing by.' Phaulkon paused while Tachard waited anxiously.

'When a royal letter reaches us from a foreign sovereign, it is given far greater prominence than the ambassador who bears it, for he is but a messenger while the letter is the royal word itself.' Phaulkon looked at the priest as if to elicit some comment from him.

'It has come to my ears, my lord, that some foreign ambassadors have felt slighted at being treated with less reverence than the letter they were carrying.'

'Precisely, Father. You must emphasize this important point of etiquette to your Ambassador. You must edify him in the customs of this country.'

'I would be glad to do so, Your Excellency,' said Tachard, perplexed. 'But how would it assist our cause?'

'I am delighted, Father, to hear you refer to it as *our* cause. If I could arrange for the Lord of Life to write such a letter, welcoming Ambassador de le Loubère to these shores, and if the Ambassador were made aware of the significance of such a missive and that it was not the custom for a Siamese monarch to displace himself for a mere ambassador – then, when I brought the letter, etiquette would require him and the French army to bow before it.' Phaulkon watched as a flicker of understanding crossed Tachard's face.

'The means to avert war, Father, will rest with you. For it will be up to you to convince Monsieur de la Loubère of the importance of our royal custom. Every man, from the Ambassador to the lowest corporal, would be required to prostrate himself before the letter and render it obeisance, just as they would to the King himself.'

A frown now creased Tachard's brow. 'But surely, Your Excellency, you would have to prostrate yourself before the letter too? The population would be up in arms if your head were above that of the royal word. Would it not be like standing upright in the King's presence?'

'It would indeed, Father. Which is why I would arrange for there to be two letters. The first from the Governor of Bangkok, who is lower than me in rank, the second from His Majesty. Both would welcome the French delegation. I could stand over the first letter with impunity, and while the French contingent bowed down before what they considered to be the royal letter, the assembled mandarins would deduce that the prostrate French army was pledging its obeisance to me.'

'But won't His Majesty's letter be written on a sheet of gold?'

'Yes, it will, but it will only be brought in after the Governor's letter.'

The Jesuit frowned again. 'But . . . but if the Governor's letter isn't written on a sheet of gold, surely la Loubère will know that it is not from the King?'

'He will know only what you tell him of our customs, Father. What if a royal letter were only written on a sheet of gold when addressed to another monarch, while to anyone else, such as an ambassador, ordinary rice paper were used?'

A look of understanding lit up Tachard's face. 'You mean you want me to convince him of certain, how shall I say, suitable customs?'

'We are working for the same cause, are we not, Father?'

Tachard nodded slowly, deep in thought. Phaulkon allowed him time before continuing. 'The royal letter, on a sheet of gold, will be timed to arrive after the French are prostrate before the first letter. I shall then prostrate myself before the gold letter. Both the King and myself will thus have been duly honoured.'

Tachard remained silent as if considering the implications carefully. Then he broke into an excited smile. 'I will do it. I will say that I was sure the first letter was from the King. That I made a mistake. I will keep the French army prostrate. War will be averted and I shall live to see the King a Catholic yet.'

'It is my most fervent wish,' said Phaulkon, advancing to embrace him. 'May the hand of God guide you, Father.'

Nine

Thomas Ivatt sat at his desk and gazed out of the window reflectively. In spite of the efforts of the turbaned Indian boy pulling rhythmically at the cord that activated the fan, he could feel the moisture clinging stubbornly to his brow. He frowned. He did not like the two letters he had received.

Samuel White was a likeable enough fellow, but Ivatt had never been able to bury his suspicions that the man would stop at nothing to satisfy his ambitions and greed. Rumours of his depredations in the Bay were increasing and hardly a month now passed without someone registering a complaint with Ivatt's office. The file on White was growing. Muslim shipping, it seemed, was being indiscriminately harassed and he, Thomas Ivatt, as His Siamese Majesty's trading representative at Madapollam on the eastern shores of India, would be directly implicated, whether he liked it or not. Worse still, the Kingdom of Golconda, whose ruler had granted Siam the right to trade on his Coromandel coast, was staunchly Mohammedan. Throughout the Bay of Bengal, the flag of Siam was taking on the appearance of a skull and crossbones.

It was true, reflected Ivatt, that Ali Beague, the despotic Governor of Masulipatam, was just as rapacious and acquisitive himself, but even his predatory tactics were not quite as outrageous as White's. Ivatt felt that he was sitting on the edge of a powder keg. Though both Ali Beague and White were careful to avoid molesting ships of the powerful East India Company, whose headquarters were two hundred miles further down the coast at Madras, it was surely only a matter of time before the two swashbucklers clashed over the same prize and turned openly on each other. And where would that leave him, as Siam's agent in Golconda? If hostilities were to break out, would he be sent home, arrested, or held hostage by Ali Beague?

Again, as he had wondered countless times before, Ivatt asked himself whether Phaulkon was aware of what was going on in the

Bay. How much did he really know of White's activities? Was it possible that Phaulkon backed him? Or was he simply turning a blind eye? It was unlikely that Phaulkon had heard nothing. He was too shrewd a politician and he had legions of spies. The truth, Ivatt suspected, was that Phaulkon was probably not aware of the full extent of White's plundering. Rumours were rife enough in the coastal towns of the Bay but Ayudhya, the capital, was far inland, a good ten days' journey through dense jungle from Mergui, the nearest port. And Mergui, via which any rumours to Ayudhya would have to pass, was White's domain. Any man speaking ill of the great Shahbandar, a friend and appointee of the Barcalon himself, would be risking a public flogging at the very least.

The Moorish traders of Mergui, once so powerful, were now cowed and silent, forced to swallow their resentment. Their leader, Prince Dai, had been crushed. Ivatt shuddered, as he did each time he remembered the fate of the Prince. He had seen him, wandering the town, followed by vast crowds, with the severed heads of his chief conspirators attached to his neck. For three days and nights the Prince had stared into the lifeless eyes, brooding over his fate and the folly of the uprising he had led, until he too had been executed. The Muslim leaders in Mergui would not soon forget the ignominy and it would be a while before they spoke out against Phaulkon – or White – again.

Ivatt had considered writing to Phaulkon, but it was a delicate matter to accuse a colleague in a report. Besides, the risk of the letter being intercepted by White's men in Mergui was great. Ivatt had eventually decided to bring the matter up in person when he went to Ayudhya next month. He was due for his annual visit and he would confront Phaulkon with the facts at that time. Ivatt did not doubt that Phaulkon had his own methods for privately increasing his personal fortune, as any powerful mandarin would have, but his great regard for the Greek balked at the idea that orders to attack and pilfer innocent shipping in the Bay could have come from him.

Ivatt had always felt a special bond with Phaulkon, and his loyalty to the man who had given him his present post was unbounded. He enjoyed his work and position. He was sole agent for King Narai's monopoly trade in India's second most

95

powerful kingdom after that of the Moguls. He received every Siamese ship, superintended its unloading and the sale of its cargo and procured other cargo for the twelve-hundred-mile return journey to Mergui. He lived in opulent style, in a large bungalow attended by a score of turbaned valets. A trilingual secretary and a dozen office boys carried out his every order and not an official function was held in Madapollam to which His Siamese Majesty's trade representative was not invited. He was presently overseeing the construction of three more cargo ships, especially reinforced for the transport of elephants across the Bay. Only the shipyards of Madapollam had the skills to build such craft, and trade in Siamese elephants was booming. The demand was seemingly insatiable at the opulent courts of the rajahs. Ivatt smiled. When they were at war with each other they needed elephants for their armies and when they were at peace they needed elephants for their weddings and their hunting parties.

True, he missed Siam, sometimes acutely. But once a year he set off on the five-week journey – three weeks' sail across the Bay, a brief rest at Mergui and then ten days by dug-out canoe, elephant and bullock cart across the isthmus – to report to Phaulkon in Ayudhya. How he looked forward to that first moment when he glimpsed again in the distance the gleaming spires of his beloved Ayudhya. Thanks to the regular visits of the Siamese trading ships, he had kept up his knowledge of the language, so painstakingly learned. For though the officers of His Majesty of Siam's merchant fleet were English, the crew were mostly Siamese. Ivatt enjoyed nothing more than the second day that a ship was in port. On the first day it was his duty to entertain the captain and his officers, but on the second he would invite the Siamese crew to his house for a feast which his Indian cooks had by now become adept at preparing. Every last Siamese seemed to have some knowledge of cooking and various crew members had in time contributed their own specialities to his cooks' repertoire. Ivatt was reputed to serve the most refined and comprehensive Eastern cuisine in the Bay of Bengal. It was from the Siamese crews – over rice brandy and garlic eels and chilli prawns and crocodile eggs – that the King of Siam's representative learned of the real goings on in the Bay, of those

96

incidents that did not appear in the official reports of Sam White's captains.

Once again Ivatt's mind turned to the two letters he had received from White. They had arrived two weeks ago but though he had acted on the official one containing a fair request to Ali Beague for compensation, he had done nothing about the second. He felt certain that to do as White suggested would unchain a series of irreversible disasters. As it was, the proud and haughty Ail Beague had made no response to his first request and he had ignored a subsequent reminder. Confrontation with the Governor of Masulipatam, Golconda's chief port, reflected Ivatt, could not but have an adverse effect on trade in the Bay. Furthermore, the East India Company, with its powerful warships, its fortifications at Madras and its trading posts in and around Golconda, would inevitably be dragged into any conflict by their very presence in the area.

Phaulkon was too canny a tactician to allow such a situation to develop. It was one thing to demand fair compensation from Ali Beague, quite another deliberately to provoke him. Ivatt had seen Phaulkon operate all too often in the past. 'Learn from the Siamese,' he would say, 'and keep all your options open. Never burn your bridges except as a last resort. Look how well the Siamese have survived. A thousand years and never an outside master.' Would Phaulkon really have suggested provoking open war with Ali Beague? Ivatt doubted it. He recalled now how brilliantly Phaulkon had manoeuvred the Governor of the southern province of Ligor when the three of them, Burnaby, Phaulkon and himself, had been under house arrest for smuggling cannon to the rebel Queen of Pattani in the south of Siam. Phaulkon had managed to convince the Governor, who was no fool, that he was a royal spy sent by the King of Siam to tour the provinces and report back on the state of contentment of the people. Who, Phaulkon had declaimed, would ever suspect a farang in that role? It was an outrageous ploy, whose discovery would have cost Phaulkon his life, but the Greek had managed it. Those were the days, reflected Ivatt with nostalgia. What adventures the three of them had had together! Sam White had not been part of the team then.

No, Phaulkon was a skilled player, a brilliant tactician. His

97

stratagems were based on the unexpected, nothing so banal as direct confrontation. The more he thought about it, the more Ivatt was convinced that White was acting on his own, while at most Phaulkon was turning a blind eye. In any event, if the recent rumours circulating in Madapollam were true, Phaulkon's attention was focused elsewhere at the moment. It was said that a large and distinguished French delegation, headed by aristocrats from the court of Versailles, was on its way to Ayudhya; Phaulkon would be fully occupied with its reception.

A series of urgent knocks sounded at Ivatt's door. It was Gopal, his secretary. He stood at the threshold, his wiry chest heaving underneath his smart white coat.

'Forgive me, Lord, but an English merchantman flying the flag of Siam has been reported near the mouth of the River Narsipore. Armed men have been spotted patrolling its decks and small boats have been plying the river on reconnaissance trips. I am concerned, Lord, that none of the officers should have come to report their arrival to you.'

'How long has the ship been at anchor?'

'Since morning, Lord. They have had a whole day to signal their presence.'

It was customary for Siamese vessels to report their arrival to His Siamese Majesty's representative at Golconda. Although Ivatt's official residence was at Madapollam, some five miles from the town of Narsipore, someone should have been sent to advise him. Dusk would soon be falling. Whoever had arrived was up to no good. A nasty feeling crept up on him.

'Isn't the *New Jerusalem* anchored off Narsipore?' he asked.

In the next instant Ivatt dismissed his suspicions as preposterous. The *New Jerusalem* was probably the greatest treasure ship in these waters. She was owned by the wealthy Armenian nabob, John Demarcora, and she often called in at Golconda to trade. On this occasion she was rumoured to be carrying a priceless cargo of rubies from Pegu, a Burmese kingdom of which Demarcora was himself a mandarin. She flew the flag of Pegu and enjoyed the protection of the East India Company, thanks to the substantial trade the Armenian conducted with it.

'The *New Jerusalem* is indeed at Narsipore, Lord. She is

anchored in the river just short of the town. Governor Beague's stone merchants have been visiting her in a constant stream.'

'We'd better go and investigate, Gopal. Prepare some transport and tell the cook to hold off dinner.'

He watched as the slight, coal-black man, always eager to please, bowed and left the room. His secretary was efficient and level-headed; his reports were not prone to exaggeration. He spoke good English, which five years in the employ of the East India Company had taught him, as well as two local dialects. Ivatt was lucky to have lured him away from Company service, he reflected, as he searched the drawer of his desk for his official papers. Then, tapping a false bottom, he extracted a musket inlaid with diamonds and pearls, a gift from the King of Golconda in more cordial times. He placed it under the sash that was wound round his ankle-length Indian robe and headed for the door.

Although dusk had fallen, the heat was still oppressive and Ivatt was wet with perspiration as he walked briskly along the mud path to the back of the house where Gopal was barking orders.

Tamil servants in dusty loincloths were preparing his gilded sedan chair, to be carried by four men, two at each end.

'That's too slow,' said Ivatt. 'Saddle the horses.'

In a few moments they were galloping towards the river, over flat, sun-baked terrain, interspersed with occasional rain trees. There were only a few moments of twilight left. The sun set quickly in the tropics, disappearing from one moment to the next as if it had slipped suddenly into some invisible precipice over the horizon. Gopal did his best to keep up with his master but Ivatt was as agile an an acrobat – which profession he had followed before coming East. By the time they reached the river it was already dark. There was no sign of any Siamese ship. They dismounted and gave the horses to a couple of young Indian boys, who materialized out of nowhere, only too eager to earn a few rupees.

Gopal ran down the steep bank to the river's edge, shouting loudly, and soon a rowing boat with two oarsmen appeared by the wooden landing stage. From the oarsmen he learned that there was a great ship anchored upriver near Narsipore.

'Head upstream!' he ordered as he followed his master into the boat. 'And hurry. You'll be rewarded for your trouble.'

'How far upstream?' asked the chief oarsman, glancing at his companion.

'Until we tell you to stop,' said Gopal firmly.

'There's trouble up that way,' grumbled the man.

'What trouble?'

'Armed men in boats, heading towards Narsipore about an hour ago.'

'I'll double your fare.'

The man turned and looked questioningly at his companion. The latter, the outline of his hunched back just visible in the gloom, spoke for the first time.

'All right, but at the first sign of trouble, we turn back.'

'Agreed,' said Gopal and he squatted by his master's feet.

The first oarsman passed over an ornate cushion. 'For the master,' he said, bowing his head in Ivatt's direction.

'What was all that about?' asked Ivatt, who had early on decided not to attempt to master any of the babel of dialects that were spoken in the Indian subcontinent. No sooner were the confines of one kingdom left behind, than whatever language had been painstakingly learned was of no further use in the next. His Siamese, by contrast, could be used all over Siam and was almost as fluent as Phaulkon's.

'Several longboats filled with armed men were seen heading upriver, Lord,' replied Gopal frowning. 'They must come from that merchantman that did not report to you.'

'Did these men see them?'

Gopal put the question. The two oarsmen conferred briefly with each other before replying.

'They say they were white men from the ship anchored beyond the estuary.'

They rowed on in silence, the way dimly lit by a single oil lantern that hung from the bow of the canoe. Vague mounds of darkness on either side of them indicated the outline of the river bank, while occasional pockets of light signalled some peasant dwellings ashore.

Ivatt was lost in thought, convinced that the merchantman was one of Samuel White's ships. If some dastardly deed had not been planned, why had no one come to report to him? And yet a few armed men in longboats could hardly expect to overwhelm the forces of Ali Beague ashore. What were they up to? Ali Beague might not possess the greatest navy in the Bay, but he had a powerful army on land commanded by fearless Rajputs, the hereditary men-at-arms of the subcontinent. Ivatt's pulse quickened. Surely White's men could not be planning an attack on the *New Jerusalem*, a ship under the protection of the East India Company?

A sudden shaft of silver light illuminated the features of the anxious oarsmen and the vague contours of the shore took on a more distinctive form. An opaque moon had risen, invading the darkness from behind a cloud and casting a hazy sheen across the river. Suddenly a cry shattered the silence, followed seconds later by another. Then a shot rang out. In the eerie silence that followed, the moon disappeared behind a cloud again. All was still. The boatmen held their oars stationary in mid-air. Gopal stared at Ivatt.

'Edge forward,' said Ivatt, in a hushed voice. 'They must be round the next bend.'

Gopal translated. The oarsmen shook their heads resolutely. They started to turn back. Ivatt reached inside his belt and drew out his musket. The oarsmen froze, staring wild-eyed into the muzzle of the gun.

'Keep rowing,' ordered Ivatt, his voice soft but firm. 'I'll tell you when to stop.'

Reluctantly the oarsmen complied, making as little sound as possible and turning with every stroke to look back at Ivatt. There was a big bend in the river just ahead. Gingerly they inched towards it. As they drew nearer, the sounds of heated voices rose suddenly through the darkness. Then, as abruptly, they ceased. The boat slowed to a crawl and Ivatt brought his musket to rest against the head of the first oarsman. The threat had the desired effect and the boat picked up speed again. Its nose turned jerkily into the bend. Ivatt stared into the darkness ahead of him. Slivers of light picked out their surroundings as the moon broke briefly through a cloud again.

Suddenly the great silhouette of the *New Jerusalem* loomed large before them in the middle of the river, her tall masts reaching up into the night sky. Around her a small fleet of longboats, attached to her by ropes, bobbed up and down, while shadows moved silently about the ship's deck.

Again the oarsmen flagged until Ivatt sank the muzzle of his gun deeper into the nape of the first rower's neck. He issued a final, terse warning and the rowers pushed on, their arms weak with fright, their expressions grimly supplicating. The little boat edged up almost to the ship's side before it was sighted. A voice rang out and in the next instant several men came running to the side, peering down at the intruder. A dozen pistols were trained on the rowboat.

'Who are you? Identify yourselves!' ordered a gruff voice in English.

'Thomas Ivatt, His Siamese Majesty's representative at Golconda.' He rose to his feet in the boat and made an incongruous bow.

He made out a number of silhouettes standing against the ship's side. They were speaking in hushed tones, in what sounded like English. Demarcora was Armenian and his ship Burmese.

'What do you want at this hour?' the same voice asked again.

'I have come to see Lord Demarcora,' replied Ivatt. 'Please inform him that I am here.' Ivatt could not see the face of the man he was addressing, but he heard him turn and give an order. Another man saluted and disappeared.

There followed an awkward silence, broken only by the gentle lapping of the water against the ship's side. The rowers stared pleadingly at Ivatt as if to coax from him the order to return. Gopal continued to gaze up in silence at the deck of the *New Jerusalem*. There was no traffic on the river at this hour, though they could not be more than a mile or so from Narsipore. Clouds continued to move across the moon, occasionally offering a glimpse of the town.

There was movement on deck again and a further exchange of whispering voices.

'Lord Demarcora is not on board. You'd better come back tomorrow.' It was the same voice that had addressed Ivatt before.

'Who is your Captain?' persisted Ivatt.

'He's not here. There's nobody here. They're all in Narsipore.'

'But what is your Captain's name?'

'Look, mister. I told you to come back tomorrow. There's nobody here now.'

'Very well then, I will leave a note. But this is most odd.' Ivatt motioned to the reluctant oarsmen to draw up alongside.

'You cannot come on board,' said the voice testily. 'I'm warning you.' Ivatt heard a pistol cock. He squinted through the darkness. The rowers froze, their oars in mid-air.

'But I only want to leave a note,' said Ivatt. 'I'm a friend of Lord Demarcora. He'll be most surprised to hear about this.'

'Perhaps. But his instructions to me were to let no one on board. He obviously wasn't expecting you. Now be off with you.'

'This is preposterous. I am Lord – '

A shot rang out. The water splashed next to Ivatt's feet as Gopal grabbed him and pulled him down into the boat. The rowers came suddenly to life and the little craft sped jerkily away.

The oarsmen needed little encouragement this time. Ivatt turned to his secretary. 'Gopal, I don't believe for a moment that was the crew of the *New Jerusalem*. I want to go to Narsipore. We're bound to find something out there. Which is the quickest way?'

'The fastest would be to walk, Lord. We can pick up the path that runs parallel to the river a little further up. I'll tell the oarsmen.'

The rowers seemed more than relieved to get rid of this troublesome duo and, a few moments later, Ivatt and Gopal were climbing out onto the river bank.

They soon became accustomed to the darkness as, aided by the moon's sporadic sheen, they made their way along a sandy path that more or less followed the river's edge. The coastal land was flat, and silhouettes of fir and palm trees rose up beside them on the narrow path. They walked in silence, broken only by the habitual sounds of the tropical night: the croaking of the bullfrogs and the squeaking of the cicadas. The flames of fireflies briefly lit their passage as they walked in single file, Gopal in the lead.

They approached a group of small peasant dwellings, whose thatched roofs flickered wanly in the light of oil lamps. The path began to broaden and signs of life became more regular. It was not late and the population had not yet retired to bed. This could hardly be the outskirts of Narsipore though, thought Ivatt. It was too soon.

All of a sudden Gopal halted, raising an arm. Ivatt stopped behind him. Voices could be heard coming down the path. They were growing gradually louder, and certainly heading in their direction. Gopal led Ivatt quickly into the shadows of a small, primitive hut which appeared deserted. The oil lamps from a cluster of surrounding huts lent some light to the scene. 'Whoever they are, they're not from here,' whispered Gopal into Ivatt's ear. 'I don't recognize a word of the language.'

Ivatt huddled a little closer into the shadows of the hut and waited, his heart beating faster. He strained to catch the sound of the approaching voices. It was not a language he had ever heard before either. There were several people in the party, by the sound of it.

In the next instant, the company came into view. Half a dozen armed men led the way, two abreast, while behind them, borne on the shoulders of four retainers, came a finely carved palanquin containing an opulent figure. A further half-dozen retainers brought up the rear.

Obviously some mandarin, thought Ivatt. But where were they heading at this hour? Narsipore was in the opposite direction and there were no other towns this way. There was only one way to find out. He stepped out onto the path before Gopal had time to stop him.

The men in the lead halted and brought their hands to their swords, while Gopal ran nervously up to his master. Ivatt extended his arms in the air to show that he was not armed, while Gopal attempted to address the men in various dialects. Both parties remained where they were until the mandarin gave an order and his palanquin was immediately lowered.

A distinguished looking, elaborately dressed man stepped out onto the path. He bowed courteously to Ivatt. He wore a Burmese-style silk coat over his printed sarong, and his fingers were adorned with rubies. He could almost be Siamese, apart from his attire, thought Ivatt. '*O senhor fala Português?*' he asked, addressing Ivatt politely in Portuguese, the lingua franca of Asian trading.

'No, sir, English,' replied Ivatt.

The mandarin looked at him suspiciously. 'You are not one of Captain Coates's men?' he asked in good English.

John Coates, the most notorious of Sam White's captains – he might have guessed. 'I am not, sir,' Ivatt replied with studied indignation. 'I am here, on the contrary, to investigate Captain Coates's activities.' He bowed. 'Thomas Ivatt, His Siamese Majesty's trade representative in Golconda, at your service, sir.'

The mandarin cupped his hands in front of his forehead and lowered his head in the Buddhist greeting. 'I am honoured to meet you, Lord Ivatt. Your name is familiar to me. I am Maung Maung Thant, mandarin of Pegu and chief aide to His Excellency, Lord Demarcora.'

'I think we have much to discuss,' said Ivatt. 'May I ask what you know of Captain Coates?'

'Very little,' replied the mandarin gravely, 'other than that he is an English pirate and has seized my master's flagship, the *New Jerusalem*. He is demanding a sum in pagodas equivalent to half the *New Jerusalem*'s present cargo of rubies. A priceless cargo, I might add. Otherwise he sails off with the ship and its entire contents.'

Ivatt clenched his fists. 'He's mad. Has he given a deadline, sir?'

The mandarin pursed his lips disdainfully. 'Midnight. I am on my way to negotiate with him now.'

'May I come with you?'

'My pleasure. I welcome the company of any man who understands the gravity of so iniquitous an act.'

'It may be necessary for me to stay out of sight initially, sir. As I am King Narai's representative, Captain Coates may not be too anxious to receive me.'

'I understand, Lord Ivatt. Let us nevertheless hope that your fortunate presence here will help to bring this brigand to his senses.'

The procession began to move again though the mandarin declined absolutely to use his palanquin while Ivatt was walking. The two men proceeded side by side.

'What happened to your crew, sir?' enquired Ivatt anxiously.

'This Captain Coates claims they are all alive and will be

returned with the ship.' The mandarin turned to Ivatt. 'I find it hard to believe such a brigand is in the service of Siam.'

'Not on a mission of this kind, I can assure you, my lord. The King would have him roasted over a slow spit if he knew.'

'Our two countries' customs are similar in many ways, Lord Ivatt,' the mandarin commented. 'Perhaps it is because we have so long warred against each other.' He looked grave. 'I sincerely hope this unfortunate incident will not be the cause of a further outbreak.'

'God forbid,' said Ivatt. 'But may I enquire as to your master's whereabouts?'

'Lord Demarcora is with Governor Beague in Narsipore, awaiting the result of my mission. The Governor is outraged that such an act should have taken place in his domain. He was in Narsipore at this time to receive my master and he will no doubt take appropriate action if my mission fails.'

'What is your master's response to Coates's terms?'

'Lord Demarcora rejects them utterly, and he has the full backing of Governor Beague. The Governor is convinced the English are behind this, in league with the Siamese.'

'That is not the case, I assure you. You will see for yourself when I question Coates. That maniac must be acting on his own.'

'I respect your opinion, Lord Ivatt, but I fear that does not absolve Siam – or England. Coates is flying the flag of Siam and Governor Beague has pointed out that most of the Captain's crew are English.'

'It will be my responsibility to prove the contrary, sir.'

A slight bow from the mandarin was the only response. The path now narrowed and they had to revert to single file again, rendering further conversation difficult. Soon they could see the lights of the *New Jerusalem* in the distance. The procession turned down a path towards the river bank. Here a couple of small boats were moored. One of the mandarin's retainers walked up to the nearest hut where curious onlookers had already gathered outside the thatched entrance to gawk at the visitors. He said a few words to their leader and a discussion ensued. Eventually, having presumably agreed a price, one of the rowing boats was put at their disposal. The mandarin invited Ivatt to climb in, followed by three of his retainers, the maximum the boat could hold. The rest of the party remained ashore with the palanquin.

They rowed in silence through the darkness. Ivatt had borrowed a length of cloth from one of the retainers who had remained behind, and he wound this round his head. In the darkness he was now indistinguishable from the rest of the crew. The dark bulk of the ship loomed ever closer.

'Halt! Who goes there?'

'A delegation from Lord Demarcora,' said the mandarin. 'We request permission to come aboard.'

'Stay where you are.' The guard disappeared. Moments later an officer returned.

'Who is the leader of this delegation?' he asked.

'I am His Excellency Lord Demarcora's chief aide,' responded the mandarin. 'I wish to speak to Captain Coates.'

'Who are these other men?'

'My servants. They accompany me wherever I go.'

'They'll have to wait in the boat. They cannot come on board.'

'In that case your Captain will have to meet me on deck, in full view of my men.'

The officer hesitated. 'All right, but that won't give you much privacy to talk.'

'I do not need privacy for what I have to say. Besides, my servants do not understand English.'

'All right, come aboard.'

The rowboat pulled up alongside while Ivatt stayed huddled in the shadows, his heart beating faster. The Burmese took hold of the rope ladder with both hands and climbed up onto the deck.

Ten

Glittering state barges decked in gold leaf, their tall sweeping prows in the shape of naga snakes and garuda birds, made their way in a grand procession from the estuary of the River of Kings to the port of Bangkok, some twelve miles upriver. Teams of eighty oarsmen, each clad in brilliant scarlet, propelled the sleek craft in rows of two, in perfect unison to the chants of the oar masters. There was no stepping out of line on state occasions such as this, for the punishment was harsh. A slicing of the crown of the head with a sharp sword would soon jog the memory of the offending sluggard. But it was a hereditary honour to row a royal barge and few were caught wanting in discipline.

The entire French contingent, ambassadors, priests, valets, engineers, craftsmen, and several hundred soldiers had been offloaded in small boats from their ships and transferred onto opulent river barges at the mouth of the river at Paknam. A skeleton crew remained behind to man the French ships, for the Siamese had assured General Desfarges that the French leviathans were of too great a tonnage to clear the bar and sail up the river.

The largest and most ornate of the barges, one of the King's very own, carried Ambassador de la Loubère who noted, with some satisfaction, that it was reserved for him alone. He sat there on a throne-like dais, elevated in the centre of the lavish barge, prostrate slaves all around him. The canopied dais had silk curtains, pulled aside to allow him to enjoy the view. It seemed as if the entire population were present at the river's edge. Both banks of the river were lined with prostrate Siamese, their heads pressed into the dust.

From time to time he glanced back at the two barges that carried Cébéret and Desfarges. They were smaller, their dais less elevated than his own, and their slaves less numerous. Behind them dozens of smaller barges, in rows of two and manned by a dozen oarsmen each, carried the remainder of the French force, some healthy, some sick, but all immensely relieved at coming ashore. The Ambassador noted that the further down the procession one looked, the less elaborately attired were the oarsmen. Protocol was certainly rigid here, he reflected, and this reception, he had to admit, was faultless, even by the rigorous standards of Versailles.

It was easier to understand now why Tachard had insisted so vehemently on the protocol that would be required of them. La Loubère had at first protested at the idea of allowing the French to prostrate themselves before the King's letter, especially when he had learned that he was expected to do the same. But when the priest had explained that the presence of the letter was like the presence of the King and that it would be a gross insult to his hosts not to bow before it, he had wavered. He had finally relented when Tachard had assured him that not only would it jeopardize the whole purpose of the mission but that the letter he was carrying from Louis XIV would be accorded precisely the same honours by the courtiers of Ayudhya, Phaulkon included, when eventually he presented it in Ayudhya at his first audience with King Narai. The priest had finally informed him that letters addressed to foreign monarchs were engraved on a sheet of gold but that he was not sure of the protocol with other dignitaries. La Loubère smiled to himself. He hoped it would be on a sheet of gold. He had never received one before!

Lavish rest houses, complete with banqueting facilities and beds from China, had apparently been prepared for them at intervals along the way in case they wished to go ashore and stretch their legs, but la Loubère had declined, saying that he wished to proceed directly to Bangkok. It was the monsoon season and the clouds were ominously grey; he was anxious to settle the men in at the fort as soon as possible.

Tachard had brought news that an Englishman was Governor of the province in which Mergui lay, and another harbour master of the port, and that several English captains were in the service of the King of Siam. That in itself denoted a substantial military presence. But what concerned la Loubère most of all was that it was Phaulkon himself who had made these appointments. The more he thought about it, the more he suspected that Phaulkon was playing one party off against the other, using them all in the process. Yet this was the man on whom he was instructed to confer the title of Count of France.

His barge moved smoothly up the broad river past small settlements of wooden houses on stilts and the occasional shimmering spire of a village temple.

No wonder Kosa Pan could swim like a fish, he reflected, as he saw children flailing towards the shore to join the rest of the prostrate population. Everyone seemed to live by the water's edge. He sighed. If only the country could have surrendered quickly and quietly, then he could have engaged in his favourite occupation – writing a treatise on the country: its geography, its history, its religion, its mores, its judicial and administrative systems, the mentality of the natives, their beliefs and aspirations. In short, a comprehensive survey that would cover every aspect of the land and serve as a reference for posterity. It was an intellectual exercise which he enjoyed, in which he knew he excelled, and through which he hoped to be remembered by future generations.

The leading boats now began to turn towards the shore. La Loubère, whose barge was in the position of honour at the centre of the procession, stared ahead of him as the fort of Bangkok came into view. Though mounting some eighty guns, it was, by French standards, a rather crude construction, clearly more suited to defend the town against Burmese crossbows or Khmer harpoons than the cannon of the Western world. The French engineers who had survived the journey would certainly have their work cut out for them. The stone façade was crumbling in parts and the bulwarks were eroded and uneven.

As his barge turned in towards the bank, la Loubère noticed a large number of small, canoe-like boats milling about the shore. There must have been at least a hundred of them. On closer inspection, he saw that the canoes were laden with market produce and steered by young women in broad-brimmed hats. La Loubère was struck by the youth and beauty of the smiling market women who wai'd to him gracefully as he passed; he found himself involuntarily adjusting his wig.

A great shout arose from behind him and he looked round to see row upon row of Frenchmen leaning over the sides of their barges and cheering wildly as the market vendors greeted them with the traditional wai. The barges of the soldiers looked as though they were ready to overturn, so heavily tilted were they. La Loubère smiled to himself despite the lack of decorum.

As his barge came in sight of the landing, a profusion of colour met his gaze. Hundreds of soldiers in scarlet tunics squatted by the quayside, while behind them loomed a regiment of Moorish cavalry armed with lances, whose Persian mounts shimmered with diamonds, rubies and pearls. Beyond them towered two hundred war elephants, richly caparisoned and in full harness, upon each of which were seated two mandarins wearing their ceremonial cone-shaped hats. One elephant, taller than the rest, stood out in front. In its canopied howdah sat a single soldier, attended by a bevy of slaves who crouched prostrate across the great beast's rump. No doubt the Commander-in-Chief, thought la Loubère, impressed.

If the Siamese had intended to display a show of strength, they had certainly succeeded, he reflected. Even the most fearless of the French soldiery would find the ranks of war elephants a daunting sight. The Siamese troops looked cool and disciplined, in contrast to the French who were irritable in the humidity and constantly perspiring.

With one accord, as the royal barge came in to dock, the whole assembly bowed low to la Loubère and a fanfare of trumpets, conch shells, bagpipes and horns welcomed him. Awed by the magnificent pageantry, and flattered by the marks of esteem, the Ambassador Plenipotentiary bowed back gallantly and descended ashore to await the arrival of the barges carrying Desfarges and Cébéret. Three gilded sedan chairs stood by, their bearers prostrate beside them.

The sun came out briefly from behind a cloud and the diamond-encrusted halters of the elephants and horses flashed and glittered so brightly that the Ambassador was forced to shield his eyes.

'Very impressive, I must admit,' said the portly Desfarges as he stepped ashore and walked across to la Loubère.

'Aren't you relieved you didn't have to fight today, General?'

'Only because my men are tired,' replied Desfarges. He gestured in the direction of the assembled troops, disciplined and motionless. 'It all looks very solid, but you have no idea what a mess my bombardiers could make of these ranks. If our warships were to sail up the river, our cannon could destroy them within hours.'

'But I understand our ships are too large to cross the bar,' said Cébéret, who had just joined them.

'That's what they would have us believe. But I'm not so sure,' countered Desfarges.

'I think we have underestimated these people, gentlemen,' Cébéret commented looking around him.

Fourteen muscular bearers, clad only in loincloths, approached and prostrated themselves on the ground before them. They pointed to the sedan chairs, indicating by signs that the largest of the gilded chairs, borne by six men, was destined for la Loubère, while the other two, with four bearers each, were for the General and Cébéret. They should perhaps have made an exception to the protocol and offered Desfarges the larger vehicle, for his bearers, unaccustomed to such a heavy load, struggled to lift him up.

It was only a brief journey to the fort, along an attractive alleyway of bougainvillea that led from the quayside to a large inner courtyard. Here some forty of the highest mandarins of the realm lay prostrate in several rows, in order of rank. Each wore his conical hat and his finest brocade coat with silk panung, and each carried a silver box containing betel nut and areca.

The courtyard was dotted with palm trees and at its far end was what appeared to be a small chamber enclosed by a red curtain, presently drawn to. The prostrate mandarins had left a clear passage between the chamber and the centre of the court-yard where a pedestal about the height of a man stood. The pedestal was draped in scarlet cloth and upon it was a golden vessel. Below and to one side of it rested a letter, written on brown rice parchment. Two low-lying, round tables on either side of the pedestal were laden with a profusion of gifts wrapped in banana leaves decorated with gold leaf. All round the court-yard rose the brick walls of the fort.

The sedan bearers deposited the French dignitaries on the other side of the pedestal to the mandarins and noiselessly departed, taking their chairs with them. La Loubère stood looking at the supine dignitaries, wondering whether he should prostrate himself too. Before he could make up his mind, a figure shuffled up behind him. It was Tachard and he was obviously out of breath.

'You must prostrate yourself before the letter, Your Excellency,' he said, panting. 'Every moment of delay is an offence to the Siamese. These are the highest mandarins in the realm.'

'Why did none of them come to greet us then?' asked la Loubère indignantly.

'Because their first duty is to bow before the royal letter. Their priority is to their King.'

'And where the devil is Phaulkon?'

'I don't know, Excellency. Please lie down, I beseech you.'

Grudgingly, la Loubère lowered himself onto his knees and elbows and took up his position before the pedestal. Desfarges, muttering under the effort, joined him, and next to him Cébéret followed suit. La Loubère beckoned to the priest. 'You'd better lie beside me, Father. You seem to be the only one familiar with all this protocol.'

Slowly, rank upon rank of French soldiers fell to the ground behind their General, the officers filling the inner courtyard and the men spilling out onto the quayside beyond. In a few moments the entire French army lay prostrate before the letter on its pedestal.

When not a Frenchman was standing, there was the sound of trumpets and conch shells, and the curtain at the far end of the courtyard was opened. A European in Siamese clothing stepped out and began advancing slowly between the rows of prostrate mandarins towards the pedestal. La Loubère squinted up at him. His handsome face was browned by the sun and his chestnut eyes had an almost feverish sparkle to them. He was dressed in what was obviously ceremonial attire, an open silk brocade robe with wide three-quarter-length sleeves and a silver panung wound round his waist and between his legs. His head was covered with a pointed, cone-shaped hat with three rings of gold round it and on his feet he wore curved slippers. The fingers of both his hands glittered with rings. He walked slowly, staring straight ahead over the heads of the prostrate French army. He did not lower his gaze until he reached the pedestal. In that instant, la Loubère's eyes met his and the Frenchman froze. He was sure he detected a look of triumph in the eyes of the Barcalon.

113

Phaulkon took his position with studied dignity behind the pedestal. He was of medium height, but tall enough for his head to be above the letter. He was not more than ten feet away from the Ambassador.

A growing suspicion came over la Loubère. 'Why is he not prostrate like the rest?' he whispered, turning to Tachard. 'You told me that no one may stand in the presence of the King's word.'

The priest glanced nervously at the Ambassador. 'I am sure he will bow down at any minute, Your Excellency.'

'Then I shall do so only when he does,' asserted la Loubère, starting to rise.

'Please, Excellency,' pleaded Tachard, tugging at his coat to restrain him. 'Protocol is all-important here. The chief minister cannot even welcome you if you do not pay your respects to the royal word.'

La Loubère hesitated. 'I thought you said the letter would be engraved on a sheet of gold.'

'It usually is, Your Excellency. Perhaps it is not so in the case of ambassadors. I am not certain. Please be patient.'

La Loubère looked unconvinced. 'If he does not prostrate himself instantly I shall rise to my feet,' he whispered angrily.

Tachard's heart beat faster as Phaulkon looked around the supine assembly for a moment longer. Then he raised a hand and the sound of conch shells and cymbals shattered the silence once more. The red curtain was again drawn open. A ripple of excitement went through the assembly as two mandarins crawled forward on knees and elbows, holding up a letter on the end of a long golden handle. The letter was engraved on a sheet of gold.

Phaulkon sank to his knees as the mandarins reverently deposited the letter at the end of its long handle inside the golden vase on the pedestal. At no time did they touch the King's word. The entire assembly remained prostrate. Tachard breathed a sigh of relief and thanked the Lord God from the bottom of his soul.

Phaulkon rose to his knees and bowed his head three times in the direction of the royal letter. La Loubère looked grim as Phaulkon extended an arm and took the first letter from below the golden vessel. It was the one written on rice parchment. Very clever, thought Tachard as Phaulkon began to read the Governor of Bangkok's letter and the full extent of his ploy dawned on him. Without reading out the Siamese, Phaulkon was translating it directly into French. The assembled mandarins, who spoke no French, would assume he was translating the Governor's letter. They would know that the royal letter was destined only for the King of France, for none but royal hands could touch it. The French, however, would think Phaulkon was reading a copy of the gold letter.

The priest glanced around him and noticed Desfarges grimace in discomfort at the unfamiliar posture he found himself in. He began to straighten up. Tachard quickly urged him to remain prostrate. There was something so awesome and formal about the proceedings that Desfarges obeyed. Tachard turned his attention back to the reading of the letter and realized that Phaulkon was in fact making up the words as he went along. It was certainly not the contents of the Governor of Bangkok's letter that he was reading out.

'We, Lord and Master of Life, sovereign of the ancient peoples of Siam and ruler of the extensive dominions which owe allegiance to our Crown, do extend a warm welcome to the ambassadors from our distinguished friend and colleague the all mighty, all excellent, all powerful and all magnanimous King of France. May God augment his greatness with continuing health and happiness. We ask the chief delegates to relay to their lord and master that we consider his royal friendship our most prized possession. As a token of that special bond we hereby place our Kingdom at their disposal and specifically our port at Bangkok. It is with much regret that we have learned of the many deaths which occurred on the long journey from France and we express the wish that those who have survived will soon be fit enough to train our own troops in the techniques of modern warfare. We know from reading the histories of Europe how greatly France excels in this field. We invite the French troops to regain their strength after the rigours of the journey and offer them our physicians and nurses to tend to their sick.

'We request that the élite bodyguard sent to us by King Louis be presented to us in Ayudhya as soon as they are sufficiently recovered, and we instruct our Pra Klang to set a date for the

115

chiefs of mission to be received in audience at our Palace. Finally we commend our Pra Klang to see to your mission's every need.'

At a signal from Phaulkon the two high-ranking mandarins who had brought the royal letter in on its long golden handle now reversed the process, crawling out backwards again, with the letter held high above them. As soon as the red curtain had closed behind them again, the assembled mandarins rose and began to disband.

Phaulkon approached the leading Frenchmen who were now once more on their feet. Behind them the ranks of officers stood waiting. Phaulkon bowed courteously to la Loubère. 'Your Excellency, the arrival here of so distinguished an embassy from France is indeed an historic occasion. As Barcalon, my master has appointed me to take charge of your reception, and it will be my pleasure to make your stay here as agreeable as possible. May I assure you of my complete devotion at all times.'

'Thank you, Your Excellency,' said la Loubère, bowing stiffly in turn. 'I am sure we shall lack for nothing. But as I am new to these parts, perhaps you could explain certain points of protocol to me.'

'With pleasure, my lord.'

'I have been informed that custom requires you to bow before a letter from your King. May I ask then why you remained standing before the very letter you were just reading?'

'Indeed. That letter was but a copy. Only the original has the Lord of Life's seal and is his sacred word.'

'It seems, however, that I was directed to bow before the copy too.' He looked towards Tachard whose eyes were firmly shut in an attitude of prayer.

Phaulkon raised his eyebrows in surprise. 'Before a mere copy? No such obeisance could have been expected of so distinguished an envoy from the court of Versailles. What a sorry misunderstanding. No doubt Father Tachard in his zeal wanted to ensure that Your Excellency was suitably prostrate before the original was brought in. Protocol is very strict here.' Phaulkon smiled pleasantly. 'To stand in the Lord of Life's presence, or in the presence of an original communication of his, is punishable by death. You would have put me in a most awkward position, Your Excellency.'

La Loubère smiled thinly and made no response. Phaulkon then presented him with a beautiful gold crucifix, inlaid with rubies, as a clear token of His Majesty's partiality for the Christian religion. To General Desfarges he presented a splendid diamond-encrusted sword, and to Cébéret a handsome model of the royal barge in gold leaf. All the officers present in the inner courtyard received gifts of value from the large pile that were stacked on the round tables.

La Loubère informed Phaulkon that the many gifts from Louis XIV were still on board the French ships. Then he stepped forward and placed a handsome silver medallion on a chain, representing the esteemed Order of St Michel, round Phaulkon's neck, intoning solemnly: 'In the name of His Gracious Majesty the omnipotent King Louis of France, I hereby proclaim you an honourary French subject and confer upon you the noble title of Count of France.'

Phaulkon bowed graciously and remained at his most engaging throughout the exchange of civilities that followed. Every Frenchman within hearing was duly impressed and even Cébéret began to wonder whether Phaulkon might not be on the side of France after all.

Before the reception ended, however, la Loubère determined to make it clear to Phaulkon from the start where France's interests lay and what was the foremost object of his mission. He looked at the Barcalon steadily.

'Your Excellency, it has indeed been an honour and a privilege to meet you. Your name is known and respected in France, not only as a friend of our nation but also as a devout Catholic who has striven unfalteringly to point out the true faith to His Majesty, the King of Siam. It is to preside over the fulfilment of this crowning ambition that I have been sent to these shores.'

Phaulkon bowed. 'Nothing could give me a greater encouragement in the achievement of my task than the arrival of so distinguished a delegation from the Defender of the Catholic Faith himself.'

The two men bowed low to each other and the assembly disbanded. The ambassadors and high-ranking officers retired to specially prepared guest quarters, while the troops returned to the barges, which were waiting to transport them back to their ships.

That evening Phaulkon presided over a sumptuous banquet in honour of the French delegation. Maria was not present, as it was not customary for ladies to attend such functions. Nor was Kosa Pan, Phaulkon noted grimly. The ambassadors were introduced to many of the country's leading dignitaries, most notably General Petraja, the Commander-in-Chief of the Royal Regiment of Elephants, whose presence la Loubère remembered at the ceremony, seated alone on the tallest pachyderm at the head of his army.

The Siamese General appeared somewhat uncomfortable during the banquet, eyeing the foreigners almost with suspicion, but la Loubère ascribed his attitude to the discomfiture of a military man ill at ease in the presence of such sophisticated visitors. When Desfarges turned to him to enquire as to the whereabouts of Kosa Pan, Petraja shot him a look of disapproval before informing him that the Ambassador was unfortunately indisposed.

But the Frenchmen soon forgot the moody General, as the feast got under way. Garlic eels in beds of aquatic chestnuts, tossed chicken in coconut husks, the cooked stems of the lotus flower, crocodile eggs, fresh river fish in lemon grass, curried prawns and a host of other dishes were complemented by the finest Persian wines from Shiraz. There followed a classical dance show in which a bevy of sleek young girls fluttered their eyes beguilingly, swung their hips, undulated their arms and arched their fingers backwards onto their wrists, to the delight of the applauding Frenchmen who never took their eyes off them.

Then came a kick boxing tournament in which lithe contestants swung their legs up at their opponents, striking each other with lightning speed or ducking blows with masterly reflex. The spectators were treated to a Siamese puppet show, a breathtaking performance of royal acrobats, and a Chinese firework display.

Later that evening, several of the officers went for a stroll along the river's edge, where they met a few remaining boatwomen apparently packing up their wares for the night. These beautiful young girls greeted them with a charming mixture of modesty and effusive smiles that went straight to the Frenchmen's hearts. The more inebriated of the men tried to approach them but the girls kept their distance, smiling all the while and portraying by sign language that they and their friends would be back tomorrow.

More than one Frenchman went to bed that night dreaming of tantalizing Siamese boatwomen offering them glimpses of paradise.

Eleven

Ivatt sat hunched in the little rowing boat that was tied to the New Jerusalem's ladder. He kept his face well in the shadows and by straining his ears he could hear everything that was being said on deck. Three of the Burmese mandarin's retainers huddled round him to shield him from view, though in the feeble light of the ship's lanterns this was probably an unnecessary precaution.

He did not have to wait long to hear the stentorian voice of Coates. Ivatt had never met him, but stories of his bloody escapades were legion. His name had figured more and more frequently in the reports that he had received. He was said to be a hulk of a man with a corpulence that belied his real strength, a blustering unscrupulous buccaneer, for whom only one man in the world counted: Samuel White. He would lay down his life for that man, and from all appearances White was taking full advantage of it.

'I am Captain Coates,' said the voice. 'Welcome aboard. So you are a messenger from Lord Demarcora?'

'I am Lord Demarcora's chief aide, Captain. I am here to extend an invitation to you from my master to discuss the return of his ship.'

'I have already informed your master of my terms. I sent the Captain of this ship with a message. Did he not deliver it?'

'He did. But my master wishes to discuss the matter with you further.'

'I don't see that there is anything further to discuss. Lord Demarcora has till midnight to pay up. Or I set sail.'

'Captain Coates, I understand your quarrel is with Golconda. Are you perhaps not aware that this ship flies the flag of Pegu?'

There was a blustering laugh. 'Not any more, it doesn't.'

'Then you accept that you wish to open hostilities with the Kingdom of Pegu?'

Coates's tone was derisory. 'The Kingdom of Pegu could

hardly be foolish enough to take on the might of England and Siam combined.'

Ivatt sat up straight in the boat. What did he mean, England and Siam combined?

'Are you saying that this act of piracy has been committed in the name of England and Siam?'

'Indeed, I am, sir. My own ship flies the flag of Siam and most of my men have been provided by the English Company in Madras. Isn't that so, boys?'

There was a chorus of assent. In the confines of his little boat Ivatt felt the perspiration mounting on his brow.

'I find it very difficult to believe, Captain, that the English would condone such an act when my master is on the friendliest of terms with their Company,' said the mandarin.

Coates laughed again. 'And I find it hard to believe that anyone in these parts could still be taken in by the duplicitous East India Company. They are masters of the dual policy.'

'I would rather believe, Captain, that you are acting entirely on your own.'

'That is your privilege, sir.' Coates's tone had turned notably cold. 'But if you have nothing further to add, then I suggest you return to your master.'

'I will do so, but I believe you should accompany me, to hear from my master's mouth the likely consequences of this act of yours. Perhaps then you would be more amenable to a compromise. Governor Beague, who also has strong views on the subject, is with him now.'

Coates emitted a raucous laugh. 'You are not seriously suggesting that I attend a meeting with Ali Beague in his own camp?'

'Have I myself not come here alone to meet you?' asked the mandarin.

'Ah, but I am a gentleman, sir, that is the difference.'

Ivatt swallowed hard as a chorus of 'Hear! hear!' erupted from the deck.

'You may bring an armed crew with you if you so wish,' offered the mandarin, ever courteous.

'Thank you, but I intend to remain on this vessel a while longer. Whether I then depart in my own ship or yours will depend entirely on you.'

The meeting was getting nowhere, thought Ivatt. It was time to make a move. He tugged on the rope to pull the boat in closer. Then he swung a leg onto the ship's ladder. He climbed up quickly. There was a guard at the top.

'I've come to see the Captain on urgent business,' he announced in a loud voice, startling the guard. 'Move out of the way.' The guard cocked his musket. 'Don't you know me? I'm a friend of Captain Coates.' He practically pushed the man aside. But the guard pressed the barrel of his gun against the side of Ivatt's neck.

'Stay where you are,' he shouted, 'or I'll shoot. Do you know this man, Captain?'

Coates squinted at Ivatt, trying to place him. He was larger even than the reports had described, and Ivatt became acutely conscious of his own diminutive stature. 'Who are you?' Coates demanded, angry at the sudden intrusion.

'Thomas Ivatt.' An image of David and Goliath rose incongruously before him. He held his head high as he repeated, 'Lord Thomas Ivatt, His Siamese Majesty's representative on the Coromandel coast.' He was having to say that rather often this evening. 'I believe you know who I am, Captain.'

Coates was visibly taken aback. 'Lord Ivatt, you here?' He forced a smile as Ivatt turned to bow to the mandarin. 'All right, guard, drop the gun.' He tried to make light of the situation. 'Lord Ivatt here is hardly going to take over the ship singlehandedly. Besides, he and I are on the same side.'

'We *were* on the same side, Captain. I'm not so sure about that now. Would you mind explaining your presence on this ship?'

Coates's eyes narrowed, turning into two tiny slits in his fleshy countenance. He glanced at the mandarin. 'I think we'd better discuss this matter in private. We'll go down to my cabin.' He turned to one of his officers, a bearded man with a deep scar across his forehead. 'Fairchild, take care of our visitor till I get back.' He nodded in the direction of the mandarin.

'Aye, aye, sir,' replied Fairchild.

Ivatt followed the burly Captain down the companionway and along a narrow passageway. As they progressed, Ivatt was sure he heard muffled cries coming from the depths of the ship.

'What was that?' he asked.

Coates ignored the question. He opened a low door, stooping to enter. 'There's some pretty decent grog on board this ship,' he said, turning to Ivatt once they were inside. 'What'll you have?'

Ivatt glanced around him. He was in a beautifully panelled sitting room, tastefully adorned with Burmese bronze figurines and a large collection of lacquerware boxes of all shapes and sizes.

'I won't have anything, Captain. It doesn't belong to either of us. But you didn't answer my question. What were those noises?'

'What noises?'

'The cries we heard when we were in the corridor.'

'I didn't hear anything. Probably the creaking of these old timbers.'

'What happened to the crew of this vessel?'

Coates's face broke into a proud smile. 'They surrendered without a shot.'

'But where are they now?'

Coates opened a glass cabinet and extracted an old bottle of brandy and two glasses. He shook his head and replaced one of the glasses. 'I forgot, you don't drink,' he said. 'Won't you sit down? I'm afraid there are only cushions here. Peguans don't seem to go in much for chairs. First-class grog this, though.' He glanced appreciatively at the bottle before pouring himself a large measure. He drained it and smiled across at Ivatt. 'The crew? Well, as I said, most of the little dagos surrendered without a shot. Never knew what hit 'em. We crept up under cover of darkness and wham.' Coates slapped his thigh with a laugh. 'There were only a couple of skullheads who resisted. We had to tie 'em up. My men are looking after them.'

Ivatt surveyed him coldly. 'So you admit to an act of piracy?'

'Piracy isn't a nice word, Lord Ivatt. We're just occupying the premises temporarily until the ransom money is paid over.'

'Under whose authority?'

Coates affected surprise. 'Why, I act under the orders of Lord White, sir.'

'And he ordered you to take over the *New Jerusalem*?'

'He sent me to Golconda to seek redress.'

'Redress from what?'

'From Ali Beague's constant harassment. He has caused great losses to the Siamese fleet.'

'But the *New Jerusalem* doesn't belong to Ali Beague.'

'It belongs to Pegu, though, and they're just as bad. Sam White doesn't like the Peguans any more than he does Beague's Golcondans. He told me so.'

'Do you realize,' pursued Ivatt, 'that you have not only seized a ship whose owner is under the protection of the East India Company, you have made a mockery of my government's policy as well? The Siamese Crown has sent Ali Beague an official demand for compensation. He has been given time to respond. That time has not yet elapsed.'

'Given time to respond! That dog's turd?' Coates laughed till his jowls shook. 'Why, you can wait till the cows come home for a response from him. There's only one thing Ali Beague responds to, and that's force.'

'That may be so, Captain, but it still doesn't explain what Demarcora has got to do with all this.'

'His ship was in Golconda waters, Lord Ivatt.'

The finer points of the argument seemed lost on Coates. The cargo of rubies was what mattered to him. Ivatt could see the greed in his face. He probably fell upon the prize by chance and just couldn't resist it.

Ivatt stared at him angrily. 'In the name of Siam, Captain, I order you to drop your demands immediately and return this ship to its rightful owner.'

'I take my orders from Samuel White and no one else, sir,' said Coates haughtily.

Ivatt tried one last tack. 'What about the East India Company? How do you think they'll react when they find out Demarcora has had his ship seized by an English captain? Do you know how long they've been trying to entice the wealthy Demarcora brothers to move their base to Madras?'

Coates grinned. 'I've taken care of all that, sir. I sailed via Madras and told the Company exactly what I was up to. They gave me ammunition and a score of lads to help me out. They're still on board with me now. Charlie Fownes even said to me that it's about time somebody gave Beague's nose a fair tweak. The Company is in this as well, you know.'

Ivatt shook his head in disbelief. 'The Company would never condone the seizure of shipping under its protection, Captain. And you know it. You may have started a series of wars in the Bay, and mark my words, you will bear responsibility for them. Now I'm giving you one last chance to reconsider.'

Coates scowled at him. 'Only one man tells me what to do, Lord Ivatt.'

'You are flying the flag of Siam, Captain, and will answer to its King for your actions. I shall make a full report.'

Coates looked at him as if he were vermin. 'You go ahead, little Lord Ivatt. And maybe you'll discover that I get my marching orders from Sam White, and that he gets them from Lord Phaulkon. You can't go much higher than that now, can you? Goodnight, sir.'

He rose and Ivatt had no choice but to follow him out. Neither man spoke. Once on deck, Ivatt walked over to the Burmese mandarin who was standing by the ship's bulwark surrounded by cut-throats.

'Excuse me, sir,' said Ivatt, 'but would you happen to know the way to Governor Beague's mansion in Narsipore?'

'I do, sir. And I should be honoured to accompany you there. I am going in that direction myself.'

'I am most obliged to you.' The two men turned and left the ship without so much as a glance at Coates. As they ushered each other politely down the ladder, Coates called after them, 'My terms remain unchanged. Just remember that, Lord Ivatt. Full payment by midnight. Nothing less.'

Ivatt did not respond and a few minutes later he was ashore once again, walking briskly behind the mandarin and his retainers along the sandy path to Narsipore. The faithful Gopal brought up the rear. They made faster progress this time as half a dozen men led the way with lighted torches; neither man used the palanquin.

Ivatt was preoccupied with thoughts of Ali Beague. Though he had corresponded with him often enough, he had never come face to face with him. Madapollam was within Ali Beague's jurisdiction but it was governed by one of his lieutenants. Beague himself was stationed at Masulipatam. He was reputed to be ill-disposed towards foreigners and had opposed from the start the granting of trading concessions along Golconda's shores. But the hereditary Kings of Golconda, who lived far inland in a great turreted palace surrounded by their opulent court, were eager for the revenue that derived from the concessions. It allowed them to indulge their passion for the hunt and to keep their bejewelled elephants in finest groom. Besides, they did not have to mix with the foreign traders, who seldom ventured inland, confining themselves to the coastal towns where they felt more secure in the knowledge of their superior naval power.

The party was approaching the outskirts of Narsipore where Ali Beague's mansion was located when a sudden sharp command in the local dialect brought them to a halt. A tall, strapping guard blocked the path and held up a lamp in the face of the mandarin. After a brief exchange the guard bowed and beckoned the party to follow. The path broadened and a moment later they were walking down the centre of a human alleyway of armed men standing rigidly to attention. Rajputs, thought Ivatt with a sinking feeling. There must have been eighty to a hundred of them. As he walked along the corridor of turbaned, red-uniformed warriors, their long swords and curved daggers glinting in the lamplight, he wondered what folly had possessed him to offer to come here. What if Ali Beague now considered Golconda and Siam at war? As a representative of Siam, Ivatt could be imprisoned, held to ransom or even executed. The presence of so many Rajputs did not augur well. They did not belong in such a small town as Narsipore. Ali Beague must have summoned them here on hearing of Demarcora's plight. No doubt more were on their way. A shiver went through Ivatt.

The twin column of trained fighters seemed endless. Ivatt tried to keep his mind alert, but his thoughts kept turning to the prospect of death. He wondered whether his bones would be cremated in his beloved Siam. He had converted to the Buddhist faith, impressed by its logic and open-mindedness and comforted by the idea of reincarnation. It was good to know that with charity and fine deeds one might return to this life once again, enjoying the rewards of one's past generosity. But they were all Muslims here. They would not even cremate his body as at least the Hindus would have done. Perhaps he could claim he was

Hindu. There were millions of them in the surrounding kingdoms.

In this bemused state, it appeared to Ivatt that the guards on either side of him suddenly grew in stature. Then he realized that there were steps ahead, leading onto a raised platform.

At the top of the steps the line of guards fanned out into a large circle. The mandarin's retainers and Gopal disappeared to the side. Ivatt stared out in front of him. Ahead was a pavilion supported by bamboo columns. At the far end, their features dimly lit by lanterns, two men sat in high-backed, throne-like chairs, surrounded by fawning attendants. They were dressed in total contrast to each other, one clean-shaven and hatless, wearing a white silk coat with a mandarin collar, the other as elaborately dressed and plumed as a peacock, with a thick black moustache. A colourful turban encrusted with rubies was wound round his head while his body was covered by a long quilted robe tied with a bright sash. Jewelled swords and daggers of varying lengths hung from his sides and curved slippers adorned his feet. Round his collar flashed a large necklace and his fingers were covered in jewels. Ali Beague.

He remained seated and immobile while his clean-shaven companion rose from his chair and came forward to greet the arrivals. Out of the corner of his eye, Ivatt saw the Burmese mandarin prostrate himself before the advancing figure and instinctively Ivatt did the same. The figure inclined itself to them both in turn and then addressed the prostrate mandarin in a strange tongue. Presumably Peguan, thought Ivatt, rising to his feet. The two men conversed for some time and Ivatt noticed the stranger glancing at him from time to time.

Ali Beague, if indeed it was him, seemed to have no intention of greeting them. Ivatt felt the haughtiness of the man and noticed for the first time that though his face was immutable, his fingers drummed impatiently against the mosaic inlaid arms of his chair. Ivatt turned his attention back to the others. The Burmese mandarin was still prostrate and his master was listening to him closely. Though it was hard to tell precisely in the lantern light, he appeared olive-skinned, almost Mediterranean in features and complexion, and he was of medium height. He bore himself erect with none of the arrogance of Ali Beague.

127

As if sensing Ivatt's gaze, he turned towards him.

'John Demarcora, at your service, sir. May I suggest, before we proceed further, that you present your salaams to Governor Beague. He is quick to take offence,' he added in an undertone.

Ivatt was a little slow to react, startled both by the man's manner and by the fluency of his English. His unexpected courtesy under the circumstances caught him offguard.

He turned to Ali Beague and bowed deeply. The Governor was known to speak no word of English nor to have any desire to learn it. He nodded his head condescendingly in recognition of Ivatt's greeting.

'Well, now that the formalities are over,' said Demarcora, 'perhaps you will tell me about yourself.'

'Thomas Ivatt, at your service, sir. I am His Majesty the King of Siam's representative in Golconda.'

'Lord Ivatt, eh? You have been in these parts some two years, I believe. We have not had the pleasure of meeting.'

'Indeed not, sir,' said Ivatt, barely recovering from his surprise, 'though your own name is of course a legend in these parts. I must apologize for the unfortunate circumstances surrounding this first encounter.' Buoyed by the Armenian's charm, Ivatt felt a surge of hope, almost forgetting his own predicament.

'I am sure it is nothing more than a misunderstanding which the two of us will be able to clear up, Lord Ivatt. Perhaps your English Captain mistook my ship for somebody else's?' He cocked an eyebrow indicating Ali Beague in the background.

Ivatt glanced at the Governor who was staring at the Armenian's back, listening with studied boredom to his aide's translation of their conversation. Another retainer stood silently behind him, while the Rajput soldiers who lined the room remained as immobile as statues. The Burmese mandarin continued unmoving in his supine position, and Ivatt had the impression he was in a wax museum with only himself and Demarcora among the living.

'I am afraid, Lord Demarcora, that though we are indeed faced with a misunderstanding, the situation is not so simple. You see, and I must stress this point, Captain Coates is not acting under the orders of my government, which in no way condones the molestation of shipping. I must apologize on behalf of the Siamese Crown and assure you that I am as taken aback by

128

Captain Coates's actions as I know you must be. It is true that our relationship with Golconda is a little strained, and that I have submitted certain claims for compensation to Governor Beague, but this is no excuse for the kind of behaviour which – '

'No one threatens Ali Beague of Golconda,' thundered the voice from the end of the pavilion. The voice of the interpreter sounded quite meek by comparison. 'No one seizes a friendly ship in Golconda's waters. You can take your requests for compensation to the devil himself for all I care.'

Ali Beague's dark eyes flashed and the Rajputs stiffened round the edges of the room. The Governor leaned over and spat into a bronze receptacle, demanding his hookah. A servant quickly stepped up from behind, placing the water pipe in front of his master.

'As for war,' continued Ali Beague, fixing his black eyes on Ivatt as he spoke, 'it is irrelevant whether the English Captain has declared one, whether the trade representative wishes to avoid one, or where the infidel government of Siam stands on the issue because I, Ali Beague of Golconda, hereby declare war on Siam. Let it be known that any Siamese ship met with on the high seas will be sunk by the ships of Golconda, and any Siamese ship attempting to enter my ports will be put to the torch and its crew summarily executed.'

Ali Beague sat back in his chair to allow the translation to sink in.

'Your Excellency,' said Ivatt, 'it is with great regret that I learn of your stand in this matter. It has been my hope to avoid war. But if your resolve is unalterable, I beg leave to impart your news to Captain Coates, so that he may be brought sufficiently to his senses to return Lord Demarcora's ship and its cargo to its rightful owner. I repeat, Your Excellency, Captain Coates is acting entirely on his own without even the knowledge, let alone the sanction, of his government.'

As soon as the words were translated, Ali Beague emitted a derisory laugh. 'My Rajputs will be the ones to impart the news to your Captain, sir, and in no uncertain terms. You yourself will remain here in my custody.'

Ivatt blanched. The Indian despots were not known for their gentle methods.

'Your Excellency,' said Demarcora, turning politely to Ali Beague, 'I must point out that Lord Ivatt is the diplomatic representative of a foreign nation. As such he is worthy of your great protection. If war has been irrevocably declared, then he should be dismissed and sent home to his country.'

Ali Beague scowled. 'Which country, pray? England or Siam? It is clear to me that the two of them are working together. My spies have informed me that this English pirate was fêted by the English Company. They even supplied him with mercenaries and ammunition. For what purpose?' Ali Beague leaned forward in his chair and raised a finger. 'I warned our gracious King and his father before him, may Allah rest his soul, that trouble would come from granting these white men trading posts on our shores, but my pleas went unheeded. "Give me proof!" His Majesty said. "Give me proof at any time of their perfidy, and I will consider your request."' Ali Beague's expression was triumphant. 'Now, at last, I have that proof and by the beard of the prophet, while there is still a breath of life in me, I will see to it that every last infidel is fed to the vultures.'

'So be it, my lord,' said Demarcora, 'but the honour of Golconda still calls for the safe conduct from your domain of a foreign representative. I know His Majesty your ruler well, and he would not approve of any other course.'

Ali Beague appeared to ignore the warning. 'You too, Lord Demarcora, would be well advised to heed my words. The English, whose protection you think you have, are behind the seizure of your ship, believe me. They want to rule our lands, and then the lands beyond ours. We must stop them.'

'I cannot speak for English ambitions, my lord, but I do not believe they ordered the seizure of my ship. They could have taken any number of my vessels in the past, if such had been their intent. They have always behaved honourably towards me, as honourably at least as anyone can be expected to behave in the Bay of Bengal.'

'Then why was this English pirate regaled by them and given men and arms before seizing your ship, Lord Demarcora?' demanded Ali Beague with a sneer.

As Ivatt listened to the exchange, he could only pray that Demarcora's views would prevail.

'Because, my lord, the English Company has a trading branch in the Siamese capital and maintains friendly relations with the Siamese King. It is only natural that they should entertain visitors from an allied country.'

'And supply them with men and weapons? Lord Demarcora, you may have been treated with honour by the English in the past, but a country's policy is not eternal. It can change when the moment is ripe, just as mine has now.'

There was a brief pause and Ivatt took the opportunity of turning to Demarcora. 'I am ashamed of Captain Coates's behaviour, sir, and mortified that his actions should be attributed to either Siam or England. I thank you for your efforts on my behalf and assure you that the beliefs you expressed will soon be justified.'

'I am just a simple merchant, Lord Ivatt, seeking the return of my ship and a peaceful environment in which to trade,' replied Demarcora modestly.

As if in mockery of his words, there erupted a deafening roar of cannon shot. It sounded ominously close. The Rajputs stiffened like hounds. Ali Beague barked an order and several of them hurried off in the direction of the river. Then he rose from his chair for the first time, reeling off a string of further orders. A wave of wailing, frightened natives began to converge on the pavilion. Taking advantage of the chaos, Ivatt turned and discreetly followed the Rajputs out, but one of Ali Beague's retainers spotted him and raised the alarm. Furious, the Governor bellowed an order. Four Rajputs shot after Ivatt. The little man broke into a run. One of his pursuers, his long legs covering the dark terrain like a gazelle, drew ahead of his companions. He was soon within arm's reach of Ivatt, who weaved and twisted like a hunted hare. Every time the man reached out for him, Ivatt wriggled out of his grasp. But his evasive action was slowing him down and soon the other three Rajputs had caught up.

Ivatt turned and crashed his head into the stomach of the first one, sending him reeling to the ground with a cry, but as he turned on the second one, his long-legged pursuer tackled him from behind, slamming him face down onto the hard earth. The other two now pounced on him but Ivatt was too stunned to offer any resistance.

The Rajputs removed the sashes from their waists and bound his arms behind his back. They dragged him, half walking, half stumbling, back to the pavilion where Ali Beague was waiting. His black eyes glared at Ivatt menacingly. He barked another order. His hands were securely tied with cord, and he was blindfolded and led off.

As he stumbled along, occasionally tripping over some obstacle in his path, Ivatt listened to the continuing pounding of the cannon, interspersed with the cries of panic-stricken natives. Had Coates's deadline expired? he wondered. The bloodthirsty cur must have decided to give Ali Beague's nose a final tweak, as he had put it, before departing.

Suddenly Ivatt's captors brought him to a halt. Hands were placed firmly on his shoulders and without warning he was given a shove from behind. He felt himself falling through air. He braced himself for the landing, wherever it might be, his body conditioned from years as an acrobat.

He landed with a thud, rolling over several times. When he came to a stop, he realized his blindfold had come off, though his hands were as firmly bound as ever. The ground was not hard, almost sandy, and he felt dazed but not hurt. He struggled to his feet. Then gradually another sensation came back from his past, from his days in the menagerie. It was the scent of a wild animal. His heart thudded and his nostrils flared. He recognized the familiar odour of the cat family. As if in confirmation, there was a deep growl from just in front of him. Ivatt felt his knees buckle beneath him.

Twelve

The majestic elephant, its diamond-encrusted halter sparkling in the sun, lowered itself to the ground to allow its celebrated rider to dismount. Three prostrate slaves slid discreetly from the beast's rump onto the earth like raindrops falling noiselessly to the ground. They lay there motionless, their heads pressed into the mud.

The wiry General, his shock of grey hair cropped short, straightened his red military tunic, adjusted his sword and strode head high into the fort. His crouching slaves followed at a respectful distance. He made for the large courtyard where his men were waiting, an élite contingent of Siam's top soldiers, five hundred of them, smartly dressed in bright scarlet tunics with matching skull caps.

The moment Petraja appeared, the squatting soldiers fell forward as one, instantly supine like an army of crocodiles.

He scanned his troops carefully and then, seemingly satisfied, walked to the far end of the courtyard before turning to address them.

'Men, you are here to occupy this fort. But this is no ordinary occupation. You will find yourselves for the first time in the company of an equal number of farang soldiers. But you must never lose sight of the fact that this is a Siamese fort on Siamese soil, and it will remain at all times a Siamese fort. The farangs are our guests, and their officers are here to impart knowledge, not to give you orders. Their weaponry is deadlier than ours because their religion, unlike ours, is a warlike one, and they are constantly called upon to perform bloody deeds in the name of their gods, whereas the Lord Buddha would not think of asking us to shed blood in his name. But know that though their arms may be deadlier than ours, their hearts are no braver. Study their science and master it. For by learning from those who seek to conquer, we can better defend ourselves and our sacred and inviolable sovereignty, if we are called upon to do so. Each one

133

of you must stay by one of their soldiers, work with him, eat with him, train with him and learn from him. Do not be afraid to ask questions, even if you have to use sign language.

'Most of the farang soldiers will remain on their ships until their quarters are ready. So to begin with, we will outnumber them. Take advantage to settle in first. You will proceed to the fort now. Officers are to seek out their fellow officers in the farang hierarchy and see to it that the men are properly assigned. Now go.'

The army of scarlet rose to its feet and, still crouching low, disappeared into the fort, a large two-storeyed edifice of crumbling brick and stone, built a century ago by the Portuguese.

Petraja waited till his men were gone. He did not follow them into the fort. The French General was indisposed and there would be no one of his own rank to communicate with. The farang officers showed no respect for their superiors. They did not even prostrate themselves before a commanding officer. What would his own men think? No matter how one might try and explain such unprecedented behaviour, it would look as if the farangs did not consider a Siamese general their superior. It was best to avoid a confrontation. He wanted anyway to check on the accommodation for the sudden influx of troops. Rows of wooden huts on stilts were being erected for his own men as well as for the farangs and he would make sure that the facilities were of equal standard.

As Petraja turned to make his way towards the large field next to the fort, where the living quarters were under construction, a figure surrounded by a retinue of slaves came striding towards him. Petraja stiffened and reluctantly prostrated himself.

'Good morning, General,' said Phaulkon. 'I heard your speech. Most impressive. But I do hope your troops won't get the wrong impression. If the Siamese were to appear in any way suspicious of their French counterparts it would only arouse similar feelings in the farangs. We would not want that, when the Lord of Life has instructed us to make the visitors welcome.'

'Indeed not, Your Excellency, but I have always made a point of training my soldiers never to relax. Their suspicions, if you wish to call them that, are merely a sign of their readiness at all

134

times. It was that very readiness, you may recall, which won us our numerous successes in the Burmese campaigns.'

'No doubt, General, but I must remind you that in that instance we were at war with Burma. We are not at war with France.' Phaulkon smiled. 'But you are on your way to the new barracks, I see. Perhaps you will accompany me?'

'It would be an honour, Your Excellency.' Petraja rose. He was a head shorter than the Barcalon so protocol was naturally observed. They walked side by side while both men's slaves followed behind at a respectable distance.

'I think the welcoming ceremonies went very well yesterday, don't you, General?'

Petraja considered for a moment. 'Indeed, Your Excellency.'

'I detect a note of doubt. You are surely not opposed to the containment of the Dutch, are you?'

'Far from it, Your Excellency. Unless one were inadvertently to replace one danger with another.'

'Between you and me, General, the size of the French army came as a surprise to me as well. Life has nevertheless taught me the wisdom of adapting quickly to a new set of circumstances. We must and will make the most of it. From your own point of view, in fact, there should be a number of advantages. Think of it this way, General. Where else could your men receive free tuition in the art of modern warfare from the world's most powerful fighting force? King Louis of France has two hundred thousand men under arms.'

'The sort of numbers a nation might require to expand its territories abroad, Your Excellency.'

'Quite so, General. Though such designs can only succeed where the territory in question is too weak to resist, or when disloyal elements within it undermine its strength. Fortunately for us, neither of these conditions exist in Siam. Ah, but here is our newborn village.' They emerged into the large field where some thousand carpenters and slaters were busy erecting two hundred huts on stilts. Each hut could sleep five men. 'It never ceases to amaze me how dexterous the Siamese are with their hands, General. These huts will be complete in a day or two. Some look as if they are already. And all without the help of a

135

single nail. Just grooves to hold the timbers together. Remarkable. I wonder what the French engineers will say to that?'

'The farangs do not have our flexibility, I think. In Siam a man can dismantle his home in a day and move it to another location.' Petraja looked meaningfully at Phaulkon. 'After all, circumstances can change, and every man knows his position may not always be secure.'

Phaulkon glanced at him. 'Yours is, I trust. When His Majesty graciously adopted my suggestion that a Siamese soldier should be placed next to every Frenchman in the fort, we both expressed our great confidence that under your experienced command and with your encouragement the soldiers of both nations would remain on the friendliest of terms, sharing their experiences and knowledge in full.'

Petraja heard the hint of a threat behind Phaulkon's words and his hackles rose. 'My loyalty to His Majesty's wishes are unquestioned,' he said coldly, 'but it may be difficult for my soldiers to welcome the French with enthusiasm, for they find it hard to comprehend why so large a farang army has arrived uninvited to our shores.'

Phaulkon swung round. 'I would like you to furnish me with an immediate list, General, of any who feel that way, so that they may be instantly replaced. I will not tolerate anyone questioning our nation's policies. Do I make myself clear?'

Petraja inclined his head, hiding his anger. 'Perfectly, Your Excellency. And while we are on the subject of policies, could you perhaps advise me of the exact chain of command? There will be both Siamese and French officers in the fort. Who has the final word?'

'The Siamese officers command their own men, and the French theirs. Given the language barrier, there is no alternative. But as I said before, the emphasis is on co-operation, not confrontation. Needless to say, the Lord of Life is in overall command of the fort, while I, his servant, will see that his wishes are carried out.'

'Of course, Your Excellency. But what if General Desfarges and myself were to disagree on some issue?'

'Then you will refer the matter to me.'

'Will the farang General be residing in the fort, Your Excellency?'

'He and the ambassadors will share a large guest house.' Phaulkon pointed to a spacious bungalow in one corner of the extensive fields. It had been used as a guest house for visiting dignitaries before and was now being extended and refurbished.

Petraja appeared worried. 'Since I do not live at the fort, Your Excellency, that would make General Defarges the most senior officer in residence, would it not?'

'It would seem so. But he will have no authority over your men. He has pledged his allegiance to the Siamese Crown. You were present at the ceremony yesterday, were you not?' Phaulkon paused. 'There is one more thing, General. As I stressed before, the French must be made to feel at home in Siam. As part of this plan, certain entertainments will be laid on for them.' Phaulkon looked squarely across at the soldier. 'I expect your full support in this matter. Now, if you will excuse me, I have matters to attend to.'

Petraja prostrated himself instantly, enabling him once again to conceal the rage that was seething within him.

Thirteen

Ivatt lay without moving, waiting for his eyes to grow accustomed to the darkness. His head pounded where he must have hit it when he fainted. His bound hands were numb. He tried to flex his fingers to get the blood circulating.

Far above him, through what seemed a narrow aperture, he thought he could see a star. It was not for some time that he realized the aperture was in fact quite large and that the lack of more stars was due to the cloudiness of a moonless night. All the while he was conscious of the presence of the beast. He sniffed its strong, primitive odour. His only consolation lay in the thought that whatever beast it was, it had to be in confinement or he would not be alive to make that sort of deduction.

He came to the conclusion that he was in a pit with sheer walls. He decided to wait for the dawn before exploring. In the meantime he would do his utmost to prise his hands loose. He groped about him in the dark until he found a sharp stone and then rubbed his cords against it in a slow methodical rhythm until he felt sure his aching wrists must drop off. But each time he was about to give up, a deep growl from close by spurred him on. It was not till an hour or two later, long after the exploding cannonballs and the cries of the natives had ceased, that the first cord finally snapped. He pulled a hand free. Pain shot through his wrists and arms as the pressure on them was released. He lay down against the soft earth and in the next instant, exhausted by his efforts, he fell into a deep sleep.

When he opened his eyes at daybreak, he found himself staring into the luminous eyes of a fully grown tiger. The beast stared back at him, then yawned nonchalantly and began to lick its right paw.

The tiger was in a wooden cage only a few feet away from him. Despite the early morning chill, beads of sweat formed on Ivatt's forehead. He well knew how such beasts were used to torture prisoners in Siam. He had seen the Muslim survivors of the

Macassar rebellion put to death by such means. The tigers were kept chained in their cages for three days and nights without food, with only the prisoners to stare at. On the fourth day the prisoners were tied to posts and the doors of the cages opened. The famished beats were given just enough chain to reach the extremities of their screaming victims. Each day the beasts were given a little more chain until eventually the prisoners were eaten whole.

Ivatt saw the chain attached to the tiger's neck. But where was the post? Perhaps it was not time yet. There were still three days to go. Who had introduced this punishment to whom? he wondered futilely.

He could hear the waking sounds of the town now, the shrill crowing of the roosters, mixed with the call to prayer of the muezzin. How sweet and precious the need to live had suddenly become.

As the light from above grew brighter, Ivatt saw that the sides of the pit were indeed sheer. He wondered whether he could climb out. He walked round the walls twice, testing their firmness at different points, but everywhere the earth crumbled beneath his toes. An occasional growl greeted his efforts. It was an impossible task. He leaned against the earthen wall and contemplated his fate. As he did so, something fell at his feet. He looked up but there was no one there. He stared at the little package wrapped in banana leaf that had landed in front of him. The beast did so too. As Ivatt bent to pick it up, the tiger snarled. Gingerly he opened it, and stared at a half-cooked chunk of meat. He contemplated it, his mind in a whirl. Was this some new refinement that the Siamese had not thought of? Either the prisoner gave the meat to the tiger and starved himself to death, or he ate the meat and was devoured by the famished tiger.

He hesitated a moment and then walked over to the cage and thrust the meat between the wooden bars. The beast swallowed it in one gulp and seemed a little appeased. At least it had stopped growling. It licked its chops and looked at Ivatt for more. He tried to recall from his days at the menagerie how much meat an animal of this size could consume. Certainly a great deal more than the paltry morsel it had just been given. The tiger continued to stare at him expectantly. Obviously it was

139

under the impression that this was just an appetizer. How could he explain that the next course might be a long time in coming?

Ivatt retreated to the side of the pit and sank down. He stayed there for a long time listening to the beast's growls, catching snatches of sleep.

When the day finally came to a close, the longest and most contemplative of his life, he dozed off for a longer period. But as the night progressed, the increasing anger of the tiger kept him awake, and when at dawn another piece of meat landed in the pit, Ivatt wondered whether any further sacrifice was worthwhile. Would the ungrateful cat be even aware that he was giving away his life's rations? The fierce growling decided him and he threw the meat into the cage. The tiger snapped it up ferociously. It licked its jowls again and waited for more.

Ivatt dozed fitfully through another day, growing weak and despondent. Then on the third night he suffered the most excruciating nightmares. He died a dozen deaths, all by tiger, and woke up screaming, his face and body drenched in sweat. He felt his hands and his toes and his crotch and was surprised to find them still intact. He was becoming delirious.

He dozed off again and was awakened by the most fearsome growling. It wouldn't let up. He opened his eyes and vaguely made out the chunk of meat lying at his feet. It was dawn once more. Weakly he forced himself to his knees and picked up the morsel. The growling rose to a crescendo. He shuffled forward on his knees and threw the meat towards the cage. He had only one wish now: to sleep and to wake no more. His dulled senses knew only one terror: to be eaten alive while still conscious. He started back to his place of rest but a deafening roar stopped him in his tracks. He looked round and saw that the piece of meat had landed just short of the cage. The tiger's paws were stretched to the full, frantically groping towards it.

Sick with fear and exhaustion, he made his way back towards the cage. The din of the howling beast hurt his ears. He bent down and carefully picked up the meat. He could feel the animal's fetid breath on his face. With his last remaining strength he threw the meat as hard as he could. To his horror he watched it sail over the cage and land on the other side, out of reach of the maddened beast.

He collapsed in a ball at the foot of the cage and passed out.

Fourteen

On the evening following the banquet, Phaulkon returned to Ayudhya with a senior French officer, Major Beauchamp, and a royal bodyguard of fifty of the fittest men in the French army. He put them all up at his own palace with the intention of entertaining them lavishly until such time as His Majesty expressed himself ready to receive them. In deference to protocol, this would no doubt occur after Ambassador de la Loubère had been received in audience. The Ambassador, meanwhile, remained on board *l'Oiseau* while the final touches were being added to the guest house. He had visited it once already and had been duly impressed. It was furnished with Persian carpets, Chinese lacquer screens, enamelled cabinets and, in the dining room, European-style chairs and table. Three spacious bedrooms contained low-lying rattan beds. La Loubère's chamber was slightly larger than that of the other two, as befitted his rank, and once again Phaulkon had noted the Ambassador's satisfaction at the observance of so important a detail of protocol. A bevy of servants stood by, waiting to attend to the visitors' every need as soon as they arrived ashore.

Phaulkon now made his way to the Grand Palace to apprize His Majesty of the latest events in Bangkok. Though he had arrived a little early at the audience hall, he was surprised to find the King already waiting for him. He prostrated himself immediately.

'High and Mighty Lord of me, thy slave, I desire to take thy royal word and put it on my brain and on the top of my head.'

The audience hall, once again void of the usual host of mandarins, resounded to the wheezing and coughing which had recently become a feature of Phaulkon's meetings with the Master of Life. He waited patiently for the royal discomfiture to ease.

'Well, Vichaiyen, how did the reception and the banquet go?

Did you manage to retain control over this great army of farangs you so unwittingly invited here?'

'August and Revered Sovereign, I, a hair of your head, am pleased to report that everything went according to plan. It was made clear to all present that the French are welcome here and that their commanding officers owe allegiance to the Lord of Life for as long as they remain on Siamese soil.'

'Good, and are you any the wiser as to their intentions?'

'Mighty Lord, their overall intentions seem to be those we surmised, but what did emerge at the banquet was the marked difference between the natures, and consequently the priorities, of their leaders. The trade director, Cébéret, clearly a pragmatist, is more concerned with commercial concessions than Your Majesty's conversion, while la Loubère is stubbornly determined to achieve what he views as the prime objective of his mission. He will be more difficult to manipulate. He is also an intellectual who considers it his duty to record for posterity the mores of our . . . er . . .'

'Pagan society?' suggested His Majesty. 'Then if such are his leanings, we should hasten to indulge him. Anything to keep him from plaguing us about his beliefs. Why don't we send him Kasem and Sarit with an interpreter?'

'August Lord, I receive your orders. Your wisdom is without bounds.' It was true, thought Phaulkon. What a brilliant idea. There was nobody who knew more about every aspect of the country than those two officials of the Ministry of Trade. Had there been universities in Siam, they would certainly have held the chair in Siamese affairs. As it was, all learning was in the hands of the temples, for the teachings of the Lord Buddha covered every aspect of life. 'I will send for Kasem and Sarit as soon as the Ambassador is settled in his new quarters, Your Majesty.'

'And what of the French General's nature, Vichaiyen?'

'August Lord, I, a hair, suspect there is more fire to his words than to his deeds. During the banquet he spoke in lofty and noble phrases about his mission, but his eyes rarely left the servant girls. I feel that it should not be too difficult to redirect his declared valour down more peaceful avenues.' A wheezing chuckle emanated from the royal balcony. 'The General is still not fully recovered from his sickness,' Phaulkon went on. 'In fact he returned to his ship shortly after the banquet. He has sent some engineers with a few of his officers to work on the fortifications, but the bulk of his men are waiting to disembark just as soon as their accommodation is ready.'

'When will that be?'

'Mighty Lord, tomorrow or the day after at the latest.'

'Good. Our own troops are already in the fort as we directed?'

'August Sovereign, they are. And I, a speck of dust on the sole of your foot, have instructed General Petraja to receive the farangs with great civility. I think he is experiencing some difficulty in coming to terms with the presence of so large a foreign force, Your Majesty.'

'No soldier likes to have the enemy within his ranks, Vichaiyen. And no doubt the General considers the French his enemy.'

Phaulkon kept silent, not wishing to say any more about Petraja. The King was, after all, beholden to the General for having harboured that good-for-nothing son of his, Sorasak, all these years. The boy was an evilmonger who had been born of a brief liaison with a northern peasant woman while His Majesty was directing the Burmese campaigns. When, nine months later, a bundle had been respectfully deposited at the palace gate, the Lord of Life had been unwilling to recognize the contents as his only son, owing to the lowly standing of the mother, and Petraja had dutifully removed the burden from him.

'And have you readied Sunida with our female cohorts?' questioned his Majesty.

'Mighty Lord, she is prepared. She has transferred an entire floating pleasure world from Samut Songhkram to Bangkok. The ladies in question are now disguised as boatwomen.'

There was laughter from above. 'Excellent, Vichaiyen. In your place we would be spending some time there ourselves.'

'Mighty Lord, I am not sure if the Lady Maria will allow it.' There was the sound of further mirth from above.

'Not even in the line of duty, eh? Well, we are indeed gratified that all is proceeding as planned, Vichaiyen.' His Majesty's tone became suddenly serious. 'We would like to have everything in place, before we consider moving.'

143

'August Lord,' said Phaulkon, taken aback, 'did you say moving?'

'We are considering the possibility, Vichaiyen. Our health is not good and we feel, as do our physicians, that the air of Louvo may suit us better.'

'Mighty Lord, then I, your slave, will move too.'

'We shall see, Vichaiyen. But do not think for a moment that even there we will not keep an eye on the affairs of state. They will remain our primary concern, and distance will not diminish our vigil. Besides, we are rapidly approaching our fifth cycle and we wish to reflect upon the question of our successor. It is a matter which has been causing us increasing concern.'

Understandably so, thought Phaulkon, who had himself been far from happy on that score. In Siam, a brother was considered to be of closer bloodline than a son, and the succession passed to the eldest living brother, but neither of His Majesty's brothers presented much of a prospect. The elder of the two, Prince Apai Tot, was mentally and physically deformed, a cripple and a drunkard, incapable of ruling his own household let alone the nation, and considered by the people to be cursed by the gods. The youngest, Prince Fa Noi, once a handsome youth, was in disgrace and paralysed from the neck down following the flogging he had received from Petraja. The young Prince had been caught red-handed with the King's favourite concubine, the lascivious Yupin. His Majesty, though furious, had declared himself incapable of passing fair judgement on his brother and had requested the Chairman of his Privy Council, General Petraja, to conduct the trial and pass sentence for him. The General had administered justice with such zeal as to leave the young Prince permanently paralysed.

The King's only daughter, Princess Yotatep, who had been in love with her uncle, Prince Fa Noi, and who as a woman could not succeed to the throne, was still unmarried. Whomever she eventually chose would, under the circumstances, have a strong claim to the succession.

'Mighty Lord, may I enquire how fares your esteemed daughter, the Princess Queen?'

'Indeed, Vichaiyen, you may. She has been much on our mind of late. Her infatuation with my younger brother seems little abated despite his paralysis. Though of course she will never marry him on account of his disgraceful behaviour towards us, her heart cannot seem to find room in it for other suitors. Yet there is one young courtier who pleases us increasingly. We wish to spend more time with him and if we go to Louvo, we will invite him to join us for the hunting season.'

Phaulkon was immediately alert. Who was this courtier?

The King did not elaborate and Phaulkon curbed his curiosity. It was not his place to ask.

'August Lord, this worthless minion begs to suggest that it would be impolitic at this stage to allow news of Your Majesty's temporary indisposition to be known. At least not until a successor to your peerless reign is firmly in place.'

'Indeed, Vichaiyen, we are aware of that. You may rest assured that, should we decide to move, appropriate reasons will be given. Our predilection for the hunt is sufficiently well known for it not to appear unnatural for us to spend more time in the finest hunting terrain in all of Siam. Besides, it will show how relaxed and untroubled we are about the French presence. Speaking of which, we will receive their ambassadors in audience next Tuesday at the usual hour. They must be given full honours. See to it, Vichaiyen.'

'Mighty Lord, I receive your orders. Do you wish to receive their General too?'

'Yes, all three of their leaders, but no more.' A severe bout of coughing ensued. 'Perhaps, Vichaiyen, after the audience is over, we will retire to Louvo for a while. And now we will rest. Return to Bangkok, Vichaiyen, and may the Lord Buddha watch over you.'

'Mighty Lord, I receive your orders.'

Fifteen

The sea was rough and the boat lurched sickeningly. The pale, emaciated man sat up and blinked, shielding his eyes from the glare. It was not the intermittent flashes of lightning in the distance that caused him to squint, but the sudden appearance of any light at all.

He had been asleep or unconscious, he had no idea which or for how long. He strained to remember, but the only thought that kept recurring was that he had died. Was this then hell? he wondered. Perhaps he was crossing the Styx. It was certainly a rough passage. He felt frail and nauseous; he lay down and closed his eyes again.

'Hey, Charles, I think he's awake.' The cavernous voice seemed to emerge from the very bowels of the ship. Was this the stentorian voice of Charon? He would have imagined it differently, a little more . . . Something touched his shoulder and he knew then that the snarling tiger had leaped. He screamed, lashing out with both arms.

'Easy now.' A pair of strong hands gripped him and held him till he had exhausted his energy. The boat swung down into a trough and he felt nauseous again.

'Where am I?' he asked weakly.

The tall silhouette loomed over him and smiled kindly. 'You have come back from the dead, sir. You're on your way to Madras. You've been summoned by the Governor himself.'

Ivatt tried to make sense of the words. 'Madras – the Governor – back from the dead . . .' He sat up with a start and shrieked, prepared again to defend himself. 'The tiger! Where's the tiger?'

A comforting hand rested on his shoulder. 'It's all right, sir. That's all over now. You're alive and after a good rest you'll be just fine. You're with friends on a ship. I'm Charles Fownes of the East India Company. We're on our way to Madras. Governor Yale is expecting you.' Seeing Ivatt's doubtful look, he added

146

with a smile, 'There are no tigers, sir. Not on the Indian Ocean, anyway.'

Ivatt stared out to sea. It was true, there could be no tigers here.

'We brought you up on deck, sir. The sea's been rather choppy lately and,' Fownes smiled again, 'you saw a lot of tigers down below, sir.'

'What happened?' Ivatt asked.

Fownes looked at him sympathetically. He would not soon forget the image of the half-starved little man lying in a bundle before the ravenous tiger in the pit.

'We received an urgent courier from Lord Demarcora that there was trouble at Narsipore, that an English Captain was firing on the town and that another Englishman had been thrown into the tiger pit. When the messenger told us who you were, sir, our Governor pledged your ransom to Ali Beague. Lord Demarcora's letter apparently assured the Governor that you had played no part in Captain Coates's actions and that, on the contrary, you had been quite opposed to them.'

'Where is Coates now?' asked Ivatt weakly.

'Unfortunately he got away, sir. He has caused irreparable damage to our relations with Golconda. No doubt the Governor will have much to say on the subject.'

'Governor Yale?'

'Yes, sir. He's expecting you.'

Ivatt looked up at Fownes. 'How did you get me out of there?'

'Well, it wasn't easy. Ali Beague would not at first agree to your release. No amount of ransom money could persuade him. He would only agree if Coates was handed over in your place. So we pledged to find Coates, to abduct him if necessary, and to hand him over.' Fownes's expression became grim. 'We shall have to find him, even if it means war with Siam. But Governor Yale will explain the situation to you. I wouldn't want to step out of line. Anyway, sir, Ali Beague finally accepted our pledge and then demanded the ransom money too, the rogue. We threw a rope ladder down into the pit, but you were too weak to climb it. So Ali Beague sent one of his Rajputs down and he slung you across his shoulders and carried you up the ladder. You were barely conscious when we brought you on board and we had to

147

feed you very slowly. You've been asleep for over twenty-four hours now. You must be hungry again.'

'Thank you, I could do with something.'

'I'll see what the cook can rustle up, sir.' Fownes turned and disappeared below decks.

Ivatt lay down again on his bed of cushions and abandoned himself to the roll of the ship. So it had been Coates who had fired on the town. And the villain had got away, while Yale had bartered his freedom with a pledge to substitute Coates. But why? What was he, Thomas Ivatt, to the Governor of Madras, that he should pay a large sum for his release? Elihu Yale must have his reasons. He was no fool. He had a reputation for cunning and strategy, as well as for getting things done. The man had not risen from a simple copier to be Governor without reason. He was a tough American from the colonies. Was it Massachusetts or Connecticut? Ivatt could not recall. Anyway, the East India Company's Siam office had recently been placed under the jurisdiction of Madras. Perhaps that had something to do with Yale's behaviour. Ivatt was, after all, Siam's representative in the area. What schemes did Yale have up his sleeve? He was said to hate Phaulkon's guts.

Ivatt adjusted the cushion behind his head. He was going to need his strength for this encounter. Yale was bound to exact his pound of flesh in return for paying the ransom. Ivatt wished he knew more about him apart from the endless gossip. Apparently he liked to boast that he would one day use his growing wealth to found a college in his native America, a college as great as Oxford, that would bear his name. His fortune was said to be already huge, amassed in private trading, a sure enough indication that he was not bound to the straight and narrow.

Governor Yale had quite a reputation with the girls too. He had married Hymmers' widow barely a couple of months after the old man's death. Ivatt had met Joseph Hymmers when he had been second-in-command at Madras. Ivatt remembered meeting his wife very well. Catherine, her name was, a striking woman. But that was some six years ago. More recently the wags had it that Governor Yale kept a mistress, none other than the famous Jeronima do Paiba, the ravishing Portuguese Jewess who was the darling of Madras. Now, there was someone he would like to meet, thought Ivatt, as he felt a surge of warmth envelop his body. He was beginning to recover, he reflected with a smile.

He closed his eyes and soon, coaxed by the rocking of the boat, he fell into a deep sleep.

When they woke Ivatt, the twin-masted Company ship was already anchored off Madras and a flat-bottomed Masula boat was waiting alongside to take him ashore. He took his leave of Fownes, thanking him profusely for his timely rescue, and gingerly climbed into the boat. A long golden beach dotted with palm trees stretched out along the shore; behind it, the crenellated walls of Fort St George rose up like some guardian angel. Madras was the Coromandel headquarters of the greatest monopoly ever created by man: the British East India Company. Cannons protruded from the fortifications to remind observers of the might of the English Crown, and sentries in bright blue and red uniforms patrolled the ramparts, their bayonets reflecting the sunlight. The Union Jack, visible from afar, fluttered at the end of a long white pole.

As the boat beached and he stepped ashore with no other belongings than the shirt on his back, Ivatt gazed around him and thanked God he was still alive. Against the imposing background of the fort, all the colour and bustle of Asia passed before him: barefooted, turbaned natives herded cattle and goats along the streets of the town, naked children sat astride bleary-eyed oxen, panting rickshaw boys pulled brown-skinned potentates in flowing white robes and broad cummerbunds, peasant women in colourful saris balanced earthenware pots on their heads, semi-naked snake charmers played their flutes. This was really where East met West. Winding their way slowly past smart cavalry officers onto the bridge that led into the fort itself were caravans of brightly festooned elephants and indignant looking camels, loaded to capacity with provisions for the residents inside. An Englishman might be far from home, but he lived like a prince in his adopted land.

Accompanied by one of the ship's officers, Ivatt entered the main gate of the fort. As he did so, the sound of trumpets and bugles filled the air to announce the Governor's passage. His Excellency never moved without his escort, even from one

149

building to the next within the fort. He travelled everywhere with the pomp and ceremony due his rank; outside the fort in the town where the natives resided, the familiar sound of the bugles instilled fear and respect. Ivatt watched the escort disappear into the imposing Church of St Mary's, which had been still under construction when he had last been here.

At Government House a sentry saluted him. The officer with Ivatt told him he was expected and would find everything he needed in his quarters – fresh clothes, linen and toilet articles. His Excellency the Governor would receive him punctually at six. A major-domo was summoned to show him to his room and the officer departed.

'Welcome back from the dead, Mr Ivatt,' said Governor Yale. He spoke with an unusual accent, somewhat akin to a West Country drawl in England.

'Thank you for providing the means, Your Excellency.'

The two men observed each other for a moment in silence. Ivatt realized he must cut a strange figure in his oversized blouse, but then he was used to having his small stature over-rated; he was barely five feet tall. By contrast, the figure across the desk from him was somewhat large, with plump cheeks, a protruding belly and the beginnings of a double chin. Yale had a long nose that made his eyes seem closer together than they actually were, and his ample wig, worn despite the excessive heat of the tropics, denoted a certain formality, a pride of office, an appreciation of the trappings of power. He was impeccably dressed and there was an air of confidence and authority about him, enhanced by the severe aspects of the former governors whose portraits lined the wall behind him. On his desk a large silver plaque inscribed with the coat of arms of the East India Company was prominently displayed: three ships on a shield with two rampant lions above them. Ivatt judged him to be close to forty years of age.

'I am pleased to welcome you to Fort St George and to extend the honourable Company's hospitality to you. I believe we once had the privilege of employing you here, before you offered your services to a foreign power.'

Ivatt bowed his head formally, without offering any comment, though the hint of disloyalty was not lost on him.

'Since you are no longer in our employ, Mr Ivatt, and since I would not dream of asking you to pay for your keep after the harrowing experiences you have undergone, I must ask you to compensate us instead by answering a few questions.'

'With pleasure, Your Excellency, though I assure you His Siamese Majesty will recompense you for any expenses incurred on my behalf.'

'I shall be coming to that later, Mr Ivatt. In the meantime, may I ask you exactly what your role in Narsipore was? What were you and Captain Coates doing there together?' Yale raised his quill and drummed it rhythmically against the surface of his desk.

'I was trying to dissuade Coates from committing further follies, Your Excellency. When I caught up with him, he had already captured the *New Jerusalem* and was demanding a ransom from Ali Beague. I ordered him to drop his demand, but to no avail.'

'As you may be aware from Charles Fownes, the *New Jerusalem* has not only been seized but has disappeared and Coates with her. She's probably on her way to Mergui at this very moment. Coates set sail with her after setting fire to his own ship the *Star of Ayudhya*.'

'He set fire to his own ship? Why?'

Yale shrugged his shoulders. 'Who can follow the workings of a demented mind? The *New Jerusalem* was no doubt a finer ship than his own. Or perhaps the fool didn't have sufficient crew to man both ships. Who knows? What exactly were the bounds of his authority, Mr Ivatt?'

'An official ultimatum had been presented to Governor Beague from the Siamese government, to which he has not yet responded. Coates's attack on Ali Beague was both premature and unauthorized.'

'Sheer, unadulterated piracy, Mr Ivatt, that's what it was. And it will not go unpunished, mark my words. Siam's policy of luring Englishmen away from their Company commissions into its own service is detrimental to the interests of the Company and hence of England. The Company is incorporated under *royal* charter. The Company *is* England, Mr Ivatt. You will forgive me for not addressing you as Lord Ivatt, but I do not recognize all these foreign titles bestowed on Englishmen.'

Yale leaned forward and his voice grew suddenly quiet. 'I was weaned in another part of the world, in Connecticut, where they fight another kind of Indian, the Mohawk. And when a white man goes over to the other side and fights alongside the redskin chiefs, we call him a turncoat no matter what grandiose title the tribe might have conferred on him.'

Ivatt did not so much as blink. 'Your Excellency, I am unable to compare the ancient Kingdom of Siam with the land of the North American Indian, of which I know too little, but I can with some authority state that no Englishman in the service of Siam has ever fought against his own country. The two nations are allies and at peace, and your Company, which you call a part of England, has a long-established trading post at Ayudhya.'

'But, Mr Ivatt, you are constantly fighting against the country of your birth. Not a war of arms perhaps, but a trade war. What difference is there in terms of disloyalty? Your leader, Phaulkon, is out to damage the Company's trade by enhancing his own, and hence to destroy the Company itself, for the Company lives off its trade. Why else has he inveigled dozens of our employees into his service, with the lure of higher wages and the promise of fancy titles and great rewards? He is a Greek, he doesn't care tuppence about the English, and I understand he is even courting the French now. He is out to destroy us, but,' the Governor pointed his quill at Ivatt, 'I intend to stop him.'

'Lord Phaulkon believes in the concept of free trade, Your Excellency, and not royal monopolies which line the pockets of the chosen few.'

'Free trade be damned!' Yale banged his fist on the table. 'Phaulkon spent too long in the company of that renegade liberal George White. If every pirate and freebooter were allowed to indulge in free trade, there would be no law or order on the seas. Just look at the activities of that buccaneer Samuel White.' Yale pulled a folder from a lower drawer of his desk. 'Look at this, Mr Ivatt, look how thick it is. This file is full of complaints about Samuel White, Phaulkon's servant. It contains a tale of pillage and plunder. The file is growing every day as new reports come

152

in. That's what you call free trade, eh? No, we are not ready for free trade yet. Perhaps in another age, but not in this one.'

The Governor had a point when it came to White, Ivatt had to admit. But he nevertheless believed staunchly in free trade himself. 'There are excesses, Your Excellency, I will not deny it. But even they cannot justify the restricting of trade to a single company. During my brief service with the East India Company, I never met anyone who did not trade for himself on the side, despite his vows to the contrary. Is that not just another form of free trade, Your Excellency, but restricted to the chosen few?'

'We all carry on a little trade on the side, Mr Ivatt. Even a hermit could not subsist on the wages we are paid.' He gestured with his hand. 'Why any one of these heathen rajahs receives ten times my stipend, though I am equal to them all in rank.' The trace of a smile formed on his lips. 'As a matter of fact, my brother Thomas is at this very moment on his way to Ayudhya with a special consignment of rubies ordered by your Mr Phaul-kon for the King. So you see, I am even prepared to do business with my enemies, if the transaction is genuine. We are all businessmen, Mr Ivatt, but we are not pirates. That is the difference. But I digress. I have brought you here for a reason.'

Ivatt smiled. 'Don't tell me you want to trade with me on the side?'

Yale chuckled with sudden good humour. As quickly, it disappeared. 'Mr Ivatt, the native governors of Golconda's coastal towns have concluded that the East India Company was behind the attacks of Coates and they have advised the King of Golconda accordingly. It is not difficult to see how they arrived at their conclusions. Firstly, Coates is an Englishman. Secondly, he was entertained by the Company, quite lavishly and ostenta-tiously, both here and at Madapollam where we have a factory. Thirdly, the Company provided him with ammunition and naval stores. The fact that he had to pay for them seems not to be of interest to them. Fourth, several Europeans, Englishmen among them, were seen to board his ship here. Lastly, in the eyes of Ali Beague and the other governors, the Company was seen to do little or nothing to deter Coates's actions.

'In vain have we pleaded that Coates is in the employ of the King of Siam, that we had no inkling of his intentions and that

153

we were taken as completely by surprise as they were. In vain, I say, because the native governors refuse to believe that a lone English captain would wage war on the Kingdom of Golconda without the full connivance of the English trading posts in the area.

'The continued existence of the English factories on these shores is now at stake. The Indian governors demand that all their stolen ships be returned to them and that full compensation for the extensive damages inflicted by Coates be made.' Yale paused and a shadow crossed his face. 'Pending settlement, Mr Ivatt, the Company's trading activities in Golconda have been suspended. The order affects every one of our factories on the Coromandel coast of India.'

Ivatt was about to speak when Yale raised a hand. 'I have not finished yet. Only this morning I received an urgent courier from the chief Dutch factor at Pulicat, which as you know is a Netherlands enclave further up the coast. It appears that Coates was in a particularly bloodthirsty mood on his way out of Narsipore and that he seized five boats belonging to Holland, burning one of them and killing a Dutchman in the process. And now the Dutch, too, are pointing a finger at the East India Company.'

Yale opened another drawer and pulled out a second file. He handed it over to Ivatt, who opened it and grimly began to peruse the contents in silence.

The document was signed by the Council of Pulicat and made a claim to the English Company for the sum of £45,000 in the name of the Netherlands Company for injuries sustained, etc. etc.

Ivatt blanched as he read on, his mind ranging over the far-reaching consequences of this disaster. It was essential that he reach Ayudhya and speak to Phaulkon. Coates would have to be arrested and brought to trial quickly.

'These particular demands are quite paltry in the scheme of things,' Yale said drily as he pulled out yet another file. 'Here is the sum total of all the compensation demanded by the various Golconda governors for damages sustained to their shores: five hundred thousand pounds!' He enunciated each word slowly.

There was a heavy silence.

'Do you still believe in free trade, Mr Ivatt?'

'Free trade, yes, Your Excellency, piracy, no. Lord Phaulkon will, I assure you, be as outraged as you are to learn of these events. I know him well. His retaliation will be swift and merciless, you can count on it, sir.'

'I intend to. I am passing these charges on to Mr Phaulkon. Do you agree to deliver them personally or shall I send my own messenger?'

'I will do it, Your Excellency. You can count on that too. Though you may think me a traitor to my country, I believe in the rule of law.'

'When may I expect you to depart?'

'As soon as you provide me with a ship. Under the circumstances I do not think it wise for me to return to Madapollam fetch my own.'

'I agree with you.' Yale smiled broadly for the first time. 'A ship has, in fact, been ready and waiting for you for some time. But first you must dine with me. Who knows when we'll have another opportunity. Fort St George might be closed down before the occasion presented itself.' Yale seemed unconscious of the incongruity of dining with a man he had just insulted as a traitor to England. His reputation for strategy and pragmatism was well founded, reflected Ivatt.

'Lord Phaulkon would never permit the closure of the Company,' he said, smiling. 'He still has a soft spot for his *alma mater*.'

'Touché,' said the Governor, rising from behind his desk. 'You know, we still keep a common table here, Mr Ivatt, with myself at the head of course and all the senior members around me. And so on down the line.' He smiled. 'Just like the old days.'

'I remember only the junior end of the table. I never got as far as the middle, Your Excellency.'

'You didn't stay with us long enough, Mr Ivatt. But today you are forgiven. You'll dine at the top, next to me. The partridge is excellent and there is a particularly fine consignment of wines in from Persia.'

'I expected no less, Your Excellency.'

The Governor headed towards the door. With his hand still on the knob, he turned round. 'Ah, but there is one more thing I forgot to mention, Mr Ivatt. I think it only fair to inform you that it is my firm resolve, should the demands for compensation not be met in full by Mr Phaulkon, to advise the senior Council at Surat to declare war unconditionally on Siam.' Yale opened the door, smiling courteously. 'My recommendations are usually taken rather seriously these days.' He took Ivatt amiably by the arm. 'Let me show you our new church before we dine. I don't think you've seen it since it was built. St Mary's we have named it. Do you know, I was the first person to be married there. My name appears at the top of the register . . .'

Sixteen

On the ninth day of the waxing moon, in the tenth month of the
year of the lizard – the morning appointed for the royal audience
– forty mandarins of the first grade arrived at the port in Bangkok
to escort the French ambassador in stately barges up the river to
Ayudhya. Entering the guest house they prostrated themselves
before the letter from Louis XIV which lay in a golden vase in
the foyer, awaiting its royal delivery. They remained thus until la
Loubère himself entered and lifted the vase from its base, taking
care not to touch the letter itself. He had not been appointed a
top diplomat for nothing. He handed the vase to a French officer
standing by, who then carried it in similar fashion to the waiting
barges.

Much to his surprise and not a little to his frustration, la
Loubère found his way politely barred when he tried to board
the main glittering barge in the wake of the letter. For this was
none other than the Lord of Life's own barge sent as a special
token of esteem to transport the royal word of his brother King
in France. None but the letter, placed high on a golden throne in
the centre of the magnificently adorned barge and surrounded by
prostrate slaves, could travel therein.

La Loubère observed the barge with undisguised awe. It had
not been part of the last procession. Both its extremities swept
skyward in the shape of a mythical animal or bird – he was not
sure which – and the dais itself was overhung by tiers of scarlet
and gold parasols, sixteen in all. At the top of the throne in the
centre, a solid gold sceptre rose high into the sky like the sculpted
horn of a unicorn. The lower half of the dais was enclosed by
beautifully graven panels. One hundred and twenty oarsmen
dressed in scarlet rested their gilded oars over the barge's side
which was carved and painted with Siamese designs. The royal
pennant flew from a golden pole at the head of the barge, its
height equal to that of the crown of the dais.

La Loubère was politely ushered into a second barge, not quite as elaborate as the one bearing the letter. He was, however, somewhat appeased to find that Desfarges and Cébéret were escorted to smaller barges still.

The magnificent fluvial procession wended its way up river and once more the Ambassador was amazed to observe hundreds of thousands of natives prostrate on both banks. The procession appeared at least as long as the previous one, for though the French army was not present this time, its missing ranks seemed to have been replaced by an army of Siamese mandarins, each wearing his finest apparel and each carrying his betel box and bearing his arms of honour: swords, scimitars or darts.

At the royal landing a splendid gilded carriage waited. But once again la Loubère discovered it was destined only for the conveyance of the royal letter; he himself was carried in a finely carved palanquin behind the royal carriage, which was both drawn by horses and pushed by men in the rear. The procession was accompanied by music throughout: trumpets, bagpipes, cymbals and horns, a singular mark of esteem as he later learned. The entire route from the dock to the main gate of the Grand Palace was lined with elephants, their riders prostrate in the saddle.

Passing through the main gate, with scores of guards prostrate on either side of it, the procession entered the palace precincts, passing through a series of courtyards. In the first courtyard, two thousand soldiers were seated on the ground in rows fifty deep, their heads and torsos bowed; opposite them were fifty elephants in war harness. In the second courtyard they encountered several dozen bejewelled Moorish cavalry, armed with lances.

With each courtyard they crossed, the harnesses of the animals and the dress of the soldiers became richer and more adorned, and in the fourth courtyard they came across the 'red arms', an élite troop who rowed the King's barges. They carried swords of gold and painted their arms red. Everywhere, the soldiers were either sitting or squatting on the ground, as it was forbidden to stand upright in the palace except when walking. As they proceeded, the courtyards began to be covered with Persian rugs, and on these were prostrated mandarins of different grades. First they encountered the fifth, fourth and third grades, and then the second.

Finally they arrived at a stairway, at the foot of which stood two magnificent elephants covered with gold and six Persian horses whose harnesses shimmered with diamonds, rubies and pearls. The procession came to a halt and only the delegation itself, accompanied by the Siamese mandarins, was allowed to proceed further up the steps to the magnificently panelled audience hall. As a special gesture of good will, an exception had been made for the French clerics, including Father Tachard, who had joined the Ambassador and his party; they, too, were permitted to enter the audience hall. There, on magnificent Persian carpets, the princes and chief ministers of the realm lay prostrate in order of rank. In the centre of this room, perched high on a golden vase, was the letter from the King of France.

Not only was it the custom in Siam for all envoys to prostrate themselves before the King, and remain in that position, but stairs had to be climbed on hands and knees, and no shoes could be worn in the royal presence. Much to the relief of la Loubère, Phaulkon had obtained special concessions for him, which would mark his visit as one of unprecedented consequence. Phaulkon had prevailed upon the King to allow la Loubère to remain standing in the European manner, with his head bowed, whereas the rest of the delegation would conform to Siamese custom. Surveying the scene now, the Ambassador was unable to resist a silent chuckle at the sight of the portly Desfarges lowering his creaking frame onto the carpet like some overfed crocodile.

There was an aura of hushed excitement as some eighty Siamese officials and the members of the French contingent waited prostrate for the King to appear.

To the same sound of music as had accompanied the procession to the palace, la Loubère watched as the curtains of an upper balcony overlooking the audience hall and surrounded by nine tiers of golden parasols were drawn aside and the King, resplendent in jewellery, appeared. He was visible to la Loubère only from the waist up. He wore a pointed crown of diamonds in the shape of a cone and a richly embroidered red vest with pearl buttons and flowers of gold. But his face was in shadow; no one was allowed to look upon his countenance. His neck and wrists were studded with diamonds and his fingers glittered with a plethora of precious stones.

The prostrate mandarins raised themselves on their knees and bowed three times, touching their foreheads to the ground. La Loubère bowed deeply in the European manner.

With Phaulkon interpreting, the King bade the Ambassador and the members of his mission a warm welcome and trusted that they had not had too tiring a journey. La Loubère in turn thanked the King for the splendid reception accorded him in Siam and extended greetings and good wishes from his master, King Louis XIV of France.

It was the custom for a royal letter to be handed up to the King at the end of an extensive golden handle, some three feet in length, by the emissary who had brought it. In this way no mortal would have physical contact with any part of the letter or with the King's person. La Loubère now performed his duty.

After His Majesty had set the letter down beside him, the Ambassador proceeded to speak, following closely the tone and content of his master's letter. After the opening courtesies, he exhorted the King to become a Christian 'since by those means Your Majesty will secure eternal welfare in heaven after ruling so prosperously on earth'. Phaulkon's translation was a masterpiece of impromptu paraphrase, neatly skirting any offending issues; the Lord of Life, and the assembled mandarins, remained unaware of the true import of the Ambassador's words in matters of religion, and His Majesty's reply, in turn, made no mention of the subject of conversion. He enquired after the state of the King of France's health and that of his family, and asked whether he had made any further military conquests of late.

After a further exchange of courtesies, the curtains were drawn to, and the King disappeared from sight, to the usual fanfare of musical instruments. The mandarins retreated and la Loubère and the members of his mission were taken by Phaulkon on a tour of the palace. They were shown the King's prize white elephant, a magnificent beast, shaded from the sun by a huge umbrella. The great white animal, a rare phenomenon and a special omen in Siam, was believed to contain the soul of a former prince and was waited upon hand and foot by a score of retainers. It drank only from a bowl of pure gold. Phaulkon informed the visitors that the farmer who had discovered this particular beast in the forests of the north had been exempted from the payment of taxes for the rest of his life, together with his entire progeny for a generation to come.

Phaulkon accompanied the Ambassador and his party to their guest houses overlooking the River of Kings and suggested they might like to rest before the banquet to be held in their honour that evening. Desfarges and Cébéret, unaccustomed to the ordeal of lying prostrate, readily agreed but la Loubère requested a few words with Phaulkon in private first. They adjourned to a spacious living room.

'My Lord Phaulkon,' began la Loubère as soon as they had settled into two Western-style chairs specially made for the French delegation, 'I would like to ask you why His Majesty made no reference to religious matters in his speech, especially when I clearly brought the subject up in my own. I believe I made it plain that it was a matter that lay very close to King Louis' heart.'

'Indeed you did, Excellency, and I can assure you the point was not lost on His Majesty. I beg you to consider the protocol of Siam, however. It is not customary in an official audience, when the entire mandarinate is present, to touch upon anything beyond formalities and a general exchange of courtesies. Siam is strict, as a man of your observation will have noticed, in questions of protocol. Matters of a more specific import are discussed in private audiences which are scheduled for a later date. I shall be glad to arrange one when the appropriate time has elapsed.'

'Very well, Lord Phaulkon, I accept your explanation for now. But I shall be grateful for an early meeting with His Majesty.'

Phaulkon inclined his head. 'I shall confer with His Majesty and will work out a convenient schedule. And speaking of customs, His Majesty will not be attending the state banquet tonight. The difficulties of protocol would be insurmountable. Nobody's head could be above that of His Majesty's, neither would etiquette permit him to address a word to anybody he had not first ennobled.'

La Loubère nodded. 'I understand. Tell me, my lord, I have heard from the Jesuits that His Majesty has not been well of late and that the air of Louvo might suit him better. Is that so?'

Phaulkon laughed. 'Siam is a great place for rumours, Your Excellency. His Majesty's attachment to Louvo is a little more pleasure-seeking than that. He loves the hunt, you see, and the forests around Louvo are among the best in the country.'

'Wild boar?'

'No, Excellency, elephants. The object is not to kill but to trap the beasts and then to tame them. It's very exciting to watch. I'm sure His Majesty will invite you to attend a performance soon enough. The noble elephant is highly revered in Siam. It supplies the army, works the teak forests and generates a great revenue in trade across the Bay. It is considered an animal of superior intelligence.'

'I must tell Cébéret about its trade potential,' said la Loubère. 'That will certainly be a new commodity for him. He is fascinated by any novelty in his field.' He paused. 'My own primary concern, of course, is to fulfil the paramount wish of my liege, King Louis. His Majesty counselled me before leaving to seek your advice on how most readily to achieve the conversion of His Majesty of Siam to the Catholic faith.'

'Your Excellency, I have no doubt that your objective, which indeed in no way differs from my own, will eventually be achieved. I must in turn counsel you, however, to proceed with caution. Like most rulers, His Majesty is not accustomed to being told what to do, nor would he take kindly to any attempt at coercion. He likes to arrive at his own decisions in his own time. The very presence of so distinguished an embassy from France will, I feel sure, have a most positive influence on his outlook. My master considers his friendship with the King of France a matter of supreme consequence.'

'Indeed, my lord, and this friendship would be irrevocably sealed by his conversion. There could be no greater display of your King's feelings than that.'

'Quite so, Your Excellency, though there may be a subtle difference in priorities here. You see, my master is under the impression that your visit is primarily motivated by King Louis' desire to express his great friendship for him. It would not seem politic, therefore, for the first overture to concern itself primarily with the subject of his conversion. That should follow naturally and in due course.'

'But when?'

'I think the question is more a political than a religious one,

162

Your Excellency. You see, Buddhism is a long-established way of life here. Though the King himself may already have seen the merits of the true faith, his people have for generations followed the old beliefs. For the King abruptly to abandon those beliefs without first preparing the nation for change could cause great upheaval. The majority of this country's courtiers and leading officials are devout Buddhists and opposition to the King's sudden conversion would be rife.'

La Loubère appeared sceptical. 'From what I have seen of Siam, Lord Phaulkon, the King is revered as a god, and if he were to exhort his people to adopt the Christian faith, their reaction would surely be to comply and not to rebel.'

'Your Excellency, though it is true that the Siamese revere their King highly, it is also true that they are a traditional people, proud of their heritage. They do not change habits easily. They have furthermore been brought up in total tolerance of other people's beliefs. There has historically been complete freedom of worship here; no one can be prosecuted for their beliefs, providing those beliefs are not in conflict with the laws of the land. It will not be a simple process, Your Excellency, to impose a mandatory faith to the exclusion of all others.'

'How then, Lord Phaulkon, do you see my King's interests being served?' There was a note of impatience in la Loubère's tone.

'If we move to break with tradition too fast, we could incite the country to rebellion, which might allow some ardent traditionalist, less well-disposed towards foreigners than His Majesty, to seize power. The King of France's interests, Your Excellency, can best be served while the present King reigns. We must proceed with caution, and achieve our goal step by step. First we must secure a political compact, an official treaty of friendship, then trade concessions, and finally the crowning glory, a religious entente.

'You must understand, Excellency, that when it comes to foreigners, the Siamese are accustomed to the expansionist policies of the Dutch and the inconsistent machinations of the English. The French are still new here. The Siamese must come to view them as their principal allies, they must come to trust France and her intentions, as no European power before her.

They must come to respect her ways, so that when eventually the King converts, the change will feel almost natural.'

'You are a skilled diplomat, Lord Phaulkon, and I follow your reasoning, but King Louis has been assured by the Jesuits here that your King is not only well disposed towards Christianity but that his conversion is imminent.'

Phaulkon smiled resignedly. 'Unfortunately, Your Excellency, in their fervour our clerics have been all too ready to read more into the situation than is yet there. They have been swayed by His Majesty's gifts of land and his generous contributions towards the erection of their churches. They have mistaken charity for a readiness to convert. But I see His Majesty every day, and I know that it will take time.'

La Loubère appeared suddenly frustrated. 'Nonetheless, Lord Phaulkon, you must make the King of Siam aware that the treaties and favours granted by the King of France are in the end dependent upon his adoption of the Catholic faith. Following that act, the largesse of France will know no bounds.'

'I shall certainly seek a politic moment to express your sentiments, Your Excellency. But in the meantime,' said Phaulkon, suddenly changing the subject, 'I have taken the liberty of sending you a team of Siamese scholars, together with an interpreter, who between them are familiar with all aspects of Siamese life and culture.' Phaulkon smiled pleasantly. 'I am aware of your noted talents in the field of literature. I am sure a man of your intellectual pursuits will find much to discuss with them. They are scheduled to arrive in Bangkok tomorrow and will remain at your disposal for as long as you wish.'

La Loubère was taken aback and clearly delighted. His face lit up. 'As a matter of fact there is nothing I enjoy more than my modest intellectual pursuits. That is most considerate of you.'

As Phaulkon had surmised, the religious topic fell abruptly by the wayside. He congratulated himself on having taken the trouble to trace the Ambassador's career through the Jesuits' well-stocked library.

'On the contrary, Your Excellency, far from being considerate, my motives are purely selfish. For I wish to make use of your renowned talents. I know of no visitor who could write a more comprehensive study of this fascinating country than yourself.'

La Loubère bowed. 'You flatter me, sir.'

Phaulkon bowed in turn. 'I must take my leave of you now to attend to the preparations for tonight's banquet. His Majesty has planned great festivities in your honour.'

The banquet was a great success. It was held at Phaulkon's palace in the great hall. Windows in the Siamese style, their large panels pushed outwards and held open by carved wooden supports, gave out onto a lit courtyard where the silhouettes of sculpted animals flickered in the torchlight.

La Loubère, Cébéret and Desfarges were accompanied by their chief aides, all of whom were spending the night as Phaulkon's guests. Phaulkon had introduced Maria to all of them before the festivities, and there was not a man who had not been instantly charmed by this porcelain beauty who addressed them in fluent French and graciously concerned herself with their every need. Even la Loubère had shed his usual petulance, while the General's gaze kept returning to her as if drawn by some magnet. Phaulkon had not failed to note Desfarges' close attentions but he was especially amused by the unexpected shyness of Cébéret who became awkward and withdrawn every time Maria addressed him. Both the General and the Ambassador more than made up for his reticence, however, and la Loubère even commented on how His Majesty of Siam could not fail to adopt the Catholic faith when so charming an advocate as the wife of his chief minister was there to impress him.

The great hall glittered with silver candelabra. As a special concession to the visitors, small stools had been provided for them to sit on. Each guest was attended by two slave girls who constantly replenished the little round tables in front of them with an endless succession of dishes. There were twenty-four courses in all, alternating between Siamese, Chinese and European delicacies, while the wines from Shiraz, subtly aromatic and of an unusual enough bouquet to impress even the fastidious French taste, were highly acclaimed.

All forty mandarins of the first grade had been invited to attend, though they were excused the discomfort of the small stools, and they filled one end of the great hall, in order of their dignity marks, the highest being closest to Phaulkon. The chief minister sat at the other end of the hall, with la Loubère to one side of him and Cébéret on the other. In the absence of any ladies, the trade director reverted to his usual confident self, displaying particular interest in the culinary delights whose novelty clearly intrigued him. Desfarges sat beside la Loubère, while six French aides and the fifty-man bodyguard destined for His Majesty separated their leaders from the throng of local dignitaries. The conversation was ever more lively and the number of compliments to Phaulkon increased in direct proportion to the amount of wine imbibed.

The acrobatic displays that followed the banquet were held in the adjoining courtyard and elicited even greater applause than the ones at Bangkok, for these were the finest performers in the country, the King's own troupe. They were succeeded by dancers wearing tall conical hats and flowers in their hair. As they swayed to the haunting music of the flutes and xylophones, arching their slender fingers backwards till they touched their wrists, the audience fell silent, captivated by the sensual grace and beauty of the women.

Phaulkon thought nostalgically of his first meeting with Sunida. He wondered what havoc her presence might have caused among these increasingly merry Frenchmen. No doubt they would have gawked at her as he himself had done several years ago, before he had assumed the manners of a Siamese. Thank God he had followed the local custom and not included any women at the banquet tonight. This boisterous crowd would certainly have ogled them and behaved in so conspicuous a manner as to have shocked the etiquette-conscious mandarins. It would have done little for the French cause. He glanced around him discreetly. Even now, row upon row of mandarins sat cross-legged, speaking in hushed tones to avoid defiling the atmosphere. Quiet and dignified, they sipped water or lime, not partaking of any alcoholic beverage. Whenever they felt a Frenchman's gaze on them, they smiled courteously and inclined their heads. They really were more refined, these adopted people of his, reflected Phaulkon. Next to Desfarges and Cébéret, whose corpulent frames spilled over their little stools, the mandarins appeared graceful and unobtrusive, a more pleasing sight to be sure.

Had he become so Siamese that even the most distinguished

166

Europeans now appeared gross in his eyes? Phaulkon watched them as they argued volubly and stared blatantly and drank profusely throughout the prolific entertainment, until the mandarins politely took their leave and he was left to try and coax the revelling Frenchmen to return to their guest quarters for the night.

Seventeen

There was a hush as General Petraja rose to speak. His youthful appearance and strong physique belied his fifty years. There was barely a wrinkle on his handsome face, nor any apparent fat on his body, and though he was short and burly he was said to move like a cat.

Petraja viewed the assembly one by one before speaking. It was not a large group. There were just five of them, seated cross-legged in a circle. To his right was Kosa Pan, today's host, whose firsthand experience of the new farang invaders was invaluable. Next to him squatted Abdullah Mafid and his brother Mohammed, bearded and wearing Muslim robes, both former mandarins disgraced when the revolt of the Macassars, their fellow Moors, had been crushed. The King had stripped them of their rank and left them penniless and embittered. But they were particularly useful to the cause, and Petraja and Kosa Pan supported them financially on account of it. They were an essential conduit to their fellow Muslims in the south, equally embittered by the loss of their historic monopoly of trade across the Bay. It was to their brothers in Ayudhya that the disgruntled Muslims of the south sent their confidential dispatches via their leader Selim Yussuf. At every meeting the latest shocking developments in Mergui were divulged to the assembly.

Next to the brothers sat two Siamese officials known only as Somboon and Virawat. They were both emissaries from the monkhood, more specifically from the powerful Abbot of Louvo, who was known to have the ear of the Supreme Patriarch himself. The emissaries were not clothed in saffron robes as any monk would be, for they were but laymen closely connected to the Buddhist hierarchy. It would hardly have been fitting for the venerable Abbot himself to appear at such a gathering. He had assured Petraja, however, that his representatives were totally trustworthy and would report back only to him. It was the first time they had appeared at such a meeting, following a request from Petraja to the Abbot. The powerful Buddhist clergy, greatly revered by the people, was increasingly perturbed by the agressive tactics of the Christian Church, and formed an integral part of the General's overall plan, dominated by his ultimate ambition to succeed one day to the throne of Siam.

After looking round the assembly, Petraja began his address.

'Honourable colleagues, you are all aware that our Pra Klang has turned the fort of Bangkok over to the visiting farang army. I need hardly tell you that Bangkok, lying as it does near the estuary of the great Menam Chao Phraya, serves as the eyes and ears of our nation. Such concessions are not new in history, they are merely new in the history of Siam. But we can learn from the history of other nations. For that history has shown that every Oriental prince who has chosen such a path has become a vassal of the same European state to which he offered his fatal hospitality. Why should we, who have kept our independence for so long, knowingly throw away that freedom in exchange for the shackles of the French? For dependence on another nation is none other than bondage. Look around you, my lords. The Macassars came to seek refuge on our shores. Why? Because the Dutch, professing to be interested only in trade, had overrun their homeland in the Celebes. Look around you to every corner where the Portuguese, the Spaniards and the Dutch are ensconced today, and ask yourselves: what happened to the princes of those lands? Where are the indigenous rulers now? They are puppets, my lords, and their subjects slaves.

'We have heard great things about the King of France, but is not our King a just and powerful ruler too? We have heard of the Christian path to God, but have we grown weary of our own faith? I ask you, my lords, have we not engineers enough to build us fine temples, and soldiers enough and ships to sail to France? Then why do we not send them to their city called Paris, and let our soldiers garrison their forts and our engineers build them Buddhist wats and preach them the sermons of our guide. Why? Because the King of France and the French mandarins would have none of it. Yet we have welcomed the foreigner to our shores. We have invited him to share our rice and allowed him to preach his faith. All this is well. The laws of hospitality require as much. But are we now to hand him over our cities and let him

169

arm them with his troops as well? Soon we will not have to think of what to give him, for he will have taken all. My lords, I say Siam for the Siamese. '

Petraja paused to let his words sink in. He looked around him at the clandestine group, joined together in its hatred of farangs and in its determination to see the last of their stinking priests and traders and soldiers expelled from Siam's shores. The group was only small; it was dangerous to recruit others, for they would weigh the proposal against the rewards of revealing the plot to His Majesty. But it was powerful enough.

Petraja thanked the assembly for its attention and invited Kosa Pan, the most recent and distinguished addition to the group, to speak.

Kosa in turn looked at the faces now turned expectantly towards him. His distrust and dislike of all farangs, and the French in particular, had if anything intensified since his ignominious return to Siam. He had been stung by a notice from the Pra Klang expressing his displeasure at his absence from the banquet in honour of the French delegation at Bangkok. It was a gross breach of etiquette, he was informed, at a time when His Majesty had clearly outlined the country's policy of showing every courtesy to the visitors. His absence had been most conspicuous, causing a number of eyebrows to be raised and giving rise to repeated enquiries by the French ambassadors. Kosa shook inwardly with rage. That swollen-headed Pra Klang had actually had the gall to recommend to His Majesty that the number of his dignity marks be reduced and that he be demoted to a mandarin of the second grade! His conical hat now bore only two rings. He had been publicly humiliated in his own land by a farang! It was preposterous.

'My lords,' he said, bridling his emotions, 'our honourable President has put it well. There is little left for me but to tell you something of my personal experiences of the French farangs with whom I spent a year in their capital city of Paris. It is as large a city as Ayudhya, and their monuments and temples are not without beauty when one becomes accustomed to the strangeness of their form. Their houses are built of stone instead of wood and cannot be dismantled and moved to another place as ours can. Their chief river, the Seine, is but a bloated stream compared with our great Chao Phraya, and they have hardly any canals, using narrow cobbled streets instead of waterways. For transport they use horse-drawn carriages instead of boats and the harshness of their climate and the hardness of their road surface force all but the poorest to wear apparel on their feet, called shoes. I have seem extreme poverty there such as no Buddhist administration would tolerate, yet in fairness I must point out that the severity of their cold season renders their requirements far greater than ours. They need many layers of clothing, much wood to keep warm, and far greater shelter to survive the cold winds. In the direst of times the waters of their rivers harden so that you can walk across them. The rain turns white and the ground is covered in a substance called snow, which is too cold even to touch. They cannot wash themselves in the river as we do several times a day, for the water is too cold, and they cannot hang their panungs in the sunshine to dry, for the sun does not heat their land as it does ours.' Kosa wrinkled his nose distastefully. 'Consequently the poor seldom bathe while the rich cover themselves with perfumes to hide their bad odour.

'No, my lords, these people are not blessed with an easy life as we are. Perhaps it is because of this that they seek to conquer other lands. They are for ever waging war but even their wars are different to ours. They fight to kill, not to capture slaves as we do. They use firearms and horses instead of harpoons and elephants and while after a fierce battle we might find twenty dead on the field, they will slaughter thousands. And whereas our gracious King calls upon his men only when he needs them, their King Rouee has a standing army of two hundred thousand men, the largest in all Europe.'

Kosa paused and his dark eyes narrowed. 'It is part of this great army, my lords, that has disembarked on our shores. We must not underestimate its strength nor the baseness of its intentions. One does not invite the hungry crocodile through the front door. And though spiritually these people are beneath us, in matters of science and weapons of war they are our superiors. You can be sure that these farangs are here for a purpose and that that purpose is not a peaceful one. For while I was received with much fanfare and curiosity in France as the representative of the Lord of Life, I discerned, through all the courtesy and protocol, the real aims of France: to subject our beloved nation to the will of King Rouee and to supplant the Buddhist doctrine by the Christian faith. And in this task they will turn to the insidious Pra Klang, for whom they have come laden with honours, gifts, medals and even a mandarinate of France.'

Kosa Pan turned his attention now to the representatives of the venerable Abbot. 'The farang faith is a greedy one, one that does not tolerate other beliefs as ours does, and one that cannot and will not rest until it has forced all those around it to adhere to its narrow path to God. No other belief may live alongside it.'

The ensuing silence was interrupted by Virawat: 'I am not a military man, my lords, but how can five hundred men hold an entire country to ransom?'

'Perhaps they cannot,' replied Petraja, 'but while they are His Majesty's guests, no one would dare lift a finger against them. We have no choice but to bide our time. Meanwhile we must start to lay the foundations for their early departure.'

Somboon, the senior of the two representatives of the clergy, turned to Kosa Pan. 'We will relay your thoughts to our revered Abbot, Your Excellency. I am sure His Holiness, the Supreme Patriarch, will be most interested to learn what you have to say.'

It was precisely what Petraja had hoped to hear. Besides His Majesty, no one had greater influence in the country than the Supreme Patriarch of the Buddhist faith. He was the only mortal not required to prostrate himself in the presence of the King.

Petraja inclined his head respectfully to the two officials and turned to the Moors.

'Tell us, my lords, what news have you from your brethren in the south?'

Abdullah Mafid scratched his thick dark beard. 'The news is not good, Your Excellency. The farang Shahbandar has taken the law completely into his own hands. Our brethren report that he behaves like a despot, answering to no one, while his pirates continue to rob the Bay of Bengal in the name of Siam. The members of the Council of Five are too frightened to oppose him and affix their seals meekly to his decisions. The farang Governor is besotted with wine and women and does not interfere either.

The Shahbandar even collects the province's taxes on his behalf now.'

'To show how far matters have deteriorated,' added Mohammed, his large round eyes indignant above his sharp nose, 'I have received a report from Selim Yussuf that the Shahbandar's new tactic is to put a series of ghost workers on the Treasury payroll and to pay their salaries straight into his pocket.'

'Do we have any proof of that, Mohammed?' asked Petraja. 'And do we know if the Pra Klang is involved?'

'We know it is happening but as usual we have no tangible proof, Your Excellency,' replied Mohammed bitterly. 'Neither do we know how far the Pra Klang is involved. But even if he were not, he would surely stand behind his appointed crony.'

'Much as I despise the man,' observed Petraja, 'I believe he is too wily to involve himself in so obvious a scheme.'

'Why can't we simply inform the Lord of Life of what is going on?' asked Varawat.

Petraja glanced at Kosa, indicating with a barely perceptible nod that he wished him to answer.

'That is the one thing we cannot do, Virawat, at least not until we have accumulated sufficient evidence.' Kosa glanced warily in Petraja's direction, before continuing, 'You see, His Majesty's infatuation with his Pra Klang is so complete that any criticism directed at him would be ascribed to General Petraja's bitterness at not having been elected to the post himself.'

There was an embarrassed silence. Petraja glanced briefly at his feet. Then he looked up again haughtily and addressed the assembly once more.

'My lords, though our forts be garrisoned by farang troops, though we have a farang as chief minister of this ancient, sovereign nation, though the farang priests enjoy special privileges, and though there are rumours that His Majesty himself is considering adopting the farang faith, yet shall we overcome. We shall gather evidence and spread rumours and sow discord in as many quarters as possible until there is sufficient chaos in the land to force the Pra Klang to retract his plan to welcome the farangs to these shores. More immediately we shall deal with that renegade Shahbandar of Mergui. He must be exposed for the blackguard that he is and taught a severe lesson.' The General

173

looked at Mohammed. 'It seems clear to me that Selim Yussuf is the man to do it. Will you see to it, Mohammed?'

'You can count on me, General.'

'Good,' he said. 'In the meantime, let discord and chaos be our watchword.' He rose to his feet. 'And now we had better disband before our absence from our posts arouses unwanted suspicion.'

Eighteen

On the day following the state banquet, la Loubère returned to the fort at Bangkok where the distinguished team of Siamese scholars was awaiting him. He was accompanied by the senior officers who had been invited to attend the official functions, and by Céberet, who was to begin the task of setting up the French trading post there. The King departed for Louvo in the royal barge in the company of his new French bodyguard under the command of Major Beauchamp. They were to take up their new posts at the palace there for as long as His Majesty chose to remain in residence.

Of all the French dignitaries who had attended the festivities, only General Desfarges now remained behind in Ayudhya. He had welcomed Phaulkon's suggestion to stay on an extra day to see the sights and examine the layout of the city before rejoining the garrison at Bangkok. Only one aide de camp remained with him.

It was the opportunity Phaulkon had been waiting for. He could entertain the Frenchman discreetly, far from the prying eyes of his officers.

General Desfarges dreamed a lot that night. He had gone to bed tired after a long but fascinating day exploring Ayudhya. The dinner that followed had been sumptuous, graciously presided over by the charming Lady Maria. Phaulkon certainly kept a fine table. The Bishop of Heliopolis from the Jesuit Seminary had been there as well and the conversation had been lively. The last thing on his mind that night as he fell asleep had been the smiling image of the Lady Maria.

He dreamed of banquets and armies and conquests and glory, and also of the Lady Maria, smiling at him. The dinner was over, the guests had left and the two of them remained alone. She led him away from the banqueting hall, walking with slow, gliding movements, and he followed behind her, marvelling at her grace.

175

Then Phaulkon's face, angry and taut, stood at the head of a huge army, blocking his way. Phaulkon gave an order and ten thousand Siamese soldiers raised their lances, aiming at him. Phaulkon shouted a further command and they let fly their weapons. The lances flew at terrible speed towards him, heading for his face, his chest, his stomach and his groin.

Desfarges cried out and sat up with a jolt in his bed. He was perspiring profusely. Thank God, it was only a dream.

He lay down again on his back. Then he kept breathlessly still. He was sure he had heard a light rustling sound. He heard it again. It was coming from the far end of the room. He looked across, straining his eyes. A tiny shaft of light filtered through the bottom of the panelled doors that led into the garden outside. It was just enough for him to make out the figure of a girl crouching on her haunches with a fan-shaped broom in her hand. He blinked. She was sweeping the room! What a strange time to choose to do it. It must be early morning. Perhaps it was the custom for a room to be made spotless before the guest woke up. He lay back and stared at the ceiling. His ear picked up a similar noise to the other side of him. He look round and made out another female figure shuffling forward on her haunches and swinging a rattan broom rhythmically from side to side.

He raised himself on one elbow. As he did so, a third silhouette that he had not noticed before emerged from the shadows and crept silently over to the window. She pushed the wooden shutter outwards, inserting a bamboo stick to keep it in place. As she turned, the light framed her naked torso, highlighting her delicately rounded breasts. He feasted his eyes on them.

A measure of light now entered the room through the open window and she glanced across at him.

She said something to the other girls and one of them handed her a strip of cloth. She walked over to his bed crouching respectfully low and smiled shyly at him. She examined his brow and began gently dabbing his forehead with the piece of cloth. It felt cool and moist and he was grateful. He wished she would never stop. She wore only a simple panung and her young breasts hung tantalizingly close to his mouth as she leaned over to sponge his face, wiping the perspiration in soft, diligent strokes from his head to his shoulders. Suddenly she seemed to notice the stains

176

of perspiration seeping through his white nightshirt. She let out a small cry and spoke to the other girls. They dropped their brooms, each picking up a cloth and dipping it in a pail of water. They came and joined her and now the three of them began to douse his perspiring body, lifting his nightshirt in different places as they worked.

Desfarges sighed involuntarily. It was an extraordinarily sensuous feeling. For a moment he wondered whether he might still be dreaming. A wave of excitement engulfed him and he felt himself growing embarrassingly erect. He was at his wit's end how to hide it. Yet the more they sponged him, the more his desire grew. He felt suddenly ashamed of his obesity. These people were all so slimly built and delicate. If only he were young and dashing again. Perhaps one of them would have liked him. He would have been hard pressed to choose one over the other. Then he chided himself for his thoughts. They were maids assigned to his room, that was all.

They continued sponging down his whole body, entirely engrossed in their task, omitting only the area around his groin. They could not fail to have noticed his unflagging desire, but they appeared to ignore it, as if it did not exist. Eventually, their task completed, they wai'd respectfully to him and returned to their sweeping.

He lay there watching them, hugely excited, his mind ranging over every possible angle of approach. He wanted them to start all over again. His whole body was on fire. He would simply have to pluck up the courage and ask one of them. But what? And how? What kind of sign language would he use? What if they laughed at him and reported his behaviour to their mistress, the Lady Maria? Imagine staying in her house, partaking of her hospitality, and then attempting to seduce her maids. He, a marshal of France!

The girls continued their domestic work, assiduously sweeping every corner of the room. Then, apparently tired, they stopped for a break. One of them drew an arm across her forehead and said something to the others. She seemed to be perspiring. Her friends fetched a couple of cloths and while one girl stood by, the other began to sponge her face and neck. Then she turned the girl round and sponged her back. As she did so, the other girl

177

came forward and began gently cleansing her breasts and stomach with the wet cloth.

He stared transfixed as each of the girls rubbed the other one down in turn. They worked together, their movements slow and graceful. It was the most erotic thing he had ever witnessed. He could barely refrain from crying out.

He raised himself higher in the bed, leaning back against the rattan headboard, and stared at them blatantly. They continued for a while without appearing to notice his curiosity. Then they turned and smiled at him. It was a smile full of promise. To his stupefaction the girls now began to unwind each others' panungs until all three stood naked before him. While the one in the centre remained standing, the other two bent down on both sides of her and began carefully sponging the areas that had been covered by the panung. As soon as she was clean, another girl took her place in the centre.

Desfarges was perspiring profusely again. He watched, unable to tear his eyes away. When all three of them had finished, they turned to face him, as if seeking direction for their next move. They just stood there, their young bodies tantalizing and provocative. He threw his arms out towards them and groaned. Slowly they approached the bed, smiling. They lifted his arms and pulled the nightshirt over his head. When he could see again, one of the girls had disappeared. He searched about him quickly, but she was nowhere to be seen. How odd. No matter, there were still two of the voluptuous creatures left. Who was he to complain?

Their smiles were so friendly and their actions so natural that he soon felt little shame for his nakedness, or even his obesity. They seemed to view his corpulent body as if he were Adonis himself. They treated him with such loving attention that he soon began to think he was. They pulled him gently down onto the bed until he lay quite flat. Then they wiped him clean again all over, this time lingering at great length over his most sensitive areas. They sponged his groin with great care, pausing whenever they felt his excitement would overflow. They had an uncanny sense of timing. They knew exactly when to stop. Delicately, as if they were handling ancient porcelain, they cleansed his genitalia and gazed admiringly at the size of his lust. He felt himself to be very special.

178

They knelt now to either side of him and rubbed a sweet-smelling oil into his skin, causing his whole body to tingle pleasantly. Then they rubbed the same oil all over themselves, helping each other to reach the difficult areas. His eyes feasted on the sinuous lines of their bodies and the olive-brown of their skin. Never had he known such ecstasy of anticipation.

Thoroughly oiled, the two girls slid on top of him, moving like serpents across his body, teasing and caressing him, their fingers delving into his every pore. He closed his eyes in ecstasy.

Just as he thought he had reached the pinnacle of sensation, a new thrill suffused him, sending further convulsions through his body. He did not at first comprehend what was happening; both girls were on top of him yet his haunches and scrotum were being erotically stroked from below with feathers. My God! It was the third girl. There must be some sort of sliding compartment under his bed. What incredible refinements these people had. They could certainly teach Western women a thing or two. All three girls seemed to be everywhere at the same time, provoking him, ravishing him, tantalizing him until the prolonged ecstasy reached the threshold of pain and his body could stand it no longer.

He felt one of the girls straddle him while the second proffered her breast to his voracious mouth and from beneath him the play of feathers grew to a frenzy. With an uncontrollable shout he exploded, uncertain whether it was the world or his amazing dream which had ended.

Nineteen

'Land ho!' shouted the lookout, high on the mast of the sleek frigate. Behind him the ship's red and blue ensign fluttered in the breeze.

The shout reached the ears of Thomas Ivatt and sent a flurry of warmth through him. In the next instant he was on deck, eager to catch a first glimpse of his beloved Siam. In the distance, in the late afternoon sun, the silhouettes of dozens of islands with their ribbons of white beach and transparent turquoise water jutted out like proud sentinels from the azure sea. The Mergui archipelago was a breathtaking sight. Beyond the islands was the harbour of Mergui, and a few miles upriver lay the ancient trading town of Tenasserim founded in 1373 by the Siamese, just after they had moved their capital south to Ayudhya from Sukhotai.

How the first European mariners, the Portuguese, must have marvelled at this sight, thought Ivatt, as the host of islands covered in forested hills drew gradually closer. Vasco da Gama had changed the world in that fateful year of 1497 when he had first rounded the Cape of Good Hope to open up another continent, vast in riches and immense in the diversity of its ancient cultures: Asia. In that moment of discovery, Venice had been unseated as the maritime queen of the West. The Portuguese discovery revolutionized the political, commercial and social history of every Asiatic nation as the greed and lusts of the European powers vied for a part of its lucrative shores.

Now, almost two centuries later, the power of Portugal was waning. The British East India Company, with strongholds all along the maritime trade routes from Persia to the Bay of Bengal, competed with the Dutch Verenigde Ostindische Compagnie, defender of the sprawling Dutch empire that was headquartered at Batavia in Java.

Ivatt shuddered. To think that war between England and Siam, unthinkable only a month ago, was now a real possibility, not to mention war between England and Holland. Coates had to be brought to justice and full compensation paid to Demarcora, Golconda and the Dutch. But would Phaulkon agree to it? The sums involved were hardly inconsequential. How would Phaulkon explain them to the King or justify such a drain on the Siamese Treasury? Would he settle the claim out of his own vast resources? Would the King ever accept the humiliation, the loss of face of having to admit to the degrading behaviour of a naval officer in his service?

Whatever happened, Ivatt knew that he had to reach Phaulkon in Ayudhya in the shortest possible time. Perhaps, with his genius for diplomacy, he would come up with a solution.

Ivatt had crossed the Bay in a record nineteen days, thanks to the fast frigate provided by Yale. He would stop at Mergui only long enough to arrange for overland transportation – canoes, porters and elephants – and to see what more he could learn about Samuel White's activities. There were bound to be rumours in Mergui. Two days should be enough for that, and if the rains were over, he could make the journey to Ayudhya in a further ten to twelve days.

The shoreline beyond the islands was now visible for the first time and as the frigate rounded a large horseshoe-shaped island, crisscrossed by sparkling waterfalls, Ivatt drew in his breath and stared, transfixed, to starboard. In the shelter of a sweeping bay, a beautiful three-master lay at anchor. There was something strangely familiar about her shape. She was flying the flag of Siam so it was possible he had seen her at Madapollam before. But something bothered him. He kept his eyes riveted on her. Judging from the activity on board she had only just arrived.

'Beauty, isn't she, sir?' Simpson, the first lieutenant ambled up to him. He held a folding telescope to his eye and whistled quietly.

'Can you make out her name?' asked Ivatt.

'I was just looking, sir, but the characters seem to have faded. Very odd. You would have thought a ship of that calibre would take more care.'

'May I?' Ivatt took the eyeglass from the officer. The characters were indeed obscure, almost invisible. He strained his eye.

There appeared to have been two words. Then the wind fresh-
ened and the angle of vision changed. The evening sunlight shone
directly on what remained of the name. Ivatt sucked in his
breath. The word 'New' was just visible now. There was another
name that appeared to have been scraped away. His heart
pounded faster. Of course he knew that ship, though he had only
seen her once, and at night. It was the *New Jerusalem*! Coates
must be totally deranged to bring her to Mergui. She had
certainly taken her time getting here. What had she been up to
in the meantime? Ivatt shuddered to think. He took a last look
at the great trading ship and then went below to pack the few
belongings Yale had given him.

The last rays of the sun caught the makeshift thatched roofs of
the sprawling harbourfront stalls and the cries of the vendors
offered the final bargains of the day as Ivatt picked his way up
the narrow winding path that led to the harbour master's spacious
house on the hill. His modest bundle was slung over his shoulder.
Soon he was on the crest of the hill, slightly out of breath. He
stared captivated at the sweep of jewel-like islands set in a
turquoise sea that stretched to the orange horizon. Here and
there hung a cloud tinged with pink. Behind him, straddling
another tall hill, was a Buddhist Pagoda, its gold leaf glistening
in the last rays of the sun.

Ivatt stopped in front of a tall gate and banged on a wooden
gong that was strapped to one of the posts. Through a slit in the
latticework he observed a tall European emerge from the house
and start across the well-kept garden towards him. The grass was
freshly cut and an archway of vivid bougainvillea and fuchsia led
from the house to the gate. The gate swung open and a lanky,
dishevelled man observed him with a mixture of curiosity and
suspicion through intense grey eyes.

'Can I help you, sir?' Noting Ivatt's stare, he ran a hand
nervously through his mop of unruly chestnut hair. Ivatt did not
know the man, but he had the same sort of accent as Yale.

'I have come to see Lord White. My name is Thomas Ivatt.'

The man stiffened. 'Ivatt? Lord Ivatt? Your name is familiar
to me from dispatches, my lord.' He stared at Ivatt rather oddly

before bowing. 'Francis Davenport at your service, sir. I am Lord White's secretary. Would you follow me, please?'

Davenport led the way to the door of the main house, which gave onto a large anteroom furnished with bamboo chairs and a long wicker table. The sound of voices drifted in from an adjoining room.

'Lord White has a visitor, sir. Mr Yale has only just arrived so I don't know how long they will be. May I bring you some refreshment in the meantime?'

'Mr Yale?' enquired Ivatt. 'Which Mr Yale would that be?'

'Mr Thomas Yale, sir, the younger brother of the Governor of Fort St George. He has just returned from Ayudhya. We also received him on his way there about a month ago.'

Ivatt now recalled Elihu Yale saying that he had sent his brother to Ayudhya with an important consignment of rubies ordered by Phaulkon for His Majesty the King. Thomas Yale was no doubt on his way back to Madras now.

'Is Captain Coates by any chance in Mergui?' asked Ivatt casually. 'I have messages for him from some friends across the Bay.'

Davenport hesitated. 'Er, I believe so, sir. I'm sure Lord White will be able to tell you more about it.' He shuffled about uncomfortably on his feet as if the subject were not a particularly salubrious one. 'Would you like some tea, sir? Or something stronger perhaps?'

'I will gladly accept tea, thank you.'

Davenport bowed and left the room. Ivatt sat in one of the bamboo chairs and stared at the wall in front of him, adorned with sketches of ships in simple wooden frames. No doubt the ships of the royal Siamese fleet under the command of the Shahbandar, he mused. The sound of voices drifted through again. They seemed to emanate from the wall directly behind the pictures. Every now and then a sentence was audible.

'Rubies of inferior quality?' It was White's voice, expressing surprise. Ivatt strained to catch the rest but the answer was indistinct. There was a lengthy mumble and then:

'Well, I'll be damned. . . . Are you going to refund the money?' It was White's voice again. It seemed to carry more clearly than that of his visitor.

Ivatt crept stealthily across the room and listened.

'Lord Phaulkon . . . every penny back . . . the rubies . . . were with me.' It was Yale's voice this time. Ivatt recognized the same singsong lilt as his brother, Elihu.

Ivatt glanced towards the door. There was no sign of Davenport or his tea. He put his ear firmly against the wall and strained to catch the words.

'But were the rubies really fake?' White asked.

'No!' exclaimed Yale. Ivatt could hear the American more clearly now. 'Lord Phaulkon claimed the King's advisers had rejected them as being of inferior quality. Between you and me, Samuel, I think the Barcalon is out to discredit my brother. There is not much love lost between them, you know. Anyway, Phaulkon refused the rubies on His Majesty's behalf and demanded a full refund.'

They certainly sounded on intimate terms, these two, thought Ivatt, pressing his ear harder to the wall.

'But if Phaulkon didn't trust your brother, why would he have sent him the money in advance to procure the rubies?'

'In order then to discredit him. It was a trap. I'm sure of it.'

'But now you've got the rubies and the money,' exclaimed White, 'it's you who hold all the cards.'

'Not really. I believe Phaulkon is counting on my brother refusing to refund the money. The Barcalon will then have the excuse he needs to discredit the entire English Company, conveniently ignoring the fact, of course, that my brother was acting privately outside the Company in this matter. The Greek will use the opportunity to persuade the King to throw in his lot with the cursed French. Already the bloodsuckers have sent some fancy embassy to Ayudhya full of Gallic pomp and false promises. They've even installed a whole army in the fort at Bangkok.'

'What army? How many men are you talking about?'

'There are apparently at least five hundred soldiers at the fort. Everyone is talking about it. I saw a great number there myself. Your time is up, Samuel. The writing is on the wall.'

There was a moment's silence before White's voice resumed. 'Constant will never replace us by Frenchmen. He appointed us all himself.'

184

'Perhaps he did, because it suited him then. But circumstances change, Sam.'

It was 'Sam' now, noted Ivatt. Very cosy. But what was this about a French army?

'What are you trying to tell me?' asked White.

'I'm trying to warn you to get out while the going's good. Phaulkon will discard you and Burnaby and all the other English here the moment he no longer has a use for you. And that moment has come. Leave Mergui before the French take it over and have you thrown out – or thrown in jail. You've had a good run here. You're a rich man, let's face it. We know all about your activities in the Bay.'

'What activities?' challenged White, a little too aggressively.

'Oh, come now, Sam, you know what I'm talking about.'

'I do not. Unless some of my captains have been overstepping their authority without my knowledge.'

Yale laughed. 'That's putting it mildly. But my advice to you remains unchanged. Get out while the going's good.'

There was a pause. 'You want me out of Mergui so you can take it over yourself, right?'

'Yes, before the French do. Wouldn't you prefer to see it in English hands, for heaven's sake?'

There was no response.

'Open your eyes, Samuel. King Louis has sent an army here. Do you think they journeyed half a year for a holiday?'

Ivatt's heart thumped in his chest as he waited for the answer. This was serious business. If Mergui were to fall into English hands and they then declared war on Siam . . . Footsteps resounded in the corridor outside and Ivatt, cursing his luck, was forced to creep stealthily back to his seat.

The door opened and Davenport came in carrying a tray. 'Your tea, Lord Ivatt. I am afraid Lord White is still in conference. May I pour you a cup?'

'Thank you.'

'Would you allow me to join you for a moment, sir?'

'By all means,' said Ivatt, masking his irritation. He noticed that a second cup was already on the tray.

'I would like to talk to you in confidence.' Davenport paused and then pulled up another bamboo chair and sat down facing

185

Ivatt. 'I am most anxious to return to my post at Madras, sir. I never officially resigned my commission in the Company and I have wanted to return all along, but do not have the means for my passage. Lord White is unwilling to help me. Terrible things have been going on here, my lord, and I worry that Madras might not believe my story anyway.'

Ivatt sat up, his interest instantly aroused. 'What sort of things, Mr Davenport? Perhaps I can be of help in your predicament.'

'Well,' began Davenport hesitantly. 'I would like you to know, my lord, that I am only going to speak out on two accounts. Firstly because I believe Lord White to be wrong, and secondly to clear my name.'

'I fully understand,' said Ivatt encouragingly. 'I will be going straight to Lord Phaulkon in Ayudhya from here. He is a fair man and I have no doubt he will view your case sympathetically. I shall certainly put a word in for you.'

The secretary perked up. 'You were asking me about Captain Coates, my lord. Well, he is indeed here, with the *New Jerusalem* which he captured along with its priceless cargo of rubies.'

Ivatt looked appropriately shocked. 'And what does Lord White have to say about that?'

'He is furious and has ordered Coates up to Ayudhya to explain his actions.' Davenport leaned forward with a crafty look in his eye. 'But while Lord White is aware of the folly of Coates's behaviour, I am not so sure he wouldn't be happy to keep the *New Jerusalem's* treasure, especially if he could get Coates to take the blame for the whole affair.'

'But was Coates acting under his instructions?'

Davenport hesitated. 'I don't think he was, in this instance. Lord White is not such a fool. But I know for a fact that he told Coates to step up his activities in the Bay, because time was running out. You see, sir, Lord White is planning to leave.'

'To leave? For where?'

Davenport looked at Ivatt appealingly. 'You will help me to clear my name, won't you, my lord, if I reveal everything?'

'You have my word on it, Mr Davenport.'

'For England, sir. There have been rumours that a powerful French fleet has designs on Siam and Lord White doesn't want to

186

be around to see the results. He wants to play safe and leave, taking as much treasure with him as he can, of course.'

Ivatt was silent for a moment. 'When exactly does he plan to leave?'

'I don't know for sure, my lord, but certainly in the next few weeks. I have been ordered to keep the *Resolution* at the ready.'

'I will help you, Mr Davenport, I assure you,' Ivatt said. 'But I need to reach Ayudhya first – and fast. It would be better, under the circumstances, if Lord White were not to be informed of my presence here. Can you see to that? And can you sneak me out of here unobserved?'

Davenport nodded.

'How soon can I get transport to the capital?'

'It so happens that I have arranged transport for Captain Coates tomorrow morning – porters and all. He is due to leave at daybreak to report his actions to Ayudhya.' Davenport grinned. 'If you were to go to the departure point, my lord, and pass yourself off as Captain Coates, why, the native porters wouldn't know the difference. You could say you had decided to leave earlier. Of course there will be some guards waiting there, because Coates is technically under arrest. But I am sure you could identify yourself once you were underway and – '

'Is the departure point down by the river?' interrupted Ivatt.

'Yes, my lord, at the wooden dock by the estuary.'

'Good, I'm leaving now before Lord White comes out of his meeting.' Ivatt rose. 'But what about Coates? White will be livid. What will you say?'

'Don't worry about that, my lord. Leave it to me. The porters are not always reliable anyway, and I'll just say they scampered off. I'll get another lot together in a couple of days.'

'All right then. And thank you, Mr Davenport.'

'My lord, when you speak to His Excellency, Lord Phaulkon, please be sure to tell him where you got all your information. I mean, if ever there is an opening in Ayudhya . . .'

'I will, rest assured. In the meantime, Mr Davenport, keep your eyes and ears open. The more information you can provide us with, the better it will serve your case.'

'I understand, my lord. Count on me.'

Ushered out by Davenport, Ivatt left by the back door.

Twenty

Tuk felt a slight tremor inside her as she watched the farang horde descend upon her and her colleagues. The shiver was triggered not just by fear of the unknown, but a certain excitement as well. She had never entertained a farang before. In fact many of the girls present here today had never even seen a farang, let alone known one.

Tuk was the star of Khun Prateep's floating willow world and if the tastes of these large visitors were anything like those of her people, there were bound to be several of them converging on her. Her own boat was in the very centre, as befitted that of the queen of the pleasure world.

She shivered again. Would these big-boned giants be gentle with her or would they crush her under their weight? Would they pay handsomely for her services or would they expect her to give herself freely to them out of a sense of hospitality? She chided herself for being so silly. Of course they wouldn't pay her. The beautiful palace emissary who called herself Lady Sunida had explained to all of them that they would be generously remunerated by the honourable Pra Klang's office and they were under no circumstances to demand any payment of the farangs. On the contrary, they were to show marked modesty and to submit only gradually. The farangs were to be flattered into believing that it was their great charm that had seduced the girls.

Nevertheless, reflected Tuk wistfully, perhaps there might be a tip or two if she performed well. And the Lord Buddha knew, the money was always useful. Her grandparents were still alive, her mother was too ill to work and her father had died of the smallpox when she was still a child. She was one of eight children, the third of six girls. As the comeliest of them all, it was her duty to look after her family. She had left her home in the provincial village of Nakon Panom at the age of fourteen, to the tears and hopes of her family, and had travelled six days to the faraway capital of Ayudhya, where her mother had a distant cousin who

188

was rumoured to be well-connected. Through her it was hoped that Tuk's looks would catch the eye of some rich mandarin.

She had indeed caught their attention, but not in the way envisaged. By now, hardly three years after leaving home, she was the favourite of several mandarins, one even of the first grade. He came to visit her regularly at the floating brothel. The distant cousin had introduced her to a lady who, she had assured her, was influential and well-connected. A sum of money had changed hands, of which Tuk had seen not one salung, and she had been taken off to Samut Songkhram. The shock had at first been profound, but she was fourteen and alone in a faraway place with no friends; she had been forced to face reality and strengthen her resolve.

The wily old mamasan, seeing her potential, had been far from unkind and had treated her as a special favourite. Tuk had listened to the advice of Khun Prateep carefully and then adapted it to her growing experience of men. Soon she was earning more than she had thought possible in a lifetime and sending back sufficient sums to feed her entire family. The initial regret at the source of her revenue was offset by the pleasure she derived every time she thought of the comforts that would surround her grandparents and her ailing mother in their last days. Never, in all her letters home, did she divulge the true nature of her earnings. Her grandparents would die happy in the belief that their grandchild had married a wealthy mandarin.

A young French officer was approaching her boat now. Tuk paddled closer in, until the prow of her little canoe touched the bank. She beckoned him to step inside. He seemed shy and she tried to reassure him with a broad smile, though her own heart was fluttering nervously. Thank God he wasn't one of the fat ones she had seen, as bloated as well-fed water buffaloes. No, this one was tall, but not a giant, and he had eyes the colour of the heavens and hair the colour of stripped bamboo. Would they have strange habits, these fair-skinned farangs, or would they behave and react like her own people? The words of the palace official, Pi Sunida, came back to her again. 'These farang men will not know what to expect any more than you do, so take control from the start. For who controls, dominates.'

The young officer stepped gingerly into the boat and looked

around him. He peered under the cloth awning at the back of the boat behind Tuk, and observed the thick rush mat, almost like a quilt, amid the pyramid-shaped cushions that surrounded it. Then he stared in fascination at the profusion of fruit that was piled up in the front of the boat: mangosteen, jack fruit, pomelo, tangerines, guava, papaya, banana, green plum, sapodilla and pineapple. He smiled at the second boatwoman, almost as lovely as the first, who squatted near them and picked up a mangosteen, carefully examining its purple skin. It struck Tuk that perhaps they did not have such fruits in his country. Tuk's assistant, Plern, came to his aid, picking up another mangosteen and slicing it with a sharp knife. She showed him the delicate white segments inside and cut one out for him. He sniffed it warily. The two women smiled with amusement and he swallowed it bravely. A look of appreciation came over his face. Plern peeled him a second one.

He glanced over at the other boats. They were not more than a few feet apart and similar scenes seemed to be taking place on each of them. Smiling boatwomen were peeling and offering fruit for the visitors to sample. Dusk was setting in and suddenly the young officer let out a cry and searched his arm, feeling it in different places. He seemed perplexed at finding nothing there. He looked around him as the whining noise increased. Then he emitted another cry and scanned his other arm.

Was it possible they had no mosquitoes where he came from? Tuk found it hard to imagine a country without these little insects whose vicious former lives had led them to be reborn as pests and parasites, hiding in the daylight and coming out only at night to sting and scourge. Still, no matter how aggravating, he should not try and swat them as he was doing now. They had souls like everyone else and one did not kill other living creatures. Tuk rose and extracted a spare mat from inside the awning, beckoning him to sit beside her on the floor. Then gently she took the arm he was scratching and rubbed a little coconut oil into it. He looked at her in gratitude, offering no resistance. He watched her as she lit a candle and placed it next to him. Then she lit a small coil and to his evident amazement the buzzing gradually ceased. She lit another coil and placed it next to the quilt. He glanced at the quilt and back at her and smiled shyly.

There was a longing in his eyes she could not mistake, but she remembered the words of Pi Sunida: 'Give in only gradually. Under no circumstances must the farangs suspect you are anything but market boatwomen.' Yet the look in his eyes excited her. She felt an urge to pull him under the awning and remove that strange-looking apparel he was wearing. How would his love lance be? Large, like the rest of him? She was suddenly consumed with curiosity.

Her instructions had been not to give in on the first encounter, but to entice the farangs back the next evening. But who knew whether the same handsome man might return to her the next day? Supposing his superiors kept him at the fort and she was straddled instead with some ogre, fat, sweaty and pockmarked? She ordered Plern to row out to midstream. Night had just about fallen and they would soon be invisible from the shore.

Plern looked anxiously across at her mistress, but she knew better than to question her will. Besides, life with her mistress was exciting and to study under such an accomplished artist was a boon to her prospects, for she met many high-ranking dignitaries. Usually she watched her mistress perform while she fanned the lovers, to keep them cool, but sometimes she was asked to pleasure the dignitaries as well. While many of the others girls could find themselves at a loose end, her mistress was in constant demand and the flow of customers unending. It was a privilege to serve under her.

She took hold of the paddle in both hands and glanced furtively around. It was almost too dark to recognize the faces of the boatwomen around her. As she began to push the paddle through the water, first to one side and then to the other, she noticed to her relief that one or two other boats were heading out as well. They were not alone in disobeying palace orders.

The little canoe was soon in midstream, drifting with the flow. Plern shifted position and began to paddle against the current. The boat made no headway but remained in place. Tuk peeled a small banana, known as an elephant's tooth, and placed it in the Frenchman's mouth. He bit off a piece, not taking his eyes off her. She could feel his desire and looked down in a show of modesty. She picked up a custard apple from the bowl of fruit in front of her. She was about to squeeze it open when he held both

191

her wrists in a tight grip and pulled her to him. She appeared surprised and pretended to resist, knowing from the strength of his grip that resistance was useless. She allowed herself to be dragged under the awning. He pushed her down onto the quilt and slid his body hungrily on top of hers. She felt the passion flow from his body to hers. She tried to calm him down before it was too late. She wanted to savour the experience and make the moment last. He was, after all, her first farang.

He was trying to place his mouth on hers, a strange habit indeed, but she turned away, gently caressing the back of his neck and placing her nose on his cheek to inhale it. No sooner did he sense that she was giving in than the tension left his body and he became in turn gentle, emulating her actions and sniffing her cheek as well. They laughed happily and he rolled onto his side taking her with him, hugging her firmly and staring into her eyes in the flickering candlelight. Slowly they undressed each other, he with her guidance unwinding the ends of her panung, she with his help unlacing his boots and removing his breeches. Soon they were naked, a symphony of white and brown, alternately holding each other close and then breaking away to stare at each other's bodies, all traces of shyness now gone. Her eyes grew wide at the first glimpse of his love lance and he sucked his breath in at the first contact with the velvet texture of her skin. They made love with their eyes, as well as their bodies, oblivious of time and place, each enthralled with the contact of an alien being, each devoured by passion and curiosity and an overwhelming desire to please.

When finally he eased his love lance into her, hearing her muffled cries and feeling her pain, he felt a swish of cool air deliciously caressing his bare buttocks. He looked round briefly to see the other girl kneeling by the edge of the mat and fanning him with a large heart-shaped fan.

What a strange and wonderful land, he thought, as the boat drifted downstream, temporarily guideless.

Twenty-one

As Ivatt's boat entered the great estuary of the Menam Chao Phraya, his heart beat faster and a wave of nostalgia engulfed him. This was the land he knew and loved. In less than a day he would be back in Ayudhya. For a moment he forgot the many worries that had been nagging him during the journey up from Mergui. He smiled at the naked children jumping with shouts of delight into the water from their houses. The children were happy in this blessed land, he reflected, and the happiness seemed to stay with them through their youth and into middle age, until in venerable old age they enjoyed the fruits of wisdom and respect which only age could bring. The elderly were revered instead of abandoned to their own devices. Ivatt had often thought that the reason the Siamese smiled so much was because their beliefs always gave them something to look forward to. Youth was a time of learning and excitement, middle age a time to enjoy the fruits of that learning, old age the time to be a respected patriarch or matriarch, and death a time to begin a fresh cycle. For the purpose of life was the renewal of life itself, just like the plants and the trees, and the quality of that new life was the direct result of the kindness and charity shown in the previous one. How pleasant to have everything so clearly defined and how conducive to a serene existence.

One day he would retire here with his women and his books and his tropical garden. He might even write his memoirs. The life of a seventeenth-century adventurer in paradise. He did not share the restless quest for power of Phaulkon or the consuming greed of White.

Ivatt was only too aware that he might be making a permanent enemy of White, and a dangerous enemy too, but there was nothing he could do about it. He had to reach Phaulkon without delay. White would surely have found a way of preventing it, had he known of his presence. Ivatt had driven the porters and oarsmen hard, and gained a whole day. He would complete the

193

ten-day journey in nine. Now that he was close to home he was himself overcome by fatigue. He looked around for a suitable spot to rest in the little sailboat he had hired for the last leg of the journey up the coast to the mouth of the River of Kings. Eventually he lay down in the shade of the batwinged sail and fell into a deep sleep.

The guard recognized Ivatt immediately and smiled as he prostrated himself before him. The little farang was after all a friend of his master, as well as a mandarin. The guard informed him that His Excellency had just returned from the palace and escorted him obsequiously to an anteroom.

Though Ivatt stayed in Phaulkon's palace on each of his annual visits home, still its grandeur took his breath away. There was something different about the interior though. Of course, it was the wonderful French mirror over the mantelpiece. It was new, as was the grandfather clock in the corner where previously a Japanese screen had stood. The beautiful set of gleaming silverware on the lacquered table was an addition too. All gifts from the French delegation, no doubt. What an extraordinary man Phaulkon was, and how he admired and revered him. Imagine the Sun King taking the trouble to send lavish gifts to a former Greek cabin boy in an exotic land seven months' distance from France. It was the stuff of legends. Ivatt's heart beat louder in his chest as suddenly he heard the familiar voice resounding from a nearby corridor.

'Is that my favourite rascal, my little giant of a man?' In the next instant Phaulkon was in the doorway, beaming a warm smile, his arms outstretched in welcome. The two men fell into a tight embrace.

'Let me look at you, Thomas. Well, I can't say that you've grown much.' Few people could tease Ivatt about his height without causing offence.

'Not in stature perhaps, Constant, but certainly in wisdom. Now let me look at you. Oh oh, is that a touch of grey I detect above the right ear there? Goodness, but there's a bit over the left ear too. They match!'

'Come now, Thomas. Can't you see that's a reflection of all the silver the French have brought me?' Phaulkon's chestnut eyes

194

sparkled. 'They've made me a Count of France you know.' He laughed heartily. 'You may now address me as le Comte de Faucon.'

'A count and a prime minister,' murmured Ivatt, suddenly overawed. 'Where will it all end?'

'With the throne of Siam, if you believe the latest rumours, my friend. That's supposed to be my next goal.' He grinned. 'I'll certainly be in need of your help there, Thomas. And the post of Barcalon would of course become vacant . . . But first the good news.' Phaulkon looked at Ivatt affectionately. 'I've obtained His Majesty's approval for you to return to Ayudhya. You are hereby relieved of your post in Golconda and will work under me here, where I can keep an eye on you. What's more, as I knew you would be racked with envy at the news that I had been created a peer of France, I have further recommended to His Majesty that you be promoted to the rank of mandarin of the second grade. This has now been approved and you will shortly be entitled to four thousand dignity marks, forty personal slaves and a place of honour in the royal audience hall.' Phaulkon paused to observe the little man's reaction and then added with a grin, 'Besides, your promotion will make it less embarrassing for me to be seen in public with you.'

Ivatt was speechless. He could not make out which pleased him more, the mandarinate of the second grade which would put him among the second forty most powerful men in the land, or the fact that he could now remain in his beloved Ayudhya and work under the man he most admired.

'But you look devastated, my friend,' observed Phaulkon. 'Is it the thought of having to leave Golconda? Have you struck up a bosom friendship with that devil Ali Beague?'

Ivatt laughed bitterly. 'We were inseparable at one point, Constant. In fact he kept me in a pit with a tiger for fear I might leave him.'

Phaulkon observed Ivatt carefully to see if he were joking. He decided he was not. 'I think you have much to relate to me,' he said, his face suddenly serious. 'Let us sit down.'

'But tell me first, Constant,' said Ivatt, sinking cross-legged onto a cushion. 'How is my beloved Sunida? Is she still pining for me? Or is she finally resigned to settling for second best?'

The two men had been together when they had first met Sunida at the Governor of Ligor's court in the south, and it was one of the many bonds between them.

'She is the one who persuaded me to bring you back, Thomas. She pestered me until I could not face her pained expression any more.' He smiled. 'She is thriving. She is as wonderful to me as ever and I bless those smuggling days that took me to Ligor. She is busy learning French now and has made remarkable progress, despite the most pronounced and quite delightful Siamese accent.'

'And Maria?'

A slight shadow crossed Phaulkon's face. 'She is as loyal – and as Catholic – as before,' he answered, with noticeably less enthusiasm than had been evident in his reaction to Sunida. 'But tell me your news, Thomas. I am dying of curiosity.'

'Your offer to remain in Ayudhya is most timely, Constant, and as usual your timing is perfect. I am more grateful than you can know.'

The two men sat opposite each other on the cushions, surrounded by priceless Oriental artefacts, and Ivatt told him everything that had befallen him, from his confrontations with Coates and Ali Beague to his discussions with Elihu Yale, his encounter with Davenport at Samuel White's house and his escape from Mergui.

Phaulkon listened in silence, occasionally frowning but never interrupting. By the time Ivatt had finished, all traces of humour had vanished from his face and a look of grim determination had replaced them. Ivatt had seen that look before and he was glad Phaulkon and he were on the same side.

'So autonomy and ill-gained riches have gone to Samuel's head,' muttered Phaulkon bitterly, 'and Eli Yale has seen his chance to control the Bay of Bengal. Both are dangerous men, Thomas. Yale is probably the cleverer of the two but Samuel is the more ruthless.' He paused in reflection. 'You know, Thomas, there have been two great loves in my life: Sunida and George White. I admit I have been weak with Samuel because he is George's brother, and whenever I suspected him of duplicity I tried to cast the thought from my mind for George's sake. I left home when I was nine and that was the last I ever saw of my father, until I met George. George was the father I never had. Better still, he was everything I'd always wanted a father to be: ebullient, wise, unconventional yet fair. I will not claim to have seen through Samuel entirely, but perhaps I did not want to see through him. Yet now I feel I have paid my debt to George. I have done everything I possibly could for that brother of his.' Phaulkon's expression hardened visibly. 'I shall have to destroy him, before he destroys me.'

Ivatt felt an involuntary shudder. He would not be in White's shoes for all the plunder in the world.

'When does Yale's ultimatum expire?' asked Phaulkon. 'Did he give you a time limit for settling the damages?'

'He used the word "immediate". He is clearly under pressure from his end. He referred only to the time it would take for me to reach you here. He certainly looked as if he meant business.'

'I have no doubt of that, Thomas. Yale is a man to be reckoned with. He has probably amassed as great a fortune as Samuel but in much subtler ways. And he will not hesitate to use it for his own advancement and my destruction. In his mind I am the epitome of the free trader and, worse still, I have succeeded in that role.'

'Are you going to pay the damages?' asked Ivatt. 'Between the demands of Ali Beague, the Dutch and Demarcora, the sums are enormous.'

'No, I am not,' replied Phaulkon decisively. Then for the first time since Ivatt had begun his relation, he saw a thin smile etch itself on Phaulkon's lips. 'Sam White is going to, and from his ill-gotten spoils.' His smile broadened. 'I have no doubt he can afford it.'

'How will you manage that?'

'You'll just have to wait and see, Thomas. Have faith. I managed to make you a mandarin against much higher odds, didn't I?' Phaulkon's sense of humour had returned and Ivatt marvelled, as he had so often before, at Phaulkon's capacity to switch moods. He could charm a snake one moment and wring its neck the next.

'Tell me something, Constant, I am curious. Were the rubies you returned to Yale really defective?'

Phaulkon looked at him. 'They were flawed, Thomas, but not

that flawed. They were certainly not worth the money I paid in advance for them. That is the difference between Yale and White, you see. Sam would have acquired some really inferior gems and pocketed the difference, while Yale obtained only slightly flawed ones. But if you are going to cheat at all, does the degree really make any difference?'

'But supposing Yale refuses to return the money?'

'If he did refuse, it would give me the excuse I need to discredit the English. If he returns the money, it will show at least that he considers Siam a country not to be trifled with.'

'But why would you want to discredit the English in the first place?'

'Because, my friend, they no longer serve Siam's purpose, or mine. They lack the flair and grace needed to treat with an ancient kingdom like Siam. Instead they send traders who are little better than cut-throats and drunkards. The Lord of Life, eager to be impressed by them, finds it singularly difficult to be so. No, Thomas, France is the right bedfellow now. And the French will not want the English around. They don't like each other. It's historical, and no doubt permanent.'

'France will replace England then?'

'Yes, Louis XIV is Europe's most powerful monarch. His ambassadors are men of style and distinction. They are not cut-throats and drunks. He has sent an army here. Far greater than anything I ever requested for the King's protection. But they are here now, whether we like it or not, so we might as well make the most of it. And the most of it is to use them to our advantage. It so happens that an opportunity has presented itself. If Yale declares war on us, we will make it plain to him that he stands to face the might of France. He was no doubt unaware of that development when he made his threat. Now, we do not want Siam to be seen to shirk its responsibilities when it is obviously at fault, so we will place the blame squarely, and with much publicity, where it belongs: on Sam White's head. He will be ordered to pay the damages incurred by Coates. If he pays them, his fortune – or a good part of it, I should imagine – will be wiped out, which to a man of his greed is punishment enough, and if he refuses to pay up he will be tried here in Ayudhya and undoubt-edly executed. I will then appoint a French governor of Mergui and garrison the town with French troops. Yale's threat of war will stick in his throat. Even the powerful English will think twice before taking on the might of the Grand Monarque.'

'What if White escapes?'

'Then he will be doomed to wander, like the ancient mariner, for the rest of his days. For he will be wanted for treason in England, in India and in Siam. Demarcora is under the Company's protection. It will be punishment enough for a man who dreams to retire as a country squire in Somerset.'

'And Coates?' enquired Ivatt. 'He is due here in a day or two, ordered by White to confess his crimes.'

'I shall not receive him, Thomas. At least not at first. There is nothing worse for a man ready to confess than to deny him his confessor.'

Phaulkon made everything sound so easy, reflected Ivatt. He seemed even casual about the French threat. 'Why did the French send so large an army?' he asked. 'Surely their intentions cannot be friendly?'

'Indeed they are not. They want to take over Siam. The Sun King has made a name for himself throughout Europe and he is now keen to expand that reputation further afield. The self-styled Defender of the Catholic Faith seeks great prizes in Asia for one, and what greater prize than Siam? The French army is here to convert every last Siamese to the Catholic faith.' Phaulkon paused. 'I suspect by force, if necessary. The ambitions of France are the greatest problem we face, Thomas. Far greater than White or even Yale. The French plan to use me as their stepping stone. That's why they have made me a Count of France. If I fail to support them, they will try and overthrow me. Our task will be a very delicate one. We must encourage the French by keeping their hopes alive. They must see the juicy grape of possession dangled before their eyes like Tantalus, but we must never allow them to reach it. Siam must remain for ever free. No one must be allowed to subjugate this beautiful land. We must use the French presence to deter the Dutch and the English, but otherwise control it. It will be a thin line to tread. That is why I will need you here, Thomas.'

Phaulkon rose. 'But I must be off to Louvo. His Majesty awaits me.' He smiled. 'We will fix a date for your investiture as a mandarin of the second grade. But don't let it go to your head, Thomas. Just remember what happened to White.'

Ivatt grinned. 'I'll wait and see if he gets away with it, before I decide how to behave. But tell me, how long will His Majesty be in Louvo?'

'Oh, a little while, Thomas. You know how he enjoys the hunt.'

'And when will you be back?'

'Tomorrow at the latest. You stay here and rest.' He glanced at the little man's outsize clothes. 'You'll need a tailor by the looks of it too.' Phaulkon turned at the door. 'You know, Thomas, though I am surrounded by hordes of admirers and sycophants, men who swear me eternal devotion, it is possible that you are my only friend.'

'Know too, Constant, that I will serve you till my death.'

Twenty-two

The Masula oarsmen looked frightened. All had the same thought as they rowed the flat-bottomed boat towards the beach at Madras. One of their colleagues had been hanged last week and four others were lingering in jail for having overturned a boat and drowned one of the sahibs. The sahib had been clearly intoxicated at the time. He had hardly been able to step off the ladder from his ship into the boat. The other passengers had not drowned. Why, even the memsahib had clung to the boat and survived. It was not fair. The fact that the sahib had been drunk had not been taken into account in the trial.

He was certainly strict, this Governor, reflected the chief boatman, and a stickler for the rules. Rules, rules, rules, ever more rules to be obeyed. And ever more taxes to be paid. Now they were building a wall round the black town and every last coolie was expected to contribute part of his pay. The last Governor, the one with the vermilion face and the wart on his nose, had left them for the most part in peace. But this one – he always wore formal clothes, regardless of the sweltering heat, which did not improve his temper. He put the fear of the gods into everybody. He was worse than Shiva in a rage. And as all-seeing as Vishnu. They had to admit to a grudging respect for him. He was certainly different from the others. He had learned their language and seemed to take an interest in their religion, but would it not be better to have a governor who was a little less zealous? They were certainly a strange breed, these white men. One of them even kept a pet tiger, attended day and night by slaves, who fed it a whole goat once a day. What extravagance, when thousands in the black town were starving!

They were approaching the bar now, about a quarter of a mile from shore. This was where the fatal accident had occurred. The chief boatman shouted an order to his ten oarsmen and six of them leaped out of the boat, three to each side, to hold her steady through the surf that swirled angrily over the reef. This time there were no mishaps and all breathed a sigh of relief and thanked the gods for their mercy as they entered calmer waters. They would row in a little further, and then the chief would jump over the side and lift the lone passenger out of the boat. He was no ordinary passenger, this one. He was the brother of the Governor himself. He looked very worried. Perhaps he had heard of last week's mishap. The chief would carry him astraddle his shoulders, to avoid his getting his breeches wet, to the beach beyond.

Thomas Yale was indeed worried as the husky boatman lifted him like a child out of the boat. He was not looking forward to this meeting with his brother. He felt the bag containing the rejected rubies. Over a thousand of them! What's more, the Treasury of Siam had ordered several bills due to the English Company to be withheld pending repayment of the monies laid out in advance for the rubies. There was also a letter from Phaulkon to Elihu. It was sealed so he had not read the contents; he did not like to think what it might say.

An army of young native boys in loincloths had gathered on the shore as they did whenever a new arrival was sighted. The minute Yale's burly porter lowered him onto the burning sand, they ran up to him, vociferously offering him sweets and trinkets. But he was in no mood to dally and he pushed past them, walking in rapid strides across the hot sand to the sea gate. Only when he began mounting the stone steps did the children abandon the chase, fearful of the guards on duty at the great fort. The sentry saluted and two soldiers escorted him directly to the Governor's office.

Elihu Yale was busy at his desk sorting out a mound of papers. He had just held his daily consultations with the chief factors of the surrounding towns and there was much paperwork to be dealt with. The excellent news he had just received would have to be acted upon right away. He answered the knock on the door more cheerfully than usual. Then his face lit up as he saw his brother standing in the doorway. 'My dear Thomas,' he said, rising from his desk to embrace him, 'welcome back! I am indeed pleased to see you. This is the second piece of good news I've had today.'

He offered Thomas one of the chairs recently occupied by his second-in-command, John Nicks, the head bookkeeper.

The thought of the news he had to impart weighed doubly on Thomas, as he observed his brother's elation. His hand nervously clutching his bag, he took the proffered seat. Elihu eyed him closely and then glanced suspiciously at the bag.

'You look uncomfortable, Thomas. Was the journey an unpleasant one?'

'No, Eli. The journey wasn't too bad. We had a bit of a scare on the overland route when some tigers killed one of our water buffaloes. A porter was dragged away screaming when he tried to intervene. And it was a constant battle to keep the swarms of mosquitoes at bay, but I must say those new coils the Siamese use are quite effective if you can keep them alight all night.'

Elihu nodded distractedly. 'We lost John Simmonds last week in a boat accident,' he said. 'The natives claimed he was drunk, but I suspect foul play after the imposition of that new tax. I had to punish them anyway. I hated doing it but I had to hang their chief as an example. It's the only way to keep order.'

Thomas was silent, glad for the moment to be speaking of anything but the results of his trip. 'But you look otherwise pleased, Eli. What's the good news you mentioned earlier?'

The Governor broke into a broad smile. 'The annual mail arrived from England while you were away, Thomas. And with it some very happy news indeed. The approval of a policy I've been advocating for years.' He slapped the palm of his hand on the desk. 'We've got a new King, Thomas, and with it a new policy. Long live King James II.' The Governor opened a small cabinet below his desk and extracted a bottle of brandy and two glasses. He filled them and passed one over to Thomas. 'To His Majesty King James,' he said, raising his glass, 'and to our late King Charles, may his soul rest in peace.'

They drained their glasses.

'For years, Thomas, we've been receiving orders from a group of dandies in London who've rarely emerged from their clubs, let alone set foot in India. They have no concept of life or conditions in these parts, as is painfully obvious from the policies they advocate. Can you imagine instructing a handful of Englishmen to extract crippling revenues from hundreds of thousands of impoverished natives so we can build another fort a few miles down the coast? They should send us the wherewithal from their own bloated purses.' Yale shook his head. 'If the natives balk, they point out jovially, have them executed.'

Yale leaned forward. 'But now Sir Joshua Childe is beginning to make sense. It seems he has at last come to hear of the piratical orgies that are taking place in the Bay of Bengal with Englishmen at the helm. His Majesty King James, long may he reign, has issued a new proclamation, encouraged no doubt by Sir Joshua's considerable contributions to the Crown. All His Britannic Majesty's subjects in the Orient are henceforth forbidden to serve a foreign liege. Every last one of them in the employ of a foreign prince is required to resign his position immediately and to report to the nearest British outpost.' Yale was jubilant. 'Where do you think that leaves the likes of Sam White and John Coates, not to mention every other sea dog that serves a heathen master in the Bay and beyond?'

'Listen to this,' continued Yale, extracting a letter from his drawer. 'We require you, according to His Majesty's late proclamation, to try all the English by martial law whom you shall find in the said King of Siam's service, or otherwise detain them in close imprisonment until our Judge Advocate shall arrive!' The Governor looked up. 'We are further instructed, Thomas, to seize all Siamese vessels off the coast of India, unless satisfactory compensation for past damages is received.' He smiled. 'We now have official sanction for the actions I have already taken.'

Thomas listened intently. His mind was churning. 'What about Phaulkon?' he asked warily. 'Does he come under that heading?'

'Would that he did,' said Yale glumly, 'but he still calls himself a cursed Greek. He's going to be a very solitary one by the time we've recalled his bloodsucking henchmen.'

Thomas stared down at his feet. It was time to tell his brother the worst. 'Eli?'

'Yes?'

'Things did not turn out as well as we had hoped in Siam.'

'Oh yes?'

'I brought the rubies back with me, Eli. They were rejected by the court at Ayudhya.'

Yale's face reddened with anger. 'Rejected? Why?'

'The experts deemed them of inferior quality.'

204

'Inferior quality?' he burst out. 'Who the devil examined them? A blind school?'

Thomas hesitated. 'After the court experts gave their opinion, Phaulkon had them shown to a leading French trader for a second opinion.' Again Thomas hesitated. 'The Frenchman expressed them inferior to anything obtainable in Paris. I have a letter here for you from Phaulkon,' he added quickly, delving into his pocket and handing over a sealed envelope. It looked very official, embossed with the royal seal of Siam.

The Governor glanced at it and put it to one side. 'A Frenchman!' he repeated again, his tone clearly disparaging. 'In the exalted opinion of some French trader – '

'Eli.'

'What?'

'The French army has arrived in Siam in force. There are five hundred soldiers in the fort at Bangkok now, under the command of a marshal of France. They have been welcomed with open arms. There is also a director of the French East India Company and an ambassador plenipotentiary from the court of Louis XIV.'

The Governor was silent. For a while the only sound was that of his fingers drumming the edge of the desk. In the distance the shrill voice of a drill sergeant could be heard shouting orders. Despite the open window, the heat was intense.

'When did they arrive?'

'At the same time as I was leaving,' replied Thomas. 'I think it was a well-kept secret.'

'Did you meet Ivatt in Mergui?'

'No, was he there?'

'How strange. He travelled on the ship I sent to pick you up.' Yale was silent again. 'How did White receive you?'

'Very hospitably, actually. I took advantage of my knowledge of the arrival of the French to sound him out. I suggested that Phaulkon was planning to replace all the Englishmen in his service with Frenchmen, hence the secrecy surrounding their true numbers.'

'How did he take that?'

'He said Phaulkon was his partner and would never do a thing like that.'

'Isn't it odd how naive rogues can be about their fellow rogues?'

'Eli,' continued Thomas somewhat nervously, 'I went a step further than that. I hinted that the Company might just close an eye on his past activities if he were somehow to co-operate in helping to deliver Mergui into our hands.'

The Governor smiled. 'Good for you, Thomas. Well, go on, how did he react to that?'

Thomas felt a wave of relief. 'It seemed like an obvious thing for me to suggest in view of the number of French troops. What would they be there for, if not to replace the English?'

'Quite. So what did he say?'

'He seemed sufficiently interested in the question of immunities to lead me to believe he might eventually co-operate.'

'I bet he would, the turncoat. But are the French there in fact to take over from the English?'

'I don't know. But they have no great love for us and the territorial ambitions of King Louis are well known.'

The Governor puckered his brow. 'Is it not just possible that Phaulkon himself was not expecting so sizeable a contingent? What if he too were taken by surprise?'

'You mean that King Louis is planning to take Siam by force?' Thomas sounded incredulous.

'Possibly. Whatever the case, that devil Phaulkon's timing is uncanny. If we declare war on him now, we could be facing the armies of France.'

'Declare war, Eli?'

'Half the world is demanding compensation from us and calling for our blood. They think we're behind Coates, damn his English blood.' Yale lapsed into thought. 'Did you at any time hear of any rumours about the French army, or any part of it, being sent to Mergui?'

'No, the entire contingent seemed firmly ensconced in Bangkok.'

'Let us hope they remain so. We must act fast. We must take over Mergui before the French discover its value as a trading post. If King Louis has sent a director of the French Company to investigate trade opportunities, it will not be long before he finds out that Mergui is the key to the area. Already the French have

206

a base down the coast from here at Pondicherry. If they set up on the other side of the Bay too, controlling the trade route into Siam, we could be in serious trouble.' Yale frowned. 'I wonder if that blackguard Phaulkon is fully aware of the extent of the damage his pirates are causing in the Bay.' He glanced at the calendar on the wall. It hung next to a charcoal sketch of his baby boy. 'Ivatt should have given my ultimatum to Phaulkon by now. How long did it take you to cross the Bay, Thomas?'

'Twenty-one days.'

'Ivatt must have gone straight to Ayudhya. So if it took him eleven days to reach the capital from Mergui he would have delivered my message some ten days ago. I demanded immediate and full compensation from the Siamese treasury. In the unlikely event that Phaulkon were to agree, it would take him a further month to have the funds delivered here. Ten days have already elapsed, so if I were to send an armed frigate to Mergui now, it would arrive when the ultimatum was expiring. I could suggest a further ultimatum to White and Burnaby, disguised of course as an offer: immunity from prosecution, safe passage to England and no questions asked about their cargoes – no matter how bountiful – in return for deliverance into our hands of Mergui and the surrounding areas. If we were to give White about three weeks to think it over, it would appear as if we had set sail only after giving the Siamese treasury due time to deliver the compensation.' The Governor smiled. 'The threat of His Majesty King James's proclamation should be an added incentive to swing White round to our point of view.'

'But what if White turns to Phaulkon and the French?'

'It will be too late, thanks to the geographic position of Mergui. I know that terrain well. There is no way an army, least of all a European one, can march overland to Mergui from Ayudhya. You've just done the trip yourself. The way is along a narrow jungle path surrounded by impenetrable undergrowth and infested with tigers, snakes, wild elephants, crocodiles and leeches. And there are rivers and rapids to ford as well. It is viable enough for a small party equipped with guides and porters, but a whole foreign army? Never.

'The only way the French can reach Mergui in any numbers is by sending their fleet along a circuitous sea route down the Malay

207

peninsula, round the Cape of Singapura, through the Straits of Malacca, and up the western coast of Siam. That's a six-week voyage at least. We could be established in Mergui in a little under that and still have time to garrison the town, even if the French fleet were to leave immediately, which is unlikely. They must still be recovering from the voyage from France. Once properly garrisoned, Mergui would be impregnable from the sea. No ships could sail unchallenged across the bar. They would be within range of the guns on the hillsides.'

Yale was visibly excited. He rang the bell on his desk and almost instantly an aide appeared.

'Ah, Marlow. Is Captain Weltden still in port?'

'He hasn't returned, Your Excellency.'

'Let me know as soon as he does. I want to see him immediately.'

'Very well, Your Excellency.' The aide saluted and left.

'Well, Thomas, you could be witnessing an historical moment. One in which you played a valuable role. Come, let us stretch our legs a little before the sun sets and the mosquitoes come out to plague us. I want to tell you about Captain Weltden. Because Anthony Weltden, I am sure, is our man.'

Twenty-three

The two men sat cross-legged in one corner of the reception hall. They had dismissed the servants to ensure privacy. The other members of the Council had not been summoned. The finely carved furniture and the priceless artefacts from both East and West denoted the residence of a well-travelled man of means.

The host spoke first. 'How are things at the fort, General? Are our soldiers becoming more skilled in the use of Western arms?'

'There is marked improvement, Ambassador, and my men have learned a lot, but the mood of the fort is turning ugly. The farang soldiers are becoming increasingly arrogant.'

Kosa Pan nodded. 'I am not surprised. The French consider themselves the chosen people of God, and the superiority of their weaponry must do little to dispel such a belief.'

'I am not displeased at this turn of events, however,' observed General Petraja, 'because the French attitude is playing into our hands. The population is gradually turning against them. Three weeks ago I said we should spread chaos and discord. Well, that is precisely what the farangs are doing for us. Their officers look down at our men as ignorant and backward peasants who should be tilling their fields, and they no longer even have the grace to disguise their feelings. They're imbibing those intoxicating liquors of theirs with growing frequency, and the more they swallow, the more they treat our men and women as their servants. Vichaiyen's idea to entertain the farang soldiers is exploding in his very face.' Petraja shook his head. 'It is hard to believe from the way they are behaving that their religion forbids them to take more than one wife.'

Kosa was thoughtful for a moment. 'General, I have made it my job to discover exactly who was involved in this scheme of using our women as bait for the French soldiers. Do you remember the rumours of a palace official being in charge of the project – a beautiful woman to boot?' Kosa stared intently at

Petraja. 'Well, that woman is none other than Sunida, Vichaiyen's concubine.'

'The one who lives at the palace?' asked Petraja, raising an eyebrow.

'Precisely.' Kosa paused. 'And as you rightly pointed out, Catholics are not supposed to keep concubines.'

Petraja's eyes slowly lit up. 'Of course. Do you know, it simply never occurred to me. It all seemed so natural in Vichaiyen's case. But now that you mention it, I can see . . .' He hesitated.

'Further areas in which to sow discord?' Kosa grinned. 'It is a God-sent opportunity, Lord Buddha be praised. Vichaiyen's deeply Catholic wife must know nothing of this arrangement, else why would Vichaiyen be concealing the girl?'

Petraja observed Kosa's arch smile. It was one of triumph and revenge, the anticipation of settling some deeply rankling score. Although the subject was never broached at their weekly meetings, Petraja was only too aware of Kosa's humiliation at the hands of the Pra Klang. Imagine being stripped of four thousand dignity marks overnight! Not to mention the demotion to mandarin of the second rank and being excluded from sitting with the élite of the nation.

'Have you any particular plan in mind?' Petraja asked.

'As a matter of fact I do, and I would like to have full charge of its implementation, if you have no objections.'

'How can I object without knowing the plan? But it is enough for me to see the fervour in your eyes. Yet that very fervour drives me to caution you. Never underestimate that dog Vichaiyen. He has the blood of Tosakan in his veins.'

'But not quite the power of that evil deity, General. He is fallible. But I thank you for your trust. My plan is simple. I intend to pay the Lady Maria a visit.'

Petraja smiled in understanding. 'It would serve our cause well if those two-faced Jesuits were to start questioning the sincerity of Vichaiyen's beliefs. I mean, his standing in their eyes, and through them in the eyes of the French delegation, would surely drop.'

'Indeed, General. And what better conduit to the Jesuits than the Lady Maria? But now tell me, what news of Selim?'

'Good news. A dispatch arrived yesterday. The excesses of the

210

farang Shahbandar have finally persuaded the members of the Council of Five to take action. The pusillanimous Moors are no longer prepared to sit back and allow the Shahbandar free rein. They have unanimously agreed to allow Selim Yussuf to take whatever action he deems necessary.'

Kosa was impressed. 'That certainly is a step in the right direction. I think the pieces of the puzzle are beginning to fit into place.'

Petraja smiled. 'Our efforts and patience have at last been rewarded. So tread carefully when you visit the Lady Maria.'

'She is the prize piece in my puzzle, General. I will not place her wrong.'

'May the Lord Buddha guide you.'

Twenty-four

Samuel White was enjoying himself. The last of the monsoon had set in and because of the difficulties of filibustering during the heavy rains he had decided to take a fishing holiday on one of the offshore islands. It was one of his favourite pastimes. Yet beneath his apparent contentment lay a deep-rooted anxiety. He still hadn't heard from Ayudhya. It was now three and a half weeks since he had sent Coates there and Phaulkon should have acknowledged his arrival by now. Perhaps he would hear something soon. Was it possible that Coates knew something he had overlooked? Yet, thought White, he had been over every angle in detail. Again and again. There was nothing, unless Coates had somehow found out about the fictitious sailors on the payroll. But how? Damn that blustering idiot. How could he have been so stupid as to take the *New Jerusalem*? Without that, everything would have been fine.

At least in the peace and serenity of the island surroundings he felt more able to relax. Even in the rains the water was translucent and the stretches of fine white sand felt exquisite to the feet. He had had a little bamboo hut built behind the glorious sweep of beach that had become his favourite hideaway. It was the only hut for miles around. It had a thatched roof to keep out the rain, and only one room; his servants slept out in the open under blankets. He could see it clearly now from where his rowing boat was bobbing gently in the breeze.

White cast his line out. As he did so, he noticed a boat rounding the rocky promontory that sheltered the bay. How strange. It was rare to see a craft in these waters. He had told Davenport he was not to be disturbed unless in an emergency. White strained his eyes. As the little boat came in closer, he recognized the figure of his secretary, his hair awry as usual. There were two other Siamese in the boat apart from the two rowers. Damn it, what did they want?

'Can't a man fish in peace these days?' he demanded gruffly as the boat came up alongside his. 'I thought I said no interruptions, Francis.'

'I'm sorry, my lord. But this gentleman here,' he pointed to the taller of the two Siamese, a swarthy man with pockmarks down one side of his face, 'was most insistent. He said he wouldn't leave until he had seen you. He's an emissary from His Excellency the Barcalon. I took the liberty of bringing an interpreter as well.' The interpreter, a small wiry Eurasian whom Samuel had used before, wai'd politely to him. The emissary followed suit, inclining himself courteously before White. Then he began to speak in rapid tones, while his expression remained unchanged.

'My Lord, I bring you an urgent summons from His Excellency, the Pra Klang. His Excellency wishes you to proceed immediately to Ayudhya and requests you to bring all your accounts with you.'

White stiffened as the interpreter rendered the translation. This was a strange summons indeed.

'Is there no written message?'

'My lord, there is none.'

White eyed the emissary suspiciously. He turned to the interpreter. 'Ask him if he has any proof of identification.'

The inscrutable emissary produced a document authorizing him to travel on official business from Ayudhya to Mergui. White could not read the Siamese but he had no trouble recognizing the Barcalon's seal at the top.

'Ask him why there is no letter.'

'He says the honourable Pra Klang told him to deliver the message orally.'

'Most unusual.' White stared at the emissary, as if to elicit some clue from him, but the man's expression remained a mask.

The emissary now addressed the interpreter again. The Eurasian turned politely to Samuel. 'He asks whether Your Lordship would wish him to accompany you on the trip back to Ayudhya?'

White controlled his anger. What damned impudence. Did they expect him to leave this minute in the middle of his fishing holiday? 'I have a few matters to attend to first,' he said, restraining himself. 'He should not wait for me.'

White now glared at Davenport who had been shuffling his

arms about nervously during the interview. 'Let us go ashore. I wish to speak to you alone.' The two boats turned to shore and a moment later nosed gently up the beach.

As soon as the parties had disembarked, White took Davenport aside. 'You'd better return to Mergui,' he said in an undertone, 'and start looking into the accounts. We may have to make a few changes.'

Davenport blanched. 'Changes, sir?'

'Don't answer in that tone, Davenport. You prepared the accounts. You're in a position to know how best they should be . . . er . . . presented.' Davenport remained silent. And I won't tolerate any more interruptions during my holiday, is that clear, Francis?'

The secretary looked stung. 'Would you have preferred me to tell Lord Phaulkon's emissary that you were not disposed to receive him, sir? You were, after all, awaiting news from Ayudhya.'

'Perhaps, but you could have told him I was on holiday, and that he should await my return in Mergui.'

'I did just that, my lord, but he was most insistent. He kept stressing the urgency of the matter.'

'All right, Francis,' said White, relenting a trifle, 'but next time *you* be more insistent, do you understand?'

'Yes, sir.' Davenport spoke to the interpreter and the party returned to the boat. The emissary kept looking back at White to see if he were following.

What incredible insolence, thought White. He walked over to where his two servants were squatting idly in the sand. 'We will spend the night here,' he said in a loud voice. 'Prepare my room.'

'My lord, we receive your orders.'

The fishing was neither a success nor a diversion. White's mind kept straying back to the visitor. Why was he not carrying a letter from Phaulkon? It was not like Constant to behave like that. What had Coates been saying? Grudgingly White recognized that he could not ignore a summons of this kind. He would have to go to Ayudhya. But he was damned if he was going to go there like some lackey with a bad conscience. He would go there with his head held high and in his own good time. Besides, he needed the extra time for Davenport to scrutinize the accounts, and very carefully this time.

The evening was gloomy and overcast, without even a decent sunset, and White's depression increased. It rained that night and he slept badly. There was a leak in the thatched roof and he woke his servants and blasted them for their incompetence. Did they not give a farthing for his comfort? They hardly understood what he was saying but it wasn't difficult to gather his gist.

Next morning, shortly after dawn, the same messenger returned again, accompanied by the same interpreter. 'He refuses to leave Mergui without you, my lord,' explained a nervous Davenport. 'He claims his instructions are of the utmost urgency.'

Barely controlling himself, White dismissed them both brusquely, saying he wished to travel to Ayudhya alone and would do so when he was ready.

This time the messenger refused to stir. He turned to the interpreter. 'Please inform the honourable Shahbandar that I shall wait with him until he is ready to travel.'

It was all White could do to contain himself. He took Davenport aside. 'What the hell is going on, Francis?'

'I don't know, my lord. But this emissary is impossible to shake off. I've tried everything. It looks as if only force will remove him. And that would seem unwise under the – '

'How are the accounts?' interrupted White. 'Have you been through them again?'

'I have, my lord.' Davenport hesitated. 'They are, er, they are as presentable as they could be expected to be.'

White grunted but made no further comment. What could Coates have said against him? Had he produced some unexpected evidence? Had Phaulkon somehow discovered that he had not been receiving his full share of the spoils? But why should Phaulkon care when he had the whole country to milk?

Davenport fidgeted beside him. 'I fear, my lord, that whether or not the accounts will bear scrutiny, we have no choice but to return to Mergui.'

White scowled at him. 'All right, Francis,' he said glancing at the emissary. 'But I shall not travel beyond Mergui in the company of so impudent a fellow.'

215

Davenport made no reply and White ordered his servants to pack his belongings.

He was sullen throughout the short journey to Mergui. The enormity of his misdeeds glided across his mind in an unending procession. My God, he had made so many enemies. Accusations and complaints against him could have come from any quarter. Suppose they had come in continuously, one after the other: Ali Beague, the East India Company, the Mohammedan merchants, the mandarins of Pegu, even the citizens of Mergui. The list was long. Yet there was no real proof that Phaulkon was angry with him. No letter, no word of reproach. But what could be so urgent that he was expected to undertake the trip to Ayudhya in the middle of the rains, when the rivers became dangerously swollen, the jungle paths slippery and the leeches and mosquitoes multiplied a hundredfold? Did Phaulkon not know that there were some who did not even survive such a trip?

For a full day White remained in Mergui, torn between confidence and doubt. He went to visit Burnaby to entrust his personal affairs to his care during his absence, giving him detailed instructions as to how to dispose of his property, in the event he should not return. He then enjoined Davenport to accompany him to Ayudhya, ignoring the secretary's repeated protestations that he remain in Mergui and insisting that he was the only one familiar enough with all the financial transactions to answer any possible charges against him. Davenport was forced to relent, though he managed to persuade White that the messenger, who had steadfastly refused to leave, would have to be included in their party.

The journey, in the wet season, was not a pleasant one, first by river and then by sedan chair and elephant. It rained heavily every day, creating swift currents, and the temperature dropped dramatically during the downpours. The mosquitoes and leeches were merciless. A second messenger from Phaulkon, on his way to Mergui to ensure White had left, was encountered en route.

It took them twelve insufferable days before they finally crossed the isthmus that separated the Indian Ocean from the Gulf of Siam. Here, at the coastal town of Phipri, two more messengers from the capital awaited them. These extreme measures to guarantee his arrival at Ayudhya began to make White

216

feel almost like a prisoner under guard. His nerves were stretched to breaking point.

From the Gulf of Siam the journey continued by sea, where the hardships of travel were reduced. White used these last days to go over with Davenport all possible loopholes in the accounting, and to prepare himself to field the various questions that might be put to him. He concluded that of all the damaging charges that could be levelled against him, his instructions to Coates to ignore Phaulkon's orders to await the expiry of the deadline to Golconda would be the most difficult to answer. The seizure of the *New Jerusalem* had already been laid squarely on Coates's shoulders in a letter he had entrusted to one of the guards accompanying Coates. Surely Phaulkon would believe that he himself had no hand in it? Yet the more he considered his situation, the more insecure he began to feel. He remembered forcing traders to sell him their imports at the lowest prices, so that he could in turn dispose of them to the local merchants at a big profit; he had even sold some of the goods to the King's own warehouses! There were so many crimes attributable to him that it was feasible he might be questioned on some he had completely forgotten about. He might be caught off guard when the questions were thrown at him. He now remembered that he had done nothing about the fortifications at Mergui, though he had received a large sum from the Treasury to erect them. Somehow the money had wound up elsewhere. And of all his oversights, perhaps the stupidest was not to have shared some of the spoils with the mandarins on the Council of Five. Now they would all testify against him.

An increasing despondency took hold of him and, weakened by the trials of the journey, he was taken ill on arrival at Ayudhya. Despite a high fever, he proceeded to Louvo where he had been told Phaulkon was in residence at a new house he had built himself near the King's palace. White acquired lodgings close by, and immediately took to his bed. He became delirious, and for a while he was close to death; he had contracted malaria. In moments of lucidity, he gave Davenport last-minute instructions in the event of his death. But on the fourth day his fever abated and his strength began to revive. Phaulkon, who was travelling regularly to and from Louvo, never once enquired after his condition. This unexpected coldness greatly perturbed White and added to his insecurity.

Finally, after a week's convalescence and unable to stand the uncertainty any longer, he had himself personally announced to the uniformed guards in attendance at the gates of Phaulkon's palace. For three days in succession he sought an audience but on each occasion, after being kept waiting an interminable time, he was told that His Excellency was too busy to receive him.

Crestfallen and close to despair, White suffered a relapse.

Twenty-five

Once again Maria felt her girth. The little kicks seemed to be occurring with increasing frequency. She looked forward to telling Constant but she wanted things to quieten down first. After all the many honours the French had bestowed on him, it should be his crowning pleasure. They would surely fight over the name; she would want a Portuguese or a Japanese one as befitted her lineage and he would want – heaven only knew. A Greek or an English, a French or a Siamese one? It would be a pleasant topic to argue over, anyway.

She entered her Portuguese-style living room. Across one wall, two large wooden commodes with transparent glass fronts were filled with delicate porcelain figures, while a long teakwood refectory table inlaid with mother-of-pearl stood in the centre of the room. Carpets with floral designs covered the floor. There were straight-backed chairs, and silk drapes hung to either side of a Goanese rent desk made of ebony. But for the teak door panels in the Siamese style, one might have been in a well-to-do salon in Lisbon or Goa.

A child might help to calm Constant's restless soul, Maria reflected as she took up her sewing, and might perhaps persuade him to devote more time to her. These days he seemed entirely absorbed in the affairs of state, to the exclusion of all else. Despite his thirty-five years, his boundless energy showed no signs of abating. At least these days it was channelled into more respectable pursuits than formerly. He had been something of a rogue in his youth. Only five years before, she had forced him to give up his harem and live the life of a decent Catholic. When he had asked for her hand in marriage she had insisted on certain conditions. Monogamy had been the chief of them. For in her heart she knew that no matter how much she loved him and no matter how different the customs of Siam might be, her beliefs would not tolerate any other way. The agonies she would suffer

219

in sharing him with other women, even as the major wife, outweighed the pain of losing him.

She smiled to herself – at least today she could smile about it; then, it had been quite another story. That rascal of a husband of hers had dismissed his harem with the exception of one girl whom he claimed was a spy planted by the palace to report on him. Sunida was her name. She was supposedly not aware that he knew of her role, enabling him to feed information, highly favourable to himself, back to the palace. How they had fought over her. Maria would never forget it. The girl was far too beautiful, and refined, to give her a moment's rest. Eventually, however, to his eternal credit, Sunida's spying role had been confirmed. Maria had felt guilty for some time after that, but he had tactfully avoided bringing the subject up, even when they quarrelled. And now, though Maria wished they could spend more time together, she accepted that there was a price to pay for being married to a public figure.

It was an exciting life, she had to admit, and she was proud to be a part of it. Until just a few days ago she had been fully occupied entertaining all those Frenchmen. Her home had practically taken on the function of an army barracks! Fifty French soldiers, destined for His Majesty's bodyguard, had actually been staying here. Of course they had been housed in another wing but she saw the officers at meal times. There had been much to talk about. She was always fascinated by the latest fashions and developments in Europe, especially France. Her French was quite fluent thanks to her upbringing by the Jesuits, and one of the officers had even spoken creditable Portuguese. They were gentlemen, these officers, refined and courteous, unlike the rough European traders she had hitherto come into contact with.

Constant was particularly busy and frequently absent these days. The King was in Louvo, the French were in Bangkok and she was in Ayudhya. And even when Constant was home, there was always some function or other to attend in the evening. Thank the Lord, though, that wives were not expected to be present. They were so boring, these official receptions. Anyway, the result was that she hardly saw her husband at all. He was exhausted by the time he returned home. Perhaps the child would change things, she reflected again, optimistically. In the meantime she had the orphanage to care for. It took up most of her time. She had just returned from there now. The roof of the long hut she had had erected behind the main house had sprung a leak in the heavy rains and she had wanted to oversee the repairs. There were always more stray children brought in during the monsoon season than at any other time of the year and the great hut was filled to bursting. The children were fed and clothed and slept on mats in long lines on the floor. She was considering erecting another building. The palace grounds were certainly extensive enough. Her only hesitation lay in the fact that she liked to get to know each child individually and watch its progress.

A discreet cough interrupted her thoughts. Ning, her little slave girl, had crawled silently into the room and the cough was her usual signal that she wished to speak.

'What is it, Ning?'

'Great lady, I, a hair, beg forgiveness for the intrusion, but an honourable mandarin awaits your pleasure in the anteroom. He has been here since early morning. He will not go away until he has seen you. He says the matter is urgent.'

'Who is he?'

'Great lady, he said his name is Lord Kosa.'

'Kosa Pan?' Maria spoke to herself more than to the girl. She knew the name well enough. She knew he had been Siam's first Ambassador to France and that he had returned unexpectedly. Constant had told her of the man's distrust of the French – and of farangs in general – and of the ignominious manner of his arrival ashore. What could he want with her? She had never met him before. Well, she reflected, there was only one way to find out.

'Send him to the audience hall, Ning. I will receive him there.'

'Your slave, my lady.' Ning crawled out backwards.

Kosa Pan had timed his arrival to coincide with one of Phaulkon's frequent absences in Louvo. He had been irritated to discover that the Lady Maria was out. If she was absent for long, it might become risky, for he did not know exactly when Vichaiyen was due back. But when he learned that she was only in the orphanage next door, he decided it was a risk worth taking.

221

'Will my lord come this way, please?' He looked up to see the slave girl beckoning him shyly.

He followed her down a long corridor lined with Burmese tapestries. In front of an open doorway she stopped and prostrated herself. Kosa stepped into what was obviously a formal audience chamber. He looked around him and drew in his breath. It was not so much the individual works of art which impressed him, but the very Siameseness of the room's proportions and decor. It was the first time he had been in the farang's mansion. Despite his contempt for the hated usurper, he could not help but feel a grudging respect for the man's taste. Vichaiyen seemed somehow to have captured the soul of Siam. There was nothing farang about the room, not even a chair. The early Ayudhya cabinets were exquisite and the faded silk of the triangular cushion rests were of an ancient design difficult to come by today. Kosa's eye swept over the sculpted bronze figurines that graced the many recesses of the room and then travelled slowly over them again, one by one. It was a collection that rivalled his own.

He did not hear Maria come in, so absorbed was he in his observations. A slight cough made him look up, and again he was impressed. The woman standing in front of him in a blue Japanese-style kimono was exquisite, as fine and delicate as any of the masterpieces that surrounded her. Her skin was flawless and her features a true blend of East and West. Her nose, straight and thin, was distinctly farang, while her high cheekbones and black, semi-rounded eyes were Japanese. He remembered hearing that some ancestors of hers had been nailed to a cross in Japan, at the time when the Emperor had forbidden his subjects from becoming Christians. The Emperor had obviously seen what troublemakers they were, these Christians. If only his own King would follow such an example. The family had then apparently moved to Siam where they had intermarried with the Portuguese Christians. More damned Christians, Kosa thought angrily. No wonder the family were all such fanatics. Then he remembered how that very fervour would serve him well in this instance, and he smiled to himself.

Maria cupped her hands in front of her bowed head and he returned the greeting. 'I'm sorry you should have been kept waiting so long, my lord.'

222

'Gracious lady, on the contrary, it is I who am intruding. It is well known, how busy your ladyship is with all your good works.'

Maria smiled modestly. 'My orphanage keeps me busy, it is true, my lord.'

'Then I will not take up more of your time than is necessary. With your permission I will come straight to the point.'

Maria eyed him quizzically. He was small and dark even for a Siamese but his movements were lithe and his searching, intelligent eyes seemed to miss nothing. She had a strange premonition that he was up to no good.

'Please proceed, my lord.'

'You must first understand, gracious lady, that I am under oath to deliver this message to no one but you. Hence my sudden, presumptuous appearance.' He bowed his head as if in recognition of his impropriety. 'As you may know I have lately returned from France. In my capacity as humble emissary of the Lord of Life I have had occasion to spend much time at the Grand Palace recently to present my reports to His Gracious Majesty.' Kosa glanced up at Maria, still framed in the doorway. He had her full attention, he noted with satisfaction.

'On the last occasion,' he continued, 'as I was leaving the palace grounds I was approached by a young page boy who informed me he was bearing a message from the honourable Pra Klang's minor wife, the Lady Sunida.' Kosa looked casually across at Maria. Though her expression remained impassive, the sudden pallor in her cheeks told him his words had found their mark. 'When I asked him what that message was, he bid me follow him. We proceeded along a series of narrow paths which led eventually to a small secluded garden where the Lady Sunida awaited me. She seemed in some distress and most eager to speak to me.'

Kosa paused while Maria, without saying a word, came forward and sank slowly onto the thick Persian carpet opposite him. She adjusted the folds of her kimono and looked at him.

'I am indeed sorry to learn of the Lady Sunida's distress,' she said. 'But what was her message?'

An expression of concern spread over Kosa's face. 'She told me, gracious lady, of her growing anxiety for the safety of her master and begged me to bring a message to you. She wished to

223

appeal to you in the certainty that you love the honourable Pra Klang with as great a devotion as she does, and in the hope that you might be successful where she has failed.'

Maria observed him steadily without offering any comment.

'You see,' continued Kosa Pan, 'the Lady Sunida told me that on her honourable master's last visit to her, only the day before, she had clearly warned him of the dangers he was facing. But in typical fashion he had shrugged them off.' Kosa leaned forward.

'The Moors in the south have written to a high-ranking colleague of theirs in Ayudhya – one of the few remaining mandarins acquitted after the Macassar trial – informing him that the activities of the farang Shahbandar in Mergui are giving His Gracious Majesty a terrible name in the Bay. Not only is the shameless Shahbandar draining the Treasury with a legion of non-existent sailors whose salaries are paid directly into his pocket, he has been plundering innocent shipping in the Bay and lining his pockets with the proceeds.' Kosa's tone dwindled now to a hush so that Maria had to strain to catch the words. 'As a result, the neighbouring provinces are preparing to rise up in revolt, and there will be terrible bloodshed unless it can be stopped. The Lady Sunida has in vain pleaded with her honourable master on each of his recent visits, but to no avail. She begs to enlist your assistance, knowing full well how highly her master regards your ladyship's advice in matters of politics.'

The pallor had grown visibly deeper in Maria's face and though she made every effort to sound calm, a tremor now entered her voice.

'And how did she . . . how did the Lady Sunida discover all this?'

Kosa was prepared for the question.

'A page attached to the royal harem where the Lady Sunida is housed is the nephew of one of the local Muslim mandarins. His uncle warned him of the dangers in the hope that the information would find its way to His Majesty's ears. As you may know, my lady, nothing remains a secret for long in the palace.' Kosa lowered his eyes modestly. 'Your ladyship is no doubt aware that no one would dare speak out directly against an appointee of the honourable Pra Klang. I am sure that your esteemed husband is ignorant of the behaviour of the Shahbandar and of the serious-

224

ness of the plot which is presently hatching there. But the Lady Sunida is convinced that the weight of your opinion could persuade him to take some action before it is too late.' Kosa paused again. 'You understand of course, gracious lady, that my only concern is for Siam. If there is to be an uprising against the established order, no matter how justified the cause, then your honourable husband must be informed of it, so he can take appropriate measures.' Kosa lowered his head respectfully. 'He and I are both servants of the great Lord of Life.'

Maria held her head high. 'I am indeed grateful to you, my lord, for coming here and displaying such obvious concern for my husband's welfare, but I am confused on one point.' Maria made every effort to retain her composure as she forced herself to utter the words: 'Since the Lady Sunida is the minor wife of my husband and not a royal consort, why is she unable to deliver this message herself? Why should she be restricted to the palace compound?'

Kosa looked momentarily surprised, as if he had not expected the question. 'Gracious lady,' he answered, feigning embarrassment, 'forgive me, I can only . . . assume from . . . from the rumours one hears that . . . I mean, the Lady Sunida is aware that you know of her position, yet she feels – or perhaps it is your husband who feels – that in view of your religious beliefs you might consider it an affront . . . er . . . I mean that it would be indelicate for her to be seen in public. Hence her confinement to the palace, and her voluntary seclusion.'

'I see.' Maria fought to disguise her pain.

Kosa felt a wave of exultation. This was just what he had planned. And he hadn't finished with her yet.

'There is one more thing, gracious lady.' He paused to savour the moment. 'The Lady Sunida had a further message. Though that message was meant for me, I will nevertheless relay it to you as it concerns the welfare of Siam. Your honourable husband had put her in charge of the boatwomen from the floating pleasure houses, who were to entertain the French soldiers on the river. It seems that one of these Frenchmen, a senior officer, has fallen in love with one of the boatwomen and revealed to her the rumours now circulating in the French camp.' Kosa's expression hardened. 'The talk is of war, gracious lady, now that the troops are sufficiently recovered from the hardships of their journey. The troops are only awaiting the order to turn on the Siamese in the fort at Bangkok.' Kosa smiled bitterly. 'The officer was obviously concerned for the future of his amorous affair.'

Maria puckered her brow. 'And why, may I ask, would the Lady Sunida reveal such information to you and not directly to my master? Surely it is he who needs to know this?'

Once again, Kosa assumed an air of embarrassment. 'Gracious lady, the Lady Sunida is aware of my long experience with the French. She was afraid to incur her master's displeasure, because he seemed so impressed with the delegation. She felt that perhaps I might be more receptive to such revelations. That,' added Kosa modestly, 'together with my ready access to the palace is no doubt what prompted her to approach me on the matter.'

Maria looked at him with growing suspicion. 'How odd, my lord, that the Lady Sunida, who is confined to the palace in Ayudhya, should be able to arrange and supervise the activities of scores of boatwomen on the river at Bangkok. Remarkable.'

This time Kosa Pan was caught genuinely off guard. 'Gracious lady, I did not enquire into the sources of her information,' he said hurriedly. 'But no doubt she has her messengers.'

Maria looked at him steadily. 'Lord Kosa, had these words come from even the most loyal servant of the Pra Klang, I should have difficulty in believing them. I find your account poorly fabricated, inexcusably vicious, wholly vindictive and quite fantastic. Your outlook and prejudice betray you, my lord. Your true motives are all too visible: you wish to vilify my husband and make a mockery of my religious beliefs. You will succeed in neither. Your hatred of the farangs is too well known.'

Kosa appeared dumbfounded as she continued, her head held high.

'Were my husband to fill this entire palace with minor wives, I should consider that preferable to spending another moment in your company. You will leave immediately.'

Maria rose and rang the bell firmly three times, looking with contempt at Kosa as she did so. He barely managed to control his anger. His face contorted and he looked almost ready to spring at Maria and throttle her.

226

The prolonged ringing brought in a bevy of retainers and even some guards.

'Show the Lord Kosa out please. His visit is at an end.'

Kosa turned at the door. 'Perhaps you would care to speak to the boatwomen themselves. They will confirm the name of the "palace official" directing them in their acts of prostitution.'

Maria remained motionless for some moments after he had gone. Then she walked, her head still held high, to her bedroom. She closed the door behind her and sank onto the divan, where she gave in to a torrent of uncontrollable tears.

Twenty-six

Samuel White lay in bed agonizing. For ten days now he had heard nothing from Phaulkon. This morning Davenport had dutifully brought the calendar in for White to tick off yet another day. Though he was still in bed, his renewed attack of malaria was less severe than the first. The air of Louvo seemed to be living up to its reputation for having special healing qualities.

Reluctant to humiliate himself further by attempting to gain access, White now dictated a letter in which he expressed great surprise at his old friend's coldness and deduced that his enemies must have poisoned his mind against him. Before dying, he wished to know in what way he had offended His Excellency, so that he might throw himself at his feet 'in the belief and confidence that his lordship would not pluck down the building which his own hands had raised'.

It was a further two days before a reply came. Davenport brought it in excitedly and White opened it with trembling hands. He scanned the lines and read the final paragraph first, hoping it would answer his most urgent question. In it Phaulkon had taken up the theme of his own letter: 'It will be no small pleasure to find you as innocent as you pretend, nor shall we ever take delight in ruining what our hands have built up. But if we perceive a structure of our own raising begin to totter, and threaten our ruin with its fall, none can tax us with imprudence if we take it down in time.'

White read the letter over and over and then handed it to Davenport. Its contents did little to set White's mind at ease.

Finally, on the fourteenth day, White received a summons to attend Phaulkon at his house. It was situated within the walled compound which surrounded His Majesty's palace and two guards in red tunics escorted him past various sentry posts. White felt uneasy in the unfamiliar, austere surroundings. Would he be able to retrace his steps as a free man this day? he wondered.

Finally he was ushered into a long anteroom. Phaulkon was

standing at one end of it, his face to the wall, surrounded by crouching slaves, some of whom were fanning him. He did not turn round and White was left to stand and stare at the handsome silk blouse covering his back.

'Sit down, Samuel,' Phaulkon said coldly, still without turning.

White sat cross-legged on a cushion on the floor, listening to the loud beat of his heart. This was hardly an auspicious beginning, he reflected. Why couldn't Phaulkon at least turn round and face him?

Without moving, Phaulkon spoke again. 'What have you got to say for yourself, Samuel?'

Samuel had rehearsed his answer endlessly. 'My Lord, what I did was wrong perhaps, but I did it for the best. I saw great profits to be made which would enrich you and the King's Treasury, as well of course as myself, but in all my enterprises I always put the greater share of gain in the way of yourself and His Majesty. If I did not carry out your orders to the letter, it was only because I was there on the spot and I thought, wrongly no doubt, that I was the better judge of the situation.'

'Like ordering Coates to ignore the terms of His Majesty's ultimatum to Golconda? When you attacked Golconda, Samuel, our ultimatum had not yet expired. In what light do you think that put His Majesty's government?'

'Coates acted on his own, my lord. He disobeyed my orders. I sent him to you to confess his crimes.'

Phaulkon swung round now for the first time, his face grim and unsmiling. There was not a trace of the old camaraderie in it. 'I have the letter containing your counter-orders to Coates,' he said coldly.

'It must be a forgery, my lord. I wrote no such orders.' For once, White was telling the truth, and his indignation was twice as righteous in consequence. 'The man would stop at nothing. He was for ever acting on his own. He commandeered the *New Jerusalem* without my knowledge too.'

'Coates is paying the price for his crimes. He has the cangue round his neck. Yet though he is a pirate and a criminal, his activities were only made possible by the atmosphere of total depravity which you created in the Bay, Samuel. You have done

229

incalculable harm to this country's reputation.' He paused. 'Next to yours, Coates's crimes are paltry.'

White's heart sank. If Coates had the dreaded cangue round his neck, what would they not do to him? He had seen prisoners wearing it and observed the suffering in their eyes. The terrible weight of the board fixed tightly over the head and shoulders allowed the victims no room to twist or turn. They did not need a prison cell; they wandered about freely, dragging their suffering with them, to the jeers and gibes of the populace. It was a most painful and humiliating punishment.

'Would you believe Coates's word, the word of a pirate, against the word of the brother of your old friend, George White?' pleaded White.

'The shocking roster of your activities has been confirmed by more sources than I care to name, and the details of your depredations fully described in the confidential dispatches I have intercepted from the Moors of Mergui to their brethren in Ayudhya. Your crimes, Samuel, are monumental and irrefutable. There is little you can do or say in your defence.'

'Then I shall die an innocent man, at the hands of my brother's friend.'

'You shall not die, Samuel, for I have no intention of disposing of you so easily. You must make amends first.' White's heart beat faster. Amends? Was his penance to be torture? The thought terrified him and he felt sick.

'I am returning you to your former post,' Phaulkon continued, 'on two conditions.'

White looked up quickly, hardly believing his ears. He didn't dare speak.

'The first is that you will mend your ways and, on pain of punishment in accordance with Siam's laws, you will at no time make it necessary for me to answer for your behaviour. The second is that you will settle in full and immediately upon arrival in Mergui the amount of damages claimed by various parties through the East India Company in Madras. In addition, you will return the *New Jerusalem* to its owner, intact with its full cargo, any deficit or damage to the ship to be made good. I have examined the claims submitted by the Company and consider them to be fair and equitable. They cover the injuries sustained by Golconda's nationals, damage inflicted on Golconda's merchant fleet and its coastal towns, compensation for cargoes expropriated from neutral shipping, redress for the loss of trade of sequestered vessels, and reparation for the murder of a Dutch national at Pulicat. The sum total is five hundred thousand pounds.' Phaulkon spoke the words slowly.

Once again, the blood drained from White's face. 'But that is preposterous,' he burst out, his terror of a moment ago swept away by the prospect of financial ruin. 'How can I be responsible for Coates's activities? And . . . and even if I were, where could I find such a sum? Why, you could buy a whole English county with that much!'

'No doubt you could, Samuel. You will simply have to lower your sights and acquire a smaller plot of land.' Phaulkon's tone hardened. 'For if you are still thinking of retiring to your beloved England, you will have to wipe your slate clean first. As things stand now, you are branded a criminal on any corner of British soil, as well as in any of the dominions of Siam, Pegu and Golconda. Because you are George's brother, and only because of that, I am giving you a chance to wipe that slate clean. Otherwise I would have had you tied naked to a tree in the swamps at dusk for the mosquitoes to feast off your body and drain the life slowly out of you through the course of the night. Think well on it, Samuel, and remember that I reserve myself that option still. Now go.'

Phaulkon turned away and White found himself once more staring at his back. He rose, his head swimming, and headed for the door.

'Come on in, Thomas,' called out Phaulkon, as soon as White was out of earshot. 'Were you able to hear clearly?'

'Every word, Constant,' said Ivatt, entering the room. 'Do you really think he'll pay up? In his place, I'd run for it and I'm not nearly as dedicated a rogue as he is!'

'The truth is, I don't know, Thomas, but I just couldn't bring myself to execute the brother of my mentor. I can't say I'm worried about what he'll get up to next, but I had to let him go. At least Davenport will report his every move back to us. Did you make the final arrangements with him?'

'I did, Constant.' Ivatt paused. 'Will you honour the debt if Samuel doesn't?'

'We'll have to, or at least a part of it. Yale's figures, you can be sure, are on the high side. Of course the Dutch at Pulicat will have to be paid, and the *New Jerusalem* must be returned to Demarcora. We can hardly afford another war with Pegu when the last one dragged on for a hundred years! Whatever happens, White cannot be allowed to continue holding sway in Mergui. His influence must be curbed, though not completely erased. Not yet. We mustn't be precipitous. He must be given a chance to pay his debts before he bolts for England. As for Governor Burnaby, he must be put out to grass. He's obviously not doing his job. I want a new governor installed in Mergui, who will in turn appoint a new shahbandar, as soon as the time is ripe.' Phaulkon looked at Thomas. 'I want that new governor to be you, Thomas.'

Ivatt's face lit up. Then a frown spread slowly across his forehead. 'I won't end up fighting the French over Mergui, will I? Didn't you tell me you were planning to appoint a French governor there?'

Phaulkon's expression turned grave. 'I had that in mind, because we must do something for the French. Their patience is wearing thin and they're becoming openly disagreeable. Things have reached boiling point. We can't present la Loubère with any religious miracles and Cébéret has concluded that Bangkok is too limited a trading post. They have their sights fixed firmly on Mergui now. But it's too important a concession. I'm going to try and appease them by giving them Songhkla instead. It's less strategic. We can't have the French taking over all our key garrisons. That is why it is essential that reparation be made to the East India Company. Yale must have no excuse for going to war. Once that danger is averted, we won't need the French as a deterrent in Mergui any more.' A thin smile spread across Phaulkon's face. 'Especially when we'll have you there to protect us, Thomas.'

'My harem in Golconda will miss me terribly, Constant. They'll be suicidal. I'd hate to leave them there alone and undefended. Can I take them to Mergui with me? And Gopal, my secretary, too – assuming he escaped Ali Beague. The last time I saw him

232

was shortly before I was forced to share my living quarters with a hungry tiger.' An involuntary shiver ran through Ivatt at the recollection.

Phaulkon smiled. 'As it happens, Thomas, they'll all be safer in Mergui. I have heard – confidentially from the Persian Ambassador – that Aurangzeb, the Great Mogul, is planning to invade Golconda. He is the Grand Monarque of the sub-continent, eager to extend his dominions. If a state of war should arise in Golconda, we can hold off paying compensation to them, and if Ali Beague were to be deposed we could probably forget about it altogether. A substantial saving for young Samuel when one considers that Golconda's claims represent, all in all, the major part of the debt.'

Phaulkon looked at Ivatt affectionately. 'I want you first to go to Madras, Thomas, and see Yale. You must prevent him from sending a force to Mergui. Don't forget the Lord of Life knows nothing of Yale's ultimatum and I would hate him to wake up one morning and find his country at war. You've got to stall Yale. Tell him you have come in an official capacity to inform him of Siam's acknowledgement of its debt and of its sincere regrets. The Treasury is presently examining the amount of the charge. As soon as that is completed, due compensation will be paid. That should keep him happy.'

Ivatt smiled. 'Then I can collect my belongings at my house before Aurangzeb's armies get to it.'

Phaulkon laughed. 'Thomas, I'm going to miss you. Get back here quickly. I will see to it that Mergui is ready for its new governor by the time you return.'

The two men embraced for a long moment and then Ivatt went to his quarters to prepare for the journey.

233

Twenty-seven

The guards fell prostrate as Phaulkon entered the walled compound of the palace at Louvo. His face was drawn, fatigue shadowed his eyes. The Lord of Life was ailing fast and despite his earlier assertions that he would exercise control over the affairs of state with as much vigilance as from Ayudhya, he was finding it difficult to cope. His increasingly laboured breathing made even the daily audiences with his mandarins too great a burden. He was relying more and more on his chief minister to be his eyes and ears.

Though Phaulkon's enormous physical and mental energy stood him in good stead, he was nevertheless overburdened, not least because his presence was now needed in three places at once. The seat of government was in Ayudhya, yet the King wished to have his most trusted servant near him at all times in Louvo to keep him fully informed. In addition, the French in Bangkok demanded Phaulkon's time and attention. La Loubère, though engrossed in his Siamese research, nevertheless repeatedly requested some evidence of progress regarding His Majesty's conversion. It was clear that the matter was still uppermost in his mind. Desfarges, too, who had returned to Bangkok to oversee the training of the Siamese soldiers, brought up the matter whenever he came to Louvo on his regular trips, ostensibly to inspect the royal bodyguard. But Phaulkon knew that his hospitality in the form of the three 'first-rate chambermaids', as the General liked to call them, was the real incentive. Phaulkon was well pleased with this. It was part of his plan to separate Desfarges from his army and distract him from thoughts of aggression towards Siam. But the situation could not continue as it was much longer. Somehow, the French would have to be appeased, and soon. The King's condition added to the urgency. If His Majesty's health gave way before the uncertainties surrounding the French presence in Siam were resolved, the consequences did not bear thinking about.

As he reached the inner courtyard, Phaulkon pressed a hand to his eyes in an uncharacteristic gesture of weariness. How he wished that Sunida could be with him in Louvo. Her company would do much to ease the intolerable pressures upon him. His visits to her during his frequent trips to the capital were now all too brief. The Lord of Life, Phaulkon felt sure, would have no objection to his bringing Sunida here, but the problem was that he was not sure what Maria's plans were in that regard. Would she want to move to Louvo too? He determined to find time to raise the matter with her when he was next in Ayudhya. It would not do to have both his wives in Louvo. The residences of the King and his first minister were within a stone's throw of each other, and it was just conceivable that Maria and Sunida would stray into the same garden at the same time – a situation which could never arise in Ayudhya. Although Sunida could always use the alibi that she was the King's consort, instinct told Phaulkon it was best to avoid a confrontation.

In spite of his deteriorating health, the King at least seemed happier in Louvo. The palace here was considerably less formal than the one in Ayudhya. The atmosphere was more relaxed and the protocol less strict. The hunting was the finest in the land and whenever he ventured out he could appear with a retinue of only two or three hundred followers instead of the twenty thousand that protocol required of him in Ayudhya. In his present state of weakness, the informality of life in Louvo was a boon.

Phaulkon walked up the wooden steps that led to the panelled audience hall. He was saluted by a couple of smartly dressed French soldiers, part of the fifty-strong bodyguard, under the command of Major Beauchamp, who were now in residence at Louvo. The audience chamber was smaller than the one in Ayudhya but just as elaborate. The sculpted walls had recently received the addition of two giant mirrors from France, a gift from King Louis. Visiting mandarins could now glance up discreetly at the magnificent frames and see their reflections as they lay before their liege.

As Phaulkon waited, alone and prostrate, the sound of trumpets and conch shells announced the Lord of Life's appearance. In the silence that followed, Phaulkon could hear gasps emanating from the upper balcony. If only there were some cure for asthma, he thought.

'Vichaiyen, we are pleased . . . to see you. The air grows thinner around us. It is not . . . pleasant.'

His Majesty paused. He spoke with difficulty, in short sentences, halting frequently to suck air into his lungs. 'Our only daughter has angered us,' the King went on abruptly, not wasting words. 'She stubbornly refuses to be wed . . . to Piya. She says she would rather die . . . than marry anyone of such humble origins.'

So, thought Phaulkon, Pra Piya was the suitor the King had had in mind when he expressed the wish to get to know a certain young courtier better while he was in Louvo. Phaulkon had noticed that Piya was among the retinue that had accompanied His Majesty to Louvo. He was not surprised at the choice. Pra Piya had been given as a gift to the Lord of Life, according to the age-old custom. Many parents from around the country, who had more than one child, were permitted to present their newborn to the King as a gift. Selections were made from as great a number of districts and provinces as possible, to ensure the continued loyalty of even the most far-flung communities. For when these children, brought up by the royal nurses until their twelfth year, returned to their place of birth, they would be for ever beholden to His Majesty and would bring great honour to their districts. The King was very fond of children. If a child cried when brought before him it would be sent home, but if it smiled, thus appearing pleased, it would remain and be brought up in the royal household. The only condition, which was strictly imposed, was that the child would not be authorized to see its real parents until it had reached the age of puberty and was by then irrevocably bound to the Master of Life who had raised it.

As a baby, Pra Piya had immediately smiled upon the King and stretched his tiny arms out to him. The King was delighted and placed him in the care of one of his sisters, to be brought up along with his only daughter, Yotatep. When the boy grew up and was found to be well versed in court etiquette, considered the height of good breeding, His Majesty was pleased and, on discovering that his father had died, adopted the young man. He was no genius but he was correctly obsequious and attentive. The King, having no son of his own, became very attached to him and he was to be seen more and more at the King's side.

Phaulkon listened as His Majesty described his latest encounter with Yotatep. '"What, Father," she said to us, "marry a man . . . whose origin is not even properly known? It is one thing to adopt a child from far away, but another to taint the royal blood with . . . the Lord Buddha knows what lineage."'

His Majesty paused for breath, clearly incensed at the recollection of his daughter's defiance.

'August Lord, I, a speck of dust on the sole of your foot, can well understand Your Majesty's displeasure. Your unworthy slave, however, begs to offer a humble suggestion.'

'Yotatep is strong-willed and stubborn, Vichaiyen. Your suggestion must contain . . . arguments of equal strength.'

'August Lord, I receive your orders.' Phaulkon hesitated. 'Perhaps the honourable Princess would be more favourably disposed towards the marriage if she thought she did not have to bed with Pra Piya.'

'Not bed with him? How could she refuse her own husband?'

'Mighty Lord, the kings of Europe often marry for convenience. I'm sure that Pra Piya would be prepared not to molest the Princess if he were told his marriage precluded any form of intimacy and was merely for the purpose of consolidating his claim to the throne. That might make the Princess more receptive to the idea too.'

'What strange rituals your farang monarchs indulge in, Vichaiyen. Still, perhaps we . . . can learn something from them in this instance. We will think on it, Vichaiyen.' Phaulkon listened to the King drawing in great gulps of air. 'How is the Ambassador from our esteemed colleague, King Rouee? Is he . . . immersed in his literary pursuits? And is he still satisfied . . . with the carrot of our imminent conversion?'

'August Lord, I fear not.' Phaulkon was silent for a moment, acutely aware of just how weak such a bald reply must sound to his demanding master. The truth was, he could think of no ready solution to the problem, and he simply had not had the leisure to bring his mind fully to bear on working one out. The silence lengthened. 'Mighty Lord and Master, we are fortunate in that General Desfarges' mind is not so much on military matters any more. He has become too fond of our hospitality. And Cébéret du Boullay, though he has not lost sight of the French goals, appears to be a man of reason. I feel we could placate him with a further gesture. I, a hair, therefore beg to suggest that were we to grant him trading facilities at Songhkla, he might be suitably assuaged.'

'How much of our kingdom do we then . . . have to give away, Vichaiyen, to satisfy the French?' The uncustomary irritation in the royal tone sent a chill through Phaulkon.

'Mighty Lord – '

'We wish to know . . . how you plan to satisfy their chief of mission in the matter of our conversion, Vichaiyen,' interrupted His Majesty. 'We understand this question to be of greater import than trade facilities.'

Phaulkon was again silent.

'Your answers . . . are less ready than we have grown accustomed to, Vichaiyen.' The King's tone softened slightly. 'Perhaps our absence from Ayudhya is placing too great a burden on you.'

'August Lord, it is an honour for this slave to serve the Lord of Life in any part of his dominions, whatever the circumstances,' said Phaulkon, stung by the King's remark.

'But surely, Vichaiyen, these . . . very circumstances must afford us some respite. We cannot believe our ardent Jesuits have not . . . informed their Ambassador of our condition. Even the French must understand there are moments when their patience must be curbed.'

'August Lord, this slave craves forgiveness for his shortcomings.'

'We want . . . to give you every assistance in these difficult times, Vichaiyen. You may offer . . . the French Songhkla. But know that this will be the last of our concessions.'

Phaulkon was both relieved and grateful. 'August Lord, your wisdom and tolerance are all-encompassing. My heart is touched. And while speaking of matters of the heart, Mighty Sovereign, I humbly beg to present a petition at the door of your divine ears.'

'Speak, Vichaiyen. The subject of Sunida always pleases us.'

Phaulkon was forced to smile. 'Mighty Lord, I, a hair, crave permission to move Sunida to the royal palace here. Her absence in Ayudhya lies heavily on my heart.'

'Have you informed the French Ambassador of your intentions?'

Phaulkon burst out laughing. 'Mighty Lord, I confess not; though judging from the behaviour of the French in these matters, I doubt they could have much objection.'

'Indeed, Vichaiyen.' His Majesty had been highly amused by the account of the General and his 'most worthy chambermaids'. He chortled wheezily. 'Very well, you may ask your Catholic . . . God to forgive you your sins. You may arrange suitable accommodation for Sunida. We should anyway like to . . . congratulate her. She performed a fine task in keeping . . . the thoughts of the French army away from matters of war.'

'August Lord, there could be no greater reward for her than to hear of Your Majesty's satisfaction.'

'Go to her, Vichaiyen. Impart the . . . good news to her while you conceal it from your Catholic wife. And in the confusion may all the different gods be with you.'

'Mighty Lord, I receive your orders.' Phaulkon crawled out backwards, marvelling at the capacity for humour in times of trial of the great master he served.

Twenty-eight

As the capital disappeared gradually from view, so Samuel White's memory of the last few weeks of fear and dejection seemed to recede with it. By the time he reached Mergui, his narrow escape was but a dim recollection, and far from being chastened by it, he determined to play his biggest gamble yet. He had had ample opportunity to consider his situation carefully on the return journey; mercifully, it had been less arduous than the last one, as the rains were nearing their end. He had concluded that his best bet was to repay the sums demanded by Yale, or at least a part of them, after some heavy plea bargaining, because he had before all else to ensure his immunity from prosecution in England. After all, what would be the point of returning home to face trial? The whole idea was to purchase a great estate, with a squiredom and all the accompanying appurtenances, and retire in comfort.

He reckoned he might scrape together just enough from the treasure he had hoarded to settle the entire compensation, but he was damned if he was going to do so from that hard-earned money. What a pity he would have to return the *New Jerusalem* with its fabulous cargo to its owner. But under the circumstances he had little choice. No, he would have to seek new victims, new prizes, but with a subtlety beyond the range of Coates. On the journey home he had conceived the ploy of hoisting the French flag on all of his ships before they attacked their prey. They would change their names to Gallic ones as soon as they had left harbour. This would tally well with the rumours that were no doubt rife about the arrival of a great French fleet. He smiled to himself. If the exact intentions of the French had been a mystery until now, that mystery would soon be solved.

As soon as he had amassed sufficient spoils, he would repay the debt and head for England, leaving the 'French' to explain their actions. He would have to move fast and his timing would have to be perfect. He would have to be prepared from the start for a rapid departure.

He had sent Davenport ahead to Mergui as soon as his interview with Phaulkon was over. He had assured his secretary that his worries had been groundless, that Phaulkon had entirely exonerated him from any blame and that only the unexpected arrival of a very distinguished delegation from the King of France had prevented the Barcalon from receiving him earlier.

Before returning to Mergui, White felt obliged to visit Coates, if only to assure him that he was doing everything in his power to obtain his release. He also wanted to make discreet enquiries among the English traders to find out exactly what the French were up to. It was essential to ascertain if there was any truth in Thomas Yale's contention that Phaulkon was planning to replace the English by the French. It was hardly a question he could have put to Phaulkon himself under the circumstances. If anyone should know, it was the local English traders.

While he did visit Coates and offer him some small measure of consolation, the English traders turned out to be of little help. They seemed to be of the opinion that Phaulkon had been as much taken aback by the size of the French army as anyone. Perhaps, reflected Samuel, it had been a ploy of Yale's to get him to surrender Mergui to the Company.

White glanced up at the great wooded hills that formed the backdrop to Mergui. It was good to be back. He tipped the smiling porters and boatmen handsomely – it was always best to stay on good terms with the local peasantry – and headed up the hill with three of his own porters. His secretary came out to greet him.

'Welcome back, my lord.'

'Thank you, Francis. What news?'

'Things have been remarkably quiet in your absence, my lord. Almost too quiet. I get the feeling that something is amiss, but I can't quite put my finger on it.'

'In what way?'

'I wish I knew, my lord. Things are just too quiet.'

'Why shouldn't they be quiet in our absence?' observed White with a smile. 'We're the only ones who make things move around here. Where are Wilkes, Jamieson and Farley?'

'Captain Jamieson is here, my lord. Wilkes and Farley are out at sea. Oh, by the way, there is one thing that occurred in your absence.'

'Yes?'

'Heavy seas brought the *Sancta Cruz* into the outer islands for shelter. She suffered some minor damage as well.'

'The *Sancta Cruz*? Demarcora's brother's ship?'

'Yes, my lord. What a beauty she is, too. A greater ship even than the *New Jerusalem*, I reckon. I went to visit her yesterday.'

White was instantly curious. 'What was the *Sancta Cruz* doing in these parts anyway, Francis?'

'She was apparently on her way to Sumatra – Acheem, I think. She was fully loaded, and it must have been a valuable enough cargo because there were a lot of guards on board. I saw the – ' Davenport broke off, staring at White. He knew that look. He had seen it before. White's eyes had glazed over, the sign that he was hatching some monstrous scheme. Oh my God. Not the *Sancta Cruz*!

'The Queen of Acheem is vastly rich, isn't she?' asked White, a feverish look in his eye now.

'Ye-es, sir. I believe so.'

White laughed. It seemed to Davenport to be the laugh of a maniac. 'So the great ship *Sancta Cruz* is carrying a cargo fit for a queen, eh?'

Davenport did not respond.

'The *Sancta Cruz* is still here, is she, Francis?'

'Er . . . I'm not sure, my lord. She was here yesterday but she was preparing to sail.'

White leapt to his feet. 'I doubt she'll have left yet in this wind. Francis, fetch me Captain Jamieson. I want an immediate word with him.'

Davenport felt limp. He would have to get word to Ayudhya. 'Very well, my lord,' he replied.

As soon as he had left the room, White began to pace up and down, his excitement mounting. If only the *Sancta Cruz* were still here. It was a wild plan but who knew when another opportunity like this might present itself. Even if the *Sancta Cruz* were guarded, she couldn't have more men than he could muster on his home ground. Thank God it was Jamieson who was here

242

and not one of those other puppies. Next to Coates, Jamieson was the finest man he had, a rugged Scot, not quite as ruthless as Coates perhaps, but not as rash either. He'd never known Jamieson to back down before a challenge. And if Jamieson were in port, so would the *Redoubtable* be, and the old *Redoubtable* was the finest of his armed frigates.

White tried to kill time till Jamieson's arrival by examining the pile of papers that had accumulated in his absence, but he had difficulty in concentrating. All he could think of was the *Sancta Cruz* and the plan that was taking shape in his mind. By the time Jamieson arrived some half-hour later, the final details were ready.

Davenport ushered the captain in. Jamieson was a stocky man of medium build with large freckled arms and a heavy auburn beard. His red hair was thick and curly and his hazel eyes were sunk deep into his weatherbeaten face. He loved his job and had a ready grin.

'Good to see you, Rob,' said White, grabbing him familiarly by the shoulders.

'And you too, Sam. Welcome back. Where were you? Ayudhya, wasn't it?'

'Yes.' He winked. 'I went to get us a few more concessions from the Barcalon.'

'Aye,' said Jamieson, 'that's the stuff.' His craggy face was wreathed in smiles.

'Rob, is the *Sancta Cruz* still sheltering in the islands?'

'Aye, I saw her there this morning. She's getting ready tae set sail, though. I reckon she'll be away as soon as the wind turns. She's some beauty, by God.'

'How would you like to sail her?'

'Me, sail her? Ye're pulling ma leg, Sam.'

'No, I mean it. Listen, we're old mates, you and I. I'm going to square with you.' White leaned forward. 'You and I are going to share the biggest prize you've ever dreamed of. Just you and me and nobody else.'

The Scotsman eyed him uncertainly. 'Ye're no' speaking of the *Sancta Cruz*, are ye?'

White beamed at him. 'The very same, Rob.'

'But she's the sister ship of the *New Jerusalem*, is she not?

243

That's what's got Master Coates in such hot water. Ye punished him yerself, Sam, or so the word goes.'

'Coates was a fool, Rob. He disobeyed orders. You won't do that. You're much too sensible.'

Jamieson observed him cautiously. 'And what might those orders be?'

'To hand-pick the best lads you've got, and take over the *Sancta Cruz* tonight after dark. She won't be leaving yet in this wind. You'll take her by surprise and sail her with your own crew. Why, you'll be captain of the finest ship in the Bay.'

'Where'll I sail her tae, Sam? She sticks out like a tree in the desert, that yin. I wouldnae get far in her.'

'You won't stay in the Bay, Rob. You'll head due south, to Acheem. Down the coast and on to Sumatra. She's expected there soon anyway. Now listen to this. She's carrying the richest cargo this side of Constantinople. You'll sell the cargo to the Queen of Acheem for a fortune in gold. She'll never know it's not the original crew.'

Jamieson's eyes grew narrow. 'But whit'll happen tae the auld crew, Sam?'

'That's a problem. We can't have them going around telling tales.'

'I don't like that part of it.'

White did his best to look sympathetic. 'Can you think of another way?'

Jamieson paused in reflection. 'I could put 'em in a lifeboat and give 'em half a chance.'

White did not want to risk an argument. There was so little time. 'All right, Rob. You put them in a lifeboat and direct them here to me. I'll take care of them.'

Jamieson laughed. 'Would they no' be safer at the bottom of the ocean?'

White laughed too. 'Don't you worry about that. They'll be off your hands, that's the main thing. Are we agreed then?'

'So long as we don't have tae harm the men.'

'It's a deal. You'll be a rich man when you return.'

White rose. 'Good luck, Rob.'

'I'll be needing it on this one.'

As soon as Jamieson had departed, White began to pace the room again. He was jubilant.

Out of the corner of his eye he saw a shadow in the doorway move. He relaxed. It was only Davenport.

If this cargo were worth half what he thought it was, he could pay off the entire debt to Yale in one fell swoop, and still have some left over, not to mention his own treasure. He must hurry and return the *New Jerusalem* to Demarcora as proof to Yale of his good intentions. He would instruct Davenport to arrange that right away. He laughed aloud. What exquisite irony. To hand over the *New Jerusalem* in exchange for her sister ship. This time he would be more careful. The *Sancta Cruz* would not be expected back at home port in Pegu for another five weeks. If all went according to plan, she would be back in Mergui in four. He would have to time his departure for England then. It was in the week before the *Sancta Cruz* was expected back in Pegu that he would have to make his escape. He would have the *Sancta Cruz* moor in the outer islands on her return, and transfer the gold to the *Resolution* out of sight of harbour. No one would see the *Sancta Cruz* return. After the transfer he would take her out to sea and sink her. It would be assumed she had gone down in a storm somewhere between Acheem and Pegu. With her whole crew, of course. Yes, he reflected ruefully, he would have to do away with her crew. He had no choice. There must be no evidence.

Twenty-nine

It was late when Phaulkon arrived in Ayudhya. He was planning to spend the night there before proceeding to Bangkok to make the offer of Songhkla to the French. He entered his quarters quietly, not wishing to disturb Maria at this hour. He would sleep in his dressing room where a couch was always made ready for such contingencies.

He stripped off his clothes and began to douse himself from the large earthenware jug in the corner of the room. He was just putting on a clean panung, which, like the Siamese, he always slept in, when Maria entered his room. He stared at her in surprise. It was not like her to enter thus unannounced. And fully clothed at this hour, what's more. She looked pale and there were deep rings round her eyes. She stood there observing him for a moment in silence as if she were assessing the value of some merchandise in a shop.

'You're up late, my dear,' he said. 'Are you all right?'

'What does it seem to you?'

'Well, you look out of sorts.'

'Good, my lord,' she answered, addressing him formally. 'I'm glad to see your sensitivities stretch that far.'

'Maria, I'm sorry to see you this way but I've had a long day. This is not the sort of greeting I expected. If something is bothering you, please say so now.'

'I'd rather you told me yourself, my lord. Perhaps you can think of something you've been keeping from me all these years? It's rather important, so think hard.' Maria's voice quivered slightly but her gaze remained firm and cold.

Phaulkon racked his brain. This was not like Maria at all.

'I give up, Maria. Why don't you tell me?'

'I've managed to control myself so far, Constant. But I warn you my scorn will be limitless if you do not come out with it yourself.'

'Come out with what, Maria?' Phaulkon felt himself losing

patience. He was tired and preoccupied with the next day's meeting in Bangkok.

She glared at him. 'You are keeping that vixen Sunida at the palace, you visit her daily and you return to me tired in the evenings. How do you think I feel about that?' Her eyes never left his face but Phaulkon's expression gave nothing away. 'Then I have your nature to consider,' she went on with icy scorn, 'the honesty, the integrity and the morals of the man I married. After assuring me, with your glib tongue, that you had abandoned your old ways and dispersed your harem, you sneak behind my back and ask His Majesty to house your women for you. How do you think it feels to know I can never trust you again?'

Her voice carried loathing as well as anger, and Phaulkon was not immune to either. 'Those are harsh words, Maria,' he said, his face pale. Some part of him had always been prepared for this, but his regret that it should be so was no less real. 'They are also unjustified.' He started towards her but she stepped away from him.

'How do you think it feels to bear the child of a liar and a hypocrite, an adulterer and a profligate? You, who profess to be a Catholic.' She scoffed. 'You're no Catholic. You became one to suit your ambitions and you married me for the same reasons.'

Phaulkon was speechless for a moment. 'Bear the child of . . .' He held his arms out to her. 'You're pregnant!' he said, with genuine joy.

'Stay away from me!' she hissed as he drew closer. 'Don't touch me. Perhaps you have come from her. Is that why you returned here so late?'

He stood still and looked at her. 'I have arrived this minute from Louvo, and I am thrilled beyond words at the news you have just given me. No wonder you're a prey to wild fantasies.'

'Sunida is no fantasy, Constant. She is the bane of my existence. She has come back to haunt me. She hurt me then and she is hurting me now. I will not rest till she is dead.'

Despite himself, Phaulkon felt a shiver go through him. 'I would not wish Sunida or anybody dead, Maria. But she has been out of our lives for so long, why resuscitate her now?'

'Because she is there at the palace, waiting for you, Constant. I know it.'

'Who has been putting these ideas into your head? God knows, I have enough enemies. Won't you tell me who it is?'

'I'll tell you nothing until you admit the truth.'

'I cannot admit to something that does not exist, even to please you, Maria. But know that there is little else I would not do for you . . . or for this wonderful gift of the gods,' he said, glancing at her belly.

'You're a practised dissimilator, Constant, as well as a very stubborn man. You care nothing for my feelings. My hurt is not yours, is it? Does it matter to you that my heart is bleeding?'

'It matters a great deal, the more so since the reasons are unfounded. Besides, this is no way to celebrate the joyful news of an heir. Come, let me open a good bottle of wine. Our child shall be initiated early. Is it a boy or a girl?'

'I hope it's a boy. No girl would be safe with you, Constant.' She was pouting now, and he sensed that the eye of the storm had passed.

He laughed. 'It's true, I would spoil her with love.' He walked over to the cabinet and extracted his best bottle of Shiraz wine.

'No doubt you will want to name her Sunida?' she said acidly.

'It's a pretty name,' he said, opening the bottle. He poured her a glass. 'To little Sunida, then.' He raised his glass.

She stared at him without drinking. 'Don't avoid the issue, Constant. She is still a part of your life, isn't she?'

'She seems more a part of your life than mine, Maria. That's the unfortunate truth.'

'You're so glib, but I do not believe you.'

'The absurdity of the matter is that if I were to look you in the eyes and say, yes, I see her every day, you would believe me. But you see,' he teased, 'I will not give you that satisfaction. You do not deserve it for doing everything to ruin such a momentous occasion.'

'You devil!' she exclaimed. 'Tell me another "truth" then. If I were to say to you, all right, Sunida can be your minor wife; I accept, as long as I remain the major one. That would suit you perfectly, wouldn't it?'

'I would not dare to hope for such a miracle, Maria.' He smiled knavishly. 'Besides, if you made it that easy, there would be nothing left for me to strive for.'

248

She threw her glass at him. He ducked and it flew over his shoulder and shattered against the wall. 'You are evil, Constant. You are a heathen at heart. You should never have married a Catholic.'

He smiled. 'Has it ever occurred to you that I married you because I knew that as a Catholic you could never divorce me. You see, I want us to be together for ever.'

'There are times, Constant, when, God forgive my blasphemy, I wish divorce were possible.'

'So you see, my dear, in reality you're no different from those Siamese ladies you profess to despise. Do you know that the biggest obstacle facing our valiant missionaries in their efforts to convert the Buddhist ladies is the fact that Catholicism does not allow divorce? The thought of being stuck for ever with a man they don't love sends them fleeing from our faith in terror. I always knew you were a Buddhist at heart.' She stared back at him, unsmiling.

'Come now, Maria, where is your sense of humour? I remember a time, not that long ago, when a Siamese lord offered you the position of minor wife in his retinue, and you teased your father – and me – mercilessly over it. What was it you said? Oh yes, what a great honour it was for you to be asked, especially as he lived in the palace, and that if you were to accept, you would slowly poison the major wife to take her place. I remember, too, that when your father failed to be amused – exactly as you are now – you appeased him by saying that in the Siamese lord's way of thinking, the offer was a great honour. Well, to return to the painful subject of Sunida, it was no different with her. She wanted to be my minor wife, but to serve under you as the major wife. She never dreamed of taking me away from you or of challenging your position.'

Maria shifted uncomfortably and avoided his gaze.

'It's not he who has been talking to you, is it?' he asked. 'That blackguard Sorasak?' Phaulkon involuntarily clenched his fists. 'He's not the one who has been putting these ideas into your head, is he?'

Maria kept silent. She flushed as he continued to look at her. Then she said suddenly, 'It was Kosa Pan.'

Phaulkon stiffened. 'Kosa Pan!' His eyes narrowed. 'I should have thought of him. My dear Maria, you have been swayed by a tongue as glib as mine. A tongue that would say anything to embarrass me, that would stop at nothing to discredit me. I have just stripped Kosa Pan of his rank as well as several thousand of his dignity marks. He hates farangs and believes every last one of us should be thrown to the crocodiles. What a reliable source of information! And how pleased that villain would be now to see how his efforts have disrupted our home. Don't you see what he's trying to do?' Phaulkon was angry now, the venom beginning to show in his eyes. 'How could you fall for a ploy like that, Maria?'

Maria had started to sob gently, uncertain what to believe any more. She felt terribly tired. She wanted more than anything for all this to be finished and done with. He walked quietly over to her, encircled her with his arms and lifted her onto the couch. She offered no resistance as he removed her clothes and lay down next to her. Her body felt cold. He caressed her gently but she didn't respond. She turned her back on him, staring at the opposite wall, her mind in turmoil. Could she really allow this woman, whether or not she existed still, to go on disrupting her life in this way? Phaulkon was, after all, her husband and they would both have a child to think about soon.

Phaulkon walked past two prostrate eunuchs into the special section where Sunida resided. She purred with delight at the sight of him. She prostrated herself, unabashedly pleased to see him. 'I was sure my lord had abandoned me. I was preparing to offer myself as food for the tigers,' she said, with her usual wide-eyed impishness.

'Those beasts would have melted at the sight of you, Sunida, as would any living creature with a soul,' countered Phaulkon.

'My lord, you flatter me, most pleasantly to be sure, but I know it's only because of the terrible guilt you feel. Don't think I'm going to forgive you that easily. Can you imagine how I felt when I saw all the chief consorts of His Majesty being transferred to Louvo?' She pouted. 'Only the shrivelled ones remained behind – and me.'

Phaulkon laughed. 'Well, the shrivelled ones will have to do without you from tomorrow, because I've obtained His Majesty's permission for you to be moved to Louvo too.'

'Oh, my lord.' Sunida was visibly touched. She lifted her sensuous body onto her knees and threw her arms gracefully round his neck. Instantly he felt the heat rise in him. No woman had ever had such an unfailing effect on him; time had not mellowed the reaction in the least.

'Sunida,' he said, his eyes devouring her.

She arched her back luxuriously, moving the weight from her knees to her haunches. The sash that covered her shoulders and chest slipped to the floor. She looked up at him, her eyes shining with desire, naked but for the panung that encircled her slim waist. 'Won't you love me now, my lord? You have left me alone so long.'

He held her close and she merged hungrily into him. Over the next frenzied moments, entwined like an erotic Hindu sculpture, they discovered each other again after their long separation, pausing only occasionally to savour the desire. Now they both rose to their knees, facing one another, their arms encircling each other's necks. Her lips were quivering. 'My lord,' she said, 'I believe I can reach the heavens without your even inducing me. That's how much I feel for you.'

He smiled at her, his whole body throbbing too. 'You may have to, Sunida. For my love lance has no resistance left.'

'Then release it, my lord, do not restrain yourself a moment longer.' She hoisted her hips eagerly onto him while he remained kneeling. Then she lowered herself gently down over him, digging her fingers into his broad shoulders for support. They remained almost still, barely moving, until moments later their bodies shook with a slow, protracted spasm. They had reached the stars with hardly a movement, so finely attuned were they to each other.

He smiled at her lovingly. 'Sunida, if reincarnation is a fact, I can only pray that in each of my future lives I may encounter you.'

She pretended to look hurt. 'You mean, my lord, you do not think you have already reached nirvana with me in this one?'

He laughed. 'I thought nirvana was the negation of all earthly pleasures, Sunida. That is hardly what I feel.'

251

'Nirvana is the ultimate state of bliss, my lord, like reaching the stars without moving. It is the end of earthly appetites and the beginning of serenity, and in that brief moment just now I felt I had reached it.'

They stayed still several moments more, interlocked like the great roots of the banyan tree. Then she lifted herself gently off him and he lay back, cradling his head in his arms, admiring her as she rose to her feet. He enjoyed nothing more than watching her move, like some feline animal, her long sensuous limbs merging into each other like the curves of the ancient Hindu goddesses. She walked over to a large earthenware water jug in the corner of the room and dipped a cloth into it. Then she returned to sponge him, attending to his love lance with special care. He watched her warily, knowing that in a few moments this innocent looking creature could rouse him to the heights of passion once again.

'You know, my lord,' she said, gently sponging the inside of his thighs, 'I am torn between uncertainties. I cannot decide whether it is better to see you every day or to deny myself that pleasure and let another few days of abstinence pass as they just have now. The explosion of feeling becomes so intense.' He was about to speak when she quickly placed a slender finger across his lips to silence him. 'But I have just decided that I prefer to see you every day.'

He laughed. 'And so it shall be, Sunida, but in Louvo this time. The royal barge will transport you under cover of darkness, before dawn tomorrow. It is all arranged.'

'The royal barge?' she cried exultantly. 'But what if I were to grow accustomed to such luxuries, my lord?'

'I have already considered that risk,' he said, looking grave. 'It will be a test of your true love for me.'

She sighed resignedly. 'I fear I know the results already, my lord. I shall simply settle once more for a smaller barge.'

He smiled. 'Speaking of barges, Sunida, how is the floating pleasure world?'

A slight frown crossed Sunida's brow. It was rare to see a line on that beautiful face.

'My lord, I humbly believe it was a success, in the beginning at least. The French troops seemed happier on the river than on

252

land. They could not wait for the sun to go down.' Her expression brightened for a moment. 'If war had broken out then, you could have placed all the ladies of the floating pleasure world in the front line of the Siamese army, and not a Frenchman would have fired a shot.'

Phaulkon smiled. 'But now?'

'Now, my lord, there are quarrels. And increasing arrogance on the part of the farangs. The boatwomen are becoming frightened, my lord, and resentful. They want to return to Samut Songhkram.'

Phaulkon was thoughtful. 'Nonetheless, Sunida, you did a wonderful job, and His Majesty himself has asked me to commend you.' She prostrated herself at the mention of the King, and replied with deep reverence as if he had addressed her personally.

'August Lord, I, a mere speck of dust on the sole of your foot, give humble thanks for having had the opportunity to serve you.'

'The Lord of Life is aware of the deterioration in French morale,' continued Phaulkon, 'and I am going straight to Bangkok to try and do something about it. The French army is increasingly frustrated, discipline is lax, and the troops need to be kept occupied.' Especially with Desfarges' frequent absences in Louvo, thought Phaulkon. Perhaps a trip to the south would provide the necessary distraction for some of the more recalcitrant troops. He would discuss the matter with la Loubère when he offered him Songhkla.

Sunida, seeing he had finished speaking of the Lord of Life, now rose onto her haunches again and looked up at him with her wide almond eyes.

'Will your honourable wife be moving to Louvo too, my lord?' she asked.

'She will be remaining in Ayudhya, Sunida.' He smiled. 'In Louvo *you* will be my major wife.'

Sunida seemed genuinely taken aback. 'Oh, my lord, I could never be that. I wouldn't dream of usurping your honourable first wife's position.'

Phaulkon sighed. If only Maria could see Sunida now. When he had left her earlier that morning, she was still confused but no longer angry. She had told him she did not want to be away from

253

the orphanage and would not move to Louvo. He wondered whether she was just using the orphanage as an excuse or whether she genuinely did not want to go.

He observed Sunida now. This wonderful creature before him wanted only to honour and respect Maria, never to replace her. Still, it was one of those questions of Eastern and Western upbringing, and he had agonized over the problem long enough to know there was no solution other than the present one. Maria's attitude forced him to conceal the truth from her and be honest only with Sunida.

'Kosa Pan went to see my wife, Sunida, to tell her all about us. Maria is still uncertain whether to believe him.'

Sunida looked downcast. 'Oh, my lord, how sorry I am to be the source of such trouble for you. But you know how I wish your honourable wife well and ask nothing more than to serve her.'

'I know,' said Phaulkon, observing her with deep affection. 'But it is written that your lives should remain for ever apart. You must never for a moment think, however, that you are a problem to me. Were the problem to be magnified one hundred-fold, Sunida, it would still be worth spending a few moments in your company.'

'Oh, my lord.' She bowed her head. Then she looked up and smiled. 'How foolish I am. Keeping you from your duties like this. I know you have to leave.'

'I do, Sunida. My barge is waiting at the royal quay to take me to Bangkok.'

She grinned at him impishly. 'Couldn't the affairs of state wait just a moment longer, my lord?' she asked, inhaling his cheek deeply. Her slender fingers brushed slowly across his abdomen and then delved lower still.

'You little temptress,' he sighed, as a wave of feeling engulfed him.

She smiled coquettishly. 'You kept me waiting five long days, my lord. I am more charitable. I will keep you only a few more minutes.'

It was not until an hour later that Phaulkon climbed into his official barge and offered the head boatman a special bonus if he could make up time on the river to Bangkok.

254

Thirty

'Captain Weltden is here to see you, Your Excellency.'

'Good, send him in.'

The two brothers were still in the Governor's office. Yale, always courteous to his subordinates until they in some way offended him, rose to greet Anthony Weltden. He was a tall man, with thick chestnut hair and a tanned complexion. He was in his early thirties, but his face was lined and weatherbeaten beyond his years. He wore a blue naval uniform with epaulettes and held his cap respectfully in one hand. He was known as a fearless sailor, a keen fighting man and at times a heavy drinker.

'Won't you sit down, Captain? You have met my brother, Thomas Yale?'

'Indeed I have, Your Excellency.' He bowed and sat down next to Thomas. 'Pretty warm weather we're having, sir.'

'Quite so, Captain, that's why I thought you might be ready for a little sea air.' Yale smiled graciously.

'I'm always ready for that, Your Excellency.' He paused. 'Unlike other folks, I get land sick.'

Both the brothers laughed and then the Governor's face became serious.

'Captain Weltden, I have an important mission for you. I have chosen you for this task for the simple reason that I consider you the best we've got. It is not an easy assignment. The East India Company has always tried to adhere to a policy of peaceful trading, avoiding political or military involvement in its areas of operation. The situation in the Bay, however, as you must be well aware, has become untenable.' Weltden nodded his agreement.

'Our president in London, Sir Joshua Childe,' continued Yale, 'is understandably enraged on two accounts. In the first place, he is determined to put an end once and for all to the outrageous behaviour of the likes of Samuel White and John Coates, to mention but two, and to the policies of that opportunist Phaulkon

255

who is luring Englishmen away from the Company into the service of the Siamese crown, with the promise of illgained spoils. In the second place, news has reached Sir Joshua that a great French fleet, consisting of seven ships of war, a thousand fighting men and dozens of engineers and priests, has left Brest for Siam.' The Governor's expression became grim. 'We now have information at this end, Captain, that this force has actually reached Siam, and that despite an unusual number of fatalities from the scurvy, it is in fighting shape. Its precise intentions are not known, but they are clearly not going to be favourable to us. The French force has been amicably received by the Siamese King and, with Phaulkon's connivance, I fear the key port of Mergui could end up in French hands. I need hardly tell you, Captain, what that would do to our interests in the Bay.'

Weltden whistled lightly. 'A thousand Frenchmen, eh? The Sun King's army is not one to be trifled with.'

'It is undoubtedly the finest fighting force in Europe,' put in Thomas.

'What do you think they're planning over here, Your Excellency?'

'To take over Siam and control all trade in the Bay,' replied Yale bluntly.

'What would you like me to do, Your Excellency?'

'I am coming to that, Captain. Outright confrontation with France must be avoided if possible, but we must capture Mergui before the French do. Fortunately, owing to the nature of the terrain, their armies will not be able to march overland from Ayudhya. They will need to take the circuitous sea route, a good five or six weeks' journey. I doubt the troops are ready to leave just now anyway, after seven months at sea. That should give you valuable time in which to strike a deal with Sam White, hoist the Union Jack and fortify the town. It must be impregnable by the time the French arrive, as I have no doubt they will.'

'What kind of a deal, Your Excellency? Sam White is hardly known for his honest dealings.'

'Indeed he is not. The one time you can count on him, however, is when his own interests are at stake. And that is precisely the position I intend to put him in. You have heard, no doubt, that we have a new King?'

'Yes, sir, long live King James.'

'Long live the King,' echoed the two brothers.

'Well, now,' continued Yale, his smile broadening, 'I have just received news of a royal proclamation demanding the immediate return to Madras of all English subjects in the service of foreign princes, of which the King of Siam is of course one. You will go to Mergui, present a copy of this proclamation to White and demand the immediate extradition of all Englishmen in his service. You will give him two weeks to round them up and bring them to you on your ship. At the same time you will discreetly request his assistance in delivering Mergui into your hands – in exchange for immunity from prosecution for past offences and a safe conduct to England for him and his cronies.'

'And if he refuses to co-operate?'

'You will arrest him and Burnaby and any other Englishman who refuses to comply with the royal edict. If his reluctance to co-operate extends only to his handing over Mergui, you will keep him occupied until my arrival. I have a few important matters to clear up here and then I'll be on my way myself, with two more frigates, to help hoist the Union Jack in Mergui.'

'Your Excellency, if I may enquire, why should I not take a small fleet with me now?'

'For two reasons, Captain. In the first place, a reasonable amount of time must appear to have elapsed before Siam fails to pay the compensation we have requested for its piracy in the Bay. In the second, Mergui is defended by Siamese warships under the command of English desperadoes who would surely panic if they saw a great fleet approaching. We would be better off trying to gain White's support and connivance first. It would not only avoid a bloody confrontation with White's men, but would reduce the risk of a stand by the native population against us as well. With White's co-operation, we could make it look as if we were allies of Siam, garrisoning the town against an imminent French invasion.'

Weltden nodded. 'I understand, Your Excellency.'

'One man-of-war should do the job to start with, Captain. It will show that we are serious without instilling panic.' The Governor paused briefly. 'What vessel is available for immediate departure?'

257

'The *Curtana*, sir. She could be ready to sail in less than two days.'

'Good. Then begin preparations immediately. Do not hesitate to contact me for anything you need. And remember, this mission is of the utmost importance. Its results will be anxiously awaited in London and its outcome will have far-reaching consequences for the Bay.'

Weltden stood up and saluted. 'I am honoured and privileged to have been chosen for the task, Your Excellency.'

'Then it only remains for me to wish you the best of luck, Captain.'

Thirty-one

La Loubère took a drink of fresh lime from a delicate cup-like bowl. The lime, mixed with water, was sour but had a refreshing bite to it. From the vantage point of his wooden terrace, raised on stilts, he could look out at the rows of identical huts that stretched to the far end of the field. He could also see the open gateway through which Desfarges would have to pass. The General should be here at any moment now. He had summoned him urgently from Louvo yesterday, to present him with his ultimatum. It would be an ultimatum without preamble.

The Ambassador wiped his forehead with a wet cloth. He had had enough of this debilitating climate and the droves of blood-sucking insects. The ever present smiles of the fawning Siamese attendants were beginning to grate on him too. The only cause for satisfaction his stay in this benighted country had so far given him was the material he had gathered for his treatise. With the help of the scholars sent by Phaulkon, he had taken copious notes on every aspect of Siamese life, and he was ready now to begin writing in earnest. The French public was avid to read of faraway places, and the ancient kingdom of Siam, he had to admit, provided material as exotic as any they could wish for. His volume, albeit too erudite for the masses, should nevertheless be received with wide acclaim when it was published in Paris – which would be soon enough, he reflected bitterly. He had made up his mind. His primary mission to Siam was getting nowhere. If Desfarges was not prepared to co-operate, he would return to France to seek further orders.

It was as well that the scholars had not yet left Bangkok when he had received Phaulkon's offer. They had gone to visit the great fruit orchards on the outskirts of the town before returning to their home provinces, and he had been in time to recall them. They had given him a full report on Songhkla. It was a convenient enough trading port for commerce with China and the Japans, but it did not have the strategic importance of Mergui. He had concluded that the offer was another example of Phaulkon's delaying tactics.

He caught sight of the unmistakable figure of Desfarges striding through the open gate into the field. He was preceded by a score of Siamese slaves, a now constant retinue that had done little to diminish the General's growing self-importance.

'Claude!' shouted la Loubère. 'Our military genius is arriving. It's time for you to join us.'

Cébéret du Boullay soon emerged from his bedroom where he had been having a siesta. The late afternoon sun was still hot. Unlike la Loubère, who continued to wear his European clothes, Cébéret had adopted the cooler Siamese fashion. A green panung was wound round his portly girth and a matching sash made a valiant effort to cover his flabby chest. La Loubère eyed him disdainfully as he sank into a bamboo chair, perspiring profusely.

The party of slaves fell prostrate to either side of the steps that led up to the terrace, forming a human alleyway for Desfarges, their master, to pass through.

'Good day, gentlemen,' he said, glancing around him amiably. He appeared in fine spirits, despite a long day's journey from Louvo. He was dressed in full military uniform, complete with medals.

The others returned the greeting and motioned him to sit down.

'I trust you had a comfortable journey, General?' enquired la Loubère. 'Good, then I will come straight to the point, as my time in Siam may be drawing to a close.' The General raised his eyebrows but remained silent.

'Lord Phaulkon was here two days ago to make us the offer of the port of Songhkla. That is the reason why I have sent for you. I have made the necessary enquiries. Songhkla is a practical base for conducting trade with the countries to the north, but it is not Mergui. And Mergui is the port His Majesty of France instructed us to secure. In my opinion Songhkla is a further concession on the part of Phaulkon to keep us happy for a while longer, and to divert us from our real objectives. Those objectives, gentlemen,' he added, looking sternly around him, 'remain unfulfilled.'

Desfarges frowned. 'But is not Songhkla a most strategic port, Your Excellency, from which the Portuguese in olden days conducted formidable trade with China?' He had been fully briefed by Phaulkon before his departure on the merits of Songhkla. He turned now to Céberet for confirmation. 'Do you not agree?'

La Loubère banged his fist smartly on the table before Céberet could reply. 'This trickle of concessions is just not good enough, General. Any more than the disgraceful condition of your army is. Discipline is virtually absent from this fort. Your men are either drunk or fighting over some woman.'

'My troops are not as undisciplined as you make out, sir. Incidents are bound to occur with every army of occupation,' protested Desfarges.

'But not on a daily basis. The Siamese are the only ones to show any discipline around here, while the French troops spend their time taunting them. Tensions have reached breaking point. You are spending too much time away from your post, General.'

Desfarges looked distraught. 'But, Your Excellency, my duties lie in Louvo as well. Am I not sworn to defend the King there? Besides, I have always left reliable officers in charge here during my absences.'

'Reliable officers?' scoffed la Loubère. 'Their behaviour is no better than their men's.' He leaned forward. 'Perhaps you are unaware that only yesterday three French soldiers died in a squabble over some boatwoman. Two of them were officers.'

Desfarges appeared taken aback. 'Who were they? What happened?'

'Frontin and Briamont. Four of them got into the same boat, after the same boatwomen. A fight broke out in the middle of the river and the boat capsized, drowning three of the Frenchmen and both the boatwoman. The fourth soldier managed to swim ashore.' He turned to Céberet for confirmation.

'I have to agree, General,' observed the director of trade. 'Whenever you leave town, things seem to degenerate. The men are constantly at each other's throats.'

'It is just not good enough. If they are going to be at anybody's throats,' remarked the Ambassador pointedly, 'let it at least be the enemy's. It is high time we enforced the dictates of our sovereign. It seems clear to me that all peaceful means to achieve our ends have now been thoroughly exhausted.'

Desfarges stared at him. 'You mean you are recommending war, Your Excellency?'

'Yes, General, it seems to me the only course left open to us. We came here with a purpose. Let us fulfil it. Besides, it would seem a most opportune time. Your men are obviously in need of action and you have had ample occasion to study the strength of the Siamese armed forces. I want you to draw up an immediate plan to take over the country.'

Desfarges continued to stare at him. 'But we are on the friendliest of terms with Siam, and my relationship with the authorities in Louvo is most cordial.'

'You mean, General, that you have become the servant of Lord Phaulkon.'

Desfarges raised himself up in his chair. 'I am nobody's servant, sir, other than the King of France's and, by his orders, the King of Siam's.'

'Yet you seem to do only Phaulkon's bidding. As head of this mission, I order you here and now to mobilize your men and draw up a suitable plan of action.'

'And I must refuse, sir, for it is against the orders of my sovereign. We have not yet exhausted other channels. On the contrary, we are making good headway. We have been here barely two months and already we have Frenchmen serving as His Majesty's bodyguard in Louvo, our men are ensconced in the fort here, we control the port of Bangkok and now Songhkla has been offered us.'

'What about Mergui, General, and our primary objective – the King of Siam's conversion? Those were our orders!' cried la Loubère.

'I have been in Louvo with the King, sir,' Desfarges persisted. 'I have seen how His Majesty insists on receiving regular religious instruction – despite his severe ill health. I have observed all that, sir. I have not been idling away my time writing dissertations.'

La Loubère's face turned a shade of purple. 'You are refusing to obey my orders, General?'

'I refuse to obey any orders that contradict the wishes of my liege.'

'Then you will suffer the consequences, General. For I shall return forthwith to France and recommend that you be court-martialled.'

Desfarges gaped at la Loubère. He turned to Cébéret. 'What say you, sir? Have we not achieved a great deal? What grounds do we have for war at this time?'

Cébéret scratched his head. 'In truth, the concessions have been slow, General. And our request for Mergui has still not been met. It is difficult to judge the value of Songhkla without seeing it first. I should like to go there myself as soon as possible. But Mergui was always our primary trade objective, and I would certainly feel more satisfied if it had been handed over instead.'

'But it has not,' observed la Loubère frostily.

'Perhaps we should give it a little more time,' added Cébéret. 'The idea of war at this stage—'

La Loubère cut him short. 'I will not be waylaid further. I will make immediate arrangements for my departure. I shall be taking fifty of the worst disciplined elements in the army back with me to France to face trial. They are not fit to serve our great sovereign abroad.' He looked squarely at Desfarges. 'It was your leader Phaulkon's idea that some of these men be moved to Songhkla, General. I shall make it appear as if I am taking them there.'

Desfarges was thinking rapidly. The threat of a court martial terrified him. 'I think I have a plan, Excellency,' he said earnestly. 'If Lord Phaulkon suggested that you take fifty men to Songhkla, why not take an additional hundred in two ships? We could offload the fifty in Songhkla, and take the other hundred to capture Mergui. Would you at least delay your departure until I have taken Mergui, Your Excellency?'

La Loubère hesitated briefly. 'No. I'm not prepared to waste any more time. You've had enough opportunity. Besides, even if you were to take Mergui, it would not fulfil the primary object of this mission.'

'But it would be a large step in the right direction, Excellency,' pressed Desfarges.

'It certainly would,' concurred Cébéret.

La Loubère became pensive. 'I'll tell you what,' he said after a long moment, 'I am prepared to assist you as follows. I will lie to Phaulkon for you. I will inform him I am taking a further one hundred soldiers back to France with me from the most undisciplined elements. This is on top of the fifty for Songhkla. I will accompany the men myself to Songhkla in two ships. We will offload the fifty men at Songhkla. Then both ships will ostensibly leave for France. As soon as we are out of sight of shore, we will transfer the remaining one hundred men onto one ship, which will slip away to Mergui, unbeknown to Phaulkon and the Siamese. I will continue in the other ship to France.'

'Who will lead the mission to Mergui?' asked Cébéret.

'What about you, Claude?' suggested la Loubère. 'General Desfarges must remain in Bangkok. His departure would arouse too much suspicion.

'I am not a man of arms, Simon,' replied Cébéret. 'You must send a military man. Besides, it will look very odd if I, as the director of trade, were not the one to go to Songhkla.'

'Who could you send to Mergui, General?' asked la Loubère.

'Commodore de Vaudricourt, is the most senior naval officer, Your Excellency. And the most capable.'

'Very well then, let us make ready for an immediate departure.' How convenient that Phaulkon had asked him to reduce the French force in Bangkok to appease public opinion, reflected la Loubère. And how fitting that that devil should thereby be the one to facilitate the French takeover of Mergui.

Thirty-two

Thomas Ivatt tipped the head boatman who had carried him on his shoulders across the surf and placed him on the beach. It was a ridiculous custom, he thought, except of course in the case of the ladies, but it was all part of the continuous show to keep up the image of the white man's stature in Madras.

It was noon and he jumped like a hare across the burning sand to the sea gate that formed the entrance to Fort St George. He passed the usual bevy of turbaned natives in loinclothes, contrasting sharply with the scarlet-faced white men in their breeches, stockings and hats. A line of graceful Tamil women clad in colourful saris and balancing large pots on their heads wound its way like some giant snake into the fort. At night they would return to their hovels in the black town to spend their meagre wages on staying alive and to snatch a few hours of well-earned sleep like the rest of the teeming natives. Ivatt had always wanted to explore the black town of Madras that had grown up in the wake of the fort and where some 300,000 natives outnumbered the white man six hundred to one. It was said to contain Chinese, Indian and European bazaars, and the residences of some of the wealthy Armenian merchants were reputed to be truly palatial. They had even erected a church of their own there.

As he approached the sea gate he was distracted by the sight of a group of semi-naked natives who were being ogled by a rapidly expanding crowd. He joined them and followed their gaze. There was something distinctly odd about the appearance of these natives on show and it took him a second or two to realize what it was. He stared at them transfixed. They had no noses! Their noses had apparently been lopped off. He felt suddenly nauseous and leant against the thick rampart of the fort to steady himself. The porters carrying his bags stopped behind him and stared impassively at the sight. Where had he read about these poor wretches without noses? Of course! Prisoners of war. It was the mark of prisoners taken by the Moguls. So the Moguls

265

had indeed invaded Golconda. Had they unseated Ali Beague yet? he wondered. He forced himself not to look again and walked unsteadily into the fort. There was another crowd there, in the courtyard beyond the gate, gaping at a dead man this time. The body was hanging from a gibbet, with a noose round its neck. It was the corpse of a white man.

Elihu Yale was in a foul mood. Fresh orders had arrived from London, the usual heartless orders that took none of the local conditions into consideration, the usual petty demands of rulers thousands of miles away who had never set foot in Madras or probably even Calais for that matter.

There was a famine looming, the plague had set in, the Moguls had overrun Golconda and were demanding a re-negotiation of the lease on the fort, and he had just ordered his valet hanged. Meanwhile, all that the mercenary directors in London could think of was a new decree limiting the number of horses that could be kept at the Company's expense. Just six of them! Ridiculous. Beyond that, every man now had to bear the cost of his own horse. It was the height of pettiness and shortsightedness, breeding discontent among the men with negligible gain to the Company. The Governor cursed. To make matters worse, the lucrative diamond trade which he and his partner, David Chardin, were engaged in on the side was at a standstill. The diamond-cutting centres of Golconda had fallen into the hands of the Great Mogul, and the demands of his jewel-hungry court were monopolizing the merchants and their rapidly dwindling stocks.

When Yale was informed that Lord Ivatt was waiting to see him, he was seething. The little man had better have brought the money owing to Siam's clamouring list of creditors. The Dutch were becoming particularly insistent, Demarcora's envoys were increasingly indignant and only Ali Beague was silent. Yale had heard rumours that his tongue had been cut out and that he was languishing in one of his own pits in Narsipore. But perhaps news of Golconda's defeat had not yet reached Siam – or Ivatt. If he had indeed brought the compensation with him, there was no reason why he should be told of Golconda's fate. If he had come empty-handed, however, he could be arrested as an English subject under King James's new proclamation. Yale began to

266

look upon Ivatt's arrival as less of a disturbance than he had at first anticipated. He ordered him to be brought to his office without delay.

'Ah, Mr Ivatt.' Yale rose from behind his desk to greet him. 'So you are back again. I trust you had a pleasant journey?'

'Very pleasant, Your Excellency, thank you. Though my first sight of the fort was a little unnerving. There was a corpse on show in the courtyard.'

'Ah yes, I had to hang my valet this morning. Tiresome fellow. Stole my horse. Horses are at a premium these days, Mr Ivatt. An example had to be made.'

Ivatt appeared stunned. 'You hanged your valet because he stole your horse?'

'You seem surprised. Things have changed since you were last here. The local judiciary is now authorized to pass the death sentence on pirates without having to waste valuable time and resources on sending the blackguards back to England for judgement. It makes life much easier, I must say.'

'Your valet was a pirate?'

Yale raised an eyebrow. 'Anyone would think I was on trial here, Mr Ivatt. But for your information, that rogue disappeared for three days with my horse, during which time he went to the Mogul camp to sell secrets. A large sum of money was found on him.'

Ivatt had the distinct impression the Governor was trying to justify himself. He decided to press the point. 'So you hanged him on circumstantial evidence, did you, Your Excellency?'

Yale's eyes narrowed. 'No, Mr Ivatt. I hanged him as a pirate. A pirate is defined in the criminal code as anyone who carries stolen goods across a stretch of water. My valet, you see, forded several rivers on my horse en route to the Mogul camp. And an act of piracy incurs the death penalty. But speaking of criminals, Mr Ivatt, how is Samuel White? Did you see him on your way through Mergui?'

'No, Your Excellency. He was still in Ayudhya, summoned by Lord Phaulkon to answer a number of complaints.' Ivatt had passed through Mergui quickly and undetected. Not wanting to be spotted by White's men, he had slipped out on a Siamese

267

vessel that was not under the captaincy of any of the harbour-master's men. Armed with a letter of authority from Phaulkon, he had commandeered the vessel which now awaited his orders outside Madras. With a bit of luck White would never know he had passed through. He would be back in Mergui to keep an eye on him just as soon as he had finished with Yale. He had sent a porter with a note addressed to Davenport urging him to continue to keep a close watch on White until his return.

Yale nodded. 'About time too. And how is our Mr Phaulkon? I hear the French are making some rather heavy demands on him. But then one hears the strangest rumours from their enclave at Pondicherry. Not that I've ever trusted the French, of course.' He smiled pleasantly.

'Lord Phaulkon is very well, thank you, and although I saw him every day in Ayudhya, that is the first I have heard of such rumours. But perhaps Madras is better informed than we are in Ayudhya.' Ivatt returned the smile.

Yale eyed the bag Ivatt was carrying over his shoulder. 'I trust you are here on official business, Mr Ivatt?'

'If you are referring to the compensation requested of my government, Your Excellency, yes I am. In fact, I am the bearer of good news. Captain Coates has been tried and found guilty in Ayudhya. He will receive the death sentence for treason. As a result of the trial, which revealed the true extent of Coates's piracy, the Siamese Treasury has acknowledged its debt. It has agreed to compensate in full anyone who can be shown to have suffered losses under Coates.'

'Ali Beague will certainly be pleased to hear that,' said the Governor, observing Ivatt carefully.

Ivatt stared back at him. 'Are you suggesting, Your Excellency, that the former Governor might use the compensation to obtain his ransom from jail?' Ivatt was taking a long shot, but he saw it hit home. Yale frowned. After all, thought Ivatt, if the Mogul armies had overrun Golconda, the chances were that Ali Beague was either dead or in captivity.

Yale recovered himself quickly. 'I was not aware that he was in jail, Mr Ivatt. To the best of my knowledge he is still in command of one of the southern provinces which has been resisting the Mogul advance. Whatever the outcome, Governor

268

Beague has the memory of an elephant, and I would certainly not count on him or his successors forgetting a sum like three hundred thousand pounds. But you were saying that the Siamese treasury has agreed to pay the full compensation: five hundred thousand pounds. May I ask when precisely?'

'You will appreciate that though Siam recognizes its debt and though it would never doubt the word of a governor of Fort St George, some of the claims have been made by less honourable individuals than yourself. The sums involved are considerable and must be verified by the Treasury. Coates's depositions are being examined to determine how far the demands of Ali Beague coincide with the Captain's testimony.'

Yale leaned back in his chair. 'A man of Coates's integrity should of course never be doubted.'

Ivatt remained impassive. 'He has been offered the possibility of a reduced sentence – to life imprisonment – if all his revelations are found to be accurate.'

Yale looked unconvinced. 'But you did not answer my question. *When* will the debt be paid?'

'Just as soon as the foregoing matters have been attended to. The government of Siam is aware of its obligations and deeply embarrassed by them. You may rest assured, Excellency, that it is anxious to remedy the situation and put this unpleasant episode behind it.'

'I seem to be having difficulty in eliciting a precise time from you, Mr Ivatt. We are being greatly pressed at this end, and we are not prepared to wait much longer. Conciliatory phrases like "as soon as possible" and "in the near future" are too vague. I need exactitude, Mr Ivatt.'

'I would say, Excellency, within two months at the latest. For that is the time it will require for me to journey back to Ayudhya and return here with the settlement.'

Yale raised his eyebrows in surprise. 'You were thinking of returning to Ayudhya, Mr Ivatt?'

'Yes, Your Excellency. Since we last met, I have been promoted to the second highest rank of the mandarinate, even though I note you continue to ignore my title. I am now the immediate assistant to the Barcalon.'

Yale steepled his fingers. 'You have not then heard of the proclamation of His Majesty King James II?'

Ivatt stared at him blankly. 'What proclamation?' He felt suddenly uncomfortable.

'Mr Ivatt, though you are in the service of the King of Siam, you are still an Englishman, I believe?'

'Yes, but why do you ask?' Ivatt answered warily.

'Because the royal proclamation I have just received commands all Englishmen in the service of a foreign prince to leave their posts immediately and to report to the nearest British settlement, which in your case would be Madras. Of your little group of mandarins, Mr Ivatt, it would appear that only Mr Phaulkon is exempt.' Yale's expression became grave. 'Anybody refusing to obey that order is to be arrested and prosecuted. The penalties, I can assure you, are harsh. His Majesty wishes to put an end once and for all to the practice of British subjects serving foreign rulers whose interests invariably differ from his own.'

Ivatt was stunned. He cursed his ill luck at having to learn of the new law from the man who would be enforcing it. Would the Governor really detain him?

'I have just dispatched an armed frigate to Mergui to bring back all Englishmen there in the employ of Siam. The commanding officer, Captain Weltden, has orders to arrest any who refuse to obey. The *Curtana* left only yesterday. You just missed her. When did you leave Mergui, Mr Ivatt?'

'Three weeks ago.'

'What a pity; had you left a little earlier, you could have observed for yourself how seriously I take my responsibilities.'

Ivatt swallowed his anxiety and looked hard at Yale. 'Governor Yale, I must caution you very strongly against detaining me here against my will. I am a high-ranking mandarin of Siam and the personal assistant of its chief minister, with direct access to His Majesty the King. Lord Phaulkon would consider my detention, as he would the detention of any other official of the Siamese government, a hostile act. The repercussions would be far-reaching. The payment of your compensation by the Treasury would certainly be delayed and quite possibly rescinded altogether.'

Yale contemplated him. 'Tell me, Mr Ivatt, as a British

270

subject, why would you want to defy a royal command? Do you not believe in King and country?'

'I do indeed, Your Excellency. Siam is my country and the Siamese King my liege. And since I am about to be unjustly arrested by the country of my birth for having committed no offence that I am aware of, I hereby renounce my nationality. I shall become a full Siamese subject, to which my mandarinate entitles me.'

'Renounce your citizenship?' Yale appeared genuinely appalled. 'Why that is not only illegal, it is preposterous! Where is your loyalty, sir?'

'Didn't your family leave England too, Governor?'

'That is quite different, Mr Ivatt. They went to New England, where I was born. It is not a foreign country. It is merely a part of the old country imbued with new ideas. I have every intention of returning there one day.' He looked at Ivatt haughtily. 'I am no traitor, sir.'

'Neither am I. A traitor is one who turns against his country. I do not turn against mine. I merely embrace another. I have lived in Siam for seven years now, I speak its language and love its people. I have become one of them in spirit. I shall now become one of them in fact. If you arrest me now, Governor, it will be an unlawful act on your part.'

Yale scoffed. 'Unlawful? I *am* the law, Mr Ivatt. I have full judiciary powers here.'

'Under which you hanged your valet, it would seem. Or rather, your pirate. A very convenient interpretation of the law, and one for which you may be asked to answer one day.' Ivatt saw Yale stiffen and knew he had touched a nerve. He pressed home his advantage. 'I understand that your predecessor, Governor Gyfford, is now on trial in England for decisions made earlier during his governorship. Yet he was well respected at the time.'

It was no secret that the Company in London was becoming increasingly petulant, questioning every decision, putting its nose into every little affair, reviewing the performances of past governors. It was said that Sir Joshua Childe wanted to put his house in order before retiring, and that he was particularly anxious to have any outstanding debts to the Company settled by then.

'I hope, Your Excellency, that you will have a suitable explanation to justify how you lost five hundred thousand pounds in compensation by arresting a high-ranking envoy from Siam, sent to inform you of his country's agreement to settle.' Ivatt leaned forward. 'If it is lawless Englishmen you are after, Governor, it is the likes of Samuel White you should be arresting, not me.'

Yale was stung by Ivatt's words. Their logic was undeniable. 'Captain Weltden already has orders for White's arrest, Mr Ivatt,' he said rather lamely, evading the main issue.

Ivatt scoffed. 'Sam White? Surrender to one armed frigate? You must be joking, Governor. He'll run circles round your Captain Weltden. Mergui is his fiefdom. He may be a rogue, but he's no fool. The only way you'll get Sam White here is if I bring him to you.' Ivatt paused. 'In exchange for my freedom.'

The Governor looked at him sharply. 'How would you propose to do that?' This was preferable to talk of losing the Company half a million pounds.

'Unlike Captain Weltden, I will have the assistance of the government of Siam. As I have already indicated, Siam wishes to maintain cordial relations with England. In the light of King James's proclamation, Sam White will be arrested and escorted here to you. I have a feeling Lord Phaulkon will welcome so unexpected an excuse to be rid of him.'

'If I were to agree, how do I know you would fulfil your side of the bargain?'

'Because you are a good judge of character, Governor, and you will have surmised that despite my apparent switch of allegiance, I am an honest man at heart.'

Yale smiled despite himself. 'I might be ready to deal on those terms, Mr Ivatt. But let us understand one another clearly. It will not be acceptable for White to renounce his citizenship and claim he is a Siamese.'

'Agreed, Your Excellency. Because in his case, unlike mine, the change would not be for genuine reasons.'

'Good. That is settled then.'

Ivatt stood up. 'Do I have your permission to leave then, Excellency?'

'There is one more thing, Mr Ivatt. This bothersome question of time again. It will take you thirty days to reach Ayudhya and

272

another ten days to return to Mergui with the warrant for White's arrest. That will be forty days in all. I will meet you in Mergui in forty days and personally escort Samuel White back to Madras to face trial, assuming of course that Weltden has not brought him back before then. Are we agreed?'

'We are, Excellency.'

'I will also expect at that time to collect the full compensation. It will relieve you of the burden of having to transport it across the Bay yourself.' And, thought Yale, should either White or the money not be forthcoming, it will give me the excuse I need to take Mergui by force. In the meantime, I will have another three weeks here to settle the most pressing of my affairs. He smiled. 'God speed, Mr Ivatt; till we meet again.'

Ivatt bowed and took his leave.

Thirty-three

The two Jesuit priests were ushered into the anteroom. They looked around them at the great French mirror, the Japanese screens, the Chinese Ming vases, the Ayudhya scripture cabinets and the wealth of artefacts from around the Orient. The men glanced at each other, unabashedly impressed. But there was more that bound these two priests together than their appreciation of Phaulkon's magnificent collection. They shared the conviction that France's greatest chance of achieving her goal in Siam lay in the person of the present ruler, that only in his reign could the ultimate objective be reached. If King Narai were to pass away before that joyful event, the future of Christianity in Siam would be fraught with uncertainty as the country plunged into chaos over the squabble for the succession. It had happened before, on each occasion when the succession had been in doubt, and it would happen again. Prince would slaughter prince, or some outside usurper would step in and seize control, marrying all the female relatives of the last king – his wife, his sisters, his daughter – to secure his claim to the throne. And as he fought to reinforce his position, Christianity would be the last thing on the new ruler's mind.

Father Tachard ran a hand through his hair and adjusted the cord that encircled his waist. He was unsure of the reception he would get from Phaulkon after all that had happened before. There was something daunting about the Barcalon at the best of times. Tachard had been avoiding Phaulkon; he had not seen him since the great banquet for the French delegation. Since his return to Siam, he had spent his time at the Seminary in Ayudhya, preaching the gospel, comforting dying prisoners, tending to the sick and meditating over the Scriptures. And during that time he had listened to the almost daily arguments of his colleagues over the question of Phaulkon's true convictions. Some believed implicitly in his mission to convert the King, while others were sceptical of his motives. Tachard, like his colleague

274

beside him, had concluded that Phaulkon, though a Catholic in name, would only act if it were politically expedient for him. The moment of truth had now come. For events had occurred and a reason presented itself which would force Phaulkon to take action.

Tachard glanced at the little man next to him, as if hoping to draw strength from his presence. Father de Bèze, small and frail-looking, was a man of strong purpose. His selfless will and the depth of his learning had earned him the unanimous respect of his fellow Jesuits at the Seminary. His retiring manner and slight build were deceptive, for he had great energy and a remarkably agile mind.

The two priests stiffened as they heard the approaching foot-steps. A dozen slaves entered the room first, crawling in on their stomachs and disappearing into various recesses like so many lizards seeking shade.

Phaulkon stood framed for a moment in the doorway, looking in at the visitors. Tachard was struck by the weariness in his face. In a moment it was gone as his features broadened into a warm smile.

'My dear Tachard!' Phaulkon exclaimed, striding forward, his mind instantly on its guard. This was, after all, the man who had tried to dupe him over the number of French troops. It was lucky for Tachard that he still needed the Jesuits or he would have taught the priest a lesson he would remember. 'My guards said that two farang monks were here to see me. But they never told me who. Why, these are no ordinary monks.' He embraced Tachard and then turned politely to his seated colleague. Tachard introduced Father de Bèze, who rose to his feet, ending barely higher than when he had first started.

Phaulkon contemplated them with a roguish grin. 'One Jesuit is danger enough,' he said, 'but two? Even the Lord God couldn't save me from such intrigue. What web have you been weaving, Fathers?' He sat down opposite them.

The priests smiled nervously. Tachard pointed to his colleague. 'Father de Bèze was on the ship from France with me, Your Excellency. Apart from his many qualities as a propagator of the faith, he is also a distinguished physician. He trained at the

275

medical college in Nantes. I would venture to say there is no more qualified physician in all of Siam today.'

Phaulkon inclined his head towards the little Jesuit. 'I am sufficiently well acquainted with Father Tachard to know that that is a great compliment.' A note of sarcasm crept into Phaulkon's tone as he added: 'He is certainly not prone to exaggeration. But I hope you have not come to tell me that I am going to be consumed by some terrible disease.'

The little priest smiled shyly and spoke for the first time, in short, staccato sentences.

'Your Excellency seems to me in exemplary health. It is His Majesty's condition which concerns me. Rumours are rife at the Seminary. Father Brouet has not been summoned once to Louvo. He used to visit His Majesty regularly at Ayudhya. We attribute this change to His Majesty's state of health. We would not want to view it as an abatement in the royal fervour to assimilate the Scriptures.'

A look of concern crossed Phaulkon's face. He had managed to convince General Desfarges that the Jesuits were continuing His Majesty's religious instruction in Louvo, but the priests of course knew better.

'The fact that no one has been allowed to see His Majesty,' said Tachard, 'has only enhanced speculation. He has received Ambassador de la Loubère only once. In view of His Majesty's great reputation for hospitality, this only lends substance to the rumours of his condition.'

'What exactly do these rumours claim?' asked Phaulkon.

Tachard looked at him nervously. 'That His Majesty is crippled by debilitating bouts of asthma and that he is increasingly incapable of governing. We have done our best to contain the speculation, Your Excellency,' he added hurriedly. 'It would be against all our interests to allow it to spread.'

'Why is that?' asked Phaulkon, knowing the answer but needing time to think.

'Because of the uncertainty of the succession, Your Excellency. We have no way of knowing how well-disposed towards our cause His Majesty's successor would be.'

Phaulkon looked at Tachard. 'You have some suggestions, Father?'

Tachard glanced at his colleague. The little Jesuit examined his thumbs before speaking. 'I studied a number of cases of asthma before leaving France, Your Excellency. There are certain new discoveries. I was fortunate enough to be privy to them. I have brought some medicines with me. Though I cannot cure the disease completely, I believe I can ease the patient's suffering. I might also prolong his lifespan by one, perhaps two years.' De Bèze paused, noting that Phaulkon's interest was visibly aroused. 'If Your Excellency would allow me to examine the patient . . .'

Phaulkon observed him for a moment. The physician priest had bright, intelligent eyes that inspired confidence. He also seemed modest and unassuming; Phaulkon guessed that he was at least as adept as Tachard claimed, and on this occasion the Jesuits' aims and his own were clearly on a parallel course. Yet it was certain that these fanatical men of God would demand their pound of flesh. Once again the King's conversion would be their price and once again he would have to stall.

'You mentioned easing the patient's suffering, Father,' said Phaulkon. 'But would His Majesty be sufficiently well to conduct regular audiences, and would his condition during such audiences appear normal to others?'

De Bèze cocked his head to one side like a bird. 'I would first need to examine the patient, Your Excellency. But if the disease is not too far advanced, it should be possible to achieve that. How long have the symptoms been manifest?'

'About four months.'

'In that case, Excellency, I do not foresee much of a problem.'

Tachard had kept his eyes on Phaulkon for some time, turning over in his mind how best to broach the real subject of their visit. Phaulkon had noticed the stare.

'Your Excellency,' said Tachard, smoothing the creases of his robe, 'there is a rather serious matter I would like to bring to your attention.' His expression was grave and did not augur well for his revelations.

'I am all ears, my friend,' said Phaulkon.

'I am telling you this in full confidence, my lord.'

'Of course, Father.'

'The fact is,' pursued Tachard, 'that there is a serious rift in the French camp. General Desfarges and Ambassador de la Loubère have quarrelled bitterly. Father de Bèze and I have come to see you today not because we are in the habit of revealing our nation's confidences, but because what has occurred has a direct bearing on the future of the Church here.'

Phaulkon was instantly attentive. 'What kind of a rift?' Perhaps this had something to do with la Loubère's request to meet him urgently in Ayudhya. Phaulkon had sent a note back with the same messenger agreeing to meet the Ambassador late that afternoon. Ayudhya was almost halfway betwen Louvo and Bangkok and he would travel there as soon as his interview with the Jesuits was over.

Tachard's grey eyes looked sad. 'The Ambassador has come to the conclusion that France is not carrying out the orders of King Louis. As head of the delegation, he must be concerned that he bears ultimate responsibility for its success. For though our King will assuredly be pleased to learn that the fort at Bangkok is garrisoned by French troops, yet the primary objective of his mission remains unfulfilled. What is more, that objective appears to the Ambassador to be no closer to fruition than when he first set foot on Siamese soil.'

'But you know full well how ill His Majesty is, Father. Have we not just been discussing his condition? I was with him only a while ago, and it was difficult for him even to speak. He was wheezing and gasping and could utter only short sentences.' Tachard had provided the perfect opportunity to play for time, Phaulkon reflected, just as the Lord of Life had instructed. 'You do not seriously expect His Majesty to convert in his present state?'

'We do understand, Excellency,' replied Tachard, 'but we are bringing up the matter now because there are very pressing circumstances.' The priest looked gravely at Phaulkon. 'Ambassador de la Loubère is so frustrated that he is planning to return to France.'

Phaulkon's expression barely changed. 'And what are General Desfarges' feelings about the Ambassador's plans?'

'He does not understand them, Your Excellency. That is where the rift lies. The General feels that France is making good progress here. He sees no grounds for, er, other action. He has

278

become quite enamoured with Siam, as have many of his officers. They have come to feel at home here. The local population has, how shall I say, showered them with favours.'

'I see nothing strange about that,' observed Phaulkon. 'We are allies, after all. At least I thought we were. I fully sympathize with General Desfarges' attitude. He is quite correct in showing restraint. For I must tell you, Father, that even if the General were not enamoured with Siam, as a military man he would be well advised to steer clear of warfare. His troops would be outnumbered one thousand to one, and such odds – even given the superiority of French arms – would be insuperable.'

'I am no soldier, Your Excellency, so I cannot argue in such matters,' said Tachard. 'But we have come to inform you that the purpose of Ambassador de la Loubère's return to France is to seek reinforcements. King Louis will not take kindly to the news of any failure. We fear he will send a grand army to invade Siam, and recall General Desfarges to face a court martial. At that stage,' added the priest dejectedly, 'there would be little room for negotiation, and our plans for His Majesty's conversion would be irrevocably shattered.'

'I had no idea your Ambassador was such a warmonger, Father.' Beneath the mask of composure, Phaulkon's brain was racing. Though it was just possible that this could be another ploy of the scheming Jesuits to get him to press harder for the King's conversion, he sensed that this time Tachard was speaking the truth. He turned suddenly to de Bèze.

'And what do you make of all this, Father?'

The Jesuit appeared unruffled by the question. 'I may speak in confidence?'

'Of course,' said Phaulkon, instinctively liking the little priest.

'In the first place, King Louis is not used to having his orders questioned. Certainly not disobeyed. His wrath will be great. The expeditionary force he will dispatch will be large enough to carry out his designs, with little chance of failure. That is why we have come to seek your help, my lord. You are our only salvation.'

'How is that?'

'Only you have the power to avoid a full-scale conflict. You

279

must persuade His Majesty to convert before the Ambassador leaves.'

'You want me to persuade the King to convert as a means of avoiding war?'

'Yes, Your Excellency,' replied both priests simultaneously.

Phaulkon considered his options. The King's conversion was not one of them. There could be advantages to la Loubère's return to France. It would at least provide a breathing space. Eighteen months or more would elapse before a French force returned to Siam. In the meantime he could seek other alliances or train the Siamese army to the standards of their Western counterparts. He had to admit, though, that neither of these strategies would be easy. And what a terrible waste, he thought, after all these years of cultivating the French as allies. Perhaps it was best to stick to the old plan. To try somehow to convince the Ambassador before he left that His Majesty really was about to convert. But how? How could he get la Loubère to believe him without an actual ceremony taking place? He silently cursed the stubborn Frenchman. First Yale and the English were threatening him with war and next it would be the turn of the French. Maybe the long-term answer to his problems lay in pitting the two rivals against each other – the English against the French. After all, it would just be the continuation of a long tradition. The germ of an idea began to take shape.

Phaulkon noticed the Jesuits staring at him. He brought his mind back to the immediate future. His priority was to restore the King's health before a host of internal problems were added to his foreign dilemma.

'My good Fathers, I thank you for your visit and for your confidences. It is in all our interests that war should be avoided, and I shall work towards that end with all my resources. But His Majesty will not convert in his current condition. It is out of the question. Our priority, then, must be to cure him of his ailment.' He smiled encouragingly and turned to de Bèze. 'Father, I shall request an immediate audience with His Majesty so that you can determine his true condition, and administer the correct medicines.'

De Bèze bowed. 'I am at your service, Excellency.'

The priests rose. Their mission had not, perhaps, been entirely in vain.

The two men eyed each other warily as they took their seats in the chief minister's study at his palace in Ayudhya. The walls were lined with books in half a dozen languages and though la Loubère's expression was dour and humourless, every now and then he glanced up at the full shelves, eyeing them avidly as a dog might a favourite bone.

Phaulkon waited for the Frenchman to speak.

'Lord Phaulkon, I have asked to see you in private to inform you of certain matters relating to my mission here. Though I am grateful for the hospitality you have extended to my delegation and myself, I must frankly express my deep disappointment at the lack of progress in the matter of His Majesty's conversion. I hear constant expressions of hope, yet I see no actual signs of headway. I must remind you that this is the primary purpose of my mission. No matter what other achievements may be fêted, without His Majesty's conversion my mission will have been a failure. And I shall be answerable for that failure to my sovereign.'

'No one is more keenly aware of your objective, or its importance, than I am, Your Excellency,' replied Phaulkon. 'Yet I do not ride as glibly over your achievements as you do. It is no small feat for two nations six thousand leagues apart and of entirely different backgrounds to exchange special vows of friendship and favoured treaties of commerce. You underestimate the progress you have made, my lord. France is now a force in the region.'

La Loubère raised his hand haughtily. 'During my sojourn here, Lord Phaulkon, not a day has passed in which I have not been told of the great influence you exercise over your liege. Were your faith in the Catholic God as firmly rooted as you would have us believe, I have no doubt you would have prevailed over His Majesty in this field as you have in virtually every other.'

'Were the shoe on the other foot, Ambassador, you might see things in another light. Let us imagine that King Louis had a Buddhist adviser at Versailles, as determined and influential perhaps as I am. Would he have had much success in converting your King? We know the answer to that. Yet despite the odds, I venture to suggest that I have come closer to realizing our goal than you are perhaps aware. Only His Majesty's present state of health prevents faster progress.'

La Loubère frowned. 'These are but words, Lord Phaulkon, vain words at which you excel, like the false promises you dangle before us to keep our hopes alive. I consider your monarch's reticence to be none other than your own. For it has become increasingly clear to me that you are not sufficiently dedicated to our cause.'

Phaulkon raised his eyebrows. 'I believe the Jesuits, and General Desfarges, would disagree with you, my lord. The General expressed his satisfaction to me only the other day in Louvo. He was impressed that His Majesty, despite his condition, was continuing his religious instruction.'

The colour rose to the Ambassador's cheeks. 'The General . . . the General has not been himself lately.'

Phaulkon waited for him to continue, but la Loubère was silent. Phaulkon decided to prod him a little.

'I would say General Desfarges has adapted extremely well to Siam, my lord, as behoves any ambassador of good will. He is well liked and understands the need for caution. There are many powerful elements opposed to the King's conversion. More can be achieved by impressing the Siamese than by threatening them. I am surprised, Ambassador, that a military man should show greater restraint in this respect than a distinguished envoy with your experience. Perhaps your isolation in Bangkok has made you unaware of recent developments in Louvo.'

La Loubère stiffened. 'Restraint!' he exclaimed. 'Cowardice, you mean.' His face turned redder still. 'Desfarges will be replaced, the minute I reach France. For I am ready to return to my country. I have had enough. I shall apprize my liege of the true state of affairs here.'

Phaulkon affected a look of great surprise. 'Return to France? I am sorry to hear that, Ambassador, especially when things are going so well. Would it not be wiser to wait a little longer? If you return to France before the great event, surely King Louis will consider your mission a failure? And it would seem a pity for that failure to be attributed to you, when in all likelihood my master will be a Catholic before even you reach the shores of France.'

'I have no doubt that further procrastination would suit you well, Lord Phaulkon, but I will not be swayed from my purpose any longer.'

'Very well, my lord. But as a Count of France, I shall myself be writing to King Louis to express my view of the situation. I have no doubt that both General Desfarges and the Jesuits will substantiate my opinions. I do not share your pessimism and I believe your mission has thus far been a success in almost every respect. Its accomplishments far outnumber its failures.'

'That may be your opinion, Lord Phaulkon,' said la Loubère frostily. 'But then we know you are only a Catholic by circumstance.' He drew himself up in his chair. 'I shall be taking one hundred men back to France with me. I have conferred with the senior officers at Bangkok and that is the number, it seems, of undisciplined elements at the fort. A further fifty men will go to Songhkla with Monsieur du Boullay. That will leave three hundred and fifty soldiers here, enough, I am sure, to uphold the honour of France until further notice.'

'A hundred soldiers, Ambassador?' Phaulkon could not believe his luck. This would do wonders to assuage the growing demand for the Frenchmen's expulsion. And it would help to still the furtive voices that were claiming he was on the side of France. 'Do you need to take that many?'

'I do. And I shall take the twelve specialist cannoneers under Monsieur Dularic back with me too. Now that the fortifications are secure, they are no longer needed.'

Phaulkon frowned. 'The bombardiers? I understood those were a gift from the King of France to my master.'

'I am afraid not. My instructions were to take them back with me should my mission be aborted, which I now consider it is.'

Phaulkon's tone hardened. 'General Desfarges has already presented them as a gift to His Majesty in Louvo. The Lord of Life would find it difficult to comprehend such behaviour.'

'The General had no right to do that. He will have to rescind his offer, because I intend to obey my instructions and take them back with me.'

'That would be considered an insult, sir. The cannoneers will have to remain here.'

La Loubère's face turned purple. 'I will order Desfarges to send them back, even if he has to escort them to Bangkok himself.'

'The General will not obey that order. It would make him look like a fool and a liar.'

'If he has the insolence to disobey me, it will further seal his fate at his court martial.' La Loubère was livid. 'And it will be further proof that you have so corrupted him with your flattery and favours that he has lost all sense of duty.'

Phaulkon controlled himself with an effort. 'He pledged allegiance to my master when he set foot on Siamese soil and he is merely honouring that pledge.'

'You have turned his mind, sir. He seems to have forgotten that he is a marshal of France and that his duties to his country come first.'

'Not while he serves in Siam.'

'The loyalties of an officer of France cannot alter, sir, no matter where he might be temporarily assigned.'

'The General has expressed himself quite satisfied with his appointment here. His assignment may be more than temporary, Ambassador.'

'Indeed? On the contrary, I will see to his replacement the moment I reach France.'

'It will be for the King of Siam to decide whether to release him when the time is ripe. In the meantime, His Majesty expects the cannoneers to remain, and remain they shall.'

La Loubère threw a last venomous glance at Phaulkon as he rose to his feet. 'We have nothing more to discuss. Good day, sir.' He stormed out of the room without a backward glance.

Thirty-four

Anthony Weltden navigated the *Curtana* through the myriad channels separating the beautiful islands that formed the Mergui archipelago. It was a welcome sight after the rough crossing. The rains should have been over. Most unseasonal. The three-week journey across the Bay had taken over a month and his provisions were very low. Storms had almost left him aground in the inhospitable Andamans. He shuddered. That was no place to be shipwrecked. He was lucky to have found shelter in a deserted bay. The Andamaners had a lusty appetite for human flesh and he had heard that white meat was considered a great delicacy. It was strange that such primitive backwaters still remained when one considered all the brilliance of the surrounding courts: the Moguls in Delhi, the Burmese in Pegu, the Siamese at Ayudhya. But then the Andaman islanders had no ocean-going vessels and so remained oblivious to the outside world.

He passed a beautiful sweep of sandy beach to starboard and emerged into a broad channel, where he came upon a large ship steering towards him, almost head on. She was a real beauty, a colossus of perhaps 600 tons, her tall masts reaching proudly into the azure sky. She was not flying the flag of Siam and he wondered who she was and where she was heading. As he drew nearer she veered to leeward almost as if she were avoiding him. He was sorry not to exchange at least a salutation with so stately a vessel.

He noticed Mason staring through his telescope at the rapidly disappearing ship. 'Ever seen her before, Mason?'

The first lieutenant nodded. 'Aye, sir. She looks like the *Sancta Cruz*, if I'm not mistaken.'

Weltden arched his eyebrows in surprise. 'The sister ship of the *New Jerusalem*?'

'Aye, sir. I recognized the ensign of the Demarcora brothers. Besides, there aren't many like her in the Bay. Built in Manila I believe.'

Mason was always a fount of information, reflected Weltden. An invaluable man to have aboard, he had to admit.

'What the devil is she doing in these unfriendly waters? I thought Coates had seized the *New Jerusalem*?'

Mason shrugged his shoulders. 'Beats me, sir.'

'I suppose we'll find out soon enough.' Weltden turned his attentions to the problem of finding a safe anchorage. The mainland to the north of the port was already visible and he did not want to anchor within sight of Mergui until he had checked the situation in the main harbour first.

The ship rounded one more promontory and entered a magnificent bay. This would be it, he decided.

'We'll anchor here for the night, Mason.'

'Aye, aye, sir.'

'Damn, damn, damn!' swore Sam White. 'What the hell are they doing here? They can't have come to claim their compensation, surely? Do they expect me to get it to them overnight? I already sent them the *New Jerusalem* with its priceless cargo.'

As soon as one of his privateers had come to report the sighting of the *Curtana* in the outer islands, flying the Company flag, White had gone into a black rage. He would have to receive these people now. Perhaps even delay his departure to England, just when he was making final preparations to leave. The compensation was right here in Mergui. That wasn't the problem. Jamieson had done a fine job. But he had only another week at the outside before the *Sancta Cruz* would be expected back in home port and an inquiry into her disappearance would begin in earnest. He had to be well on the way to England by then. To think he could be thwarted now when his goal was in sight. He had taken every possible precaution. He had even kept the *Sancta Cruz*'s return secret from Davenport and transferred her spoils, the bulk of it ashore to cover the compensation, the remainder onto the *Resolution*, in the dead of night and at a safe distance from shore.

As prearranged, Jamieson had sent a lone rower to inform him of the *Sancta Cruz*'s return. They had worked undisturbed by moonlight and White had been back in his bed before dawn. The *Sancta Cruz* was now out at sea being scuttled, and with her would disappear all trace of his activities. Jamieson should be returning with his men in one of the lifeboats shortly. The *Sancta Cruz*'s original crew were all in the grave and there was no one around to tell their story. Four weeks ago Jamieson had landed them at a deserted beach beyond the outskirts of Mergui, where his own guards had been waiting to escort them across a patch of dried swampland to the Tenasserim River. The jailers in Tenasserim could have had no idea who the prisoners were when they found them, mysteriously poisoned, the following day.

If only the Company hadn't come snooping right now. Their timing was uncanny. The *Curtana* couldn't have spotted the *Sancta Cruz*, could she? White's stomach turned at the thought. It would have been a close call. The great ship only left the outer islands at dawn this morning. Much would depend on which route the *Curtana* had taken late yesterday.

He would tell these untimely visitors he was just on his way across the Bay to take the compensation to Yale. They were bound to spot the *Resolution*, fully loaded with his belongings and his hoard of treasure as she was, in deep waters and ready to sail, and that would be his excuse. The Company frigate, his spies had told him, was heavily armed. He could hardly afford an armed confrontation at this time. What infernal luck.

Whatever happened, he had no choice but to receive them. He would send Davenport out right away in a boat to welcome them to Mergui and enquire after their mission. He would tell him to stall them, to give him a little more time to tidy things up. Certain documentation had to be destroyed.

Apart from that, it occurred to him that it would be wise to attend to the town's fortifications, which he had sorely neglected, using the Treasury funds earmarked for it elsewhere. There would be less chance of a confrontation if the Company frigate were to see that the town was properly defended. He would order his men to go right away into town and spread the word that well-paid jobs were available immediately for all able-bodied men. The Shahbandar was known to be generous when he needed something in a hurry and the response among the peasants would be rapid and prolific. He would order thick stakes to be sunk into the mouth of the river to prevent ships from entering, and wooden stockades erected along the hillsides from which a score of cannon would protrude. The actual half-dozen

287

cannon on the hilltop would be cleaned and oiled and their barrels covered in gold leaf to ensure they glinted in the sun. They would be clearly visible from the sea. Next to them, along the entire hilltop, a line of fake wooden gun barrels, similarly covered in gold leaf, would be quickly constructed to give the impression of an artillery force far in excess of its real strength. The town might not appear impregnable to the discerning eye, but it would present a sufficiently daunting sight for a single man-of-war out at sea, however well-armed.

It was essential that Davenport should forestall any advance party from coming ashore before he was ready for them and before he could establish what their intentions were. He rang the bell on his desk.

Thirty-seven miles up the Tenasserim River, in the ancient trading town that bore the river's name, Selim Yussuf sat cross-legged in his reception hall, deep in thought, his wiry frame hunched. It had been some weeks since he had first received the call for action from his Muslim brothers on the secret council in Ayudhya, but he had thus far been unable to rouse his colleagues to any initiative; they were too frightened of the powerful and ruthless Shahbandar. This time they would have to take notice.

Selim's black eyes smouldered. He smoothed the pointed end of his copious black beard, a sure sign of his agitation, and considered his enemy. The Shahbandar was a dangerous man. He had spies everywhere, spies who would sell their very souls to the devil for the kind of rewards he paid. But he, Selim, had spies too, and what they had now reported was very interesting news indeed. He would be discussing it soon with the Council of Five. He had called the meeting through his brother Hassan, who sat on the Council. Of course only three Council members had been invited. The other two were the Shahbandar and the farang Governor. They had no place at today's gathering.

Selim stared across at the opposite wall, at the framed pictures of Shiraz by moonlight and the marketplace at Isfahan, and his thoughts turned to his ancestors who had been executed. Had they all died in vain? Not one of the fathers or uncles of the three members of the Council who were about to visit him had escaped execution in the wake of the Macassar rebellion. They had all

288

been implicated and it was that devil Phaulkon – who was said to have felled the Macassar chief, Prince Dai, with his own hand – who had sealed their fate. Worse than that, he had sealed the doom of all the Moors in the south who for centuries had run trade across the Bay, replacing them with his farang cronies, crooks and infidels all. Selim felt a surge of pain and fury at the thought of his own father, unable to control his screams as he was slowly fed to the tigers. He had vowed to avenge that death one day.

Selim called for his servant and ordered his hookah to be brought in. In the next instant the water pipe was brought before him and he inhaled deeply. He felt the smoke permeate his lungs while the familiar gurgling sound momentarily soothed his nerves.

His servant re-entered with a look of studied importance and announced the arrival of his visitors.

Selim rose and bowed, as one by one the bearded party filed in, looking anxiously about them, as if the Shahbandar's spies might be hiding behind the very fabric on the walls. They were all dressed in the long flowing robes of the Moors. First came Fawzi Ali, whose uncle had once been Shahbandar, then Ibrahim Tariq with his great beaked nose, and finally Selim's elder brother Hassan. There was a marked facial likeness between them, but there the resemblance ended. Hassan was plump and slow-moving, Selim lean and restless.

'Peace be with you, Selim,' said Hassan, his black moustache bristling.

'And with you, Hassan,' replied Selim, and turned to greet the others.

They sat cross-legged round a low circular table inlaid with mosaics. Hookahs were passed round. Selim glanced at his guests, and tried to conceal his disdain. They seemed so abject and frightened, these new mandarins, such a far cry from their dauntless forebears. Thank God that among the local Moors there were some real fighters who were ready to serve his purpose.

All now looked to Selim to speak. Though he was not a member of the council, they knew that by force of character he was their rightful leader, and they had accepted him as such.

289

'Brothers,' began Selim, 'we all know from our informer at the jail in Tenasserim that the men who were murdered last month were from a ship seized by the Shahbandar. They were brought here in the dead of night and poisoned. We know the name of the ship from the lips of a dying crewman who spoke Malay. It was the *Sancta Cruz*, owned by the Armenian trader, Demarcora.' Selim looked around him. 'The Demarcora brothers are under the protection of the East India Company. Up till now the Shahbandar has been careful not to molest shipping that is friendly to the Company, but this time the infidel pig has overstepped the line. He must be getting desperate.'

Ibrahim Tariq raised his beaked nose a notch or two, a sign that he wished to speak, but Selim ignored him.

'I have just now learned that the Shahbandar has given orders for every able-bodied man to be put to work on Mergui's fortifications. Stakes are to be driven into the river mouth, and wooden ramparts erected. Clearly the stakes can only be to prevent ships from entering. The danger, whatever it might be, lies therefore from the sea, not the land.' Selim leaned forward. 'The Shahbandar must have heard that the English plan a reprisal for his abduction of the *Sancta Cruz*. Perhaps they are sending armed vessels from Madras to chastize him.'

'Selim, you are right,' broke in Tariq. 'An armed frigate belonging to the Company has been reported hiding in the outer islands. I—'

'You saw it?' asked Selim, unable to control his excitement.

'Not personally. But Hussein did. You know, the one assigned to keep a watch over the Shahbandar's movements. He saw the Shahbandar's secretary row out to sea and had him followed. When our man saw the frigate in the distance he turned back to report to me. He caught me just as I was leaving to come here. It was most fortunate.'

The others stared at Selim, impressed that he had concluded correctly without even knowing of the arrival of the armed frigate. Selim lived after all at Tenasserim, the second city of the province, five hours' distance from Mergui.

'Is it not possible,' ventured Fawzi Ali timidly, 'that the arrival of an English frigate is coincidental? I mean, what proof do we have that the two situations are connected?'

290

Selim stared at him. How pathetic he was compared to his uncle, the former Shahbandar. What a great man he had been, before His Majesty, under the prodding of the farangs in Ayudhya, had discovered his links with the Macassar uprising and sentenced him to death. Now his nephew lived in terror of sharing the same fate, trembling at the very thought of defying authority. No wonder, thought Selim indignantly, that Ayudhya had so readily approved his appointment to the Council.

'We do not know for sure that the two are connected, Fawzi,' said Selim, restraining himself, 'but we must act as if they were. We will be better prepared that way. There must be a reason why Mergui has been ordered to arm itself, don't you think?'

Fawzi remained silent, staring glumly at his feet.

'What are you going to do, then?' asked Hassan, who till now had not uttered a word. Even in childhood he had been in awe of his younger brother, alternately hating and worshipping him.

'I'm going to change places with you, Hassan. We look fairly much alike.' Selim grinned. 'I'll try and eat a little more and look as prosperous as you. You must stay here at my house, while I move to yours in Mergui. Most people won't know the difference. There's too much happening in Mergui for me to remain here any longer.'

'But doesn't the Shahbandar have you watched?' asked Ibrahim Tariq.

'Yes, but he'll be watching my brother Hassan instead.'

Hassan forced a smile. 'You won't do anything to give me a bad name, Selim, will you?'

Selim laughed. 'You'll be the most wanted man in the province by the time I've finished, brother.'

The others smiled weakly, glad that it was not them that Selim was changing places with.

'In view of the latest developments I would like to leave without delay,' said Selim rising. 'We shall meet again as soon as I have more information.'

Fifteen hundred miles away in Madras, Elihu Yale picked up the bell on his desk and rang it decisively. 'Fetch me Captain Perriman,' he ordered. The aide ran off smartly. Governor Yale was not a man to be trifled with. He was strict and his attention to detail proverbial. It would not be good enough to report back that Captain Perriman was nowhere around. He would be expected to continue the search until he had tracked him down, however long it took. The Governor never took no for an answer.

Yale settled back in his chair and considered the situation. No time would ever be perfect for his departure, he knew, so it might as well be now. At least the Moguls had decided against attacking. He smiled with satisfaction. He had conscripted two men from each Hindu family and one from each Portuguese the moment he had heard that the Mogul armies were amassing outside Madras. By making a daily show of their training and a public display of their prowess, he had ensured that the rumours of the strength of the British forces grew in the telling. The constant booming of the cannon interspersed with the regimented strains of the military bands had done the rest, and a suitable degree of fear had now been instilled in the minds of the aggressor. The Mogul armies had stopped short of Madras and resorted to pillaging the surrounding countryside instead. In true diplomatic form, Governor Yale sent emissaries to the Court of the Great Mogul to congratulate him on his continuing successes.

Yes, he reflected, it was time to leave for Mergui. The worst of the famine was over and he had settled a host of problems that had been plaguing him. He had ordered all slaves employed on Company business to register their names and have their histories properly recorded in an official book, without which they would now be prohibited from work. He would soon put an end to the disgraceful practice of stealing children from their parents and selling them to the fort as slaves.

At the risk of arousing the wrath of the penny-pinching directors in London, he had prepared New Year gifts for all the potentates and merchants doing business with the Fort. He had rewarded officers and slaves alike for long and loyal service to the Crown, and he had left the natives gratified in the knowledge that he respected and would continue to respect their customs.

Lastly and most significant of all, he had shown the impartiality of British justice. When the irascible Scotsman, Fraser, had cut off a black boy's ear, he had had him apprehended despite his family connections to Sir Joshua Childe. And when six English sailors from the *Royal James* had taken absence without leave to pillage native settlements along the coast, he had had them tried and convicted. One of them had been hanged at the yard arm and another on the gibbet, on consecutive days. The following day a third had been shot by firing squad at the fort gate. The three remaining sailors, subordinates who pleaded that they had only been following orders, had been punished in full view of a vast crowd that had gathered at the sea gate. Hundreds of natives had converged from all around to witness the letter P for 'pirate' branded with red-hot irons on the foreheads of the accused before they were ignominiously dismissed from service. British justice, of which the natives had witnessed an unforgettable spectacle, had been seen to be both firm and merciful. The natives would know that they could turn to the Company for a fair hearing.

There was a knock on the door and Captain Perriman was announced. He was a tall, strapping seaman with numerous tattoos on his body which even his elaborate uniform was unable to conceal.

'Ah, Captain. Is everything in order?'

'Yes, Your Excellency. Both ships are ready to sail. The men are standing by.'

'Good. We sail for Mergui in the morning.'

'Aye, aye, sir,' replied the seaman with obvious relish. This would be a good time for reward and promotion.

It was mid-afternoon when the Shahbandar's official barge bearing Davenport came in sight of the sleek frigate. It was still some distance away. As he strained his eyes, the secretary noticed a launch heading in his direction. It must have left the frigate before his own boat had come into sight and was presumably on its way to shore.

The two boats converged slowly on each other, four sailors rowing the launch, and six men pulling the oars of the Shahbandar's barge. In the back of the launch a man was sitting stiffly upright in a typical officer's posture, staring in Davenport's direction.

Davenport doffed his well-worn hat, revealing the untidy mop of hair beneath.

'I bring you greetings from Lord White, harbour master of

293

Mergui. He presents his compliments and asks how he can be of service.'

'I am on my way to see Lord White now,' said the officer formally. He spoke with authority and Davenport saw that he was wearing the uniform of a lieutenant. His brass buttons gleamed and his whole bearing struck Davenport as being rather severe. 'I am Lieutenant Mason. And you are – sir?'

'Francis Davenport, secretary to Lord White. I think, Lieutenant, we had better return to see your Captain.' Davenport eyed Mason resolutely. White's orders had been clear. He was to ascertain what the ship's intentions were. If they were friendly, he was to invite the Captain ashore; if they were not, he was to hurry back and report the position. But apart from those instructions, Davenport had reasons of his own for wanting to see the Captain. He would decide on his best policy when he had met him.

After a brief moment of indecision, Mason ordered his men to turn round. Both boats headed back to the frigate. Before long Davenport could make out the name of the ship, the *Curtana*. As they approached, the larger boat bearing the secretary drew ahead and came alongside the frigate first. The Captain was standing by the bulwark, in his blue uniform, observing them expectantly.

'Welcome to the *Curtana*, sir,' he said with a friendly smile. 'Won't you come aboard?'

'Thank you, Captain,' replied Davenport.

As he climbed the boarding ladder, he could not help observing the double rows of gun ports along the ship's sides. There were enough cannon on this ship, he mused, to blow Mergui's makeshift defences to pieces. He would have to play his cards very carefully.

He bowed courteously to the Captain. 'Francis Davenport, at your service, sir.'

'Captain Weltden, at yours.'

'I have been sent by Lord White to enquire after the nature of your visit. The harbour master is not accustomed to receiving armed frigates on his shores, especially unannounced.'

'Perhaps you'd care to come down to my cabin, Mr Davenport? We'll be more comfortable there, I'm sure.'

Davenport followed him through the hatchway, and soon they

were in a small cabin which obviously doubled as a sitting room. On one side, below the porthole, was a well-polished mahogany table and to the other a couch which could be turned into a bunk whenever the Captain felt like a rest. Weltden offered Davenport a chair while he himself sat on the bunk.

'Now then, Mr Davenport, you were enquiring about the nature of my business. Very well. I will come straight to the point. I am here on behalf of the Crown of England. I have come to acquaint Lord White of the new proclamation of His Gracious Majesty King James II.'

'The new proclamation, Captain?' This was clearly a serious matter or the Company would not have sent an armed frigate to announce it.

'Yes, Mr Davenport. A royal edict requiring all Englishmen in the employ of foreign princes to resign their positions immediately and report back to the nearest British base, in this case Madras. I am here to oversee its prompt implementation.'

Davenport gaped at Weltden. The order presumably applied to him too. He recovered himself quickly, his mind made up.

'I myself was an employee of the Company, Captain, until circumstances forced me to take up a position as Lord White's secretary. I would be glad to explain myself more fully another time, but at this moment there are more pressing matters.'

'Indeed?'

'Yes, sir. I think you should know that Lord White has seized the *Sancta Cruz*. He is now awaiting her return from Acheem to sail for England with the proceeds of her trip. Lord White's own ship, the *Resolution*, is already equipped for a long journey.'

'The *Sancta Cruz*, did you say, Mr Davenport? That is a serious allegation indeed.'

'She is expected back any time now, Captain. In fact, she is overdue and Lord White is becoming increasingly anxious.'

'The timing of my arrival would seem to be opportune.' Weltden observed Davenport quizzically, wondering how far the man was to be trusted. After all, he seemed to have been in White's employ long enough. Was it perhaps the new proclamation that was causing him to reconsider his situation? He decided to say nothing of his sighting of the *Sancta Cruz* until he was surer of Davenport's motives. It seemed strange for a start that

295

he should be unaware of the *Sancta Cruz*'s return. Or did he have his own reasons for omitting to mention it?

'Tell me, Mr Davenport, how do you suppose Lord White will react to the news of the royal proclamation?'

'Sir, I believe Lord White is anxious to avoid a confrontation with the honourable Company, if at all possible. Especially as he plans to retire to England. But I must warn you that he is a desperate man with a violent temper who will stop at nothing.'

'But will he obey the proclamation?'

Davenport looked thoughtful. 'He might, sir, if it could be made to suit his retirement plans. But if he had an inkling that you might be here to arrest him, you can expect every form of resistance. He is in fact improving the town's defences at this very moment.'

'How strong are the town's fortifications?'

'There are half a dozen cannon on the hillside overlooking the Bay, Captain.'

'Does Mergui have a standing army?'

'Not as such, but Lord White could probably muster a substantial native force in short order with the help of a few bribes. He is still very much master of Mergui.'

'And what about naval power?'

'Three or four of his small sloops patrol the outer islands, but his men-of-war are out on missions just now.'

Weltden considered for a moment. The fortifications did not sound extensive though they were perhaps sufficient to deter one ship, especially if the privateers were sent to harass the *Curtana* from behind. When Governor Yale arrived with two more armed frigates, however, that would be different. Anyway, for the time being his instructions were to try to enlist White's co-operation, not to confront him.

'Mr Davenport, would I be right in thinking that your mission was to sound me out before deciding whether to invite me ashore?'

'That is correct, Captain.'

'Then I suggest we proceed there without further ado. I am anxious to meet Lord White.'

'Of course, Captain. I trust that my, er, revelations will remain strictly confidential.'

'Naturally, Mr Davenport. You may count on it.'

Thirty-five

The fat Portuguese priest turned down the sandy path that cut a narrow passage through the lush vegetation. Pushing aside banana trees and ferns and palm leaves that grew over his path he headed for the great beach. Almost every day now, at the same hour, for the past twenty-two years of his sojourn in Songhkla he had taken this same path at sunset to contemplate the vastness and beauty of God's creation. He had sat on the same old tree stump and watched the sky light up in a great crimson tapestry of ever-changing designs. Marvelling at the sight, he felt each time cleansed, ever grateful to the everlasting Father for his bounty. Every day, too, towards late afternoon, he would look up at the sky and place a little wager with himself. What kind of a sunset would it be today? Would it surpass the one of yesterday? Would there ever again be one to compare with the miracle of that November evening nine years ago when he thought the face of the Lord himself must appear through the clouds to speak to him, so wondrous was the beauty of the firmament.

He stopped suddenly short. Were those voices he had heard? This had never happened before. Had someone discovered his spiritual hideout? It was most unusual for the Siamese to linger on the beach. The wide stretch of sand led to deep murky waters where all the worst devils lurked, especially at this hour of day when the monsters would come out to play. He stepped forward a couple of paces and strained to catch the words. It was certainly not Siamese they were speaking. He knew the local language intimately. Neither was it Portuguese. He removed his sandals and crept silently forward along the sandy path. Though he was not more than a dozen steps from the beach, the thick foliage screened him completely from the strangers. He stopped, well within earshot now. Of course, it was French! The men must be part of the newly arrived contingent of soldiers and traders who had come to disturb the serenity of his beloved Songhkla.

297

Involuntarily he clenched his chubby fists. First it was the Dutch with their blasphemous Protestant ways and now the imperious French – though at least they were Catholic. How his soul yearned for his country's glorious past when Portugal was the unchallenged queen of Asia, her caravels holding sway from the coast of Hindustan to the Japans. Why, even the devil Spanish had been restricted to their little enclave in the Philippines, unable to vie with the might of the empire that was Portugal.

The men were laughing now. The priest had a limited knowledge of French from his days at the seminary in Ayudhya where the Jesuits from France were numerous, but at least he could understand a great deal more than he could speak. He heard them laughing again and curiosity got the better of him. He listened carefully.

'What happened after that, Jacques?'

'Well, then Dumas said: "Anything's better than returning to France with that old sourpuss. Even going to Mergui to fight the Siamese!"' There was general laughter.

'Do you know what my friend Chambert told me?' said another. 'He said the only reason we French are invading Mergui is because la Loubère couldn't persuade a single man to return to France with him!' Again laughter. The priest was listening attentively now. 'The old boy had to do something with the surplus men, because only fifty of them were expected to disembark at Songhkla. So he packed the rest of them off to Mergui, all hundred of them!'

When the laughter had died down, another said, 'Do you think we'll have any trouble taking over Mergui?'

'I shouldn't think so. The Ambassador won't be there to give the wrong orders!' Again general laughter.

'It should be a certainty,' said a voice. 'The Siamese will be taken completely by surprise. Just like we were when we were told of the change of route. Did any of you know the boys wouldn't be returning to France?'

'No,' replied one. 'I don't think anyone knew. The brass certainly kept it a secret. Duvalier told me his boys were only informed after they had reached Songhkla. Some of the Songhkla contingent were given the chance to volunteer for Mergui.'

'I see you jumped at the opportunity, Murot.'

'Just as you did, Croissard.'

'But I hear the English are ensconced in Mergui,' said another. 'Those lobster faces could be a problem.'

'I doubt it. They're traders, not soldiers. What would they know about fighting?'

'The English learn to fight from birth. It's in their barbarian blood.'

'Your mother was English, wasn't she?'

'Go to hell, Gérard. At least I know who my mother was.'

'That's enough, you two. But what about Desfarges? Is he going to take over Ayudhya at the same time our boys seize Mergui?'

'I think that's the plan. It would make sense to seize both cities simultaneously.'

'That's not what I heard, Jacques. The word is that the old General quarrelled with the Ambassador, because he didn't think it was right to turn against Ayudhya like that.'

'Fancy the military advocating peace.'

'The old man was right though. We could spend the rest of our lives trying to hold our positions against hordes of restless natives. They seem pretty independent to me, these Siamese.'

'To tell you the truth, I like them. They've got a certain charm.'

'You mean the women, no doubt, Jean. You've never noticed anyone else.'

'Get lost, Gérard. You couldn't tell the difference.'

The priest waited a while longer, transfixed. Then seeing that the conversation was steering away from matters of politics he forgot about the sunset for the first time in twenty-two years and quietly retraced his steps.

If Siam were to become a colony of France, what would be the fate of his four thousand countrymen whose ancestors had laid claim to a stake in this land almost two hundred years ago? But more worrying still, what would happen to the priests and missionaries of Portugal who had laid down their lives in Siam for the greater glory of God? Would the French Catholics edge them out and take over their long-held positions?

The priest hurried along, his mind in a whirl. He had to reach the Barcalon. He had only met him once. But the great man spoke fluent Portuguese and had expressed great affection for his country at the time. And, more significantly still, when financial restrictions had forced the Bishop of Goa to reduce the flow of funds to all outlying missions, Lord Phaulkon had come to the rescue with a most generous donation to the Portuguese mission here. The grateful priest had vowed to repay him one day if such a thing were possible. And now the Almighty in His wisdom had presented him with just such an opportunity. He quickened his pace. If there were a boat readily available he could be in Ayudhya by the week's end.

Thirty-six

Captain Weltden followed Davenport up the hill to the Shahbandar's house. As he climbed the path he could not help
noticing the considerable activity taking place on the hillsides
behind the town. In the distance, long lines of bare-chested
coolies were carrying planks of timber up the hillside on their
heads, and builders were busily erecting barricades and gun
emplacements along the ridges.

Weltden had made contingency plans in the event of foul play.
Looking around him, he was glad he had. If he were not back by
sundown, Mason was to come ashore with a team of armed men.
And, in the worst instance, the *Curtana* was to sail into harbour
and threaten the town.

They reached the house where a guard ushered them through
a gate and across a spacious garden to the main entrance.
Weltden was left in an anteroom while Davenport excused
himself to inform his master of their arrival.

It was some time before Davenport reappeared and ushered
Weltden into the harbour master's office. The Captain blinked at
the sight of the berobed figure sitting at the desk, smiling
amiably. Above a flowing brocaded robe the debonair face
peered up from beneath a tall, conical hat. The hat had a ring of
gold round it.

'Captain Weltden, I believe,' said the figure rising. 'Welcome
to Mergui. Samuel White, harbour master, at your service, sir.'

Weltden bowed. 'I have heard a great deal about you, Lord
White,' he said, still staring fascinatedly at the Englishman's garb.

White turned and dismissed Davenport before addressing
Weltden again. 'I see you are wondering about my outfit,
Captain.' He smiled broadly. 'I am afraid my rank of office
entails considerable responsibilities in this province. You see, I
was out early this morning collecting His Majesty's taxes. On
such occasions it is expected of me to wear my official robes of
office.' He sighed resignedly, waving an arm through the air. 'It

is not easy being a mandarin of Siam. But tell me, to what do we owe the pleasure of this visit?'

'I am afraid, Lord White, that the tidings I bear may not be altogether pleasant, especially for an English mandarin of Siam.'

'I presume you are referring to the new proclamation. My secretary mentioned it to me.'

'Indeed, Lord White. I have come to present you with an edict from His Majesty James II, directing all his subjects in the service of foreign princes to resign their positions immediately. In the case of Siam, all such persons are required to return to Madras and report to the Governor there.' Weltden paused. 'That includes you, my lord, as well as Governor Burnaby and all the other English officers in the service of Siam.'

White was silent for a moment. Then he broke into a genial smile. 'You may be surprised to learn that the edict will come as a great relief to many of our countrymen here, Captain. You see, most of them are homesick and have already expressed to me a desire to return to their country, but they feared retaliation by the Siamese authorities to whom they feel indentured. With an official excuse to return, they will no longer have that concern, for no Siamese could expect them to refuse an order from their liege.' White's smile broadened. 'So it would seem, Captain, that contrary to your expectations, the tidings you bring are joyful. I personally am delighted by the news. I will of course need a couple of days to tidy up my affairs but I shall be ready to return to England and serve my King just as soon as it is feasible.'

Weltden contemplated him for a moment. 'I am afraid it will not be that easy, Lord White.'

White appeared surprised. 'Why is that?'

'There are certain matters outstanding, Lord White, particularly with reference to the past conduct of your men. A number of the captains in your service are wanted for a variety of crimes ranging from piracy to treason.' He looked severely at White. 'Not one of them would be allowed to return to England until they had first been investigated and cleared by Madras.'

White's surprise increased. 'Indeed, Captain? What acts are you referring to specifically?'

'There are as many accusations as there are witnesses, Lord White. The trials will be lengthy. I would not count on returning

302

to England in the near future, though of course that will be a matter in the end for the authorities to decide.'

'So the purpose of your visit, Captain, is to round up all the English in Mergui? Well then, I shall assist you, sir. Permit me to suggest that the local English residents will heed my call sooner than they would a stranger's.' He smiled amiably. 'I will round every one of them up for you.'

'That is most co-operative of you, Lord White,' said Weltden cautiously. 'But there is also the question of a large sum of compensation due for damages inflicted on various injured parties.'

'Indeed, Captain, of that I am painfully aware. Captain Coates has disgraced me by his behaviour. I was only recently called to Ayudhya as a witness in his trial. It seems that Coates lost his head and attacked everything in his path, from Golconda's coastal towns to Dutch factories to a flagship of the Demarcora brothers. Outrageous. The Malays have a word for such sudden madness: amok. The government of Siam is deeply embarrassed. Coates has been stripped of his rank and ordered to wear the cangue round his neck until his final sentence has been passed. He will almost certainly be condemned to death. As regards the compensation, Lord Phaulkon asked me to oversee its passage to Madras, which I had intended to do shortly, as soon as the trial is complete and the final costs confirmed. It should not be long now. In the meantime, the *New Jerusalem* has been restored to its rightful owner and any missing cargo made good.'

'Lord White, I appreciate your offer of assistance but I must tell you that there are many in Madras, not least the Governor himself, who believe that a captain is responsible for the behaviour of his men. As such, you will be called to account for the actions of Coates. In all fairness, I should warn you that there is likely to be a consensus against you in Madras. And given the gravity of the crimes, the sentence is likely to be severe.'

White's smile was thinner this time. 'I understand, Captain. Naturally I shall defend myself as best I can, but I do not expect to be entirely exonerated.'

Weltden remained wary, but despite himself he was not unimpressed. 'Finally, Lord White,' he said rising, 'I have been given two weeks to conclude my business here. That is to say, two weeks in which to round up all Englishmen, yourself included, in the service of Siam and to escort them back to Madras with me.'

'I think that should give me sufficient time. I shall put the matter in hand right away. But perhaps you will do me the honour of dining at my house this evening with some of your senior officers?'

Weltden bowed. 'Thank you, sir.'

White escorted him to the gate, where Davenport appeared as if from nowhere to accompany him out.

White returned to his office, closed the door and began pacing up and down the room furiously. For a brief moment he considered whether he should not just make a run for it. The *Resolution* was after all ready to sail, his treasure was on board, and he knew these waters well enough to elude the *Curtana* if she should give chase. Besides, his sloops would lend him a hand. But the futility of such a plan quickly stared him in the face. How could he ever retire peacefully to England if he were wanted as a criminal there? He would be condemned to wander abroad or seek asylum in some godforsaken land where he knew neither the language nor the people. No, there was nothing for it but to stay and face the music. Perhaps there was a chance that he could clear himself. Especially if he paid the full compensation to Yale and was careful to cover his tracks. There was in fact only one area in which he felt particularly vulnerable. If in the worst instance he had to account for his activities in an English court of law – either in Madras or in England at some future date – he felt plagued by his lack of written authorization from the Siamese government for his actions in the Bay. Not everything could be blamed on Coates. The thought continued to harass him until he suddenly stopped pacing and stood staring out of the window. In that instant he made a spontaneous decision. He went over to his desk and rang the bell.

Immediately a servant appeared. Davenport was obviously still absent.

'Send me the Captain of the Guard,' said White in Siamese. It was one of the well-worn phrases he was by now familiar with.

The servant bowed low and retreated reverently backwards. As soon as the door had closed behind him, White extracted a blank document from his drawer. It bore the official seal of the Shahbandar's office. Taking his time and pausing frequently with the quill between his teeth, he wrote himself an authorization in English on the lower half of the document, to the effect that all orders issued by him to His Majesty the King of Siam's men-of-war in the Bay were given on the express authority of the Council of Tenasserim under the direction of His Excellency the Barcalon in Ayudhya. He backdated the document, using English dates, to a time prior to Coates's first predatory attacks on the coast of India. He used the correct date for today, but not the correct month or year.

By the time the Captain of the Guard knocked respectfully on the door, the English half of the document was ready. The Eurasian officer, half Portuguese, half Siamese, bowed and then stood to attention awaiting orders. He looked pleased. A summons from his master usually meant some new assignment, for which his master always paid well, insuring the officer's steadfast loyalty.

'Ah, Rodriguez. I have a job for you. It's confidential, so I want you to handle it yourself.' The guard smiled and inclined his head. He was not a man of many words. He made up in loyalty what he lacked in intelligence.

'I want you to take this document to the three Moors on the Council of Five for their signature. I will see to Governor Burnaby's signature myself.'

Rodriguez took the proferred document, wondering what was so important about it. Then he saw that the Siamese translation was missing from the top half of the document. Most unusual. Especially when the Moors couldn't read English.

'You are to advise the mandarins that my usual translator has been taken ill and that I require these signatures urgently,' White went on. 'The document refers to a request by an English Company ship to enter Mergui's waters. I have ascertained that though the ship is armed, its intentions are not hostile and it would be both provocative and discourteous to refuse it entry. Ask the Moors to affix their seals to the bottom of the blank translation as well. It will be filled in just as soon as my translator has recovered.'

305

White saw Rodriguez' eyebrows arch. He had probably noticed the English date at the head of the document. White was counting on the fact that the English months and years would be meaningless to the Moors, who measured their dates by the Mohammedan or Buddhist calendars. At least the day of the month, which they might recognize, was correct. Rodriguez could draw his own conclusions.

'You shouldn't encounter any problems, but if you do, you are authorized to apply a little pressure. But no violence. I'll leave the details to you. Just bear in mind that I require the document urgently. You must go immediately. Try Lord Ali's house first.'

Rodriguez bowed and then appeared to recall something. 'I go quickly to my house first, Excellency.' His English was heavily accented. 'I just remember I have other letter to deliver Lord Ali.'

'Another letter? From whom?'

'From Lord Ivatt, Excellency. Mr Davenport give it me. He have no time to deliver himself. Your Excellency send him on mission.'

White froze. Thomas Ivatt? When was he here? What letter? Why had Ivatt not come to see him? He could hardly appear ignorant of Ivatt's visit in front of Rodriguez. It would make him look like a complete fool. And he could hardly ask to see the letter either. That would be going too far. Ivatt was a fellow mandarin, after all. Damn the little man's slippery guts.

White looked up at Rodriguez and smiled. 'Of course, I'd almost forgotten he was here, his visit was so brief. I didn't even have time to receive him. He got off all right, did he?'

'Yes, Excellency. One week already. Mr Davenport make all the arrangements. Like you say, Lord Ivatt, he in a big hurry.'

'All right, Rodriguez, you'd better be off now. And by the way, the document you are carrying should not be shown to anyone, no one at all. You will get a special reward for bringing back all three signatures.'

Rodriguez grinned. 'Thank you, Excellency.'

'And tell whoever's on duty that I want to see Mr Davenport as soon as he returns.'

Rodriguez bowed and left. White waited a couple of minutes. Then he rose from behind his desk and began systematically breaking every item in his line of vision. Only the silver betel box

306

presented to him by His Majesty the King was spared. Then, partially assuaged, he sat down again. There was nothing he could do about Ivatt, but he would see Davenport rot in hell – or at least the next best thing, Tenasserim jail. Yes, that was the place for the double-dealing wretch, until he decided how best to dispose of him for good. White turned his mind to planning the special welcome he intended to give Captain Weltden and his officers that evening.

Some fifty leagues upriver from Tenasserim, Thomas Ivatt watched as his rowers leaped skilfully over the side of the boat to guide it safely round the rocks in the shallow, swirling waters. Soon they would reach the end of the navigable part of the river where the rapids took over, and he would have to transfer onto elephant back to negotiate the overgrown paths that wound tortuously through the dense jungle and across the narrow isthmus to the Gulf of Siam. If there were no unforeseen hazards, in another two or three days he would be in Ayudhya. He had to reach Phaulkon as quickly as possible to warn him of White's seizure of the *Sancta Cruz* and his plans for departure, not to mention Yale's moves to enforce the edict from King James and his own undertaking to see White arrested.

He had determined to pass through Mergui quickly and discreetly, without even arranging a meeting with Davenport. Had he attempted to see him, Sam White might have been alerted to his presence in the port, and Ivatt wanted to avoid that. He was, after all, on his way to Ayudhya to obtain a warrant for White's arrest. In the event, he had run into Davenport by chance on the harbour front. And what a stroke of luck that was, given the news the secretary had had to impart.

Ivatt had not been so fortunate with the note he had scribbled to the Moors on the Council of Five. He was just handing it to Davenport when Rodriguez appeared on the scene. He kept glancing suspiciously at the letter until Ivatt was forced to reveal to whom it was addressed. Years in White's employ seemed to have made Rodriguez wary of his own shadow. His suspicions were well justified this time though, for the letter contained a request to the Moors to send an independent assessment of events in Mergui directly to Ayudhya instead of through the

307

normal channels. The normal channels were of course Sam White, who habitually ensured that the contents of all reports were harmless, or else destroyed. Ivatt had decided that he had better gather as much information for Phaulkon as he could. Davenport tried to allay Rodriguez' suspicions by asserting that Lord Ivatt had written the short note to apologize for not having sufficient time to see them on his way through Mergui. When he then handed the note to Rodriguez asking him to deliver it himself, the Captain of the Guard had seemed satisfied that the letter must indeed be innocuous. Ivatt could only hope that it would not occur to Rodriguez to mention his presence to White.

Dusk was falling fast now, and the tall rain trees on either side of the river bank seemed to be closing in on him. A few energetic monkeys clambered along the notched boughs that overhung the river to get a closer look at the intruders and to add their chorus of screams to the growing orchestra of the night.

It had been an exhausting journey. The perilous crossing of the Bay had been the worst he had ever undertaken. Ivatt would not soon forget the gigantic waves that had flung themselves furiously at his ship. For three terrifying days, sick from the heaving and tossing, they had been pounded mercilessly, unable to do anything but pray and hold on for dear life. But the sturdy vessel, whose hull had been heavily reinforced for the elephant trade, came through the storm intact, and at last they had sighted the tranquil haven of Mergui's archipelago after only twenty-three days.

He wondered how the *Curtana* had fared in those waters. Since she had left Madras only a day or two before him, she must have encountered the same violent storm. He had scanned the horizon repeatedly as soon as they had reached calmer waters, but he had not spotted her anywhere. Perhaps she had foundered. More likely she had taken shelter somewhere in the Andamans. Any delay to her mission would be only too welcome; it would give Phaulkon more time to prepare a strategy for Mergui.

A shout from the boatmen made Ivatt look up. They had spotted a safe place to moor. He declined any food – he was too tired to eat – and lay down in the boat. Here in the primeval forest, abounding in tigers and rhinoceros, it was too dangerous to camp ashore. They would sleep in midstream in the safety of the boats, attached to rocks by ropes. Only later, where the jungle paths began, would there be clearings for the elephants and humans to rest ashore at night. Ivatt covered himself in a cotton blanket to keep the mosquitoes at bay and was instantly asleep.

Thirty-seven

Phaulkon was exultant. He had just returned home from a lengthy audience with His Majesty and for the first time he had heard no wheezing from the upper balcony. There was no question now that the royal health had taken a marked turn for the better. His Majesty himself was in high spirits, joking as before, gently teasing Phaulkon and generally taking a livelier interest in everything around him. Father de Bèze was indeed worthy of his medical reputation. The Jesuit had warned him, though, not to expect a permanent cure. This was only a temporary alleviation of the patient's suffering.

Phaulkon was nonetheless delighted, and very relieved, by the progress, both for personal and political reasons; for it had distressed him to hear the suffering in the voice of the man he admired and respected, and for whom he had a deep affection. And now the increasing rumours about the Lord of Life's wellbeing could be quelled. His Majesty had agreed to receive all the mandarins of the first grade in audience the following morning. They would see for themselves the miraculous transformation of their liege. And Phaulkon would make sure that the news spread far and wide, aware of the effect it would have on the superstitious Siamese. Most would consider it no less than divine intervention. Obviously the gods did not see fit to allow the great King's soul to pass on while the question of the succession was unresolved and while a farang army still lingered on Siamese soil.

Phaulkon smiled. The Jesuits' single-minded and inflexible approach to matters of the spirit clearly did not preclude a profound and wide-ranging knowledge of the body. He had rewarded Father de Bèze with a lavish contribution towards his pet project: a school to prepare young Siamese for the medical profession, with scholarships to France for the most deserving students.

Not least among the causes of Phaulkon's elation was the

knowledge that the priest's success would do much to improve the standing of the French in the community. Father de Bèze's name would be on everybody's lips, and it might even be construed that the gods had actually brought the French here with a purpose. The past behaviour of their troops would soon fade from memory; the worst elements had anyway departed, and with any luck the remainder, under the pro-Siamese Desfarges, would share their duties with their Siamese counterparts at the fort in Bangkok in a new spirit of co-operation.

General Petraja and his cronies would have to bide their time now. As it was, Petraja was keeping a low profile and Phaulkon's spies had reported nothing new in the secret meetings of their council. Nothing new in Ayudhya at least. Mergui was another question. There were some renegades there, he knew, working against the government's interests, notably one Selim Yussuf, a disgruntled son of one of the executed leaders of the Macassar uprising. And as for Sam White, who knew what that rogue might be up to? Phaulkon was anxiously awaiting news on that front from Ivatt. He should be back soon.

Phaulkon could not leave Louvo yet, not until His Majesty had once more resumed his daily audiences with his mandarins and it could be seen that the reins of government were firmly back in royal hands. In the meantime, at least there was Sunida to relieve his anxieties and nurse his restlessness.

She would be expecting him about now. He could already feel her exquisite touch on his knee, the tips of her fluttering fingers climbing slowly higher, and he felt a surge of desire. Then he thought of his darling Supinda giggling happily at the sight of her father, and his heart filled with pleasure. He was just rising to his feet when he heard Bashpool's discreet cough in the doorway.

'Forgive me for disturbing Your Excellency, but there is a priest here to see you. He refuses to go away until you have received him. He says the matter is most urgent.'

'Who is he?'

'He says his name is Father Coelho, Your Excellency. He has just come from Songhkla, and claims to have met you before. He's a chubby Portuguese, with thick black hair.'

Phaulkon could picture him already. He never forgot a name, especially when it belonged to somebody he had helped out in the past. He clearly remembered the look on the priest's round face when he had agreed to provide the means to rebuild the Portuguese church in Songhkla after a storm had all but razed it to the ground.

'All right, Bashpool, send him in.'

'As you command, Your Excellency.'

Captain Weltden, accompanied by only Andrew Mason, the first lieutenant, arrived at White's residence at sundown on the evening of their first day in Mergui. The two men were ushered on to a broad terrace. It was a beautiful evening and the view of the setting sun across the Bay was breathtaking.

In a moment White appeared and greeted them cordially, offering them a glass of arak, a powerful local alcohol made from the fermented husk of the coconut. Weltden accepted but Mason, despite repeated attempts to persuade him, declined.

'Tell me, Lord White,' said Weltden, 'is your secretary, Mr Davenport, joining us this evening?'

White smiled pleasantly. 'I am afraid I had to send him on an urgent mission to Tenasserim where a small riot has broken out between, would you believe, two groups of feuding noodle vendors.' He laughed genially. 'My duties as harbour master are never dull, I can assure you, gentlemen.'

In the next instant there was the sound of a bugle and a bevy of servants flocked onto the terrace and fell prostrate on the floor, forming a human alleyway to the door. Moments later a lanky, stooping figure shuffled in. The solemnity of his look was accentuated by the sallowness of his skin and his tall stature only added to his appearance of emaciation. There were deep pouches under his eyes, and the few strands of white hair remaining on his head were carefully combed to cover the maximum area. Yet despite his deteriorating physique, there was still an air of authority about him.

Governor Burnaby smiled courteously as he was introduced to the two naval officers. He had been thoroughly briefed by White that afternoon, and one of White's servants had discreetly ensured that Burnaby arrived sober, his mind not unduly dulled by either alcohol or opium.

Now that the Governor had arrived, a gong was sounded for

dinner. A sumptuous banquet awaited them, all the more lavish as it had been prepared for double the number of guests. An excellent French wine, recently appropriated from a merchant-man in the Bay, accompanied the meal.

Governor Burnaby was seated at the head of the table and was at his most charming, relating stories of his earlier days in the Company when he had first arrived to open the Siam office. He recounted the story of how the young Phaulkon, who had been his number two then and a remarkable linguist, had learned Siamese in a matter of weeks, applying himself to the task for hours at a stretch. He had engaged the services of three ladies of somewhat dubious repute to be his teachers, finding it, as he put it, a most 'pleasurable way of learning'. When he thought he was reasonably fluent he went out proudly to test his skills on the local population, only to find that those he addressed either laughed at him or turned politely away to conceal their mirth. Eventually a kindly market vendor brought round a transvestite to see him. It was then that he discovered that the personal pronoun varied according to the gender of the speaker. The word for 'I' entirely differed according to whether a man or a woman was speaking. Phaulkon, having copied the speech of his 'teachers', had only learned to use the female 'I'.

Weltden burst out laughing and they all had a jolly moment at the expense of the Chief Minister of Siam. Even Mason emitted a restrained guffaw.

The dinner proceeded with increasing hilarity and Mason took to observing his Captain with increasing concern. The guests offered glowing compliments on the quality of the guinea fowl which arrived with its plumage intact, colourfully displayed around the edges of large silver platters. Every now and then White cast a cautionary glance at Burnaby to ensure that he kept within the limits of sobriety.

As the servants began distributing the brandy, Weltden decided that the moment was ripe to approach his host on a subject that had been uppermost on his mind. The Captain had not been blind to the bustle of activity in the port. He had seen hundreds of natives milling around, transporting building materials from one place to another, and he had noticed a suspicious number of small boats, a type of canoe, mustering at the mouth of the river. He had felt uncomfortable at the rapid fortification of the town and decided to question his host on the matter. Yet despite his suspicions, he had to admit that Sam White, whatever the authorities at Madras might think of him, had shown himself to be a reasonable man so far – and certainly a fine host.

'Lord White, it could hardly have escaped our notice that the town is strengthening its fortifications at an extraordinary speed. May I enquire the reason why?'

White had been expecting the question. 'Rumours have spread that you have come to blow our little town to pieces,' he answered amiably. Mason was suddenly very attentive. White continued: 'But I am counting on the fact that when the people see that you and I are on friendly terms, the panic and rumours will subside. I hope, in fact, that you will do me the honour of dining with me every night for that very purpose, apart of course from the pleasure I derive from your company. But rumours aside, the garrisoning of the town and the strengthening of its defences were ordered by His Majesty long before your arrival. The appearance of your armed frigate has merely added an element of urgency to the process. Once these rumours start it is difficult to quell them, though I can assure you that no harm will come to you or any of your men while you are seen to be on good terms with me. So have no fear, Captain. Let us drink to a most enjoyable stay.' White raised his glass and his guests followed suit.

By the time the Burmese women arrived, the company, with the exception of Mason, was most receptive to their charms. Entering demurely at first and inclining themselves respectfully in the Oriental fashion, the women were soon swept literally off their feet into the laps of the enthusiastic carousers. Mason cast a look of disapproval at his commanding officer, but Weltden took little notice and the noise of laughter and revelry was heard far into the night.

Captain Rodriguez ran a hand through his thick, cropped hair as he knocked on the door of Hassan Yussuf's house on the outskirts of Mergui. It was not the first time he had been to the homes of the three Moors on the Council of Five. Neither was it the first time he had requested their signatures on his master's behalf. Such requests, invariably referring to the routine dispatch of a ship across the Bay, were not unusual. But the lack of a Siamese translation on the upper half of the document was. Nevertheless, he had obtained the first two signatures, though Lord Tariq had shown some reluctance initially. He had had to stress the urgency of the matter twice, and even add a warning of his master's considerable displeasure before Tariq had agreed to comply. And now there was only one signature left.

A servant came to the gate and appeared to recognize the Captain of the Guard.

'I have come to see Lord Yussuf.'

'My master is out, honourable Captain,' said the servant with a trace of nervousness. 'Would you like to leave a message?'

'No, I will wait for him here. The matter is urgent.'

'Er, my master said he would be absent for some time, honourable Captain.'

'Then perhaps you had better show me to the waiting room.'

The servant hesitated. 'Would it not be better to come back in a few days, honourable Captain?'

'In a few days? I told you, the matter is urgent. I require a signature. I will wait here.' How could he be absent for days, wondered Rodriguez, when his duties were here in Mergui? Who did this servant think he was fooling?

The servant, scratching his head in confusion, led the way across a courtyard into the house. Like all Siamese houses, it was built on stilts and the waiting room was an open terrace at the top of the wooden steps that led up to the first elevation. Rodriguez squatted down on the floor of the verandah and prepared to wait. The servant disappeared and returned with some cold tea.

Rodriguez could hear voices inside the house and he strained to catch the words. But they were too faint. He had the impression that they were being kept deliberately low, and his suspicions were aroused. He should have asked the servant where Hassan Yussuf had supposedly gone for so long. The man had looked shifty enough when he had mentioned the nature of his errand. If Hassan did not appear shortly he would summon the servant and interrogate him more fully.

315

He did not have to wait long. A man soon appeared. His face seemed familiar enough, but it wasn't Hassan, surely. Hassan had never been as thin as this, not since he'd known him, anyway. The man squatted down in front of Rodriguez.

'You wanted to see me?' he asked in Siamese.

'Lord Hassan?' said the guard hesitantly.

'Were you expecting somebody else?'

'Your servant said you were out.'

The man stared at Rodriguez. 'I told him to say that to any visitors. As you can see I am not well. I haven't eaten for days. What can I do for you?'

Rodriguez eyed him suspiciously. 'You certainly have lost a lot of weight, my lord.' The man's thin moustache twitched. Rodriguez did not remember it doing that before. Perhaps he really was ill. 'I'm sorry to disturb you. I was going to await your return. It's just a routine matter. His Excellency the Shahbandar requires your signature on a document. The other members of the Council have already signed.'

'What document?'

Rodriguez produced it from under his red tunic and handed it to him.

The man examined it briefly. 'Where is the Siamese version? I can't read this.'

'The translator has unfortunately been taken ill. His Excellency asked me to tell you that as the matter is urgent he would appreciate your immediate signature. The Siamese will be filled in as soon as the translator is well again.'

'Surely there are other translators?'

'Not official ones. Although this document is routine, it is still official. I explained that to the other members of the Council. They understood. Please add your signature now.'

'What does the document say?'

'It refers to an English Company ship which is requesting permission to enter Mergui waters.'

'What is the name of the ship?'

'I don't know.'

'Why is it urgent?'

Rodriguez was getting annoyed. Lord Hassan was not usually

as aggressive as this. He looked at him closely. Or as thin. Was it really the same man?

'My lord, His Excellency the Shahbandar does not want to offend the English Company by keeping one of its vessels waiting. His Excellency feels it is in the best interests of Siam to oblige them promptly. You have his assurance that the translation will be filled in later.'

'This is highly irregular. You'll have to leave the document with me. You can come back for it tomorrow.'

Rodriguez could barely restrain his indignation. 'Tomorrow will be too late,' he burst out.

'I'm sorry to hear that, but I must do what I consider my duty.'

'Your duty is to your country, Lord Yussuf, and you are failing in it.'

'How dare you speak to me like that. I shall report your impudence to the Shahbandar. Now leave my house instantly.'

The burly Eurasian rose to his feet, towering above the Moor. He wanted to swat him like a fly but a cautioning voice kept telling him he would not obtain any signature that way. He also recalled how his master had admonished him to use persuasion but not force.

'Lord Hassan, let us not argue over so small a matter. His Excellency is asking you for a favour for which you will be duly rewarded. You know his generosity in such matters. I'm sure you will not regret it. As you see, the others have all signed.'

'That is their privilege, just as it is mine to decline. I have already told you that if you leave the document with me you can collect it tomorrow.'

'With your signature?'

'Most probably.'

'Then why not sign it now? What's the difference?'

'The difference is that I would like to know the contents first.'

'Are you then doubting the Shahbandar's word?'

'I am not doubting anybody's word. I just like to do things the right way.'

'The Shahbandar does not look favourably on people who thwart him. I would not like to be in your shoes.'

'You would hardly fit in them,' came the retort.

Rodriguez' fists curled into a ball. He felt an uncontrollable

317

fury rising in him. He spun on his heels and stormed out before he did any irreparable damage.

Selim watched him go, wondering about the contents of the document.

Thirty-eight

'Good morning, General. I trust you had a pleasant journey.'

Desfarges felt a flutter of unease as he stood before Phaulkon in the entrance to his audience hall at Louvo. The engaging smile was notably absent and there was something cold, almost hostile, in the chief minister's ritual greeting. The peremptory manner of his summons did not help to dispel his disquietude either. It was no ordinary messenger, but Phaulkon's secretary who had come to fetch him at Bangkok. He had been told to pack his belongings and prepare for a prolonged absence. The secretary had offered no explanation and in answer to Desfarges' repeated enquiries had merely shrugged his shoulders.

'The journey was fine, my lord, though the departure a little rushed,' said the General, attempting a smile.

'And you brought some changes of clothing with you?'

'Yes, my lord, as your secretary instructed.'

'Good.' Phaulkon stared at him, his expression unyielding. Then, unexpectedly, the flicker of a smile entered his eyes, as if they were mocking the Frenchman's obvious discomfort. He waved a hand towards some cushions. 'Won't you sit down?'

As Desfarges sank heavily into the cushions, Phaulkon walked away from him to the marble mantelpiece at the end of the room. He stopped, his back to his visitor. Desfarges waited in silence, listening to the beat of his heart.

Suddenly Phaulkon swung round. 'Do you realize I could have you imprisoned? Or even executed?'

The General went pale. Imprisonment? Execution? Whatever was this all about? Surely Phaulkon could not know? No, it was impossible. The French had left for Songhkla less than two weeks ago. They would have to sail down the entire east coast of the Malay peninsula before rounding the Cape of Singapura and turning north again up the west coast. And even then it was still some distance to Mergui. They couldn't possibly complete the journey in less than four or five weeks even if the winds were constantly favourable. Besides, once they had arrived it would take a further ten days for news of their arrival to reach Phaulkon in Ayudhya.

'I, er, I don't understand, Your Excellency,' said Desfarges fearfully.

'Don't understand what, General? How I could possibly know? Well I do.' Phaulkon eyed him unflinchingly, willing him to respond.

Desfarges was perspiring openly now. He had never underestimated Phaulkon but this was too much. How was it possible that the man could know? Even if the *Gaillard* had been sighted, there would be nothing odd about that. The way back to France was round the Cape of Singapura anyway.

'My lord, we have known each other for some time now,' pleaded the General, 'and I, er, venture to say that we are, er, that there exists a certain friendship and trust between us. In the name of that friendship, I beg you to tell me what the matter is.'

Phaulkon frowned. 'My trust, and my patience, are fading fast, General.'

Desfarges' mind was spinning. What if he were to come clean with Phaulkon? His conscience felt strangely eased at the thought of it. If Phaulkon knew the worst already, though heaven only knew how that could be possible, he might still be able to save himself. While if Phaulkon did not know, he would be aborting a plan he was at odds with anyway. The more Desfarges thought about it, the more he found merit in confessing.

He forced the words out. 'The *Gaillard* is headed for Mergui, my lord.'

Phaulkon glared at him. 'Go on.'

'Ambassador de la Loubère was dissatisfied with the extent of French progress in Siam. He ordered me, er, to resort to military force. I was against doing so. He then threatened me with a court martial in France. I still would not agree. Finally he and Cébéret overruled me and Commodore de Vaudricourt was ordered to take Mergui.'

'Why did you not tell me this if you were so opposed to the plan?'

'I was, er, well, I actually thought of doing so on a number of occasions, my lord, but . . .' Desfarges appeared lost for words.

'But?'

'But I was unsure. It is not easy to turn on one's fellow countrymen.'

'It was easier to allow the Siamese in Mergui to be slaughtered, was it?'

Desfarges had no answer.

'Tell me, General, what was to be your role in all of this?'

Desfarges hesitated and then made his decision. Having got this far, he had best come out with it all. 'I was expected to turn on Ayudhya. But I assure you, Your Excellency, I would not have complied.'

'You would have me believe that if the French had taken Mergui, you would have refused to carry out your side of the plan?'

'I was against it from the start.'

'I know that, General. You were the one who advocated peace.'

Desfarges' jaw dropped. 'You knew that?'

'There is nothing you have told me, General, that I did not already know.' The Portuguese priest had been very thorough. 'But what you do not know is that Mergui has since been heavily fortified and garrisoned. One French ship, however well-equipped, will never take it. Your men will be massacred, General.'

The General blanched. 'What if I were to go to Mergui, my lord, and rescind the order?'

Phaulkon looked puzzled. 'I thought the order came from the Ambassador and that you had been overridden, General?'

'If I warned them of the strength of your garrisons in person, they would take notice. They would know the matter was serious.'

Phaulkon shook his head. 'I will be the one to go to Mergui, General. You will be going to prison instead.'

The blood drained from Desfarges' face. 'To . . . to prison, my lord?'

Phaulkon ignored the question, his mind elsewhere. 'Unless . . .' he began. Then his voice trailed off, as if he had thought better of the matter.

'Unless what, Your Excellency?' prodded Desfarges in growing desperation.

Once again Phaulkon ignored the question. 'Does Lieutenant Dularic know of the French plans for Mergui?' he asked.

Desfarges considered for a moment. Dularic had not left his post at the King's palace in Louvo for some weeks now. He had certainly not been to Bangkok recently, and la Loubère had not visited Louvo before his departure. It was unlikely that the two of them had communicated.

'He is not senior enough to have been told of the plan, Your Excellency. It was a closely guarded secret. La Loubère wanted to ensure complete surprise. Even the men were not to be told until they reached Songhkla.'

'I will tell you, General, how you can prove your good faith.'

Desfarges appeared anxious. 'How is that, Your Excellency?'

Phaulkon eyed him steadily. 'You will order Dularic and his cannoneers to accompany me to Mergui. It will be more fitting that the order should come from you.'

Desfarges began to perspire more profusely than ever. Surely Phaulkon was not seriously considering asking Dularic to fire on his own men?

Phaulkon seemed to read his mind. 'As soon as the cannon are properly installed on the hillsides above Mergui, Dularic can return with his men to Louvo. He need not fire a single shot. There will be time enough to achieve all this before the *Gaillard* arrives. It is not that Mergui does not have adequate defences to deal with one ship, you understand, but trouble is brewing there from another quarter as well. I want the town to be impregnable from the attack of an entire fleet.'

Desfarges seemed lost in thought. 'But couldn't I just order Dularic to hand over the cannon to you here? Why would he and his men have to go to Mergui with them?'

'Because the cannon will have to be transported overland, which will entail hauling them over difficult jungle terrain. It is bound to cause damage. I want them in perfect working order when they reach Mergui, and I do not trust our local engineers to effect the necessary repairs. After all, we are talking about the most sophisticated weaponry from France. You have my assurances that Dularic and his men will be allowed to return here as

322

soon as their task is completed. I have enough men of my own who know how to fire cannon.'

Phaulkon observed Desfarges' torment. 'Unless you find the idea of a local prison more appealing, General, I suggest you waste no time in informing Lieutenant Dularic that I have received secret intelligence from Mergui that the English are planning an attack and that we need his men and artillery there urgently.'

Desfarges was silent for a long moment. 'I will do as you ask, Your Excellency,' he said finally.

Thirty-nine

Anthony Weltden stretched his arms in a luxurious yawn as he strolled up and down the deck of the *Curtana*. He was enjoying himself immensely. What a congenial fellow Sam White was turning out to be. Like most rumours, the ones surrounding him appeared to be grossly exaggerated. For the last three nights Weltden had not returned to his ship but stayed over at White's house. He found the company of the pliant Burmese women very agreeable. The tall one, rather buxom for an Oriental, gave him particular pleasure. She would first undress him, and then, lying him down on the bed, she would produce a bottle of coconut oil and rub it gently into his skin. Her skilful hands moving over his body alternately aroused and relaxed him. Standing over him, her breasts unashamedly naked, with only a colourful sarong tied neatly round her waist, she was the picture of feminine grace. Whenever he smiled, she smiled broadly back, and when she saw that he was roused to a point that was no longer comfortable for him, she unwound her sarong and climbed slowly on top of him. How wonderful to combine business with pleasure in this way, he mused.

Two days ago he had obtained both White and Burnaby's signature in acceptance of the proclamation. They had signed it willingly, without the least objection; White had jokingly remarked that he could hardly counsel his flock to sign if the pastor himself were not willing. He was clearly sparing no effort to round up the various Englishmen and make them sign the proclamation – Weltden had seen it with his own eyes – but they were such an eclectic lot that he suspected, despite White's protestations to the contrary, that the harbour master was not having as easy a time of it as he had intimated. Weltden had repeated his offer of help but White had declined, assuring him that he could handle the matter himself.

Soon he would approach White on the delicate question of delivering Mergui over to the English. Yale had allowed him two

324

weeks to conclude his business; with only five days gone, things were moving along nicely, though certain of his officers, led by Mason, felt that White was absolutely not to be trusted. They had presented a whole series of arguments, pointing out that apart from the general fortifications, the natives were inserting tall stakes across the mouth of the Tenasserim River to block its entrance. Another of the officers reported seeing a group of natives gathering up empty glass bottles and filling them with gunpowder. When lit, these could be hurled at a target with deadly effect. The ship's steward had reported finding it increasingly difficult to purchase provisions for the *Curtana* because the natives were herding their cattle and other livestock out of town.

Weltden listened to them attentively, but he saw nothing sinister in what he considered were normal defensive measures. After all, news must have spread that an armed frigate from a foreign power had arrived. How were the natives to gauge whether its intentions were hostile or not? Sam White had made the point himself, and Weltden was inclined to believe his assertions that no harm would come to anyone who was seen to be on friendly terms with him.

This morning, as soon as he had returned from his three-day stint at White's house, Mason had come to his cabin to appeal to him privately.

'I do not wish to question your orders, sir,' Mason had begun, 'but the consensus of your officers is that Lord White is planning to attack us. I feel it my duty to bring their views, and mine, to your attention.'

'I know what your views are by now, Mason,' answered Weltden wearily. 'Have you something new to add?'

'Yes, I do, sir.'

'Well?'

'We would like to point out, sir, that while Lord White sent us his pilot boat yesterday to guide us over the bar into the harbour, his own ship, the *Resolution*, is still anchored in deep waters. We are the only ones lying in port, sir. Even the three Siamese privateers that returned here yesterday quickly departed again. We are all of the opinion, sir, that Lord White is assuring himself of the means for a quick getaway after his attack. We, on the

325

other hand, would be stuck here at the mercy of the flood tides, unable to pursue him.'

'What exactly are you suggesting, Mason?'

'I am suggesting, sir, that by inviting the *Curtana* alone into port, Lord White has made it look as if *we* are the ones preparing some act of aggression. We are heavily armed, and our guns are now within range of the town.'

Weltden reflected for a moment. 'What would you propose we do about it?'

'That we commandeer the *Resolution* and sail her over the bar to anchor next to us, so we can keep an eye on her and continue to display our brotherly relations with the harbour master at the same time.'

'Commandeering a friendly ship would hardly be a brotherly act, Mason. The co-operation which Lord White has thus far shown us does not call for such harsh action.' Neither would it endear the Company to White, reflected the Captain, when he came to broach the subject of handing over Mergui to him.

'Are our orders not to seize enemy shipping and hold it hostage until our terms have been met, sir?' For the first time there was an open note of impatience in Mason's tone.

'Yes, if we encounter resistance, which I fail to see is the case so far.'

'But, sir, can we not at least take some precautions? Just in case our suspicions are justified?'

Weltden sighed inwardly. He would have to make some small concession to get Mason off his back. 'I will not risk offending Lord White while he continues to show every co-operation, but I promise to bring up the subject of the *Resolution* when I next see him.'

Mason seethed inwardly. How could the Captain be so blind? Had the over-indulgence of his sexual appetites addled his brain? Mason decided to talk things over with the others. If they were in agreement, perhaps they might take matters into their own hands.

'Right then, Mason, that'll be all,' said Weltden, dismissing him.

*

Ivatt looked about him in bemusement at the frenzied activity of the royal dock at Louvo. Scores of war elephants were being harnessed, smartly dressed officers were shouting orders and dozens of soldiers and slaves were running about in every direction. Had war been declared? he wondered in alarm.

Even the guards at the entrance to Phaulkon's palace, who recognized him as he approached, would not let him pass without checking with their master first. It was several minutes before one of them returned at the double to ask Ivatt to follow him.

Phaulkon was in his study reeling off a string of orders to Bashpool. As soon as Ivatt was announced, however, he dismissed his secretary and rose from behind his desk. 'Come in, Thomas,' he cried. 'I was worried you wouldn't make it in time. I am so pleased.'

'What's going on here, Constant? Are you trying to impress me by looking busy?'

Phaulkon laughed. 'Events are catching up with me, Thomas. You'll need all your good humour about you when I tell you that you're just in time to turn round and head right back for Mergui.'

'Oh no,' groaned Ivatt. 'I must be the world's expert on that stretch of jungle by now.'

'That's why I'm going with you, Thomas. I want to be with the best.' Phaulkon's expression turned serious. 'There's trouble in Mergui. Serious trouble. We're leaving at dawn.'

'You already know?' Ivatt sounded genuinely amazed.

'About the French you mean? Yes. But I'll tell you the full story some other time. We'll have plenty of leisure on the trip.'

'The French? What do you mean?' asked Ivatt, his stomach suddenly hollow.

'The French are planning to invade Mergui, my friend. They're heading there by sea now, so we have to arrive first. I was just wondering how you could have known, actually. But tell me your news. We haven't much time, so make it brief. You can save the details for later.'

'Well, for one, Sam White hasn't taken his dressing down too seriously. He's up to his old monkey tricks with more verve than ever. He has seized the *Sancta Cruz*, swapped its crew for his own and sent them to Acheem to dispose of the original cargo.

327

The *Resolution* is ready to sail for England with him as soon as the *Sancta Cruz* returns with the spoils.'

'When is she expected back?' asked Phaulkon quickly.

'Any time now, according to Davenport, if she isn't there already. In the meantime, Yale has sent an armed frigate to Mergui to arrest every Englishman there. There is a new decree from King James commanding all his subjects to return to the fold immediately.' Seeing Phaulkon's frown he added pertly, 'I've applied for Greek nationality.'

Phaulkon grinned. 'Even the Ottoman Turks wouldn't have you. But when did Yale's frigate leave Madras?'

'The day before I did. Funnily enough, she wasn't in Mergui when I arrived. There was a fearful storm during the crossing, so who knows what might have happened to her?'

'Well, I'll be damned,' exclaimed Phaulkon. 'As if I didn't have enough problems in Mergui already.'

'But how are things here, Constant? And in Ayudhya?'

'That's a more cheerful tale, thank goodness. That Jesuit physician, Father de Bèze, is a genius. He has greatly relieved His Majesty's suffering. I took my leave of the King this morning. His health is so recovered that he has agreed to return to Ayudhya and resume the reins of government during my absence.'

'Can his health really take it?' enquired Ivatt, with concern.

'You wouldn't recognize him, Thomas. He's almost his old self again. I'm sure he'll be fine till I get back. In the meantime, the latest rumour is that General Petraja is retiring to a monastery in Louvo. I think it's only a temporary measure, but evidently he considers it prudent to enter the monkhood while His Majesty's new-found health puts a check on his plans. He'll either use the time to consolidate his friendship with the powerful Abbot and rally the influential clergy to his cause, or he is looking for an alibi while his cronies in the south hatch out their plans. My spies tell me that Selim Yussuf is chiefly involved, but the exact plan remains a secret. I shall have him arrested as soon as we reach Tenasserim. Apparently that is his base of operation.'

'How are we going to head off a French invasion though? You must have a lot of faith in the bamboo fortifications of Mergui, Constant.'

'I've made arrangements, oh ye of little faith.' Phaulkon smiled. 'The invaders will be facing their own artillery. Dularic is coming with me.'

Ivatt stared at his friend in disbelief. 'You mean to say you've managed to split the French forces? Whose side is Desfarges on then?'

'He's neutral. A genuinely torn man. At the moment he's back in Bangkok under surveillance. I don't expect any trouble from him though. I've convinced him of the need to maintain the status quo in the rest of the country, especially as his troops know nothing of the invasion of Mergui. And I've prevailed upon him to write an interesting letter, which I am taking with me.'

'I don't understand.'

'I'll explain everything on the journey, Thomas. I must leave for Ayudhya now. I want to say my farewells to Maria. I will be spending the night there. You must leave here at dawn and collect me on the way.'

'Shall I look after Sunida tonight then?'

'That won't be necessary,' replied Phaulkon with a grin, 'though I thank you for your concern, Thomas. I had enough trouble preventing her from coming to Mergui as it is. She'd probably twist you round her little finger. I couldn't risk it.'

'I could always distract her with other things.'

'I can't think which is worse. No, you'd better get a good night's sleep instead, Thomas. I have a feeling you're going to need all the strength you've got by the time we reach Mergui.'

'All right,' said Ivatt pouting. 'I'll have to deprive her of my charms yet again.'

Phaulkon left the room grinning.

Anthony Weltden's assessment of White's efforts to comply with the new proclamation were accurate. From the very first day he had learned of it, White had begun to make out a list of all the English residents in Mergui: merchants, sailors, officers and engineers. There were some sixty in all. He had met practically all of them at one time or another. He had considered the list carefully, poring over it, wondering which ones might be willing to sign the proclamation, and which ones were likely to oppose it. It had taken him longer than expected to gather any sizeable

329

group together. Some were absent and others had simply not responded, as if they suspected some trick on his part. Rumours, of course, were rife and heaven only knew what they might have heard.

Now, five days later, he was ready to give Weltden a good showing. The Captain had agreed to join him for dinner that evening, and White was anxious to surprise him. It was essential that he convince Weltden of his sincerity, that he lull him into lowering his guard, the more easily to give him the slip en route to Madras. For the idea of standing trial before Judge Yale had begun to appeal to White less and less, especially since that fool Rodriguez had failed to obtain the third signature – from Hassan of all people, the meekest sop of the lot. He would deal with that impudent renegade when, or if, time permitted.

White calculated that if he were to pay the compensation in full and his behaviour remained at all times exemplary, perhaps when he gave Weltden the slip there would not be such an outcry against him. And if he were then to keep a low profile in England, the matter might eventually be forgotten. But he was more than ever anxious to get himself, and Weltden, away from Mergui as soon as possible. His ever present fear that the inevitable inquiry into the whereabouts of the *Sancta Cruz* would entangle him was now compounded by Davenport's evident collusion with Ivatt. Thank God the *Sancta Cruz* – or at least its return – was one exploit Davenport had not been privy to. Nevertheless, he could have fed Ivatt a great deal of damaging information. He had of course denied being in Ivatt's pay, but White had no intention of waiting to find out the truth of his secretary's protestations of innocence. More immediately, though Jamieson and his crew were safely back on the *Resolution*, there was always a risk that one of them – with a drink too many under his belt – might let something slip to a member of the *Curtana*'s crew. White was beginning to feel like a juggler with too many balls in the air. Any one of them might hit him in the face at any moment.

By sundown that evening there had gathered together at White's house the motliest group of Englishmen – some half of all those summoned – ever seen in one place in Mergui. They hung around the large terrace and spilled out into the garden.

With the help of three of his clerks whom he had summoned to keep order, White read out the proclamation to them. He tried to set their minds at ease by telling them they had done no wrong and that they would only be breaking the law if they refused to sign their names on the lists provided. There was nothing to fear. The new King had decided for the good of his country that his subjects should cease to remain in the employ of foreign princes. The edict was not retrospective; they would be punished only if they failed to comply with the new regulations in future. Captain Weltden of the East India Company would be along shortly, he told them, to answer any questions they might have.

When the party from the *Curtana* arrived, Weltden was pleasantly surprised to find so large a gathering to accede to the proclamation.

The men eagerly clustered round him.

'Has war then been declared on Siam?' asked a bearded man anxiously.

'How soon do we have to leave for Madras?' asked another diffidently.

'We won't be put in jail there, will we?'

'Or in labour camps?'

'Why can't we return straight to England?'

'Who will pay our passage?'

Weltden lifted a hand for silence. 'You are all required to report to the Company's headquarters at Madras. I will be taking some of you back with me in the *Curtana*, while the rest will go with Lord White on board the *Resolution*. There will be no passage to pay for any of you. We will be leaving as soon as the rest of your compatriots have come to add their names to the proclamation. You must tell them that there will be no reprisals, that no one will be prosecuted. On the contrary, you will be warmly welcomed in Madras.'

There was a general murmur all round and then, slowly, the men began to form long lines. One by one they stepped forward to sign the proclamation, some putting their names, others, unable to write, marking a cross next to which a more literate companion would print their name.

Weltden continued to answer questions as the lines gradually diminished. He wore a distinct air of satisfaction. Thirty-six men

331

in all signed the proclamation. When the last of the signatories had departed, he handed the list to one of his officers – Mason had remained on the *Curtana* – and all then joined White on the terrace, gladly accepting the refreshment their genial host offered them. It promised to be another jolly evening, Weltden mused.

Forty

At about the same time as the Englishmen were gathering at White's house in Mergui, a huge procession left Ayudhya and headed inland to begin the strenuous crossing of the densely covered isthmus that separated the Gulf of Siam from the Bay of Bengal. A battalion of two hundred and fifty war elephants, each bearing two soldiers, one mahout and one slave, marched in single file along the narrow jungle paths, while Phaulkon's large escort of soldiers and slaves followed behind them. Phaulkon himself rode in the middle of the procession on a magnificent, richly caparisoned elephant, the tallest of the troop, in a howdah enclosed by four carved posts and covered with a gold awning to shield him from the sun. Behind him and his escort came Lieutenant Dularic and his twelve bombardiers. As many bull elephants, the strongest of the herd, hauled the reinforced carts that supported the latest French artillery. Despite the enormous weight, the great beasts looked like so many children pulling toys on a string. Their plodding, steady pace would barely slow the procession, not until the jungle paths had ceased anyway. Behind them, dozens of slaves carried Phaulkon's personal belongings as well as his favourite palanquin, in case he should feel like a change of rhythm during the journey. The baggage carts, filled with provisions, followed next, and five score guards brought up the rear.

At each settlement they passed, the local population fell to the ground, awed by the passage of so elevated a potentate. The chiefs of the villages offered their finest victuals and their most valued possessions to the illustrious Pra Klang, but Phaulkon's chief aides thanked them graciously and moved on. His Excellency was in a hurry to reach Mergui, the aides explained. Even the tigers and wild elephants seemed impressed by the pomp of the procession and refrained from attacking, restricting themselves to emitting intimidating growls and bellows as they prowled around the outskirts of the huge camps at night.

On the fourth day at sunrise, the men transferred onto a fleet of one hundred and fifty river canoes which had been commandeered by an advance party. Here the men and beasts parted ways: the men took the shorter and more manageable river route; the elephants and their mahouts continued overland via a treacherous and seldom used jungle track. Despite Phaulkon's warnings about the rigours of such a journey, Dularic and his men insisted that they, too, continue on elephant back to oversee the safe passage of the cannon. The plucky Dularic seemed almost elated at the thought of being perhaps the first European to have undertaken this particular crossing. It might take them two or three days longer to carve their way through the primeval forest, but eventually they would join up with the rest of the expedition in Tenasserim. That was the prearranged meeting point from which, in another week or so if all went well, the great Barcalon and his entourage would make their grand entrance into Mergui.

On the evening of the day after the signing of the proclamation, Captain Weltden went alone to White's house, in order to broach the question of Mergui's future with him in private. It was obviously going to take a few more days for the remainder of the Englishmen to be coaxed into adding their names to the proclamation, but White had shown sufficient signs of good faith. It was time now to ascertain exactly where he stood on the question of Mergui.

Weltden settled into a chair on the terrace and accepted a glass of arak from his host. He glanced across at the shimmering ocean. In a few moments there would be another gorgeous sunset.

'My dear Samuel,' said Weltden, 'I have a request to make of you.'

'By all means. You have only to ask.'

'My officers and I are worried that the presence of the *Curtana*, so close to shore, with her guns pointing at Mergui, could give rise to some misunderstanding among the natives. I notice, too, that your three sloops, only recently returned, have left port again. I would be grateful if, as a token of solidarity, you would order the *Resolution* to be moored alongside the *Curtana*. It would be an unmistakable display of our friendship, for all Mergui to see.'

Weltden thought he noticed a shadow flit across White's face but in the next instant it was gone.

'It will be a privilege for the *Resolution* to lie alongside the *Curtana*, Anthony. After all, we are sister ships now. Consider it done. I will attend to it as soon as I have a moment.'

'Thank you. I appreciate that. I must say you have been most co-operative throughout.' He surveyed White carefully. 'Which brings me to another point. I should tell you first that some of my officers have been expressing doubts as to your intentions. Needless to say, I have no such misgivings. In fact I have told them that I will prove your integrity once and for all.'

White appeared surprised to learn of the officer's suspicions. 'You may rest assured that I will do whatever you say to put their minds at ease. Such unfortunate misunderstandings must not be allowed to fester.'

Weltden waited till the servants had finished pouring another drink. Then he leaned forward confidentially.

'Samuel, I am going to ask something of you.' He paused while White eyed him amiably. 'In the name of His Majesty King James of England I request that you deliver Mergui into English hands.'

White's smile contracted and then faded altogether. 'I think you must explain yourself.'

'Of course. The East India Company is greatly concerned over the sudden rise of French ambitions in the area. It fears that Mergui may fall into French hands. While it is a Siamese enclave, there is no problem of course, but now that the rumours of a great French naval force have been confirmed, the outlook has changed. The Company thought that perhaps you, as an Englishman in a position of power here, might see the merits of . . . er . . . steering Mergui towards English rather than French hands.'

White raised a hand. 'You must realize, Anthony, that though I have willingly signed the royal proclamation, I am nevertheless indebted to my late employers. It would hardly be a gesture worthy of a gentleman – if I may call myself that – to turn and stab his former benefactors in the back. I can hardly deliver a port, entrusted to me in full confidence, into the hands of an

335

outside power. Even if that power is England.' He smiled. 'I would not want your officers' poor opinion of me to be vindicated.'

'I understand and respect your position, Samuel. But apart from the moral aspect, would there be any other considerations?'

White pondered the question. 'Well, there would obviously be some practical considerations.'

'Such as?'

'Well, for example, though I myself am now prepared to serve the interests of my own country once more, in the eyes of Siam I would be branded as a traitor if I were to undertake the actions you contemplate. There would be a price on my head, and I would have to consider what protection the Company was prepared to offer me. There is a big difference between obeying the new proclamation of my King and committing an act of treason against my former masters.' He paused. 'Under the circumstances, I would be most reluctant to spend any time in Madras. It is too close to Siam for comfort. I would only really feel secure in England.'

The prospects were not looking bad at all, Weltden thought with satisfaction. White's implied conditions were well within the bounds of his authority to grant. 'What if I were to give you my full assurance that all your conditions would be met?' he said.

'We can only speak hypothetically, Anthony, while the moral obstacles remain.'

Weltden eyed him steadily. 'Of course. Let us speak hypothetically. What if you were to turn a blind eye while I dealt with Mergui? I can see no obstacle to your sailing to England on the *Resolution*, with a safe conduct from the Company.'

'The moral premise would unfortunately remain unchanged.'

'Even if the safe conduct were to include absolute discretion as to the nature and contents of the *Resolution*'s cargo? And complete immunity from prosecution once in England?'

'A man would hardly want to turn against a country that had exonerated him from any crime to embrace another that would try him instead.'

'Quite so. As I said, complete immunity from prosecution.'

'And Madras?'

'There would be no need to stop in Madras.'

336

White checked himself. Was he showing too much enthusiasm too soon? He could not believe his luck. Unless perhaps Weltden was just testing him.

'I have no fear of an English court, you understand. I have more than enough evidence in my possession to show beyond doubt that Coates acted entirely on his own. But my conscience would not allow me simply to stand by while you sacked my beloved Mergui.'

'I would not need to sack it if you were to hand it over peacefully. I have seen the great respect the natives have for you, Samuel. If you were to explain the French threat to them and the fact that the English and Siamese are allies . . .'

White shook his head. 'I am afraid I don't – '

'Why don't you think it over,' put in Weltden quickly, 'before making a final decision?'

White hid his elation. 'Very well, I'll agree to think it over.'

'Splendid, perhaps we can discuss it again tomorrow. By the way, I meant to ask you. Is your secretary back yet?'

White was caught off guard. For a moment he could not exactly recall what he had told Weltden about him. 'You mean Davenport?'

Weltden looked at him oddly. 'Yes, your secretary. Didn't he go off to quell some riot somewhere?'

'Oh yes, Tenasserim. Er, he's not back yet. Did you need something?'

Weltden smiled. 'I was just going to enlist his support in persuading you to co-operate with us, that's all.'

White concealed his relief, pretending instead to be horrified. 'Oh, I wouldn't do that. He's so prim. He'd be terribly shocked. I can see I'm going to have to keep him well away from you when he returns.' He raised his glass. 'Let us drink to another beautiful sunset.' He stood up and turned towards the horizon where the last rays were throwing brilliant streaks of orange and vermilion across the evening sky. He looked out to sea, and his mouth opened wide. 'What the devil?'

Weltden walked over to him and followed his gaze. 'My God,' he said. 'It's not possible!'

'It is,' said White, turning brusquely on him. A look of deep suspicion had entered his eyes.

'Did, er, did you order your ship to be moved?' stammered Weltden, as the horrible truth began to dawn on him.

'Of course I didn't, Captain, how could I? You only just made the request yourself a few moments ago.'

'Do you think your crew might have moved her for some reason?'

'No,' White snapped. 'Apart from Coates, my men never disobey my orders.'

'I cannot understand what has happened. If you will excuse me, I will return to the *Curtana* immediately to make enquiries.'

'I will await your return then,' said White coldly.

Selim Yussuf was having trouble sleeping. His messenger had reported that the Shahbandar's ship, the *Resolution*, had been moved alongside the *Curtana*. He had sneaked out at dusk and observed the fact with his own eyes. This had to mean the attack would come soon. The two infidel collaborators would open fire on the town, while their farang brethren ashore assisted them in the betrayal. Everyone was aware of how the farangs had gone en masse to the Shahbandar's house to be briefed about the plan of attack.

Gone were the days when Selim and the others had believed the *Curtana* had come to chastize the renegade Shahbandar. Perhaps that had been the original intention but it had since become obvious that the two men had struck a deal. The rumour was rife that the farang King had ordered all his subjects home. No doubt that pig of a Shahbandar had agreed to assist in the takeover of Mergui in return for the Company's absolution for his piracy in the Bay. He had sold his soul to the devil.

Selim's stomach felt raw from worry and his nerves were on edge from lack of sleep. Every night for the last week he had slipped out under cover of darkness to sow the seeds of his plan. His men were almost ready now. They knew the exact location of every Englishman in Mergui and the usual time to find each of them home, and they had spread the word among the people. How he wished he could simply overwhelm them now, instead of having to wait for the farang ships to fire the first shot. But the fate of the leaders of the Macassar rebellion held him back; he knew he could not afford to be labelled as the aggressor. When

338

the authorities in Ayudhya initiated a full inquiry, as they were bound to, into the events that were soon to take place, he would have to be able to show that the town had acted in self-defence. The Shahbandar was after all still the legal authority in Mergui, the official appointee of His Majesty. Only when he had actually fired on the town could an uprising of the natives against their farang oppressors be justified. In the meantime, there was nothing to prevent their getting ready.

Selim cringed as he thought of how much damage the first volley from those monstrous weapons on the ships might cause, before his men could retaliate. However well prepared they were, there was bound to be a lapse of time between the first volley and the response, crucial moments before they had completed their task and were ready to retreat into the hills out of range of the cannon. If the enemy remained on their ships, they would be firing into an empty town, while if they ventured ashore, they would be overwhelmed by force of numbers. Besides, the natives could hurl their exploding bottles over almost as great a distance, and with as deadly an aim, as those terrible farang firearms.

The very natives that the Shahbandar had trained to defend the town, those he thought were on his side, would be the ones to turn against him. It was the Burmese women who had done the trick, aided by the fact that every last native had heard the gossip about the Shahbandar and the English Captain, how the two cronies were seen every night in each other's company, carousing into the early hours. These women of pleasure, who were regularly summoned to the Shahbandar's house, had confirmed that the two farangs were on the friendliest of terms, poring over maps of the area together. And with a little prodding from Selim, one of the least shy of the girls had divulged that she and her companions had been made to lie naked in different corners of the room, each girl representing a prominent landmark of the town. She herself had been designated as the fortress and attacked by the two men simultaneously. They had roared with laughter as they pretended to assault her buttress and scale her ramparts. This salacious titbit, which grew in the telling, did more than any other rumour to convince the native population that the two men were truly in cahoots. It spread like wildfire

339

and the raucous laughter which emanated nightly from the Shahbandar's house did everything to confirm it.

How restless he was tonight, despite his exhaustion. He had been to Tenasserim and back with barely a rest in between. Twelve hours' travel there and back. But at least now all the exits were properly guarded. At last his pusillanimous brothers on the Council had agreed to take tangible action. With their written authority, he had been able to close off the road to Ayudhya. A thick rope of hemp lay stretched across the river beyond Tenasserim, and two guard posts, each manned by a dozen armed men, had been erected on either side of the river. All traffic in and out of Ayudhya would now be stopped and thoroughly searched and no one without a very good reason would be allowed through. The Shahbandar and his cronies would not be able to send false reports to Ayudhya, neither would any farangs who inadvertently fled the massacre be able to escape that way.

Selim turned over on his side and tried to close his eyes once more.

Forty-one

'What the devil did you do that for, Mason? Have you gone mad? Do you realize you may have sabotaged the most delicate negotiations?' Weltden was livid. 'I'll have you court-martialled for this, I promise you. And wipe that smirk off your face before I take the law into my own hands.' They were in the Captain's cabin on the *Curtana* and Weltden's fists were still clenched, as they had been from the start of this interview.

Mason had freely admitted that he and two young officers by the name of Weld and Hoddy had taken a dozen men and boarded the *Resolution*, pistol in hand. They had seized the ship in the name of King James of England. The Captain, it seemed, had been absent ashore and the crew had been caught so totally unawares that they had offered no resistance. They had been forced to weigh anchor and sail the ship over the bar alongside the *Curtana*. As soon as Mason and his men had returned to the *Curtana*, the duty officer on the *Resolution* had gone ashore to seek instructions from White. Weltden remembered in fact seeing a boat heading for shore as he himself was rowing out to the *Curtana*.

'Well, Mason, have you nothing to say for yourself?'

'No, sir, I did what I thought was right.'

Weltden banged his fist on the table.

'Who do you think's in charge here, Lieutenant Mason? You're coming with me this evening, and Weld and Hoddy too, to present your abject apologies to Lord White. You blundering cretin, I had already obtained White's consent to move the *Resolution*. Just as I said I would. Or had you forgotten?'

'I had not forgotten, sir, I just thought it might not be at the top of your priorities. We took a vote here and – '

'You took a *what*, Mason?' thundered Weltden. 'This is not a parliament, this is the Royal Navy, the finest navy in the world, with a system of ranks, so that subordinates like you do not

341

assume responsibilities they are incapable of handling. You are relieved of your duties until further notice, Mason. You will – '

There was a knock on the door. 'Who is it?'

'I'm sorry to disturb you, sir. It's Malvern, sir, the officer of the watch.'

'Yes?'

'There's a message from the *Resolution*. It's just been delivered. I thought it might be urgent, sir.'

'All right, Malvern, bring it in.'

The cabin door opened gingerly and a red-faced young officer saluted and handed Weltden a note. He tore it open and read it. Then he turned pale.

'That'll be all, Malvern.'

'Aye, aye, sir.' The young officer saluted and left.

Weltden glared at Mason as the blood came rushing back to his cheeks.

'Get out of my sight, Mason. This instant.'

Mason shrugged his shoulders and left. Weltden glanced once more at the note and then leaned across the table, burying his head in his hands. Samuel White had excused himself from seeing the Captain again that evening. He was indisposed.

The 600-ton *Gaillard* sailed up the Western coast of Siam on the final leg of its journey to Mergui. Captain Saint-Clair stood on the quarterdeck admiring the magnificent scenery. The shoreline was wooded and hilly and every now and then ribbons of white sand intruded into the forests of green. They had just passed a beautiful island called Junk Ceylon, or Phuket as the Malays knew it, surrounded by rocks that jutted out of the ocean like an army of monoliths, and clear water that was the colour of sapphire. From time to time great clusters of islands dotted the shore, their pristine beaches bright in the sunlight. He was heading due north now towards the groups of islands whose exotic names he had memorized from the Portuguese charts: the Badracan and Pulo-Tavay islands, to the south of Mergui. The timber from their dense forests was reputed to be well suited to the construction of ships, and Monsieur du Boullay had asked for a report on them. Saint-Clair sighed. If the islands looked anything like Phuket, he would have no difficulty in lingering there after the province of Tenasserim was proclaimed a territory of France and Commodore Vaudricourt was installed in Mergui as Governor.

Saint-Clair had made good time. The winds had been favourable. The *Gaillard* had left Songhkla just three and a half weeks ago, and if the Portuguese charts were correct, she should reach Mergui in another four or five days, almost a week ahead of schedule.

Saint-Clair took another look at the luxuriant coast, marvelling at the wealth of bays and inlets and the occasional meandering river whose estuary broke up the shoreline. Then he descended below decks to report to the Commodore. The sojourn in Bangkok, followed by the fresh sea breezes and the calm coastal waters had done wonders for the men's spirits and morale was high. With a bit of luck there would be no battle for Mergui. The daunting sight of this great ship, with fifty-two head of cannon protruding from its sides, should put off even the most determined of garrisons.

Saint-Clair prayed it would all turn out peacefully. For if Mergui had as much charm as the rest of Siam, and the inhabitants were not hostile, it would without question be the most pleasant posting he had ever served in.

Phaulkon and his party spent the night on the river opposite a tiny cluster of houses known optimistically as the village of Jelinga. The local headman, overwhelmed by the honour of receiving the Pra Klang, had insisted on giving Phaulkon his little house on stilts while he himself slept on the ground under the raised floor. His awe-struck daughters, their mouths stained red with betel nut, waited on Phaulkon hand and foot and executed their last remaining chicken before he had time to stop them. It was an honour that would be recounted from one generation to the next in this little community of farmers. No Pra Klang in living memory had ever visited them before.

Phaulkon rose before dawn and left a couple of gold coins hidden under a mat, where the headman's family would only discover them after he had gone and it was too late to protest. He washed in the river while his slaves kept a watch for crocodiles. Slowly, the huge procession of boats, moored at various intervals in mid stream, came to life.

For the last two days on the river Phaulkon had journeyed with Ivatt next to him and the two men had talked continuously, catching up on past events and speculating on those to come. But today, as they departed in the early light of dawn, surprising even the bird life and the sleeping monkeys in the trees, Phaulkon was in a solitary mood. He looked around him in awe. There was something haunting about a jungle river at dawn, shrouded in thin mist and serenaded by the chanting of the frogs and cicadas. It was a scene that seemed to hark back to the beginnings of time, resurrecting some primeval magic. He wished Sunida could be here now to share the beauty. And he thought of Maria as well.

She had just returned from the orphanage when he had arrived in Ayudhya to bid her farewell. She was now visibly pregnant and spoke openly and with pride about the heir who would be the owner of five thousand hectares of land in Catholic France, graciously bestowed on him or her by King Louis himself.

He had told her of the latest developments in Mergui and explained the need for him to be there. Her brow had furrowed as she had said: 'I fear for your safety, Constant – I never did trust Samuel White. Did I not warn you time and again against him?'

He had looked at her fondly and with respect. His relationship with her had been much calmer of late.

'You did warn me, Maria, and you were right. I tolerated him because of his brother George, and gave him every chance out of a spirit of charity.'

'It was not charity, Constant, but the payment of a debt. And now that debt is more than fully cancelled. Promise me that you will leave it at that?'

'You have my word on it, Maria.'

He saw her now, her hands delicately folded in front of her stomach, as she bid him farewell: 'Go with God then, Constant, and come back to me soon.'

A dark log slid into the water from the bank. Several others followed it. What dark predators lay before him in Mergui? he

344

wondered. He would know soon enough. In another three days they would reach Tenasserim. There, while they waited for the elephants to arrive, he would organize a scouting foray into Mergui.

Forty-two

Samuel White kept Weltden waiting for two full days. On the third day he sent a message to the *Curtana* inviting the Captain to dine ashore with him that evening. He calculated that by now Weltden would be desperate for a response to his offer, and that should make him more pliant. For White wanted to make certain amendments to Weltden's offer. He had spent the time canvassing for additional signatures to the proclamation, and now he had ten more with which to impress Weltden and, he hoped, to use as a bargaining point. The wait had not pleased White any more than it had Weltden, as the one was increasingly anxious to leave Mergui before his misdeeds caught up with him, and the other wanted concrete results to show Yale before he arrived. But White had considered the two-day interval a necessary part of his strategy.

As he stood on his terrace now, gazing at the ocean, he imagined himself aboard the *Resolution*, bound for the Cape of Good Hope and England. If only it could be tomorrow. He must persuade Weltden to accept his terms right away. He kept an eye on the path that led up the hill to his house. There was no sign of traffic on it. Was Weltden purposely late? he wondered. Or had he decided not to come at all?

The sun was setting fast now and White could no longer see the path clearly. He let out an angry oath and returned to his study to brood over his plans once more. He might just have to amend them again.

The lead boat slowed to a crawl and the pilot stood up, straining his eyes. Then he raised an arm in the air. The long procession of boats slowed to a halt.

The pilot continued to stare ahead. A large rope of reeds was stretched across the length of the river in front of them; it was attached to the thick trunks of banyan trees on either bank. There were what appeared to be guardhouses on either side. In the next moment Phaulkon's boat came alongside the lead canoe. 'What's happening?' he asked.

'Mighty Lord, I, a hair, am not sure. It looks like some sort of checkpoint.'

Just then the vague silhouette of a soldier peered out from one of the huts in the distance and shouted something, but the words were indistinct.

'You'd better go and investigate,' said Phaulkon to the officer. 'But be careful. And try to avoid revealing who I am.'

'Mighty Lord, I receive your orders.' The lead boat moved away.

Phaulkon waited silently in his boat. Ivatt was seated next to him. Two oarsmen kept the boat stationary while two more lay prostrate before the mighty Pra Klang.

A few minutes later the lead canoe returned.

'Well?'

'Mighty Lord, they say the river is closed. We must turn back.'

'Closed? Did they give a reason?'

'Mighty Lord, they did not.'

'Did you not ask why?'

'Mighty Lord, I, a hair, did. They told me to go back where I came from.'

'Did they ask you who you were?'

'Mighty Lord, they did. I, the dust of your feet, said we were traders from Ayudhya.'

'How many of them were there?'

'Mighty Lord, I, a hair, counted a dozen of them on this side of the river alone. They were all armed. I saw two or three firearms and many harpoons and swords.'

'Did they threaten you?'

'Mighty Lord, not as such. But I felt they would have done if I had disobeyed them.'

'All right. We'll try one more ploy. Thomas,' he said, turning to Ivatt. 'Have you got your official hat?'

'I never travel without my cone,' quipped Ivatt. 'It instils the fear of God into most living creatures, even the animals sometimes.'

'Let's hope its power is undiminished. Wear it now and get into the lead boat. Tell that guard you are a mandarin from

347

Ayudhya on a royal mission to Golconda. You must be allowed to pass.'

'What if he refuses?'

'Tell him that he will be answerable to the Lord of Life and that he had better think twice.'

'And if he still says no?'

'Come back here and we'll get the soldiers to deal with him.'

Ivatt was away for quite a while. They could see him at a distance arguing with the guards. At last he returned, a frown on his face.

'Your powers of persuasion are losing their strength, are they, Thomas? What happened?'

'I almost broke him, Constant. I had him really worried anyway. But he said he had official orders from the Council of Tenasserim not to let anyone through in either direction. There were to be no exceptions, he had been told, but in view of my elevated rank he would send someone to request special clearance from the Council. Did I have any official document to prove my mission? I said I would fetch it.'

'That won't do,' said Phaulkon. 'We don't want the Council alerted to our arrival so soon.'

Phaulkon considered the matter. He sent for his senior captain, Vitoon. Moments later a score of canoes containing one hundred élite fighting men headed off towards the checkpoint. Another one hundred and thirty boats with six hundred men followed slowly behind them, keeping their distance but making their presence known.

There was a brief exchange of gunfire and then the guard posts surrendered. Two guards were dead and one of Phaulkon's men slightly wounded.

'I want these men bound and kept under surveillance,' said Phaulkon in an undertone to Vitoon. The row of anxious prisoners gaped at him. 'I do not want rumours of our arrival to spread just now. Send a contingent to check out the jail at Tenasserim. We might leave them there later. We don't want to be encumbered with them for long. Do you know how far Tenasserim is?'

'Mighty Lord, one of my men is from the area. He says we are near the outskirts now.'

'Good. We will pitch camp as close to the town as possible, keeping out of sight. Send some men to find a suitable spot. I plan to investigate the town myself after nightfall.'

'Mighty Lord, I receive your orders.'

An hour later the slaves were pitching camp on a broad stretch of sandbank along the Greater Tenasserim River. Beyond the bank, as far as the eye could see in either direction, stretched endless mangrove swamps populated only by iguanas. The presence of even so large a gathering as this one was likely to pass unnoticed here.

Less than a league distant, situated on level ground at the confluence of the Greater and Lesser Tenasserim rivers, was the ancient trading town of Tenasserim. Despite his fatigue, Phaulkon felt a sudden elation. Ancient Tenasserim! An inalienable part of Asia's past. He had always wanted to visit this old river port where trade had flourished with the West since 1373. Tenasserim still exchanged spices, drugs, silks and musk for copper, quicksilver, scarlet cloth, coloured velvet, and rosewater from Mecca in little bottles of tinned copper. And Tenasserim wine, made from a local nut, was famous all over Asia – an especial favourite with the harems of India, whose inmates drank it to seek solace from the inattention of their masters.

As Phaulkon waited for his slaves to finish erecting his spacious tent, made of bamboo with cotton awnings, the soldiers who had been sent to reconnoitre the local prison returned. They appeared to have a prisoner in tow. He was a strange sight as he stumbled along, his clothes in tatters, his long, thin legs barely able to support him. His face was obscured by his unkempt hair which stuck out in all directions like the quills of a disturbed porcupine. It was all Phaulkon could do to make him out as a farang.

'Mighty Lord, we found this man in the jail at Tenasserim,' said the officer in charge, prostrating himself before Phaulkon. 'When he saw our uniforms, he kept babbling that he was a friend of the honourable Pra Klang's. He was so insistent that we thought we'd better bring him back to Your Excellency.'

'Perhaps you don't recognise me, sir,' croaked the man feebly. 'Francis Davenport, at your service.'

*

When Weltden arrived at White's house it was already quite late. The sun had long since set and only a dim glow remained on the horizon. Weltden was still furious with Mason. He had had yet another violent argument with him. When he had insisted that the first lieutenant accompany him to White's house to apologize, Mason had argued that since he had been relieved of his duties, he could no longer be expected to obey orders. Only when the Captain had threatened to have him strung up on the yard arm there and then had Mason acquiesced. The confrontation had made them very late.

'Lord White, Mason here, with these other two, have come to present their apologies to you for their unforgivable behaviour in the matter of the *Resolution*. I have relieved them of their duties and I will see that they answer for their actions when we return to Madras. They will be court-martialled for acting against orders.'

'If that is to be their fate, Captain, it would seem to me that they deserve at least a decent meal.'

Weltden bit his lip and forced a smile. 'You are too gracious, Lord White. But there is no need for that. They have only come to apologize.'

White held up his hand. 'I insist, Captain. I am not a man to harbour resentment. It's getting rather late, so shall we go straight in to dinner?'

Before Weltden could protest further, White led them in to the dining hall. The officers muttered a stilted apology and they all sat down.

Throughout the meal White avoided the subject of the *Resolution* and remained formally courteous towards both the officers and Weltden. The Captain became progressively more disconcerted. What the devil was White up to? Was he trying to win Mason over? But to what purpose? It made no sense. It seemed almost as if White didn't wish to be alone with him. Had he decided to reject the offer?

Weltden's fears seemed to be confirmed when, at the end of dinner, as if by prearrangement, Mason and White rose from the table simultaneously. Mason politely thanked his host for dinner and excused himself, pointing to the late hour. White concurred, saying that he too had had a long day. Turning to Weltden, he expressed the hope that the Captain would join him again tomorrow. Before Weltden could reply, White began ushering the party to the gate. The Captain had little choice but to follow.

White bade them all a courteous goodnight and turned back into the house. He had not failed to notice Weltden's discomfort and he could only hope that this last gamble of his had paid off. Though he had lost another precious day, the substantial amendment to Weltden's offer that he planned to demand required the maximum flexibility on the Captain's part, and one more day of suspense should help to put him in the right frame of mind.

It was a beautiful moonlit night. It had rained that day, a brief, heavy downpour typical of the tail end of the monsoons and the air was clear and fresh. As Weltden and the officers rounded a corner, they noticed a large number of small boats, filled with men, at the mouth of the Tenasserim River on the far side of the harbour. Their outlines were clearly visible in the distance.

'What a strange hour for so many boatmen to be about,' remarked Mason to no one in particular. 'I can't believe this is normal.'

As they reached the harbour front, Weltden stopped. The party came to an abrupt halt behind him. He stared about him, his eyes turning repeatedly to the mouth of the river. The night was strangely still. Despite the multitude of boatmen some hundred yards' distant, the only sound was that of the croaking bull frogs and the chorus of the cicadas. There was no movement anywhere. To one side was the sea, gently lapping against the shore, and to the other the rows of makeshift stalls whose owners lay sleeping under their thatched roofs. Behind the huts loomed the wooded hills, their craggy silhouettes a deeper black against the night sky.

For the second time that evening Weltden felt unsettled. He wondered whether the boatmen had indeed increased in number or whether it was the clearness of the night that simply made them conspicuous this time. He turned to Mason. 'Go back to White's house. Inform him that though we do not suspect treachery, we are nevertheless surprised by the boats milling about the river's mouth. Ask him if he is aware of their presence in such numbers. We will await your return here.'

'Aye, aye, sir,' said Mason, saluting for the first time in a long while and setting off at a rapid pace. The Siamese guard who had been sent to escort them hesitated, uncertain whether to follow Mason or to stay with the Captain. He decided to remain where he was. Weltden was unable to communicate with him or he would certainly have asked him the meaning of all these boatmen at this hour. The group waited, Weld and Hoddy glancing about them uncomfortably. The occasional cry of a wild animal shattered the silence.

After several interminable minutes, they heard the sound of raised voices. White's irate voice cut through the night air. 'I told you a hundred times that I am in command here. The natives obey me and no one else. Why is it that you simply cannot take my word for it? You are again questioning my honour, it seems.'

'Your suggestion, sir, that these hordes of natives should fear an attack from us or that they should have come to sell betel nut at this hour of the night is preposterous. You cannot tell me this is normal. I urge you to send a messenger to ask them what they are about.' Mason's voice had lost all pretence of restraint.

'Ridiculous!' exploded White. 'Since you apprehend danger where there is none, I will personally escort Captain Weltden to his ship and be his guard.'

White now strode into view, dressed in his nightshirt. On catching sight of Weltden, he quickened his pace and reached the wharf breathing heavily. He marched up to Weltden, gesticulating wildly in the direction of the river mouth.

'I invite you to order a search of all the native boats, Captain.'

Mason slipped in front of White. 'Lord White has informed me,' he said, 'that in these boats are nothing but a parcel of harmless fellows come to sell a little betel nut! Now, I ask you, Captain, at this hour of the night?'

White swung round angrily. 'I was only joking, you fool.' He turned back to Weltden and in a voice quivering with indignation repeated his invitation to him to order a search of the native boats.

'That will not be necessary, Samuel,' said Weltden quietly. 'Why don't you join us on board the *Curtana* for a nightcap instead?'

White hesitated, caught off guard. He glanced at the Captain

352

and then at his nightshirt. Then, to the consternation of Mason, he shrugged his shoulders and climbed into the *Curtana*'s launch.

'Cheer up, Mason,' said Weltden, somewhat startled himself that White should have accepted his offer but greatly relieved to have diffused White's outrage. His shifts of mood were quite the most unpredictable and volatile he had ever encountered in a man. 'You look dreadfully glum. As Lord White pointed out, those men are just part of the town's defences. If they had had any evil designs, they could surely have attacked us at any time. We were like sitting ducks, wouldn't you agree?'

Mason made no reply. Before long the party was climbing on board the *Curtana*. The startled duty officer couldn't tear his eyes away from White's nightshirt.

The officers excused themselves and Weltden led White to his cabin. He filled two glasses with his best whisky and before long he and White were in the best of spirits, toasting each other repeatedly and beginning to make cryptic references to the success of their mission.

Outside Tenasserim, Francis Davenport was being brought back to life again. Phaulkon had ordered his cooks to prepare him a nutritious meal while his barbers had been instructed to put some order into the secretary's unruly mop. Then his slaves had bathed and massaged him and by sundown Davenport was almost recognizable again. The deep lines under his eyes and his generally emaciated appearance remained, but it was agreed that a good night's rest on soft ground with clean covers would do much to restore his strength.

Phaulkon had not learned much from Davenport that he did not already know, but there was no question that his appearance was a stroke of luck. Davenport knew every inch of Mergui, as well as the exact locations of the houses of the Moors on the Council. It had also come to light that he knew a couple of the officers on board the *Resolution*. This could come in handy indeed if, as Phaulkon hoped, the frigate was still in harbour.

Phaulkon had planned to leave for Mergui before dawn the following morning, but he would now depart in the late afternoon, to allow Davenport more time to rest. This itself had advantages, since it would mean his reaching Mergui at night, when most of the town should be asleep. With Davenport's knowledge of the terrain, he could now spend the night in Mergui itself, instead of camping outside it; Davenport had assured him he could arrange discreet accommodation.

That evening, Phaulkon and Ivatt discussed the next day's strategy at length. Ivatt was concerned that Phaulkon should await the arrival of Dularic and the war elephants before proceeding to Mergui. Though the French warship was unlikely to have reached Mergui yet, in Ivatt's view White still presented a serious danger. He was a desperate man and if he were still around it was surely wiser for Phaulkon to enter Mergui at the head of a grand army than with only a small band of bodyguards.

But Phaulkon was adamant. He did not want to lose another two or three days waiting for the elephants. No one knew exactly how long the abandoned jungle route might take them, or what unexpected hazards might have delayed the travellers. The timing had to be guesswork, and Phaulkon's instinct told him he should reach Mergui as fast as possible. Even the brief delay on Davenport's account was a source of worry to him. Ivatt found there was nothing he could do or say to dissuade him. Phaulkon would go ahead incognito with a score of his toughest men, while Ivatt would follow with the rest of the force as soon as it arrived.

It was very late when Vitoon and the handful of men Phaulkon had sent to Tenasserim to learn what they could of the whereabouts and activities of Selim Yussuf returned. But Phaulkon had instructed Vitoon to report to him no matter what the hour. The captain came quietly to his tent and woke him, and what he had to say sent a chill down Phaulkon's spine. With the help of extensive bribes they had eventually learned that Selim had recently changed places with his brother Hassan, and moved to Hassan's house in Mergui. Selim had not returned to Tenasserim for some days, while Hassan had disappeared completely. More ominous still, the arrival in Mergui of a heavily armed English man-of-war had made the native population very restless. They had been arming themselves steadily over the past day or two.

Forty-three

When White woke up the following day it was already afternoon. His head was pounding fiercely. He looked around him at the unfamiliar, dimly lit room. He tried desperately to recall where he was. He saw that he was wearing a nightshirt and that he was stretched out on a bunk, but he was clearly not at home. The room was far too small. It was only when he noticed the porthole that it dawned on him that he was on board ship. With that first clue, the events of the night before came slowly back to him in confused sequence; the main events at least, for the details remained stubbornly blurred.

What a night of revelry it must have been. He remembered now that it had taken place on board the *Curtana*, which was where he obviously was now. He seemed also to recollect at one point trying to dissuade Weltden from ordering the ship's guns to be fired in salute at each new toast. Had he succeeded? Weltden had certainly been in a rollicking mood. But what had they been toasting so boisterously? Of course, their new alliance. They had drunk to each clause of the new compact. White racked his brains now, trying to recall the exact details of their agreement. He had certainly consented to the garrisoning of Mergui by the Company. And there was something about Yale too. Oh yes, Weltden had said that Yale was coming. But why? His stomach felt suddenly queasy. Yale in Mergui? What did he want here? Had he come to arrest him? He strained his memory. No, it wasn't that. Yale was coming to oversee the smooth transfer of power, because he, Samuel, was going to hand Mergui over to the Company. That was it. He remembered now asking Weltden to absolve him, in return for his co-operation, from repaying the compensation. That was one of his conditions. He remembered sticking firmly by it. Yes, he was only prepared to hand over Mergui if Weltden agreed to overlook the matter of the compensation and if he, Samuel, were allowed to leave for England before Yale arrived. But what had Weltden replied? For the life of him he couldn't recall. How could he forget so crucial a point?

White cursed and raised himself up on one elbow. Immediately the throbbing in his head grew worse. Still, he had better get up now. He wondered what time it was. He had a terrible urge to relieve himself. He groped about the floor until he found a chamber pot. He emptied himself for what seemed an eternity. Was it possible that a man could store so much liquid? he wondered. If only the pounding in his head would stop. He searched the cabin for some clothes, but without success. There was nothing for it but to go outside and seek out the Captain. He opened the door and stepped out into the blinding light.

Anthony Weltden's head was pounding too. He chided himself for having let himself go thus. He looked across at the clock on the mantelpiece. Good heavens! Three o'clock in the afternoon! Had he really slept that long? Vaguely now he recalled watching the sun rise before he retired. White certainly knew how to drink. Thank God he had not tried to keep up with him entirely. He had had quite enough as it was.

Despite his headache, Weltden broke into a sudden smile. The events of the night before were coming back to him in quick succession, and he recalled with pride that he would be master of Mergui in the morning. Well, perhaps not in the morning. It would have to be the next day now. He remembered the crucial points that he and White had finally agreed to. There had been only one serious bone of contention and that was over the matter of the compensation due to the Company. White had been adamant on that point but he had been reluctant simply to waive an item of such significance without consulting Governor Yale first. He had eventually consented to bring the matter up with the Governor as soon as he arrived. The problem with that was that White was anxious to leave *before* Yale arrived, so the matter had somehow to be resolved beforehand. Though White had not said so in as many words, Weltden had had the impression that the compensation might already be available and that what White was seeking was official sanction to take the wealth with him back to England.

356

Weltden recalled now the prolonged and often heated discussion over this question, until it had become apparent that the whole deal would actually founder over the one point. In the end he had been forced to meet White halfway. Yale had after all given him a certain flexibility. He had agreed to accept half the compensation, providing it were handed over immediately and providing White conceded on all other points. The wily harbour master had argued for a while longer, almost as if it were a matter of principle to him that he should do so, before capitulating.

The deal had been sealed! It only remained now for them to go over the points once more in the sober light of day. For Weltden wanted to satisfy himself that White had not changed his mind or reneged on any of the points. Though why should he? It was clearly in his interests not to. The general plan that the two of them had devised was mutually beneficial. White would inform the mandarins on the Council of Five that he had received an urgent dispatch from Ayudhya, warning that the French navy was on its way to capture Mergui. The English Company, not wanting to see France take over one of the key trading posts in the Bay, had offered to help defend Mergui against the invaders. In the interests of Siam, the Shahbandar had accepted the offer. It seemed a credible enough explanation to Weltden. By the time the truth were revealed, the *Curtana*'s men would be well-ensconced on the hillsides with sufficient defence measures in place to ensure their survival until Governor Yale's reinforcements arrived, which would be at any moment now. As soon as they did arrive, the Union Jack would be hoisted over the town, and the English residents would be given the choice of staying on under Company hegemony or returning to Madras; for the moment Mergui was in British hands, King James's proclamation would no longer apply to them. They could remain if they pleased.

Weltden hoped that White would be in a condition to visit the Council of Five today. If not, the occupation of Mergui would have to be postponed for another day. He dressed quickly, intent on locating White. He was just pulling on his shoes when there was a knock on the door and a very bleary-eyed harbour master stood before him.

*

357

Around four o'clock that afternoon, at the camp outside Tenasserim, Phaulkon was making last-minute preparations for his
journey to Mergui. Davenport had slept until past midday and
was looking considerably better. Some colour had returned to his
pallid cheeks, and his grey eyes were animated.

Ivatt meanwhile was making a last attempt to dissuade Phaulkon from leaving.

'Just give it two more days, Constant. If the elephants have
not turned up by then, you can be off and I won't say another
word.'

'No, Thomas, my mind is made up.'

'If you won't listen to reason, then let me at least accompany
you. I know Mergui well.'

'That's precisely why I want you to lead the army there.
Besides, Thomas,' he added with a grin, 'who would look after
Sunida if anything happened to me?'

'That's an unfair argument, Constant. It leaves me truly torn.'

'You see, Thomas, my demise would have its bright side too.
But I am serious, you know. If anything should happen to me, I
want you to look after Sunida. And I also want you to see that
Maria goes to France as soon as our child is born. I wouldn't
want to give my enemies the chance to make her suffer on my
account. If His Majesty were to suffer a relapse, she would be
particularly vulnerable.'

Ivatt was pensive. 'You know I would carry out your wishes to
the letter, Constant. But it won't be necessary, you'll see,' he
added, brightening. 'Now tell me instead how long I have to wait
here for those damned elephants? What if they take a liking to
the jungle and decide to set up home there?'

Phaulkon laughed. 'Give them three days, Thomas, at the
outside. If they don't show up by then, bring the army to Mergui.
I am only going on a reconnaissance trip anyway. If I find things
quiet there, I may even come back and lead the army myself.
Mergui is only about seven hours upstream. In any case, I'll get
a message to you as soon as I arrive. Meanwhile, stay put right
here. It's a well-concealed spot. You should send a scouting party
out regularly to keep an eye out for the elephants. It shouldn't
be difficult to spot two hundred and fifty of them emerging from
the jungle.'

'I'll do my best to recognize them.'

Phaulkon gave Ivatt a last slap on the back and summoned Vitoon. Then, with twenty of his best men, he and Davenport embarked in six swift boats. There was about an hour of daylight left. The party should reach Mergui around ten o'clock that night.

An hour before sunset that afternoon, White and Weltden were still seated in the master cabin, nursing their heavy heads. They had gone over the details of their agreement once more and both men had been relieved to find that their recollection of the pact of the night before had been much as they had thought.

Owing to the queasiness of his condition, it was agreed that White would convene a meeting of the Council first thing the following morning. Messengers would be sent this evening to the homes of the Council members requesting their presence at the Shahbandar's house no later than seven o'clock. There would be nothing unusual about that. In the sultry climate of the tropics, meetings were often called early in the morning.

While White warned the Council of the imminent French attack, fifty of Weltden's men would be standing by to occupy the stockades which had been almost completely rebuilt during the past few days. Another fifty would remain on board the *Curtana* to man the guns which would be trained on the harbour in case of trouble. Once it had been established beyond doubt that the takeover would be peaceful, White would be allowed to leave. The document which Yale had prepared, granting him safe conduct to England and immunity from prosecution there, would be handed over to him in exchange for an amount in gold or some other negotiable commodity to the value of £250,000.

Both men then agreed that it would be politic to invite Mason, Weld and Hoddy ashore again on this last night, to apprize them of the plan. The renegade officers could hardly be in a position to object to the implementation of Governor Yale's original orders. Apart from that consideration, it would not do for Weltden to find his ship infiltrated by subversive elements when so much was at stake in the morning. Finally, it was agreed that the dinner at White's house would be held early enough for all to retire at a reasonable hour.

359

'Well, my dear Anthony,' said White, smiling despite the relentless pounding in his head, 'it remains only for us to drink one final toast to the successful conclusion of our little enterprise.'

Weltden rubbed his forehead. 'I don't think I could manage another drink. I have a better idea. What about a real salute? What more fitting conclusion than to fire the guns – six loud volleys in honour of British Mergui?'

'An excellent idea, as long as you fire out to sea,' said White grinning. 'Long live King James!'

'Long live his newest dominion!' responded Weltden.

He summoned the officer of the watch and gave an order. Soon after, there was a loud report followed by five more in even succession. The massive booming of the *Curtana*'s guns reverberated around the Bay and beyond.

It was shortly before dusk. The little food stalls along the harbour front were filling faster than usual. People seemed to be converging from every direction. When the stalls were filled to capacity, a swarthy, thin-ribbed native wandered casually along the whole length of the waterfront. His hand kept returning to scratch the back of his neck as if he were suffering from an insect bite. Gradually a handful of men detached themselves from the clusters of natives and followed him. The vast majority of the peasants continued where they were, pulling on their thick cheroots and conversing in hushed tones. All had heard the guns and all knew it was the signal they had been waiting for. Tonight would be the night.

The handful of peasants trailed the thin-ribbed native along a dusty path overhung by rain trees to a small hut behind the harbour front. It was a typical peasant's hut, with a raised floor and a thatched roof. It was bare inside but for a large water jug and a thin mat of reeds. They entered and squatted silently in a circle, barely able to squeeze into the narrow space.

In the centre of the room Selim Yussuf looked around him at the tense assembly. 'All right, men, the Shahbandar and the farang captain have gone up to the house on the hill now. You know what to do. We start immediately. Are you all prepared?'

The men nodded awkwardly. Then a nervous, pock-marked

man spoke out, stuttering heavily. 'The . . . the . . . the . . . guns, great lord . . . were they . . . they . . . firing at us?'

Selim's dark eyes flashed. 'The treacherous Shahbandar and his foreign ally were celebrating their victory in advance,' he said, fixing the man with his powerful gaze.

There was a general murmur all round. Then gradually the men rose and disappeared. One of them headed back to the waterfront where a score of natives quickly joined him. Following behind him, they made their way stealthily to the warehouses by the wharf, where they soon overpowered the guard and hid inside the building. It was the building adjacent to the path that led down the hill from the Shahbandar's house.

'Land ho!'

It was the twentieth day out of Madras and the *Pearl*'s lookout had just sighted the western shores of Siam, about a day's sail from Mergui. Captain Perriman was informed and he in turn advised the distinguished passenger below. The *Pearl* changed course and proceeded southwards along the coast.

Not for the first time, Perriman wondered how the *Curtana* had fared and whether Mergui might already be in English hands. One could never be sure of course in this turbulent part of the world, where storms and pirates and tropical diseases conspired to foil even the best-laid plans. His orders were to assist Captain Weltden in capturing Mergui, should this be necessary. He was also to see to the arrest of Samuel White, if this had not already been effected.

Perriman heard a familiar step climbing the aft companionway. He turned to salute. As he did so he thought he heard a faint peal in the distance. The figure at the top of the companionway paused and raised an eyebrow. His Excellency had heard it too. Then, barely audible in the distance, came five more peals in even succession. To the experienced ear that sound, however muted, was unmistakable. It was the distant boom of cannon.

Forty-four

The evening supper at White's house was less jovial than usual. Both White and Weltden were tired and hungover, and anxious to get a good night's rest. After the plan to hand Mergui over to the English in the morning had been revealed to the officers, the conversation had become sporadic. Mason, especially, seemed morose. He had offered little comment on the planned takeover.

When dinner had finished, Weltden declined the services of the buxom Burmese beauty who usually awaited his pleasure. He did not feel in the mood for play that night. He was anxious to return to his ship. There was a strange tension in the air, and the harbour front on arrival had seemed to him even more active than usual. He stood up from the table, and his officers followed suit. White rose too. It was still only around eight o'clock, and he offered to accompany them as far as the wharf.

It was a dark night with no sign of a moon, yet there was an unusual absence of torch bearers. Perhaps they had not expected the party to retire so early. Two of White's guards lit the way instead. The party headed silently down the hill in single file and approached the warehouses by the wharf.

The vague outline of the *Curtana*'s launch loomed just ahead of them. In the general silence the voices of the crew were clearly audible. White stopped short of the first warehouse and bid his guests goodnight. He turned and started back up the hill.

There was a sudden scream. White looked over his shoulder, turned and broke into a run, heading towards the launch. In the next instant someone threw him to the ground and pinned his arms behind him. A hand closed over his mouth. He struggled briefly before recognizing his own guard. What the hell was the man doing? He had a grip of iron. Was he trying to save him or kill him? Piercing shrieks continued to split the air and there was the sound of running feet. White twisted his head and watched spellbound from the ground as a mob of dark shadows raced out of the nearest warehouse and fell upon Weltden and his group,

362

who were still on the wharf. He recognized Weltden by his hat and saw him knocked brutally to the ground. White's second guard now charged into the fray, his torch briefly lighting up the scene. Mason and one of the junior officers lay writhing on the ground. The other was fighting for his life surrounded by half a dozen men.

White tried to get up but his guard continued to pin him down. He was forced to lie there, listening to the screams. Through squinting eyes he saw the second officer overwhelmed. Then his heart lurched as the attackers glanced in his direction. One of them shouted something. They ran towards him. There were four or five of them. His second guard tried to intervene but they clubbed him to the ground. His torch fell and went out. It was pitch black again.

White lay there motionless. One of the men kicked the guard holding him. White felt his grip loosen. Then they kicked White, rolling him over and kicking him again. He felt a searing pain in the back of his neck. He kept his eyes firmly closed so as to preclude any natural reflexes. Again and again they came at him, taking turns to boot him. With a supreme effort he willed himself not to flinch. Waves of agony coursed through his body, until finally the attackers muttered a string of obscenities and moved on.

He waited till they were out of sight. There was no one else around. He got up slowly and, crouching low, hobbled in the direction of the launch. His battered body screeched in protest at the movement. Suddenly he heard a shout. Then another. The voices came from behind him. They grew louder and more frantic. Someone was pursuing him. He struggled through the shallow water and lunged towards the boat, his hands groping for the side. 'Help!' he cried. But there was no response from within. With a superhuman effort he hoisted himself over the side. He landed on a pile of bodies. There must have been three or four of them lying motionless at the bottom of the boat. Several broken oars were strewn around them. Quickly he grabbed an intact one. There were hardly any left. In the same instant one of the bodies rose up. It was wielding a curved knife. White spotted the man just as he lunged. He brought the oar crashing

363

down over his head; it snapped in two and the man slumped forward.

White grabbed the only remaining oar, thrusting it frantically into the water. The boat swerved to one side and then the other, while his pursuers closed in. Then one of them fell, screaming. In the next instant two more went down. White recognized his first guard, hacking away at his pursuers from behind. So the man had been trying to save him after all. There were only three attackers left now. The guard shouted to White to keep rowing. Two of the attackers fell on the guard while the third continued to pursue the twisting boat.

White thrust his oar into the water, first on one side, then on the other. The boat jerked forward in semi-circles. The pain in his back and shoulders was agonizing, and he was gasping for breath. His pursuer now cut him off and made to grab the boat. White veered to one side but the man's hands latched onto the edge. White glanced in vain for some weapon in the boat. It was too dark to see. The man was trying desperately to scramble aboard. White raised his last oar, aiming for the man's head. He missed but caught a hand instead. The man screamed and let go of the boat. The oar smashed against the edge, leaving White holding a shattered stump. He threw it into the water, grabbed the remains of the first oar and resumed his frantic rowing. It was a while before he realized there was no one following him.

He put the broken oar down and sank his head into his arms. His heart was thumping painfully. He could hear a growing commotion in the town. There were shouts and screams and what sounded like rallying cries. He turned weakly and peered into the darkness behind him. The *Resolution* was nowhere in sight. Neither was the *Curtana*. He let out a string of oaths and lay down among the bodies in the boat, his strength ebbing fast.

Richard Burnaby heard what sounded like yells and shouts coming from the harbour. At first they were faint and he ignored them. No doubt a pack of stray dogs or some howling infant, he thought. The little sixteen-year-old next to him heard them too and nestled deeper into his shoulder. She lay alongside him, fiddling with the white hairs on his chest. The honourable

Governor was old enough to be her grandfather, thought Plern, but he was kind and appreciative and he rewarded her well. The proceeds went to her esteemed grandparents, people as old as His Excellency. Both her parents had died, together with her five brothers and sisters, when their little boat had capsized in the rapids of the Tenasserim. Too young to travel, she had been left at home that terrible day, with her grandparents. They had brought her up and cared for her, and now that they were too old to work, it was her turn to feed them. It was hard work, she had to admit, making the ancient Governor reach the stars, for his love lance was mostly limp, but she persevered until either success came or he fell asleep, exhausted by the effort. Tonight, however, she had been successful. She lay by his side, waiting for him to doze off. As soon as he did so, she would slip out and return home. Her grandparents lived on the edge of town, some distance away from the central marketplace where they seldom ventured. They were still under the impression that their little grand-daughter helped run a food stall at the night market. Each time the messenger from His Excellency came to summon her, she would say that there were so many customers at the stall, her colleague needed assistance.

Burnaby opened his eyes briefly again as the cries resumed, but Plern stroked his temples in a rhythmic motion, soothing him back to sleep. She lay alongside him on the broad mattress, her small brown body smooth against his wrinkled skin. She glanced down the length of his lanky body. He was so tall that it always made her laugh to see her little feet dangling near his heavenly parts. She could easily tickle his love lance with her toes. How often had they not joked about this, how in his country, where the cold season apparently lasted most of the year, she would have been able to keep only half his body warm at any given time. Which half would he have preferred? she would enquire teasingly.

Now she sat up startled, as a series of shrill screams pierced the night air. An ominous chill ran through her. There had been so many rumours of late and the town was restless. What was happening? She was suddenly anxious to return to her grandparents. She glanced at the Governor. He was wide awake now, listening to the screams. She saw the look of fear in his eyes. He

365

got up slowly, wrapping a panung round him. He opened the door that led onto the terrace. From there a series of steps descended to the garden. The terrace commanded a magnificent view of the town below. He stared into the night, transfixed. Plern joined him, following his gaze. Some hundred paces distant, the flames of the Shahbandar's house rose in a sweeping blaze into the night sky, accompanied by a chorus of sharp cracks as the wooden timbers disintegrated. They watched spellbound as the roof caved in and a great shout went up. A moment later the crowd became visible behind the crumbling edifice, cheering and shouting. Others came streaming up from the town.

Burnaby gazed in horror as the mob surged towards his own house, wielding knives and bottles. In the garden below a group of his servants huddled together like frightened animals caught in the glare of a torch light. Plern wrapped her trembling arms round the Governor and buried her head deep in his waist. Emerging from his stupor, Burnaby shouted to the servants to be off and then ordered the girl to run for it as well. But she stood rooted to the spot, watching spellbound as the crowd surged closer. In the next instant the mob was in the garden. The majority of the servants had taken to their heels but a few still remained, armed with swords and harpoons. They stood valiantly on guard at the gate. As the gate was flung open they were struck down by a series of blows that didn't cease until their bodies had been hacked to pieces.

The leader of the mob eyed the Governor and his half-naked girl with disdain. She was sobbing now, still clinging desperately to him. 'Run, you whore,' shouted the leader angrily. He was a slight, frail-looking man with feverish eyes. 'Run, before you share your master's fate.' She seemed unable to move, her body shaking violently. The mob began to jeer, until with a great shout it surged onto the terrace.

Burnaby thrust the girl aside and ran to the bottom of the steps. 'Stop, I command you,' he shouted in broken Siamese. 'In the name of your King . . . I command you . . . I am your Governor . . .' His words died in the instant that his neck was severed. The girl fainted as they set about mutilating the Governor's body beyond recognition. They ran past her, more interested now in the contents of the house than in her. They

366

were still ransacking the building when she regained consciousness and quickly slipped out.

Over the next two hours, in various parts of the town, waves
of crazed natives swarmed into the houses of the Europeans,
thirsting for blood. Every Englishman was systematically flushed
out of his house and butchered. As the mob was unable to
differentiate between the English and other farangs, a number of
Spaniards and Portuguese perished also in the slaughter. But the
English constituted the majority. Not even those who threw
themselves at the natives' feet were spared.

The boats carrying Phaulkon and his men headed steadily
towards Mergui. Tall trees and dense jungle lined the riverside,
leaving all but a thin strip of night sky visible above them. As
they rounded a bend, the river broadened and the vegetation
grew sparser.

There was a sudden cry from the lead boatman. The outline of
his arm could vaguely be seen pointing upwards. They all looked
up. Ahead of them in the distance a glow lit up the night sky. It
was as if God had illuminated the firmament in the direction they
were going.

Fire. What else could light up the night sky like that, and in
precisely the direction of Mergui. Something terrible was happening there.

Phaulkon urged the oarsmen on. Strangely, the glow seemed
to diminish the closer they got to their destination. At around
ten o'clock they sighted a wooden structure whose outline jutted
vaguely out onto the river. It was the pier, Davenport informed
them. They were nearing the mouth of the river that formed the
boundary of Mergui. The rowers, exhausted and panting, lay
down their oars and let the boats drift towards the wooden
landing. Here and there in the distance were what looked like
the remnants of camp fires but the glow in the sky had now
virtually disappeared.

The canoes edged up to the landing. The oarsmen and guards
crouched low as they helped Phaulkon out of the boat, making
sure not to let their heads stray above the level of his. The pier
was deserted at this hour. Davenport climbed the wooden steps
and joined Phaulkon on the landing. He was to lead them via a

367

circuitous route to the home of the local mandarin, Hassan Yussuf. This was familiar territory to Davenport; he had run innumerable errands here for his master in the past – Hassan's signature was always being required on one document or another. He was to arrive at Hassan's house ahead of the others, ostensibly to request an urgent signature, in fact to ascertain who was the present occupant of the house, Hassan or Selim. Phaulkon and his guards would surround the building, and at the first shout from Davenport the guards would rush in.

Hassan's home was situated on the far outskirts of Mergui at the edge of the tall hills that rose up behind the town. The route they took was dark and deserted; it circumvented the harbour front completely. Judging by the sounds of festivity that emanated from that quarter, some sort of celebration was taking place.

Davenport raised a hand now and stopped. The house was ahead of them. At a signal from Captain Vitoon, the guards fanned out and Davenport walked slowly towards the gate. The sounds of revelry could still be heard in the distance and occasionally a great shout rose up through the night. What exactly were they cheering? Phaulkon wondered.

A startled voice challenged Davenport. He stopped before the gate and identified himself. Phaulkon heard the voice assert that Lord Yussuf was not at home. There was no mistaking the gruff tone when the voice added that this was hardly an hour to come disturbing the master anyway. The guard refused to answer any further questions and Davenport had little choice but to leave. As he retraced his steps, another great roar came from the direction of the harbour front.

Davenport made his way over to Phaulkon and whispered, 'The man looked at me as if he had seen a ghost. Perhaps White told everyone I was dead. I found it strange, however, that there was only one guard on duty. Most unusual. There was no sign of servants either, though at this late hour they might have been asleep. But a man in Hassan's position would have several guards, not just one. I don't understand it.'

More cheers resounded from the waterfront. Phaulkon's mind was racing. He whispered something to Vitoon who squatted reverently by his side and in the next instant twenty guards were closing in noiselessly on the house. Vitoon remained by Phaul-kon's side, not wishing to leave his master unattended.

There was a brief shout followed by a muffled cry and then all was silent again. A guard came running back to Vitoon. He crouched low. 'We have him, sir. He seems to be the only one around. Should we proceed now?'

Vitoon turned to Phaulkon, who nodded. The guard ran off again. Phaulkon walked towards the house, Vitoon and Daven-port at his side. By the time they had entered the anteroom where visitors were received, Hassan's man was firmly trussed up with palm cord. A light had been thrust in front of his frightened face. His eyes grew wide as he caught sight of Phaulkon. It was just as Davenport had said. The man's eyes registered more surprise than fear, as if he had just seen a ghost. He could hardly know who Phaulkon was. The Barcalon's guards had been given strict orders not to reveal his identity. So why the surprise?

The man was still staring at Phaulkon as Captain Vitoon stepped up to him. The prisoner's gaze shifted now to the large flat banana leaf in Vitoon's hand, which served as a tray. This time there was no mistaking the look of terror in his eyes. Slivers of bamboo lay in neat rows on the banana leaf. One of Phaulkon's guards came forward and stood by Vitoon. With rhythmic chants he intoned a prayer to the Lord Buddha asking for forgiveness for the suffering he was forced to inflict on his fellow creature.

The sharp slivers of cane would be inserted into the most sensitive areas of the body, and out again, until the pain became unbearable. Rare was the victim who could withstand the perfor-ations and refuse to talk.

The guard explained to the prisoner that as they needed answers fast, they would have to break with tradition and start with the groin instead of the neck. The prisoner began foaming at the mouth as his panung was removed and his knees were forced apart. Vitoon then offered him a choice of sticks, for custom dictated that the victim should pick his own instrument of torture. The prisoner's eyes rolled from one sharp cane to another. Vitoon came to his aid, lifting a long thin sliver from the tray and holding it up before the victim's eyes. Then he handed it to the guard who had intoned the prayer, who in turn looked to Phaulkon for permission to proceed.

Phaulkon stepped forward. 'Who do you work for?'

The prisoner hesitated. The torturer brought the sharp end of the cane to within a hair's breadth of his groin. The prisoner instinctively attempted to close his knees but four burly hands kept them prised apart. Sweat poured from his brow.

Phaulkon nodded briefly to the torturer who gave a swift jab to the prisoner's genitals. The man howled with pain.

'Who do you work for?' Phaulkon repeated.

This time the prisoner did not hesitate. 'Lord Selim Yussuf, Mighty Lord.'

'Where is he now?'

'In town, Lord.'

'What is he doing there?'

'Er, co-ordinating matters, Lord.'

'Why all the fires?'

The man hesitated. The torturer gave him another jab and his face creased with pain.

'I asked you the meaning of those fires.'

'They have set fire to the houses of the farangs, Mighty Lord.'

'All of them?'

The man nodded, his face racked with fear.

Phaulkon tried to keep his voice steady. 'Are they all dead?'

'I don't know any more, Mighty Lord. I thought, er, they might have been until Your Excellency and the other farang arrived.'

'How many farangs were there in Mergui?'

'Sixty-two, I believe.'

'Is the Shahbandar dead?'

'I don't know, Mighty Lord. Truly. Songhkram was supposed to relieve me of my duties, but he never turned up. I have been at my post since dusk.'

'Is the Shahbandar's ship still in port?'

'It was there this afternoon, Lord. It was moored next to the farang invader's. I saw them both myself.'

'How many ships in the invader's forces?'

'I don't know, Mighty Lord. There was just the one in port.'

'Who organized the killing of the farangs?'

The man stared at his feet. A powerful jab made him scream. 'Mighty Lord, it was Lord Selim,' he whimpered.

'How many men did he use?'

The man appeared puzzled. 'Many men, Lord. Everybody.'

'When did it start?'

'Just after sunset.'

'When is your master due back?'

'He didn't say, Mighty Lord. He just told me to wait here.'

'You are alone?'

'Mighty Lord, yes. The servants all left with the master.'

There was only one more question to settle.

'We are leaving now,' Phaulkon said to the quivering prisoner. 'Do you want to come with us?'

The man hesitated, just long enough for Phaulkon to make up his mind. He took Vitoon to one side. 'He is not to be trusted,' he said. 'We can't afford to be straddled with him. We have too much to do. And we can't leave him here to blabber either. You'll have to get rid of him. But I want it to be painless. See that he never knows what hit him.'

Vitoon inclined himself respectfully and walked over to the prisoner. He untied him and led him outside.

Phaulkon summoned Davenport and spoke to him urgently and quietly for some minutes. The secretary's eyes grew wide as he listened to Phaulkon's plan. It was not for nothing that the man had been named Barcalon of Siam.

When Vitoon returned, Phaulkon ordered the party to head back to the boats. As they made their way towards the wooden pier where the oarsmen were waiting, only the prisoner was missing.

Captain Weltden came slowly to his senses. There was a dreadful thumping in his head and his body felt numb. Shouts and screams emanated from the hills around him. He saw his hat lying next to him and reached across for it. The crown was slit. It must have been a sword blow. He touched his head and felt sticky blood. Thank God for the thick material of his hat. He felt weak and dizzy.

As his eyes grew accustomed to the darkness, he made out a number of bodies scattered about him. He could not see their faces but he feared the worst. Fires burned at varying intervals along the ridges of the hills and he thought he saw some glowing embers at the top of the hill where White's house was. He rose painfully to his feet and headed towards the nearest warehouse. Beyond it was the path that led up the hill. He stepped back quickly into the deeper shadow of a tree as a group of armed natives converged on the path. He watched them go up the hill towards White's house.

Weltden turned back towards the sea. He reached the water's edge and peered out in front of him, looking for his launch. It was not by the wharf but after a while his eyes made out a craft weaving across the water in slow, jerky movements. It seemed to be cutting across to the far end of the harbour. He decided to follow the shoreline on foot and try to hail it from where the land jutted out a little further to the right. The shouts from the hills had receded and the harbour front appeared deserted. He proceeded painfully, his head pounding with every step. By the time he reached the little promontory, he was quite exhausted. He made out the line of the boat moving across just in front of him. Gathering his remaining strength, he waded out towards it. The muddy bottom made the going slow and drained his strength. He saw that in a few more moments the boat, despite its slow pace, would have moved beyond his line of approach.

He stood there breathing heavily, swaying with dizziness and pain. He wasn't at all confident he could make it back to shore. There was nothing for it. He would have to shout. He knew it was risky but it was preferable to drowning in thigh-deep water. He cupped his hands and cried out as loud as he dared: 'Help!'

Davenport left the mouth of the Tenasserim and entered the bay at a wide angle, entirely avoiding the harbour front. There was no sign of the *Resolution* in the darkness, but tonight no ship's officer in his right mind would advertise his position by showing a light. Four of Phaulkon's guards rowed the large canoe while Davenport silently went over his lines again, determining the responses he would give to the questions he felt sure he would be asked.

They headed straight out to sea, following the left arm of the bay. They would cut across only when the harbour was well behind him. After some time Davenport raised a hand and peered into the darkness in front of him. A dark shape loomed ahead. Could it be the *Resolution* already? Perhaps she had moved away from the harbour. There was a growing swell at this distance from shore, but nothing that the sturdy canoe, carved out of a single trunk of teakwood, couldn't weather. Davenport was still straining his eyes when a sudden flare from one of the fires ashore caught the outline of two large vessels just ahead. He signalled the oarsmen to head for the channel between them. Which one was the *Resolution*? he wondered.

Samuel White heard the cry for help just as he was struggling with his last breath to put sufficient distance between him and the harbour. When dawn came he hardly wanted to find himself in the middle of it like a sitting duck. There were some mangrove swamps to the north of the town which he would try and reach and where he planned to spend the night. At first light he would see if the *Resolution* were still around, and if it was, he would make a concerted effort to reach it. He had been rowing for a good hour now, using his stump of an oar, and he was exhausted. Only the sight of the fires on the hillside and the certainty that his house was among them, had kept him going. He had watched with sinking heart as new fires broke out as quickly as the old ones died. With each new conflagration had come an eerie chorus of cheers which had sent shivers down his spine. He continued pulling on the oar, marvelling at the feats the human body could perform under duress. He had actually rowed a full league with half an oar, and a very splintered half at that. But why were the devils burning all the houses anyway? And who were the leaders?

A second cry for help distracted him. It was considerably louder this time. Whoever the fool was, he would soon alert everyone to his presence. The sound seemed to emanate from somewhere in the swamps ahead, not more than thirty yards away. It was an English sound, so the chances were it was friendly. Only the natives had gone berserk.

'Who is it?' he called, not too loudly.

There was no immediate response, then the voice boomed across the water again: 'Help me, please.'

White cursed. The damned idiot would warn the whole town. 'Keep quiet. I'm coming.'

'I'm over here,' came the voice, more subdued now.

With his half oar, White began to head towards the sound, praying that this wasn't some trap. It took him almost twenty minutes to reach the victim and twice more the voice called out, thinking it had lost him. As he drew nearer, White suddenly realized he knew the voice. But that was impossible. He had seen Weltden killed.

'Anthony?' he whispered excitedly. 'Is that you?'

There was a moment's silence. Then a delighted voice said: 'Samuel! What a Godsend. Am I glad to see you.'

'Keep your voice down. There may be native boats around.'

'All right. I'm over here.' Weltden splashed a hand about in the water to indicate his position.

At last White reached him.

'Anthony, thank God you're alive. I saw you knocked to the ground.' He grabbed the outstretched arm but neither of them had any strength left and Weltden fell back onto his knees in the water. White passed him the half oar and after repeated attempts Weltden finally managed to haul himself aboard, half dead with exhaustion. Both men lay there panting, unable to speak.

Eventually White said: 'I thought they'd killed you back there, my friend. I was coming to your rescue when I was knocked out cold myself.'

'What the hell is going on, Sam? A full-scale uprising?'

'Your guess is as good as mine, but it certainly looks that way.'

'We've got to reach the *Curtana*. I'll help you row.'

'With half an oar between us, Anthony? That'll be quite an undertaking.'

'Half an oar?' asked Weltden.

White showed him the splintered stump of his oar. 'Now you know why it took me so long to reach you.'

'What happened to my crew?'

'The ones in this boat, you mean? Butchered to a man, I'm afraid. I had to heave the bodies overboard.'

Weltden was silent.

'We'll take turns with the half we've got,' said White, and wearily began to row in the direction of the *Curtana*, praying she was still anchored in the harbour. But after fifteen minutes, they had progressed only a few yards. Then gradually a squall arose and they found themselves drifting helplessly away from their destination. White cursed his stupidity. At least in the shelter of the mangrove swamps they could have held their ground. They didn't have the strength to make it to the *Curtana* anyway. The only slim consolation was the thought that the squall would be scattering any native canoes that might be on the prowl as well.

After a while they drifted into another mangrove swamp and came to a halt amongst some bushy trees. Weltden wanted to venture ashore but quickly changed his mind when White warned him of crocodiles. They decided to remain in the boat till morning.

Exhausted by their efforts, they lay down. Despite the ever present danger, the thought of sleep afforded considerable relief. White glanced once more towards the hills; smouldering piles were still visible at intervals. Shouts and cheers of raucous celebration continued to puncture the stillness of the night. The two men closed their eyes and fell instantly asleep.

'Boat ahoy!' challenged the officer of the watch. 'Who goes there?'

Davenport signalled to his oarsmen to hold the boat still.

'Francis Davenport, Lord White's secretary. I've just escaped from shore. I'm looking for the *Resolution*.'

'This is the *Curtana*. The *Resolution* is to starboard.'

'Have you seen Captain Weltden anywhere?' It was a voice of authority this time, no doubt an officer. 'He went ashore to dine with Lord White.'

'No, sir,' replied Davenport. 'It's absolute chaos ashore.'

'I know, we sent a boat to look for our captain, but we had to turn back. We're planning to investigate again at first light.'

'Very wise, sir, it's far too dangerous now. I'm lucky to be alive. Well, if you'll excuse me, I've got to get to the *Resolution*.'

'You can't miss her. She's just to starboard. I am sorry I can't give you any light, but we're not anxious to reveal our position. Good luck.'

'Thank you, sir.'

Davenport pointed the oarsmen in the right direction. Only

the vaguest outline loomed ahead of them. They proceeded with caution until gradually they came alongside the frigate.

A voice challenged Davenport and he identified himself.

'Wait there,' ordered the man.

Davenport did not have to wait long. He heard hurried footsteps on the deck and then a hushed voice enquired excitedly, 'Be that truly ye, Davenport, me lad?'

Davenport would have known that voice anywhere. So Rob Jamieson was back. With the treasure no doubt. This was interesting news.

'It's me all right, Rob. May I come on board?'

'Permission granted,' said the voice affably.

Davenport climbed up the ship's ladder.

'What news o' Sam?' Jamieson asked, with a worried look.

'He's alive, Rob. But he'll only stay that way if we rescue him. Can we go to your cabin to talk?'

'Aye, Francis. Follow me.'

Jamieson led the way down the companionway into a sparsely furnished cabin. They sat down on a couple of stiff-backed chairs.

'To tell ye the truth, Francis, I didnae think anyone had survived that inferno. Where is Sam?'

'In hiding, a secret place he knows just up the coast. It's a small cave well concealed from any path. He managed to escape there with a couple of his retainers. Almost all the Europeans are dead. Massacred. The idea was for me to try and reach you. White gave me four of his best men. They're with me now. He can't move from his hideout without a boat, he's short on provisions, and the natives are after his blood. How many men have you got on board, Rob?'

'Twenty-four, but most o' them are crew.' The Scotsman frowned. 'Besides, I need them to guard . . . I've got some valuable cargo on board.'

'White told me about the treasure, Rob. He suggested that maybe you could use his men to guard it, the ones who are with me now in the canoe. We need your boys to rescue White. This is no job for the Siamese.'

Jamieson eyed Davenport sceptically. 'Are yer men to be trusted?'

376

'Of course they're to be trusted. They're White's men. Some of his finest.'

'Dae I ken them?'

'You might do. No, on second thoughts . . . they would report directly to Rodriguez, not White. You might have seen them around though.'

'I'm anxious to rescue Sam but I cannae leave only four men tae guard a treasure o' that size.'

'I understand.' Davenport paused. 'Wait a minute, I think I have an idea.'

'What's that?'

'During my escape I ran into a wealthy Portuguese trader who was fleeing too. He had a substantial retinue of guards with him. He told me that though the natives were out to kill the English, they couldn't tell the difference between one European and another. None of the Portuguese felt safe. He asked me if he or any of his friends might seek refuge on board the *Resolution*. Their little church is already crammed full. I told him I thought it would be all right. His men were in the process of commandeering some boats when I last saw him. If he makes it here, perhaps we could ask his guards to look after the treasure as well? I am sure he'd be delighted for any opportunity to show his gratitude.'

Jamieson shook his head. 'Leave the treasure in the hands o' strangers? Not on yer life.'

'But what about if you were to leave another four of your men here? Together with my men, that would be eight to guard the treasure. The rest could come with us to rescue White.'

Jamieson liked the idea a little better. 'Maybe I could ask the *Curtana* tae lend me some o' their men? Though I'm nae sure how far they're tae be trusted either.'

Davenport shook his head. 'I wouldn't do that, Rob. The *Curtana*'s going to need every available hand to man her guns, if the rumours are true.'

'What rumours?'

'The word is that scores of native canoes are planning to creep up on us at first light and overwhelm us. That's why we've got to rescue White tonight.'

377

Jamieson scowled and then a thought struck him. 'Are ye absolutely certain Sam's alive still?'

'Quite certain, Rob. I was with him myself.' He leaned forward. 'But there is something else you should know, confidentially of course.' Davenport lowered his voice. 'White and Weltden have struck a deal.'

Jamieson raised an eyebrow. 'A deal?'

'Yes. White had received special authorization from the Company to transport his treasure unmolested, in return for certain . . . well, never mind, that is irrelevant. Obviously a share will be going to the Company. But the point is, the deal has been sealed and White has the necessary papers with him.' Davenport spoke the words slowly. 'The cargo will be *legal*, Rob. The papers refer specifically to White and no one else, which is yet another reason why we have to get him out.'

Jamieson sat up straight. 'Ye mean we could get out o' here if we brought Sam back, before daybreak even?'

'Yes. The minute White is aboard, we sail. With the treasure.'

The Scotsman appeared torn. 'But hasnae the bloody town risen up in arms? The *Curtana*'s men had tae turn back. What chance would we have? And tae leave such a treasure behind, almost unguarded . . .'

'Our chances would be good, Rob, I know the terrain well. We would avoid the populated areas. White's hiding up the coast, not in town. And even if we ran into the odd native, with twenty armed Europeans we wouldn't have any trouble. The Siamese respect numbers.'

Jamieson frowned. 'But why couldnae Sam hae come straight here, like ye?'

'He didn't think he'd make it. He knew the harbour front would be well guarded because the natives would expect him to try to reach the *Resolution*. With bloodthirsty mobs marching up the hill burning every white man's house, he had to make a quick decision. He reckoned his best bet would be to avoid the town. So he escaped northwards to the cave. He was desperate to get a message through to the *Resolution*, that's why he decided to risk giving me his best men.'

Jamieson was pensive. 'I'd still like tae leave four o' my men here as well.'

378

'You do that. We'll manage all right with the other twenty.'

'Ye're sure ye know the way, Francis? We dinnae want to run into some native ambush.'

'Don't you worry, Rob. I am as keen to return here as you are.'

'All right then, I'll gather the lads.'

'And Rob, please warn the remaining guards that the Portuguese trader and his retinue might turn up. They shouldn't shoot at them or anything.'

Jamieson laughed. 'We'll give 'em hospitality, Francis, dinna ye worry.'

Forty-five

When White opened his eyes, dawn was almost breaking. He stretched his aching muscles and yawned. His whole body was stiff, partly from the unaccustomed effort of rowing, partly from the beating he had received and partly from having spent the night on the wooden floor of the launch. It had not been cold, but the hard floor had been very uncomfortable.

He peered over at Weltden lying at the other end of the boat. He was lying on his side, his knees curled up and his head resting on his cupped hands. He seemed sound asleep; either that or he was unconscious. The top of his head was crusted with dried blood.

White was just leaning across to try to wake him up when he froze, straining his ears. The sound of voices drifted plainly over the water. It was hard to tell from what distance. The voices were native ones and, from their casual tone, they had not yet spotted them. He had to wake Weltden quietly. He felt his heartbeat quickening. The voices were drawing nearer now. He crawled forward on his knees. The boat creaked under his weight and he prayed the sound would not carry far. On a branch above Weltden an iguana scurried along, then paused to listen, its throat heaving.

He was almost upon Weltden when he stirred and a loud snort started from his mouth. White lunged forward, thrusting his hand across his mouth and cutting off the tail end of the sound. Weltden opened his eyes and stared, bewildered, at White. The native voices ceased all of a sudden. Weltden's breathing was laboured and White removed his hand to let him breathe more freely. He put his finger quickly across his lips in a gesture of silence.

The voices had ceased but the sound of paddles pulling through the water was unmistakable. Though dawn had not yet broken, the darkness was getting thinner. The sinewy outlines of the mangrove bushes were clearly visible. White crawled back to his end of the boat and picked up the oar stump. He could see that Weltden had heard the sound too.

The sound of paddles ceased abruptly. Voices whispered and then the paddling resumed.

The two men lay low as the canoe edged towards their boat. White's grip tightened on the oar. He lay there breathlessly, waiting for a head to appear. It did, but at Weltden's end. In the next instant Weltden's fist smashed into the man's face. He reeled backwards, screaming. White sat up, just as another figure rose up out of the canoe, wielding a curved knife. He grabbed the edge of the launch to steady himself and prepared to lunge at Weltden. Just then he spotted White and thought better of it. He exchanged his knife for a paddle and the sight of it propelled White forward.

He landed on top of the man with a thud, nearly capsizing the canoe. 'Grab their oars!' hissed White to Weltden.

There was no sign of the other Siamese. The man in the canoe sank his teeth into White's shoulder and he yelled with pain. White was by far the heavier of the two but the Siamese was lithe and his reaction instant. Both men lunged for the knife lying on the floor but the Siamese was quicker. As he bent down, White brought his fist into the back of his neck. The man slumped forward with a grunt but he held on to the knife. He wheeled round and lashed out blindly at White. The knife struck White just below the shoulder. As the man pulled back for another lunge, Weltden loomed up behind him, his blouse held taut in his hands. He brought it over the man's head and round his neck, jerking it tight. The man's eyes bulged as he tried desperately to loosen the stranglehold. White saw his chance. He smashed his knee into the man's groin. The Siamese dropped his hands, howling with pain. The noose tightened until the man went limp.

'Let's get out of here,' said White, quickly. The first flush of dawn appeared faintly on the horizon.

They threw the body of the dead man overboard and paddled back towards their launch. It had drifted away during the struggle. There was still no sign of the other native. At least they had two reasonable paddles now. They were shorter than the oars of a launch but they were a considerable improvement on the stump. Weltden took the dead man's knife from the floor and

381

thrust it into his breeches. They came alongside their boat and climbed into it. They did not notice the figure hunched on the floor of the boat. Weltden took the blouse that had strangled the native, and began to tie it round White's shoulder to stem the flow of blood. His mouth opened wide as White suddenly kicked him violently in the chest. He flew backwards, smashing into the Siamese. The native buckled up, winded, as White rushed at him. Together the two men overpowered him but the Siamese slithered out of their grip like a snake and plunged overboard, disappearing quickly into the mangrove swamp.

The Englishmen headed away from shore, paddling as fast as their remaining strength would allow them. The squall had risen again but the wind and the tide were behind them this time and they made rapid headway. As they emerged into the bay, the first rays of sun appeared behind Mergui, lighting up the hills from behind like some majestic theatrical set. The *Resolution* and the *Curtana* were visible in the distance, moored beyond the bar. Scattered across the bay were scores of canoes. Their launch was horribly conspicuous. Quickly they turned back to the shelter of the mangrove swamps before any of the native boats spotted them.

Selim did not return to his house till the early hours of the morning. All was finally quiet in the town. He felt both elated and exhausted. Elated at the thought that once again the Moors might resume their rightful place in Mergui, and exhausted by the carnage and the difficulties of controlling the near hysterical mobs.

It bothered him that no one had actually seen the Shahbandar die, but one of the peasant leaders assured him that the Shahbandar's house had been burned to a cinder. 'Not even that infidel dog could have survived such a roasting,' he commented with a grin.

As he entered his gate, Selim was surprised to find that the guard was not at his post. Perhaps he had gone off to celebrate with his companions. He heard the servants stirring. At least they had come home.

Soon he would return to Tenasserim where he would lie low until Ayudhya had concluded its investigation into the uprising.

He felt confident that the evidence against the farangs would be overwhelming. There was not one Siamese who would not attest to the fact that the farangs had fired first.

He entered his chamber and lay down on the mat of rushes. He would snatch a couple of hours' sleep before dawn. His last thoughts were for the few farangs still alive on their ships. He doubted whether the men of the *Resolution* or the *Curtana* would dare to take action when both their masters were dead. The boat they had sent out had beat a hasty enough retreat when its men saw the insurmountable odds against them. And when dawn broke, the two ships' crews would see two hundred war canoes prowling the bay. With no friends ashore, they would surely leave.

The months of careful planning had paid off. Yet now that it was all over, Selim felt a strange emptiness and sleep eluded him until shortly before dawn.

White and Weltden located the abandoned canoe caught up in some low lying branches at the edge of the mangrove swamps. There was no sign of the second Siamese; without a paddle the canoe was little use to him.

They switched boats quickly and headed out to sea again. If only they could come within hailing distance of the *Curtana* or the *Resolution* before one of the native craft accosted them. Weltden reckoned the *Curtana* was about half a mile away. None of the canoes seemed to be moving about at the moment; the sun had barely risen and presumably the boatmen had not yet begun their patrols.

Unaccustomed to the native dug-out, the two men made slow progress until they learned to synchronize their movements. White sat in the prow, paddling with his good arm and wincing from the pain in his shoulder. Weltden had to complete one stroke to his every two to maintain an even rhythm. Within thirty minutes they had covered almost half the distance. Sweat streamed down their faces and White was looking increasingly pale.

They travelled a further fifteen minutes without incident. They knew that it was only a matter of time before one of the canoes hailed them, for they were now closer to the ships than any other canoe. The natives were bound to wonder why one of their own craft was approaching the farang vessels. They continued to head in a straight line for the nearest ship, the *Curtana*, about two hundred yards away.

They completed another fifty yards or so, before the dreaded shout came, from somewhere to their left. The two Englishmen looked at each other and simultaneously redoubled their efforts. Their canoe surged forward, but the unco-ordinated change of pace caused it to zigzag to left and right. The two men cursed as they lost precious moments adjusting to the new rhythm. The pain in White's shoulder sharpened.

To their horror they noticed that their efforts had edged their boat closer to the nearest canoe. It was less than forty yards away, and the distance was closing. Others, alerted by the shout, took up the chase. Soon a dozen canoes were heading towards the Englishmen, the natives bellowing exhortations to each other.

White and Weltden were not more than a hundred yards away from the *Curtana* and it seemed impossible that the shouting would not be audible to her crew. A moment later they heard the unmistakable cry of an English lookout. Their flagging spirits lifted and White redoubled his efforts, his eyes feverish, the pain in his arm pulsing agonizingly. Then Weltden put down his oar. White stared at him in disbelief. The canoe began to turn in a circle.

'What the hell . . .'

Weltden ignored White and cupped his hands in the direction of the ship. 'Help, it's your Captain. Help. Quick!'

White swore. Why did the cretin have to do that? The ship had seen them anyway. They had lost precious seconds.

Two of the native boats were now neck and neck no more than fifteen yards away, while the Englishmen were still ninety yards from the *Curtana*. The race seemed all but over. Then suddenly a ship's siren pealed across the water, followed seconds later by the roar of cannon shot. The lead canoes slowed. Then the *Resolution* blew its horn too. White almost wept with joy at the familiar sound. Shouts of encouragement came from both ships.

'They're lowering a boat,' yelled Weltden. 'Come on, Sam. You can't give up now.' But White's strength was failing him. His face was ashen, the makeshift bandage round his upper arm wet with blood. The paddle slipped from his grasp and he slumped forward.

Another cannon shot boomed across the bay. Weltden looked back as he paddled. One canoe was sinking, others were turning back to shore. Only the five nearest were still in the race. The ship had not dared fire on them for fear of hitting him. The lead boat was less than ten yards away. The sweat poured down Weltden's forehead, blurring his vision. He paddled like a madman, knowing that the moment the lead boat caught up with him he was a dead man. Seven yards, six . . . five . . . In front of him he could see a longboat in the water now. A dozen men propelled her. He drew on his last resources and with a super-human effort kept his distance from the lead boat for another minute. Then he too collapsed with exhaustion.

The longboat raced on, white water foaming at her bows. She was forty yards away. Second Officer Wells raised his musket and took careful aim. The shot landed just short of the lead canoe. The gap continued to close. Wells's second shot felled one of the two native paddlers in the lead canoe. It slowed abruptly. The second paddler dropped his paddle and dived towards Weltden's boat. In three rapid strokes he had grabbed the edge and hauled himself up. He drew his knife. Weltden looked on helplessly, the strength drained out of him. Two cocked muskets were raised in the longboat. The Siamese lifted his knife and lunged. Both muskets exploded. The Siamese toppled forward burying his knife into Weltden's thigh.

The occupants of the other four canoes ducked for cover as the muskets turned on them. Then, as the longboat came alongside the Englishmen's canoe, they turned back. White and Weltden were lifted aboard the *Curtana*'s boat.

Wells looked at the limp figures of his Captain and Samuel White and sighed with relief. He had been vindicated at last. For he had stood behind Captain Weltden all along. He had feared the worst when the mangled corpse of a white man had floated by at dawn and been identified as Mason. He was sure that the gruesome sight would provoke a mutiny on board. But now the appearance of White, wounded and in worse condition even than Captain Weltden, clearly showed that it had been an uprising of the natives against the white man and not some conspiracy of

385

White's. He glanced at the distant hills where the sun shone on the charred remains of what once had been men's houses. As soon as they reached the *Curtana*, he would send an armed boat to the nearest native canoe with a message for their leaders ashore, offering to redeem any surviving Europeans for gold.

There was a great cheer from the assembled crew as Weltden was carried aboard ship. A surgeon was standing by. White had regained consciousness but was still stretched out in the longboat, having insisted on being taken to the *Resolution* without delay. Though she was not more than a hundred feet away, there was a strange absence of men lining her decks. Quite a different reception to the one on the *Curtana*, he noted, puzzled.

The boat pulled up alongside. Two sailors looked down at White and saluted. Their faces seemed grim.

'Cheer up, lads,' called one of the oarsmen, 'he's only wounded. I don't think he's in any danger.'

'Can we give you a hand with him?' asked another oarsman as the sailors stepped into the boat.

'No thanks. We can manage.'

They lifted White by the feet and shoulders. He yelped with pain. They carried him carefully up on deck, and then down through a hatchway. The *Curtana*'s boat pulled away. The sailors brought White before the door of a cabin. One of them knocked.

'Come in,' said a voice.

White was immediately alert. He knew that voice. His stomach turned.

The door opened and a figure clad in a black blouse and panung greeted him with a smile. White's eyes dilated. The sailors laid him down on a bunk and left.

'Welcome aboard, Samuel,' said Phaulkon. 'I hope you haven't had too rough a time of it. But you must tell me all about it.'

386

Forty-six

Phaulkon had been on board the *Resolution* for almost twelve hours now. He had had no trouble passing himself off as a Portuguese trader the night before. He spoke Portuguese fluently and could imitate their English intonations perfectly. He even looked the part. He and his sixteen guards had made no attempt to molest the four crew members that Jamieson had ordered to remain on board. They had been allowed to sleep soundly until, in the hour just before dawn, two of the men had died silently. The other two had been disarmed and spared, after they had revealed Jamieson's name. Phaulkon needed them anyway as a front. They had professed to know nothing of the fate of the *Sancta Cruz*, swearing that they were part of the *Resolution*'s original crew. Captain Jamieson had appeared one day with a crew of his own and taken over the ship, they told Phaulkon. The Captain had left earlier that night with Mr Davenport to rescue Lord White ashore. Beyond that they knew nothing.

Phaulkon had slept for only an hour or two. After White's arrival, he spent the early part of the morning alternately observing the movements of the native boats in the harbour and checking on White's condition. On both fronts things were quiet. The native boats kept their distance, apparently waiting to see what the two big ships would do. White had not stirred. He had fainted on arrival and had then passed into a deep sleep. At about noon a boat from the *Curtana* had come to enquire after his health and been told he was still resting. In the latter part of the morning Phaulkon had investigated the ship's hold where he had discovered stacks of crates and rows of large sea chests. The crates contained a small fortune in gold bars, probably enough to pay the full compensation requested by Yale. The sea chests, filled to capacity, contained an extraordinary assortment of treasure, obviously accumulated over a period of time: priceless vases and rugs, pieces of eight, Japanese gold bars, Spanish doubloons, rubies, diamonds, golden crucifixes, and a variety of weapons inlaid with mother of pearl. In one chest he had even come across tiger skins and rhinoceros horns. The gold in the crates was still marked from Acheem. Clearly, Jamieson's mission with the *Sancta Cruz* had been successful, but her cargo must have earned more than these bars represented. And where was the *Sancta Cruz* now?

Phaulkon decided to take another look at White. It was now early afternoon; surely he must be stirring.

The sound of a door closing penetrated White's consciousness; but he gave it no thought; his mind was preoccupied with the throbbing ache in his shoulder. Then he heard a board creak and he opened his eyes. He looked around him, bewildered. Phaulkon's face swam into view. The sight prompted instant recall of his circumstances. He shut his eyes again and groaned inwardly, trying to muster his wits. Phaulkon waited patiently, saying nothing.

'They took me by surprise, Constant,' White said eventually, beginning with the obvious. 'I wanted to defend Mergui against the enemy, but the natives must have misunderstood my intentions. Perhaps they thought I was plotting with the English. Thank God you're here, Constant.'

Phaulkon pulled up a chair and sat down beside the bunk. 'What happened exactly, Samuel?'

White's face clouded over. 'The natives ran amok. They . . . set fire to the houses of the Europeans without warning. I had armed them, you see, to defend Mergui. But they turned on us instead. It was terrible, terrible. We were taken by complete surprise.'

'But what triggered the massacre, Samuel?'

White considered the question. 'I think it was the firing of the guns. I did try to stop that fool Weltden.'

'Weltden?'

'Yes, the Captain of the *Curtana*, the Company ship that came to commandeer the town.' White spoke slowly, labouring under the strain. 'You see, I had to pretend to go along with Weltden in order to stop him from going through with the attack. I even said I would co-operate with him. I had to, to stall him, until I could strengthen the town's fortifications. But before I could prevent him, the maniac ordered the *Curtana*'s guns to be fired in celebration of our compact. The . . . the natives must have thought that . . .'

'That you were celebrating your victory in advance?'

'Well, yes. After the volleys were fired I quickly returned ashore to convene a meeting of the Council. I wanted to explain what had happened. But . . . two of the members were absent and I had to leave messages for them to come to my house first thing in the morning. That was this morning.' White's face contorted with bitterness. 'By then . . . it was too late.'

'Do you know where Selim is?' asked Phaulkon suddenly.

'Selim Yussuf? The brother of Hassan?' White frowned. 'A bad egg. I had him under surveillance in Tenasserim.'

'He was the ringleader. He must be found and arrested.'

'The ringleader? I knew he was not to be trusted, but I was so involved in manipulating Weltden, I had no time to look into his activities personally. I had to rely on my men.'

White was beginning to feel desperate. What did Phaulkon know? What was he doing aboard his ship? White felt sick to his stomach when he thought of the treasure in the hold. What had brought Phaulkon to Mergui anyway? Something Davenport had said to Ivatt? Where the hell was Jamieson? A thousand questions pressed in on him, yet he was forced to play Phaulkon's game of cat and mouse. Always, Phaulkon had to prod and poke and tease before he pounced. Why couldn't he just come out with what he knew and be done with it?

Phaulkon watched the agitation in White's face. He was like a cornered beast, unsure of his tormentor's intentions. He was a pathological liar. His exposure might stare him in the face, but Sam White would try and turn it to his advantage. Even in his present weak state he was capable of spinning tales indefinitely. Phaulkon had no time to listen to them.

'Jamieson told me all about his mission,' he said coldly, 'but I'd rather hear the facts from you. Where is the *Sancta Cruz*?'

'The *Sancta Cruz*?' White's eyes shifted about uneasily. 'I wish I knew myself, Constant. There have been many rumours. And some accusations too. But I honestly haven't had time to investigate them. The safety of Mergui has been my one concern. You have no idea what it's been like. That fellow Weltden is quite unstable. One minute he wants to raze Mergui to the ground and the next he asks for my co-operation in a takeover. It has been a constant war of nerves. Where is Jamieson anyway?'

'In a safe place, don't you worry. He told me that you ordered him to scuttle the ship.'

White had grown very pale. 'He said that?' He shook his head incredulously. 'The last I heard of her she had gone off to Acheem. That . . . that was the rumour anyway.' He appeared to search his memory. 'It was even said that Jamieson had seized her and taken her there. But I find that hard to believe. Only Coates would be mad enough to do such a thing. You know, Constant, so much has happened in Mergui in the last few days that – ' Phaulkon cut him short.

'Some of the spoils of the *Sancta Cruz* are below in the hold. I have seen them myself.'

White was ready for that. 'The treasure aboard this ship, Constant, is from the *New Jerusalem*, not the *Sancta Cruz*. I was about to return it to Madras, when the arrival of the *Curtana* forced me to delay my plans.'

'The *New Jerusalem* contained rubies, not gold, Samuel. The markings on the crates containing the bars have been effaced but the gold itself still bears the seal of Acheem.'

White looked wide-eyed at Phaulkon. 'Acheem? That's extraordinary. Unless of course some of the *New Jerusalem*'s treasure came from there. I never really checked.'

Phaulkon looked at him as one might a hopelessly wayward child. 'You will have plenty of time to unravel the mystery, Samuel. I'm going to – '

There was an urgent knock on the door.

'Yes?' said Phaulkon.

'Mighty Lord,' replied a respectful voice in Siamese, 'you asked me to inform you if anything unusual happened. I think Your Excellency should come up on deck.'

'Come in, Vitoon. Take Lord White down into the hold and let him contemplate his treasure. Double the guard.'

'Mighty Lord, I receive your orders.'

Without a backward glance at White, Phaulkon climbed hurriedly up on deck.

*

390

A gig was heading towards the *Curtana*. Phaulkon shifted his gaze out to sea, shading his eyes from the late-afternoon sun. In the distance two ships were anchored in deep waters. They were too far for him to distinguish their ensigns, but they looked like English men-of-war. He turned to look towards the harbour. The scores of native canoes were still keeping watch, though cautiously maintaining their distance.

The gig pulled up alongside the *Curtana*. In it were five men. One of them stood up and spoke to the officer on duty. The newcomer was wearing the uniform of a British naval officer. The rest were oarsmen. There was a brief exchange and the officer on board saluted and marched off. Minutes later a senior officer appeared on deck, walking with a pronounced limp. Captain Weltden no doubt, thought Phaulkon. He climbed slowly down into the boat, which then turned and headed out to sea again.

Moments later a small boat from the *Curtana* was lowered into the water. It started out towards the *Resolution*. Phaulkon retreated behind the main mast, ordering Jamieson's two English sailors to greet the *Curtana*'s boat. The majority of the *Resolution*'s crew was known to be English and Phaulkon did not want to rouse the *Curtana*'s suspicions by allowing any of their crew to see so many Siamese on board. Two of Phaulkon's guards stood with him in the shadows behind the mast, their muskets trained on Jamieson's men to ensure their co-operation.

The little boat came alongside. One of the men stood up in the boat and greeted the two English sailors. Then he handed them a piece of paper. The oarsmen enquired after White's health and, after exchanging a few pleasantries, departed again.

The note was brought to Phaulkon. It had been folded in a hurry, and was addressed, somewhat lopsidedly, to Lord White. Phaulkon opened it. The message read: 'Governor Yale has arrived. Don't worry, our agreement stands. Await my return.' It was signed Anthony Weltden.

Phaulkon scanned the note again. What agreement was he refering to? he wondered. And why should White not worry? It sounded as if Yale's arrival might threaten some scheme the two men had concocted. Besides, why had Yale arrived with *two* men-of-war? With the *Curtana*, there were now three armed

Company vessels in Mergui's waters. It did not augur well. Yale's intentions could hardly be friendly. And as far as Weltden was concerned, his ally was still in command of the *Resolution*. God knows what rash decisions he might make as a consequence.

The more Phaulkon considered the matter, the more he concluded that he could not afford to wait for Yale to make the first move.

He ordered one of the *Resolution*'s boats to be lowered.

Forty-seven

'Boat ahoy!' The voice of the *Pearl*'s lookout challenged the little boat as it edged towards the huge man of war. Phaulkon counted forty-eight gunports. Not far to leeward was the other English warship. Phaulkon could just make out the name: *Hawk*.

'Constantine Phaulkon, Barcalon of Siam. I have come to see Governor Yale.'

There was a moment's silence. Then abruptly the deck of the *Pearl* came to life. A dozen crewmen converged on the ship's side to stare at the craft carrying the legendary figure of the Barcalon. The officer of the watch ran below to inform the Governor. There was a buzz of excitement as more and more sailors came to stare. Could it really be the great Barcalon in a simple boat with only two oarsmen, both of them now prostrate before their master?

It was some moments before a portly figure in knee breeches and laced coat strode onto the deck and peered down at the boat. Next appeared two men in the uniform of captain. Weltden and the skipper of the *Pearl*, thought Phaulkon. He looked at Governor Yale. He was an imposing sight, if over-dressed for the climate. An expansive grey wig adorned his head. It was parted in the middle, sending even waves of curls to either side.

'Lord Phaulkon?'

Phaulkon bowed. 'At your service, Governor.'

The Governor continued to look down his long nose at his visitor. 'You must forgive my incredulity, sir,' he said, 'but I was always given to believe that the Barcalon of Siam travelled with a sizeable retinue.'

'He usually does, Governor, unless the circumstances dictate otherwise. In this instance, it seemed advisable to exercise restraint. I would not have wanted my customary escort of over a hundred men to have made your heavily-armed crew nervous.' He smiled. 'May I have permission to come aboard?'

'Permission granted.'

Alone, Phaulkon climbed the ship's ladder under the eyes of the *Pearl*'s gaping sailors. Soon he stood face to face with Governor Yale. The two men could not have presented a more striking contrast. The one bewigged, plump and wearing formal European dress, the other straight-combed and lean, in a panung and mandarin blouse. Common to both of them, however, was an almost tangible air of authority and self-assurance.

'May I introduce you to Captains Weltden and Perriman?' said the Governor.

Phaulkon bowed to the two officers. 'Captain Weltden's exploits in Mergui are much talked about,' he said with a thin smile.

The Governor made no comment. 'Shall we go below to my cabin?'

'An excellent idea, Governor, if you mean just the two of us.'

Yale stared at Phaulkon, then gave a curt nod of dismissal to Weltden and Perriman.

The Governor's cabin was both practical and opulent. A comfortable divan from Persia lined one wall, and heavily carved chairs from Goa stood in various corners of the cabin. Vases, plates, urns and statuettes from around the Orient adorned little tables and niches. A mahogany desk took up the middle of the room.

Yale sat behind the desk, motioning his guest to a chair opposite him. Phaulkon was the first to speak.

'Governor, I can only presume you have arrived in such force to claim your compensation.'

'That is correct, Lord Phaulkon.'

'Your coming here in person indicates a certain lack of faith in Samuel White. I must say that I sympathize. He has become a thorn in the side of Siam.'

'It is a shame that he has represented your country for as long as he has,' remarked Yale.

'Indeed, Governor. But his tenure is now at an end. I am ready to hand him over to you, together with the full compensation due.' Phaulkon smiled. 'Your mission here will have ended almost before it has begun.'

'It might, had I not just learned that several dozen of King James's subjects have been brutally massacred by the Siamese.'

394

'The culprits are rebellious Moors, not Siamese, Governor, and their uprising is an internal matter. The guilty will be dealt with by the government of Siam. My troops are rounding them up at this moment. Your concern, Governor, must be confined to the object of your mission: the securing of the compensation and the arrest of Samuel White.' Phaulkon read the doggedness in Yale's eyes. He would not be put off that easily. 'Either you realize your objectives, Governor, and leave, or you remain to face the fury of the Moors and the full force of the French. The former are bent on killing every Englishman in sight, and the latter's fleet will not look kindly upon the presence here of three English men-of-war.'

'What French fleet?' asked Yale with derision. 'I did not see a single French ship in the harbour, unless they have taken to riding around in canoes now.'

'The ships left Songhkla over three weeks ago and will be here any time now.' Phaulkon smiled. 'That is why I am here – to greet them.'

'What convenient timing. But permit me to suggest that you are here rather to deal with a full-scale uprising of the local population.'

'How dare you question my word, sir!' said Phaulkon, suddenly angry. 'I have no need to explain myself to you, or to anyone else. But for your edification, Governor, the massacre occurred last night. I could hardly have known about it when it takes ten days to travel here from Ayudhya.'

Yale observed him carefully. 'So you're planning to hand over Mergui to the French?'

Phaulkon controlled his anger. Yale's supercilious tone and manner infuriated him.

'No, Governor, I am not,' he said with outward calm. 'I am giving them a trading concession. They're coming in force because I asked them to bring a large contingent of men to relieve the fort at Bangkok, where discipline has become lax. No, sir, Ivatt will be Governor of Mergui, and not any Frenchman.'

Yale's interest was clearly aroused. 'Thomas Ivatt?'

'Yes, you know him. And you know how devoted he is to Siam. He would be as unwilling to see Mergui dominated by the French as you would. More importantly, *I* have no intention of allowing Mergui to remain under any but Siamese hegemony. Ivatt is here already,' Phaulkon went on before Yale could speak. 'He will be appointed Governor forthwith and the perpetrators of the local uprising will answer to him for their crimes. But speaking of local problems, Governor, I think you have one on your hands yourself.' He searched inside his blouse. 'This message was sent by your Captain Weltden to Samuel White aboard the *Resolution*,' he said, handing Yale a note. 'I intercepted it. I don't know what it is that these two men have been planning together, but I am sure you will want to deal with it.'

Yale looked at the note and frowned. Things were not turning out quite as he had planned. In the first place he had hardly expected to find Phaulkon here. Or the French so soon. Or this note.

With Sir Joshua Childe in London currently calling to account any senior employee, past or present, who in his opinion tainted the Company's reputation, this was hardly the time to have accusations of underhand deals directed at one of his captains. Weltden was, after all, under orders from him to do some sort of deal with White, and the Captains of both the *Pearl* and the *Hawk* were, of necessity, aware of the overall facts, if not the detail.

Perhaps he should cut his losses and leave, as Phaulkon urged. At least he would have the compensation – and White. He would not have Mergui, but then neither would the French if Phaulkon were to be believed. And though he was certainly wary of this canny devil in front of him, instinct told him that Phaulkon was telling the truth. It was common knowledge that the French were heavily ensconced in Ayudhya and it was only logical that they would want to extend their influence to Mergui. What alternatives were open to him anyway? To lose the compensation and White? And to face the French and the Moors and Phaulkon's troops simultaneously? Decidedly the odds were not good.

Phaulkon had been watching Yale's discomfiture, and judged it time to make his departure. He rose to his feet.

'If you will excuse me, Governor, I have pressing matters to attend to. I will send you the compensation and White immediately, so that you can slip away before the French fleet arrives.'

Yale looked at him with grudging respect. Deep down he knew

he had met his match. He made his decision. If Phaulkon did in fact deliver White and the full compensation to him, he would return to Madras. If not, he would stay and call Phaulkon's bluff.

He rose as well. 'You do understand, Lord Phaulkon, that His Majesty King James would look upon any occupation of Mergui by an outside power as a serious threat to English interests in the Bay of Bengal.'

'As indeed would the King of Siam with regard to Siamese interests,' replied Phaulkon.

Rob Jamieson woke up in a foul temper. This was his second night away from the *Resolution* and his nightmares were getting worse. He sat up in his boat and rubbed his eyes irritably. Dawn was approaching. What a merry-go-round it had been. He had begun to wonder whether Davenport knew what he was doing. He and his men had spent the first night in their boats at the edge of an iguana-infested mangrove swamp, unable to locate the cave where White was supposedly holed up. But Davenport assured him that he would be able to find it by daylight and they set out again before dawn. They continued for three more hours up the coast. Only the thought of the document that White had in his possession, kept Jamieson going.

Eventually they disembarked and, after a lengthy walk across a maze of rice paddies, they arrived at a great cave in the side of a rock. They encountered no one en route and even this place, despite the neighbouring rice fields, had appeared deserted. Davenport ran in first, shouting for White. Minutes later he emerged holding a small water flask and looking very dejected.

'He's gone,' he said. 'All I found was this.'

Jamieson swore roundly and refused to continue the search even though Davenport said he knew of another cave further up the coast.

'I've had enough. I canna blame Sam for gettin' oot o' this hole. Mebbe he's gone tae check the treasure we put in the warehouse, though I canna believe he'd be so stupid.'

Davenport gaped at him. 'I thought the treasure was on the *Resolution*.'

'Some of it is, including my share, and I want tae get back tae it.' Seeing Davenport's puzzled expression, he went on, 'He didna tell you aboot the treasure we put in the warehouse, then? Aye, we did, the big one at the end o' the wharf. Something to do wi' keeping the English happy. Must ha' bin that document you mentioned, though it's a mighty expensive piece o' paper if that's the case. But we canna stand aboot here, prattling. I want tae get back tae the *Resolution* before nightfall.'

Davenport was thoughtful as they got back into the boats and began to retrace their journey.

To Jamieson's acute exasperation, Davenport lost his bearings among the profusion of seemingly identical rice paddies. By the time they reached the sea again and located their boats some distance further up the coast, there were only a couple of hours of daylight left and they were exhausted. They were forced once more to seek the safety of the mangrove swamps.

Jamieson now woke his men up sharply. 'Come on, lads, we've got tae reach Mergui before dawn and head oot tae the *Resolution* before the native canoes spot us.'

In the other boat, Davenport unwound his long legs and stretched. The men gathered their oars and started rowing again, taking turns to ensure maximum speed. But Jamieson had miscalculated the speed with which the dawn broke in the tropics. They were only just entering the bay when a pink glow began to light up the sky.

Jamieson emitted a series of oaths. Would the harbour still be teeming with native craft, or would they have time to make a run for it before the light made it certain they would be spotted? Jamieson looked up at the crest of the hills behind Mergui where the sun would first appear. He started. What the hell . . .? He screwed up his eyes to concentrate his vision. Along the entire length of the hill was a line of slowly-moving dark objects, looming gradually larger as they reached the crest. He waited spellbound. His men were staring up at the hills too, and Davenport held his hands together as if in prayer. Suddenly the sun's ball cleared the horizon and the objects were distinctly silhouetted. War elephants! The first rays of dawn glittered on their harnesses. They stretched as far as the eye could see, over two hundred of them, in line abreast.

Jamieson turned quickly to his men. 'I'm getting oot o' here. Let's go, lads.' Some started to row again while others hesitated.

They looked out into the bay, scanning the water for native canoes, but the view was obscured by a promontory just ahead of them.

'We can make it, lads,' said Jamieson, encouragingly. 'Are ye coming, Davenport?'

'No, I'll take my chances ashore, thanks.'

Good riddance, thought Jamieson. 'Off we go then, lads.'

Davenport waded ashore, intent on finding some way of joining the elephants. He picked his way painstakingly through the swamps, keeping a watchful eye out for crocodiles, and eventually emerged on harder ground. He climbed a tall sand hill and turned to observe the progress of Jamieson. The light was now considerably brighter and from his vantage point he had a clear sweep of the bay. The colour drained from his face. Behind the small promontory were a score of native canoes. Jamieson wouldn't have a chance. He stood rooted to the spot, not daring to shout a warning, until voices behind him sent him ducking for cover. He lay face downwards in the sand, hardly breathing. The voices approached and then grew gradually fainter and disappeared. He stayed in the sand for some time longer. When he finally stood up again, there was not a sign of Jamieson's men. Only a few overturned boats were scattering in the wind. He shuddered.

He scanned the bay once more. In the distance, a little to starboard of the *Curtana* and the *Resolution*, was a third ship. She was a large man-of-war, and by her profile he knew she was not English. He turned and hurried on. The sooner he reached Ivatt the better.

Ivatt sat up straight in his elaborately decorated howdah and stared at the devastation below him. His heart sank. Everywhere he looked he saw the burnt remains of dozens of houses. What on earth had happened? He scanned the hill where White lived. His house had simply vanished. His eye wandered upwards. Burnaby's house had gone too. A feeling of nausea gripped him. Everywhere along the hillside were pockets of charred emptiness. Only the harbour front seemed to have been spared. The warehouses on the wharf were intact and the foodstalls with their makeshift roofs were still there. He had arrived the night before at dusk, too late to see anything unusual and had camped just behind the crest of the hills to await the dawn.

As the sun rose behind him now and his field of vision increased, he stared across at the shimmering ocean. The harbour was teeming with canoes. He watched as a score of them intercepted four boats that appeared to be heading out to sea and fell on their occupants. What was going on? A terrible foreboding gripped him. The canoes were of native design while the boats were the type used by Europeans.

In the distance he saw the *Resolution*. Her tall masts and well-rounded stern were unmistakable. Next to her lay another three-master, almost as tall. But some way to starboard of both ships lay a real colossus. His heart beat faster as he recognized that sweeping design. She was French. De Vaudricourt had arrived. Suddenly the whole picture became clear. Of course, it was the French man-of-war that had devastated Mergui's hillside, leaving pockets of emptiness everywhere. No doubt she had stopped firing her cannon at dusk. With the dawn she would resume the attack. Strange that he had not heard any firing though. Perhaps it had not been yesterday but the day before, and the town had already surrendered. Either way, there was no time to lose.

He spoke quickly to his mahout, who tapped his elephant with a sharp goad. The great beast swung round ponderously and began walking along the crest of the hill. As Ivatt progressed through the ranks, he gave out a string of orders. The cannon were to be brought forward and made ready for immediate action. Thank God Dularic and his bombardiers had gone back to Tenasserim the night before. They had done a fine job. Only three of the cannon had had to be abandoned during the difficult jungle crossing, and they had made good time with the rest of the artillery – nine long-range cannon. Dularic, assuring Ivatt that all was well, had excused himself on the grounds that General Desfarges' instructions to him had been to return to Bangkok immediately upon the completion of his mission. He would spend the night in Tenasserim on the first leg of his journey home.

When Ivatt saw that the cannon were all in place he gave a final order to the mahouts to rein in their beasts. Then he pointed towards the French ship. 'That is your target. Take careful aim!'

His newly trained cannoneers made some final adjustments. Ivatt raised his right arm, and a moment later the sound of two hundred and fifty bugles shattered the calm of the Bay. Then he gave the order to fire.

The *Resolution*'s boat headed smoothly towards the huge French warship. Phaulkon's heart quickened as the mass loomed ever closer.

It was getting lighter by the minute. He looked back and saw that Vitoon was on his way to the *Pearl*, carrying his note to Yale. In it Phaulkon had explained that the first of the French ships had arrived and that he had gone to greet it. He added that he had ordered the transfer of the gold to be temporarily halted, as he wanted to supervise the loading himself. The ferrying would be resumed as soon as he returned to the *Resolution*. In the meantime, the *Pearl* and the *Hawk* should remain where they were and make no suspicious moves. He intended to reassure the French that the English mission was a purely commercial one.

In reality, Phaulkon now needed the presence of the English a little longer, and the balance of the gold provided the perfect inducement. Not quite half of it had been ferried across to the *Pearl* the evening before. The bars were heavy and dusk had fallen before his last two boats could complete enough journeys to cover the full compensation. Fortunately, too, Phaulkon had not yet handed over Sam White, not out of any judicious foresight, but more because he found it fitting to have White witness his diminishing fortune. The idea had greatly appealed to him. What more appropriate punishment than for the former harbour master to sit in the hold watching crate after crate of his treasure disappear?

'*Qui va là?*' The voice cut through the morning twilight.

Phaulkon stood up in the boat. 'Le Comte de Faucon. I am alone and unarmed. I must speak to Commodore de Vaudricourt urgently.'

'*Attendez là.*'

Phaulkon ordered his oarsmen to stay still. Then he heard a gradual bustle of activity as a number of officers came to peer over the side at him. When they had ascertained that he was indeed alone and unarmed, he was invited on board. Moments later he was on the quarterdeck, facing a wide-eyed de Vaudricourt in leather breeches and white silk stockings. Captain Saint-Clair, sunburnt and bare-headed, stood next to him.

'My Lord, this is . . . er, most unexpected,' said de Vaudricourt. 'What brings you here?'

'I will speak plainly, sir, as there is not much time. I came to warn you. You are in grave danger. The English are here in force to defend Mergui. I know you have only one ship, General Desfarges told me. The English, on the other hand, have four. You can see two of them now.' He pointed in the direction of the *Curtana* and the *Resolution*. 'The others will be visible in a moment when the dawn breaks fully. Both the others are men-of-war with forty-eight guns apiece. They are expecting you and they will not hesitate to fire.'

De Vaudricourt glanced apprehensively in the direction of the *Curtana* and the *Resolution*. He took Captain Saint-Clair aside and conferred with him. Moments later the Captain summoned his first lieutenant. 'Have the guns loaded and run out,' he ordered.

'Captain, listen to me,' said Phaulkon resolutely. 'Not only are you surrounded at sea, my armies are awaiting you ashore. The town is well fortified. You haven't a chance.'

Both de Vaudricourt and Saint-Clair looked towards the harbour and then out to sea again. The morning haze was rapidly clearing, and in the distance two more shapes were slowly coming into view.

'Masthead,' bellowed Saint-Clair, looking upwards. 'What do you see to leeward?'

'You cannot take the English on from the sea and the Siamese from the land simultaneously,' Phaulkon persisted, his eyes flashing angrily. 'It's madness. I tell you this as a friend of France, to give you a chance to save yourselves.'

De Vaudricourt wheeled on him. 'If you were such a friend of France, sir, you would not have made this deal with the English. And as for our chances, they cannot be as bad as you say, not while we have you on board, anyway. No ship will fire on us with you here.'

'Two men-of-war, Captain, one forty-eighter and one – ' The

voice of the lookout was drowned by the sound of scores of bugles echoing shrilly across the bay.

All heads turned in the direction of the distant hills, where a long row of miniature elephants lined the ridge. In the next instant there was a loud report. A plume of water shot up into the air not far from the *Gaillard*'s stern.

De Vaudricourt grabbed Phaulkon by the arm. 'This way,' he said, half dragging him down the hatchway. At the bottom of the steps, Phaulkon wrenched himself free, just as another volley shook the boat. Saint-Clair's voice bellowed an order above them: 'Hard a-starboard! Prepare to take aim!'

'Listen, Commodore,' said Phaulkon, speaking rapidly, 'if you leave now, France can retain its position of influence in Siam. If you stay, you and all your men will die, and the wrath of my liege, King Narai, will know no bounds. General Desfarges is in Bangkok under guard. He will not be leading his men to capture Ayudhya.' Phaulkon fumbled inside his blouse and produced a letter. 'Here, read this.' It was a letter that Phaulkon had forced out of Desfarges before leaving. In it the General thanked Phaulkon for sparing his life and for allowing him to stay on in Bangkok despite the revelations of French treachery.

De Vaudricourt scanned the letter and looked up at Phaulkon in dismay.

'The artillery on the hill is not aware of my presence on this ship, Commodore. The cannon will sink us. If you return fire, the English will open up as well. Now order Saint-Clair to leave or we all die together.'

An explosion threw them both against the bulwark. De Vaudricourt pulled himself up first, rubbing a bruised temple. He ran up the companionway.

'Captain,' he shouted. 'Give the order to set sail.'

Phaulkon followed after him. There was chaos on deck. The last shot had shattered the stern bulwark and slightly injured two men. Officers were trying to assess the damage, crew were leaping to obey Saint-Clair's orders to make sail, everybody was shouting at once. No one took any notice as Phaulkon ran to the ship's side and climbed down into his boat.

He ordered his terrified oarsmen to start rowing. They stopped bailing water and gripped the oars. As the boat pulled away,

Phaulkon looked ahead of him with a sinking heart. A good hundred yards separated him from the *Resolution*; he would be a sitting target for the cannon ashore to practise their new-found skills. He closed his eyes and prayed.

Davenport redoubled his pace as he heard the bugle call that preceded the first cannon shot. The crest of the hill was just above him now. He was out of breath and his legs felt weak from the climb but he had to reach Ivatt to warn him that Phaulkon was on board the *Resolution*. If Phaulkon were to die now, all Davenport's hopes and aspirations would perish with him.

He heard a second shot and pushed himself onwards. He could see one of the elephants just above him now. With a last concerted effort he reached the top, just as another shot boomed, almost shattering his eardrums.

He scrambled onto the ridge, his chest heaving, and looked down the long line of elephants. The stench of gunpowder was overpowering. The soldier nearest him swung round. He stared at Davenport suspiciously.

'Lord Ivatt,' muttered Davenport feebly, 'take me to Lord Ivatt.'

The soldier beckoned him to follow. Davenport struggled on, his knees ready to give way.

At last he stood at the foot of a giant elephant. Ivatt looked down from his howdah.

'Francis! What are you doing here?'

'Hold your fire,' Davenport called up to him desperately. 'Lord Phaulkon is on board.'

Ivatt did not need to be asked twice. He gave the immediate order to cease fire. It never occurred to him that Davenport was referring to any but the French ship.

Phaulkon could not believe his luck. His prayers had been answered. The cannon fire had stopped.

As he came alongside the *Resolution* he turned to look at the French ship. The *Gaillard*'s sails were filling and she was heading out to sea. He sighed with relief. She would probably put in for repairs at Pondicherry.

He climbed aboard the *Resolution* and gave orders for the

404

immediate resumption of the transfer of gold to the *Pearl*. Every available boat was to be used to accelerate the process. Then he wrote another note to Yale explaining that his batteries ashore were manned by Siamese who, though skilled marksmen, were unable to tell the difference between an English and a French ship. The arrival of yet another armed vessel had obviously made them jittery and they had opened fire. He added that he was anxious to go ashore himself to avoid further misunderstandings, and to that end he requested additional boats from the *Pearl* to accelerate the ferrying of the gold.

Phaulkon judged it unlikely that Yale would infer any rift between himself and the French; even if his explanation of the recent attack sounded odd, it would be believed for want of a better interpretation. Besides, what choice did Yale really have? He had seen for himself the power of the cannon ashore and the long line of war elephants clearly visible along the crest of the hills. It would be a daunting enough sight. He looked up now – and squinted. The beasts were gone! What the devil was Ivatt up to?

Phaulkon now put every available man on the job of ferrying the gold and offered each of them a whole bar as reward. The men worked like fiends. Rarely had he encountered such ant-like industry. Teams of rowers and crewmen moved the heavy bars without interruption from the hold of the *Resolution* to the deck of the *Pearl*.

At last the job was done and the final consignment – in the shape of a morose and haggard Samuel White – emerged blinking into the sunlight. He turned as he was escorted past Phaulkon to the waiting boat.

'This is no way to treat the brother of your benefactor, Constant. May God punish you for such betrayal.'

'He may punish me for a lot of things, Samuel. But I doubt this will be one of them.'

They were the last words the two men exchanged. The boat headed off towards the *Pearl* and Phaulkon gathered his guard and prepared to go ashore.

The sun was high overhead. Phaulkon pulled his conical hat forward over his forehead to shield him from the glare. As his boat approached the landing he stared at the dazzling sight ahead of him. Along the entire harbour front the full regiment of war elephants stood abreast facing the ocean. They were magnificent to behold, side by side adorned in red cloth blankets brocaded with gold and covered in a variety of splendid plumage. The beast in the centre was taller by a couple of feet than the rest, and across its back swayed an elaborately decorated howdah. The howdah had as yet no occupant.

A mahout and two soldiers sat astride each of the beasts, and as the Barcalon's boat came to a halt, scores of soldiers raised their bugles and blew an official note of welcome. Then they prostrated themselves across the elephants' backs. As Phaulkon emerged from his boat, the majestic beasts prodded by their mahouts, went down on their knees in unison.

Then the giant elephant in the centre rose to its feet and lumbered towards him. It stood before Phaulkon and stretched out its trunk. He advanced towards it. With one deft movement it wound its trunk round the Barcalon's waist and lifted him off his feet. He was lowered with remarkable gentleness into the stately howdah. The elephant turned to rejoin the ranks, and from his new vantage point Phaulkon could see row upon row of Mergui's population lying prostrate behind the line of animals. Order, through fear, had been restored.

The elephant turned once more to face the ocean. As it did so, Phaulkon's smile broadened. The *Curtana* under a full press of sail was heading out to sea. In the distance both the *Pearl* and the *Hawk* were making sail.

'Thank you, Thomas,' said Phaulkon, glancing at the kneeling beast next to him. 'But I am curious. What on earth made you hold your fire? Especially when my death might have seen you the next Barcalon.'

Ivatt smiled. 'It was Davenport who ruined my game, Constant. He told me where you were.'

'You'll have to reward him.'

'I'll give him a gold bar. Apparently there's a warehouse full of them to our right. It seems White really did intend to pay the compensation.'

'You must use it to rebuild the town, Thomas. I'm sure Sam

White would approve. You can keep the cannon and the elephants too. I want Mergui to be the greatest stronghold in the Bay and Siam's most impregnable fortress. Those are your first orders as Governor of this province. You won't let me down, will you?'

'Trust me, Constant. I intend to be the best Governor since Sam White.'

Phaulkon grinned. 'Don't forget, you have no elder brother to keep me in check.' Then his expression sobered. 'And now I must bid you farewell, my friend. There is much that awaits me in Ayudhya.'

'God speed, Constant.'

Phaulkon gave an order to his mahout and the majestic animal turned and made its way along the ranks of kneeling elephants from one end of the harbour to the other. Behind them the entire population of Mergui pressed their heads further into the earth. Not until the great beast had passed out of sight did they at last rise to their feet.